GETTING GOOSED

Ben thrust the binoculars into Marjorie's hands. "You'd better take a look—through the south wall there, about half-way up."

"Do you mind telling me what this is all about?"

"Look, dammit! Now!"

Marjorie was about to flare at Ben, but something in his face stopped her, and instead she brought the binoculars up and focused through the glass to the south. The flock of geese was a little over a mile out now, and closing steadily. Marjorie stiffened.

"You're the zoologist," Ben said. "Will they veer off?"

Marjorie gnawed her lip for a moment; then she brought the glasses down. "I don't think they can see the biosphere. The glass is transparent. They'll look right through it. All they'll see is the snow on the other side of the pyramid."

Ben rolled his eyes. "Jesus!"

Carin Callisch and Beau Culpepper got out of the tram and crossed the sand to the edge of the dune. "What's going on?" Callisch asked.

Ben said, "We'd better get everybody under cover. If those geese come through the wall, it's going to be raining glass knives in about two minutes."

"Raining knives?" Culpepper echoed. "What the hell are you talking about?"

"There's a formation of Canada geese flying directly at the biosphere," Marjorie said. "The birds are going to crash through the glass."

Tor/Forge books by Richard Moran

The Empire of Ice
Earth Winter

EARTH WINTER

Richard Moran

A TOM DOHERTY ASSOCIATES BOOK
NEW YORK

EARTH WINTER

Cover art by Tim Jacobus

A Tor Book
Published by Tom Doherty Associates, Inc.
175 Fifth Avenue
New York, NY 10010

Tor Books on the World-Wide Web:
http://www.tor.com

Tor® is a registered trademark of Tom Doherty Associates, Inc.

ISBN: 0-812-53012-8
Library of Congress Card Catalog Number: 94-46577

First edition: March 1995
First mass market edition: February 1996

Printed in the United States of America

0 9 8 7 6 5 4 3 2 1

For Glenna Goulet and Del Goulet, whose encouragement, support, and caring sustained me through the creation of *Earth Winter*. No truer or more loyal friends have ever trod this earth.

NEW YORK
• • • • • • • • • • •

2:15 p.m.–April 3, 2001

THE FIRST WOMAN PRESIDENT of the United States stared down glumly at ice-bound Manhattan Island as Marine Corps One lifted off from the United Nations helipad beside the East River and headed west across midtown.

Despite the sixty-eight-degree temperature in the cabin, Kathleen Piziali shivered involuntarily at the sight of the freezing city below. The coldest winter since the last Ice Age had left huge, dirty snowbanks lining the streets of New York, and the tops of the skyscrapers were a broken quilt of white squares and rectangles beneath their caps of drifted snow.

Two minutes later, the chopper reached the Hudson River and flew out across the ice. The great waterway was frozen solid from the Verrazano Narrows facing the sea to the source of the river far upstate.

The President pointed down at a long line of rectangular barges stretching for miles along the center of the river ice. "What do you suppose those are?" she asked the tall scientist in the seat opposite her.

Benjamin Franklin Meade craned toward the window to see. "Garbage scows. The Sanitation Department drags them out on the floes by tractor. When the ice melts, they'll settle into the river and be towed out to sea."

"Doesn't do much for the view," the President said wryly. "How'd you like to have one of those expensive riverside apartments and be staring out at miles of garbage scows?"

"It could be worse, Madam President. Can you imagine if the sun were shining, heating up all those rotten eggs and half-eaten anchovy pizzas? The damn stuff would stink all the way to Ohio."

The President looked up at the leaden sky. "We don't have to worry about that, do we, Ben? If the projections you gave the U.N. today are right, the northern hemisphere won't see the sun for another fifteen years."

"That's best-case, Madam President. The atmospheric conditions could continue even longer. What worries me is that only the industrial powers are doing any long-term planning. Most of the third-world countries still think they can rely on the U.S. to supply them with surplus food. Well, we can't. Our days as the breadbasket of the world are over."

"I think you made that chillingly clear. It was as quiet as a tomb in the General Assembly while you were listing the crops we can't grow anymore."

"You addressed the same issues in your own speech, Madam President. You didn't pull any punches."

"True, but even as President of the United States, I'm still viewed as a politician. Whatever I have to say, it's assumed that political considerations are mixed in with the facts. The U.N. members needed to hear those projections from a respected scientist, someone with your credentials."

Ben Meade was a renaissance scientist, equally at home in the fields of geology, oceanography and climatology. He was also the founder and president of Meade International, the world's foremost developer of geothermal energy. The geothermal fields he'd brought in around the world had made him a multimillionaire and given him an international reputation.

The President crossed one well-shaped leg over the other. "Ironic, isn't it? All those years during the Cold

War, we worried about a Soviet-American nuclear war filling the atmosphere with dust and debris that would block out the sun."

"The 'nuclear winter' scenario," Ben said, shifting his lanky six-foot, four-inch frame so he wouldn't be staring at the President's legs. Men often stared at Kathy Piziali, for the President of the United States was beautiful. At fifty, she looked ten years younger, with shoulder-length, straw-colored hair framing large, blue-green eyes, a chiseled nose, and full lips that parted when she smiled to reveal even, white teeth.

Everything about the President said "Class." She dressed with an understated elegance, had an intimate knowledge of art and design, and preferred the company of intellectuals and writers to the normal Washington gatherings of politicians and lobbyists. It was said that Kathy Piziali had brought style back to the White House for the first time since the days of John F. Kennedy's Camelot.

Yet for all her sophistication, Ben knew her to be one tough lady, a seasoned politician who wasn't above twisting arms and kicking ass to get a bill through Congress.

"Yes, a nuclear winter," the President said, her fingers worrying the strand of pearls that gleamed against her forest-green wool suit. "God, during the seventies and eighties, that was all you heard from some of the environmental groups."

She gave a short, bitter laugh. "And what happens? The Soviets dump their Communist system; the Cold War ends, and the nuclear bombs are dismantled. Then, *kaboom!* A monster volcano erupts in the middle of the ocean and saturates the atmosphere with more dust and debris than the bombs we all feared."

"We've entered a volcanic winter, Madam President, as sunless and cold as the worst nuclear winter we could have imagined."

"It's the rural areas of the country I'm concerned about most, Ben; northern New England and the western states. The people are too scattered and the roads too snow-clogged to get food and fuel in."

She shook her head sadly. "We haven't released the figures for fear of panic and looting, but our low-ball estimate is that fifty-five thousand Americans have frozen or starved to death over the past two winters."

Ben's mouth tightened. "I didn't know it was that many."

"It's at least that many. And that's only a fraction of the number of people who've perished worldwide. I saw a C.I.A. report yesterday that estimates eight hundred thousand dead in Eastern Europe, another six million in Asia."

"It will only get worse, Madam President. Average temperatures in the northern hemisphere have plunged fifteen degrees in the past year, and they'll continue to fall as the snowcap expands down from the Arctic."

The President thought that over for a moment. The United States had less than a year's supply of grain and powdered milk left in reserve. Meat and vegetables were already scarce enough to bring premium prices on the thriving black market. There had been food riots in several cities during the past winter. The scientists' plans for intensive indoor agriculture had goddam well better work.

"I remember your prediction that R-Nine would erupt," she said finally.

"You have a good memory. What was it, ten, eleven, years ago?"

"Nineteen-ninety. I was on a Senate subcommittee overseeing the National Oceanographic and Atmospheric Administration when you appeared before the panel."

Ben looked down at the snow-covered New Jersey countryside passing beneath the presidential helicopter. "Your committee wasn't much interested in my predictions. I remember one fat senator, from Georgia I think, falling asleep halfway through my appearance."

"We should have listened to you, Ben. Somebody should have. We could have been preparing the country for a volcanic winter, stocking food and fuel, insulating our homes and offices. A million other things."

"I've always been curious; why didn't you listen? I spread the evidence right out on the committee table; the lava samples, the chemical analyses, the seafloor charts. Facts are facts."

The President gave Ben an appraising glance. With his tousled light-brown hair and clear blue eyes, he didn't look much older than he had ten years ago. Only the laugh wrinkles edging the mantle of his eyebrows and the slightly weathered texture of his face marked the passing of the years.

"I think it was because you were so young then . . . in your early twenties," the President said. "That and the fact that older and more eminent geophysicists disagreed with you."

"You don't hear much from those 'eminent geophysicists' these days, do you, Madam President?" Ben asked, a caustic edge to his voice.

Scientists had known for almost thirty years that a five-hundred-mile chain of volcanic mountains was rising from the depths of the mid-Atlantic. Yet for the first two decades after the discovery of R-9 and her sister peaks, most geophysicists argued that the volcanism was the result of a normal upwelling of magma through the mid-Atlantic Ridge.

The ridge was part of a great fracture in the earth's crust through which molten magma was rising continuously from the planet's fiery interior to become new ocean floor on both sides of the fissure.

Then, in the summer of 1990, twenty-three-year-old Ben Meade dove to the base of R-9 in a French research submersible. When he returned to the ocean surface several hours later, he brought back evidence of the magma source that startled the scientific world.

Ben's analysis of the submarine lava turned up a composition rich in alkalies and volatiles, evidence that the magma had risen suddenly from great depths. Coupled with the immense volume of material being erupted, the chemical clues suggested the existence of an immense hot spot beneath the volcanoes, a megaplume of superheated magma rising from far down in the earth's mantle.

Ben pointed out that hot spots with a far slower rate of eruption had formed Iceland to the north, and the Hawaiian and Galápagos islands in the Pacific. Now a new island chain was about to be born.

While most of his scientific colleagues had continued to insist that the volcanoes would soon go dormant, the young geophysicist had predicted that the suddenly active megaplume would build the entire five-hundred-mile range of volcanic peaks to the surface within fifteen years. There was little doubt, Ben concluded, that the largest of the mountains, R-9, would break through the waves by the year 2000.

"One thing I'm curious about, Ben," the President said. "When you appeared before the committee, you predicted that the coming blast from R-Nine would be as titanic as the eruption of Toba in Indonesia seventy-three thousand years ago."

Ben nodded. "From the satellite readings we're getting of the debris and gases in the stratosphere, R-Nine was even bigger than Toba."

"Yes, but you said that the clouds of ash and gases from Toba blocked out sunlight all over the world, sending temperatures plummeting in both the northern and southern hemispheres. Yet the eruption of R-Nine is only affecting the planet north of the equator."

"It's a matter of geography, Madam President. Toba was close to the equator. When the volcano blew, the debris spread out evenly over both the northern and southern hemispheres. R-Nine rises through the sea at fifty degrees north latitude, farther north than any part of the United States but Alaska. The winds at that latitude will keep the ash and gases circling the earth above the equator."

"So for the next fifteen years at least, we'll have two worlds," the President said. "A northern hemisphere shrouded in volcanic clouds and ten degrees colder than normal, and a southern hemisphere with normal sunlight and seasonal temperatures."

"Life isn't fair, Madam President, and neither is nature."

"Goddamn it, doesn't volcanic debris adhere to the law of gravity? You know, everything that goes up must come down."

Ben dug at his collar. He preferred his usual flannel shirt, lined khaki pants and sturdy work boots to the suit, tie and polished wing tips he'd had to wear for his U.N. appearance.

"Sure, the volcanic debris will settle back to earth in a few years and there'll be some increase in the sunlight reaching the northern hemisphere. But not much."

The President furrowed her brow. "I don't understand. I thought it was the ash that was blocking out the sun."

"That's a common misconception. Actually, our loss of solar radiation is due far more to the gases from the eruption."

"I'm not a scientist, Ben. Boil it down for me."

"When R-Nine blew, along with the ash, it blasted a huge plume of volcanic gases into the stratosphere, seven to twenty miles above the earth. Those gases are mainly water vapor, hydrochloric acid and sulfur dioxide."

"Sulfur dioxide? Isn't that what car engines emit?"

"Same stuff. Now, what happens is that the hydrochloric acid dissolves in water and rains out of the atmosphere. But the sulfur dioxide reacts differently. Over time, it's converted into sulfuric acid and then condensed into a mist of fine particles called sulfate aerosols. It's the aerosols that reflect the sun's radiation and cool the atmosphere. And the aerosols will be up there long after all the ash has drifted back down to earth."

The President looked glum. "My private secretary, Nicole Noland, is in her early thirties. She has a baby. Little boy named Zachary. She brought Zach into the Oval Office the other day and I looked at that tiny face and I thought, Jesus, that kid won't see the sun until he's fifteen years old."

"No, he won't see the sun. But he will have a warm environment where he can play outdoors. He'll have fields where he can smack a baseball around, hills to hike, trees to climb, streams to fish."

"You mean in Biosphere America?"

"Yes, Madam President. In Biosphere America."

Biosphere America was the huge, glass-enclosed artificial environment nearing completion outside Princeton, New Jersey. Developed in the British Isles the year before, the biosphere was an immense, self-contained mini-Earth that combined intensive agriculture with high technology. Totally sealed off from the earth's atmosphere outside, the biosphere was designed so that everything the inhabitants ate, drank and breathed was recycled. Even the energy to heat and power the biosphere was renewable geothermal power drawn from deep below the earth's crust.

Ben looked at his watch. "We should be over the biosphere in about five minutes. I appreciate the ride home."

Piziali waved a deprecating hand. "I have a speaking engagement in Philadelphia tonight. It's on the way. Besides, it's the least I could do after you interrupted your busy schedule to speak at the U.N. today. Thanks."

"Any time, Madam President. If you hadn't backed that funding bill in the Senate, there wouldn't be a Biosphere America. Doctor Glynn and I are both very grateful to you."

"Speaking of Doctor Glynn, how is your fiancée?"

Ben stared down at the snow, not knowing how to answer the question. Things hadn't been going well between himself and Marjorie lately; both were conducting mind-numbing research that kept them working eighteen or twenty hours a day.

The strain, the lack of sleep and the setbacks were wearing them down, making them find fault and snap at each other over the least little thing. It wasn't helping that Ben was often away. They hadn't made love in a month.

"Marjorie's under a lot of pressure," Ben said carefully. "Her plant-genetics research has forced her to spend more and more time in the lab. She's near exhaustion."

The President looked thoughtful. "Anything I can do? More research assistants? Funding?"

"I'll ask her, but I don't think either would help. She has a full staff, and money isn't a problem at the moment. It's simply that DNA plant research is grueling, time-intensive work."

One of the four Secret Service agents on board the helicopter spoke briefly to the pilot, then came down the aisle and leaned toward the President. "We're approaching Princeton, Madam President. We'll be landing at Biosphere America in a couple of minutes."

The President smiled at the agent. "Thank you, Mike." Then she looked back at Ben. "I haven't been to the biosphere since the week after my inauguration. I can't wait to see the progress you've made."

Ben glanced out the window. "We're still above the clouds. Be another minute before you can see it."

"My science adviser tells me that all five ecosystems are in."

Ben nodded, continuing to stare through the frosted glass. "Pretty much. The rain forest, the marine environment and the savanna are complete. The desert's in, too, except for a section of cacti from Baja. We're also shy a couple dozen animal species."

"How many species are there altogether?"

"Counting the fish and insect families, over a thousand."

The President shook her head in wonder. "You know what the biosphere reminds me of, Ben? Noah's Ark."

Ben looked across at the President and smiled. "The Ark only had animals, Madam President. Biosphere America contains entire ecosystems; soils, plants, microorganisms. Even the microclimates are authentic. That's why Marjorie named it after the earth's biosphere, the envelope of air, water and land in which living things exist on this planet."

The helicopter broke through the snow clouds and Ben turned back to the window. "There it is, Madam President. Biosphere America."

The President sucked in her breath sharply at the sight of the titanic step pyramid below. Rising in three tiers like a colossal Mayan temple, the eight-hundred-foot mountain of glass dominated the New Jersey countryside.

"God, I'll never get used to how immense it is," Kathy Piziali breathed, awe in her voice.

"A mile long and three-quarters of a mile wide," Ben said. "Fourteen billion cubic feet. The largest artificial environment ever constructed. That series of arched vaults on the south side houses the Intensive Agriculture Biome. The white-domed building on the right is the Human Habitat."

The President looked puzzled. "If I recall your projections, each biosphere is designed to feed and shelter a hundred thousand people. But that habitat down there doesn't look like it could house a tenth that many."

"That's only the first of the sixteen habitats each biosphere will have," Ben said. "Marjorie and I and the other scientists working on the prototype live there. Eventually there'll be four habitats on each side, and all sixteen will open directly into the biosphere through glass pressure locks."

"Why so many separate habitats?"

"We want to give people the feeling that they're living in small cities instead of in one big beehive. The architects have done wonders. The front window in almost every biosphere apartment is part of the pyramid wall. Depending on which side they live on, a family can sit in their living room and look out at a jungle, a savanna, a desert, a marsh or a miniature ocean."

"What about the biospheres planned for the rest of the country? Are those on schedule?"

"We've had some delays, but most of the site work's been completed. We'll start putting up the steel and glass on the first phase as soon as the snow melts. Late June, probably."

The helicopter was only two hundred feet above the summit of the pyramid now, and Kathy Piziali could see the green canopy of the rain forest through the glass. "How many biospheres are planned for the first phase?"

"A thousand. It'll be the largest concerted construction effort ever undertaken in the country. The pyramids themselves should take about six months to put up. Figure another three months to bring in the plants and animals for the different ecosystems."

"So you estimate that we can start moving the first hundred million Americans into the biospheres in January of next year?" the President asked.

Ben thought for a moment. A thousand things could go wrong: bad weather, construction delays, problems with transplanting ecosystems from the tropics. "That's the target date. We could run weeks, even months, over."

The President's mouth set in a hard line. "We've

wasted the entire year since R-Nine erupted, thanks to the so-called experts at the Department of Agriculture. God Almighty, it's snowing in June and the egghead agronomists continue to insist that we can still grow enough crops in the southern states to feed the country. We never should have listened to them. We should have started our biosphere-building program at the same time the British did."

"The agronomists were as wrong as those 'expert' geophysicists were back in ninety." Ben shrugged. "There's nothing we can do about it now but build biospheres as quickly as we can."

"When do you start construction of the second phase?"

"We'll spend next winter doing the site work, then start putting up the main pyramids as soon as the weather breaks. We should have all two thousand Biospheres completed by January of year after next."

The President cocked her head. " 'All two thousand'? Did I miss something here? Two thousand biospheres will shelter two hundred million people. Right?"

"Right."

"But there are two hundred and fifty million Americans, Ben. What happens to the other fifty million people?"

Ben avoided the President's eyes. "Our computer projections say that twenty percent of the population won't come in. We need only two thousand biospheres."

The President looked at him sharply. "Twenty percent! Jesus Christ, that can't be right."

"We got the same numbers before we started building biospheres in Britain last year, and they turned out to be accurate within a point or two. One out of every five people will refuse to move into the biospheres for one reason or another."

"What kind of people would choose a life of cold and privation on the outside when the biospheres offer food and warmth and security?"

"They run the gamut, Madam President: farm families that won't leave their land, suburban homeowners with every penny they have tied up in their houses, old people who'd rather die in a world they know than move into a futuristic and frightening new environment. Then there're the fringe groups: drug gangs, bikers, survivalists, street whores."

"I don't give a damn whether they're farmers or whores, we have to find a way to bring everyone in."

Ben exploded in frustration. "What the hell are you going to do, send out the Army to round them up? We tried that in Britain and it didn't work. People see a military helicopter or a truck convoy coming, they hide. All the British Army brought back were bodies. A thousand a week sometimes. You politicians think you can legislate people into doing what you want them to do. You can't. People are people: stubborn, perverse, often stupid individuals."

The President laughed. "You don't have to tell me, Ben. Half the politicians I deal with in Washington are congenital idiots."

Ben grinned sheepishly. "I didn't mean to put people down." His face turned serious again. "It's just that in England and Ireland, I saw so many needless deaths. There was always some father with young kids and a misplaced sense of self-reliant pride who refused to move his family into a biosphere. His attitude was 'I can take care of my own family.' Two months later, the Army would bring in their bodies. The dead kids really got to me."

"I like a man who's passionate about a cause, Ben. There are too many gray people in Washington, yes-men only interested in covering their asses. I prefer hearing the unvarnished truth."

"The unvarnished truth is that twenty percent won't come in. You can take that to the bank."

They felt the helicopter touch down on the snowy helipad beside Biosphere America. Ben unhooked his seat belt and rose. The President looked up at him, her eyes intent. "And all those millions of Americans who won't come in? What happens to them?"

"They'll freeze, starve, kill each other over a sack of flour or a gallon of gas. What difference does it make, Madam President? Fifty million people will take a chance that they can survive outside the biospheres. And most of them will die."

CODY, WYOMING
••••••••••••••••••

1:15 p.m.–April 4, 2001

DICK JEROME WATCHED ACROSS the cluttered ranch-house kitchen as his young daughters, Jody and Emily, played with Sonny, their little gray cockapoo. Then he turned away in anguish at the thought of the terrible thing he must do after nightfall.

He crossed to a window and stared out into the blizzard that had been raging for the past two days. God in heaven, would the snow never stop? On the windward side of the house, the drifts sloped up over the eaves, and across the buried farmyard, he could see the snow piled twenty-five feet high against the side of the weather-scoured barn.

The blizzard was only the latest in an endless series of storms that had lashed the ranch unmercifully over the past seven months. The fences and feed bins had long since disappeared beneath the ever-thickening white blanket, as had every shrub and small tree on the place.

Only here and there did the winter-bare branches of a tall tree stick up through the drifts, like the fleshless fingers of a corpse reaching out of a snow-covered grave. Dick leaned forward and rested his forehead against the icy windowpane, seeking cold relief from the constant headache that burned behind his brow.

It was almost unfathomable to him that a single volcano—thousands of miles away in the middle of the Atlantic Ocean—could change the weather like this.

In the state of Wyoming, there were thousands of families like the Jeromes: trapped in their homes by impassable roads, their telephone and electric lines downed by fierce winds, their food almost gone.

Dick sensed a presence behind him and turned as his wife Diane joined him at the window. She avoided his eyes, looking past him at the snow.

"We should have gotten out last fall," she said with the bitter resignation that had edged her voice for months now.

Years ago, he'd fallen in love with her voice, with the way words tumbled from her in a giggly, effervescent flow, like water bubbling up from a spring. No more. The deprivation and despair of the past two years had stolen the laughter from her voice and the youth from her face. Her once luxuriant black hair was now dull and streaked with gray and her thirty-five-year-old face was creased with deep worry wrinkles. Most days she looked fifty.

Dick knew that he'd aged, too. He'd run out of razor blades six months ago and it had shocked him when his beard grew out almost pure white. Tending to his chores in the constant cold outside had left his face like dry leather, and although he was only forty-two, he already had arthritis in his hands and arms.

"We should have gone to L.A. with your brother and his family," Diane said. "Or at least moved into Cheyenne like they told us to."

"Maybe," he said.

"Maybe!" she mocked, turning back for her wood stove. "*Maybe* we won't starve to death."

Last summer the governor had ordered rural families to leave their farms and evacuate to Cheyenne or Laramie, where they could be fed and housed in Red Cross centers. He warned that the coming winter's fierce winds, cold and snow would ground most helicopter flights, and even if the choppers could take off, they would never be able to supply all the widely scattered cattle and sheep spreads.

Dick had talked it over with his brother John, who owned half the ranch and lived with his wife and kids in a double-wide mobile home down near the county road. Truth was, John had never intended to spend his life ranching, which was why he'd insisted on living in a trailer with four kids instead of building a real home on the place.

"I'm not going to risk another winter out here," John had said. "I'm taking Sheila and the kids out to L.A."

Despite Diane's misgivings, Dick had talked her into staying. After all, he'd argued, the Jerome family had survived fierce winters on the ranch for three generations now. Besides, at least half of their neighbors had also decided to ignore the governor's warning, trusting they had enough food and fuel to get them through until spring.

"You were singing a different tune last Christmas when the food riots were raging," he said to her back. "How many cities were burning, huh, how many? New York, Chicago, L.A., Memphis, Miami, a hundred more. Over a thousand dead the radio said before the damn batteries died. That's what happens when you stuff people into warehouses and feed 'em nothing but bread and soup three times a day. You can't tell me it was wrong to stay out here."

"It was wrong for the Russells."

She had him there, and he let out a long sigh and turned back to the window. It had always been a small comfort for Dick to go out for wood in the morning and see smoke rising from the chimney of the Russell ranch just beyond the eastern horizon. It was a sign that the Jerome family was not alone out on the snowbound high prairie.

Then, one morning in March, there had been no smoke. There were a lot of possible reasons to explain why the Russells' fire had gone out; maybe they'd run out of wood or food, or fallen sick. Snow might have collapsed the roof and crushed them, or the wolf pack Dick had spotted out beyond the barn the week before could have smashed in through a window and torn the family to pieces.

Or maybe the isolation and the endless cold and snow had finally driven them crazy and they'd killed themselves. Whatever the reason the smoke had stopped rising from the Russells' chimney, it could mean only one thing. The temperature fell to forty below zero at night, quickly sucking the warmth out of a house. Without a fire, a family couldn't survive for more than a few hours. Don and Susan Russell and their ten-year-old twin boys were dead.

The thought that his own family might soon join the Russells in death sent a surge of primal fear through Dick. They had enough wood to last them through the rest of the winter, the roof was sturdy, and he'd nailed heavy mesh guards over the kitchen windows on the day he'd spotted the wolves. But they were almost out of food.

There was virtually nothing left but six or seven potatoes, half a sack of cattle feed and an almost empty box of raisins. They had to have protein, and there was only one source of protein left to them. Dick forced the thought away. Tonight. He would face that horror tonight.

"Daddy, come see the new trick we taught Sonny," six-year-old Emily sang out from the corner opposite her parents' queen-sized bed. Last fall Dick had brought the bed down so he and Diane could keep the kids warm between them when the fire in the stove burned down at night.

He'd sealed the kitchen off from the rest of the house to conserve heat, then brought in the porta-potty—formerly used on long trips in the van—and turned the pantry into a bathroom. This was their world now, an eighteen- by twenty-five-foot womb of life amidst a universe of endless snow.

"Watch this, Daddy." Emily beamed as he crossed to the blanket-covered corner where the girls played with their dolls each day. "Sonny, fetch Kevin. Go on."

The small cockapoo bounded five feet away, picked up Emily's doll by the arm and brought it back to the corner. The chestnut haired little girl clapped her hands in delight. "You see, Daddy. Isn't he smart?"

"Can we give him a treat?" eight-year-old Jody asked, her thumb in her little Cupid mouth as usual.

Dick knelt next to his daughters. "We don't have any treats left, sweetheart," he said, easing the thumb from Jody's mouth. "You're going to make your teeth crooked."

"We could give him some of our food," Jody said, pushing back the wheat-colored hair from her forehead with her red and wrinkled thumb.

"No!" Diane said, whirling around from the stove where she'd been stirring a thin gruel of cattle feed and potatoes. "That dog eats too much as it is."

"Maybe just this once," Dick said, meeting his wife's eyes across the room. The thought of what they knew he must do tonight passed between them and she sighed and reached for the box of raisins. "You can give him two."

Emily squealed with delight and tore across the room, the dog on her heels. She took the raisins from her mother and held them out to Sonny. The cockapoo gobbled the morsels of fruit, then licked the last trace of sweetness from her tiny palm.

"He has the tickliest tongue," Emily giggled.

Diane's lip began to quiver and she fled for the bathroom alcove. From behind the curtain, they could hear her sobbing.

"Why's Mommy crying?" Jody asked, fear in her round hazel eyes as she jammed her thumb back in her mouth.

"Maybe she has a tummy ache." It was all Dick could think to say. "You know how you cry when you get a tummy ache."

"No, she doesn't have a tummy ache," Jody said, her too-wise eight-year-old eyes looking straight at her father. "She's crying because we don't have any food and we're all going to starve to death."

"Where'd you ever get such an idea?" Dick asked.

"I heard Mommy say it last night after we went to bed."

Dick sighed. He and Diane always tried to keep to a whisper the things the children shouldn't hear, but last night she'd been on the verge of hysteria and several

times her voice had risen. Besides, the bed was only ten
feet from the table where they sat.

"If we die, will we go to heaven and see Grandma and
Grandpa?" Emily asked, picking up Sonny and carrying
the struggling dog back across the kitchen.

"When we die, we will," her father said. "But that
won't be for a long time. Mommy didn't mean what she
said last night. Now put Sonny down and let's play a
game. How about Parcheesi?"

"No, Monopoly," Emily said, dropping poor Sonny
with a thud.

"You can't count the money," Jody told her.

"I can count the ones and fives."

"It's all right, I'll be the banker," Dick said, sitting
down cross-legged on the blanket. "This'll be fun."

They didn't hear Diane return. A while later, she was
just there at the stove again, mechanically stirring and
staring down into the gruel while Dick and the girls
played Monopoly.

There were no sunsets anymore. The light just gradually faded behind the ash clouds, and the moonless, star-
less night closed over the Jerome home cold and black. At
five o'clock, they ate gruel for the fourth time that week.
At eight o'clock, the girls put their nightgowns on over
their thermal underwear and two pairs of pants and
sweaters.

The four of them knelt down beside the bed, and Jody
and Emily began their prayers. "God bless Grandpa"—
frozen to death when his truck was mired in a snowdrift
on the road to town last winter—"God bless Grandma"—
dead because of missing Grandpa—"God bless Aunt
Sheila and Uncle John and Cousins Jennifer, Sara, Amy
and Johnny"—moved out to L.A., and who knew if they
were still alive after the food riots?

"And God bless Sonny." At this, Diane grabbed her
husband's hand and held on so tight that her nails dug
into his palms.

Finally, mercifully, the prayers were over. They kissed
the girls and snuggled them beneath the five blankets.
Later, Diane would climb in on one side and Dick on the
other. Their love life had been one of the early casualties

of the Earth Winter. With unceasing worry over how to survive, sex was not a priority.

"Sonny, c'mon." Emily clapped her hands. The little dog gave a happy yelp and jumped up onto the bed, working his way into the warm hollow between the two girls. He slept there with them every night, sharing the space with dolls Kevin and Kate.

"Daddy, aren't you going to say it?" Jody grinned.

Dick pretended not to know what she meant. "Say what?"

" 'Get that miserable, fat little furball off my bed.' You say that every night."

Dick scrunched up a fierce face. "Get that miserable, fat little furball off my bed."

The girls laughed, as they laughed every night, and Emily rolled over and threw her arms around Sonny. "No, no, no. He has to sleep here or he'll get cold."

"All right, just this once," Dick said, as he said every night.

He bent and kissed his daughters gently on the cheek, his rough hand stroking their foreheads. "Sleep tight, girls. I love you."

"I love you, Daddy," Jody said.

Emily asked, "Aren't you going to tell Sonny you love him? If you don't, he'll have hurt puppy feelings."

"He's not a puppy. He's a full-grown, fat little furball."

"He's my puppy. He'll always be my puppy, even when I'm old like Grandma."

"Dogs don't live that long, sweetheart."

"Sonny will."

"Stop it!" Diane burst out, her lower lip quivering. "Both of you, go to sleep."

The girls stared at their mother, shock and hurt on their little faces.

"I'm sorry." She bent and kissed them. "God, I seem to say that to you all the time nowadays, don't I?"

"You don't have to be sorry, Mommy," Emily said. "We know you have a tummy ache."

"Happy dreams, girls," Dick said, rising from the bed. He put his hand on his wife's shoulder. "How about some tea?"

Diane rose wearily. "Optimist. That damn bag's been used fifty times."

"I like weak tea."

"We don't have any sugar. You know that. Much less cream."

"Hot is all I care about."

Diane poured water from the kettle she kept simmering on the back of the stove, and they took turns dipping the forlorn tea bag, each avoiding the conversation they knew must come.

She brought the teacup up and let the steam waft around her face. "God, I wish I could take a hot bath. I stink like a pig. Worse than a pig."

"Remember that aging hippie couple who worked the hay harvest four summers ago? They called it their 'body bouquet.'"

"It was six years ago, and they smelled terrible. I couldn't bear to go in the bunkhouse. And now we smell just like them."

"A little b.o. won't kill us."

"No, that's not what will kill us."

Dick took a last sip and put down his cup. "It has to be tonight," he said, keeping his voice low in case one of the girls was still awake. "You know that."

"There must be another way. Maybe you could try hunting again."

"There's nothing out there, Diane. Nothing. The cattle have all frozen to death on the range. Their bodies are deep under the snow. I couldn't even find them with dogs. No deer, no rabbits, no squirrels, no ducks. Nothing but wolf packs. It has to be tonight."

"We have a few potatoes and that sack of cattle feed left. Well, half a sack, anyway."

"You think I want to do this? We haven't had any protein in a month, and the feed won't last out the week. Tonight. That's the end of it."

"Why don't you just cut their little hearts out and be done with it?"

For a terrible moment, rage boiled up in him and he had to fight not to backhand her across the face. Just knock her sanctimonious ass right out of that chair. But he had never struck any woman, much less the mother of his children, and nothing she could say would ever turn him into a wife beater.

"We've got to make it through to the middle of May," he said. "By then, the snow will have melted enough for me to walk out and get us some help. I'll make it up to the kids. I promise. I'll make it up to them."

"I'll be the one holding them tomorrow morning while they're crying and screaming."

"What do you want me to do? Cut off my arm? We could eat my arm. How about a leg? That might last us a month."

"Just get it over with. Will you please just get it over with?"

Dick rose and walked to the bed. Jody and Emily were fast asleep, their faces soft and angelic against the pillows. Waves of love and fear churned in his gut like the clash of opposing seas. He vowed to himself again that he would keep his children alive, no matter what he had to do.

From his place between the two girls, Sonny lifted his curly gray head toward Dick, his tail thumping the bed.

"Sonny, come here," Dick said softly.

The dog popped up from his warm nest, leaped over Jody's sleeping form and jumped down to the floor. He stood with his forepaws on Dick's leg, an eager hope that he was about to be fed in his trusting eyes.

Diane pushed back her chair and walked to the stove. She dipped a wooden spoon into the dinner gruel and put some of the thin liquid into a small glass jar, then crossed the room and handed the jar to her husband.

The little cockapoo smelled the food and began circling eagerly.

"It'll take about twenty minutes," Dick said, putting on his coat. "You'll have the water boiling?"

Diane nodded slowly.

He pulled a thick woolen cap down over his ears and lit the lantern, then crossed to the door and picked up the stainless-steel bucket he used for bringing in snow to melt for water.

"Good-bye, Sonny," Diane whispered as Dick opened the door.

The little dog started toward her in response to his name, but Dick slapped his leg. "C'mon, boy," he said, then stepped out into the dark freezing night and yanked the door shut behind them.

The cockapoo dashed over to his favorite spot and urinated against a snowbank, then followed his master around the corner of the house to the lean-to where the firewood was stored.

Dick hung the lantern from a nail, then knelt and stroked the dog's head. "I'm sorry, boy. If there's another place after this earth, we'll see you there."

He began to sob as his fingers kneaded the warm fur. "I'll get you rawhide toys; I'll let you sleep with the kids every night, even if you do chew up their blankets. We'll even take you for rides in the car. Would you like that, Sonny?"

The little dog lifted his floppy ears, perplexed by the mixture of pain and promise in his master's voice.

Dick reached into his pocket and took out the jar of warm gruel. He unscrewed the lid and spread the food over the top of the chopping block. Then he stood and reached for the ax.

The cockapoo sniffed the gruel, then looked up at Dick expectantly. He knew he couldn't take food unless he was told to.

"Go ahead, boy," Dick said, his voice cracking.

The hungry little dog whirled around and began to lap the gruel from the wood. Dick braced his feet, the ax held near his shoulder as he waited for Sonny to extend his neck over the block. *Now!* He brought the ax down and severed the dog's head in one blow.

The head rolled away into the snow, and Dick bent and quickly knotted a rope around Sonny's tail. Then he hung the warm carcass upside down from a rafter and let the blood run from the severed neck into the stainless-steel bucket. Nothing must be wasted.

For several minutes, Dick stomped his feet and blew into his gloves while the blood drained from Sonny's body. Then he cut the dog down and began to skin him.

In the morning, he would tell the girls that the wolves had taken Sonny when he let the little cockapoo out to go to the bathroom the night before. Jody and Emily would sob their eyes out as they ate the stew that had mysteriously appeared, the food that would keep them alive for another few weeks.

Buenos Aires, Argentina
•••••••••••••••••••••••••

4:30 p.m.–April 4th

THE MOST POWERFUL MAN south of the equator made love with his socks on. His mistress had always assumed that it was simply an odd quirk and had never mentioned the socks for fear of embarrassing the proud and reserved Argentine Colonel General Ramon Saavedra de Urquiza.

This time though, the two glasses of wine she'd had before their lovemaking dissolved the normal reticence of Maria Echeverria, and her curiosity bubbled to the surface. As the general rolled off her and lay breathing heavily with his hands crossed behind his head, the dark-haired beauty dug her toes into one of his wool stockings and pushed the calf-length hose down over his ankle.

"Why do you never take your socks off, Ramon?" the nineteen-year-old giggled, her full melon breasts brushing his leg as she reached down and triumphantly pulled the thick stocking the rest of the way off. She dangled the sock over his face, grinning in triumph, just brushing the tip of his nose with the wool.

De Urquiza frowned and flicked the sock away. "Stop it."

"Not until you tell me," she said, trailing the sock

down over his hairy barrel chest and fleshy midsection. "What is it with you and your socks? Are they like your security blanket? Perhaps when you were small, you had little wool booties and they made you feel safe."

The general grunted and scratched one of his massive, hairy shoulders. "Stop trying to psychoanalyze me. You're an art student, not a shrink."

"You think I don't know anything, do you?" she said, lifting his now-flaccid organ with one hand and slipping it into the sock. "Except how to please you in bed."

De Urquiza felt ridiculous with his penis in a sock. "Stop it or I'll give you a spanking."

She began to knead his organ through the fabric. "You'd like that, wouldn't you?" she teased, leaning over to trace his lips with her tongue as her fingers slipped inside the sock. "Bare bottom over your knee. With the video camera going."

The general shifted uncomfortably and reached for a cigar on the nightstand. "I could use a cognac. And not in one of your chipped tumblers. I almost cut my lip at lunch. I don't see why you don't buy new glassware. God knows, I give you enough allowance."

"You don't want a drink, Ramon. You just want me to stop talking about our sex games. In the height of passion, you'll do and say anything. I swear you'd have a circus in bed with us if I let you. But afterward, you're ashamed you did anything but the missionary position. Like you are now. You're probably dreading confessing to the priest all the things we do."

"It's impossible to shock a priest. Nowadays they have heard everything."

"Still, the guilt is there, eh, Ramon. It was programmed in with the catechism when you were a boy. Oh, you forget about the Church and everything else when you're fucking."

"Must you use that language?"

"You prefer what the Church calls it, then? Procreation. Is that what you say in confession? Last night I procreated my mistress three times?"

"Really, Maria, you go too far. The Church is not a fit topic for the boudoir."

"It is you who brings the Church in here. In your head. I think you wear the socks when you make love so you won't be totally naked, totally sinful. At least your feet are pious, eh, Ramon?"

"Goddammit, that's not the reason. You and your psychobabble."

"Then why?"

The general lit his cigar and exhaled angry clouds of smoke. "It's from the time when I was a boy."

Maria grinned in vindication. "I knew it."

"You know nothing. I was born and raised in Ushuaia, at the southern edge of Tierra del Fuego. I've told you that."

"So?"

"It's the southernmost tip of South America, less than seven hundred miles from Antarctica. Twelve months a year, a freezing wind howls up from the bottom of the world. We were poor. A wood stove in the house, that was all. You had to wear your socks to bed or your feet would be ice in the morning."

"Ushuaia, the city of the socked ones."

"You think it's funny? I had a cousin, a girl. She kicked a sock off in her sleep one night and her toes stuck out and got frostbitten and had to be cut off. A thing like that, no one would marry her."

The general gazed up into the smoke from his cigar. "I remember her dragging herself around on stick crutches, her face so sad you could weep just looking at her. One day, I was nine or ten, she went to mass in the village and never came home. They followed the little holes—you know, the ones the stick crutches made in the ground. They led down to the beach. She had hobbled into the sea."

Maria sighed and slipped the sock off his penis and put it back on his foot. "I'm sorry I teased you."

She should have known that the mystery of the socks was part of his beginning. Everything that made him who he was today flowed from the poverty and striving of his youth. He had clawed his way to the top, becoming one of the few cadets from the remote reaches of Tierra del

Fuego ever accepted at Escuela Militar de la Nacion, the Argentine military academy.

As a young lieutenant, while his fellow junior officers played polo and pursued the nightlife of Buenos Aires, Ramon Saavedra de Urquiza had studied military doctrine and trained his men. He soon had the finest company in the Argentine Army. During war games, his unit always won. Always.

He had been a thirty-two-year-old captain in 1982 when Argentina seized the undefended Falkland Islands, four hundred miles off her southern coast, from a surprised Britain. The Argentine junta then in power had expected Britain to complain bitterly to the United Nations but to take no further action to regain the Falklands. After all, the islands were but a tiny backwater at the remote fringe of the South Atlantic, and of almost no economic significance to England.

The junta had not anticipated the fierce nationalism of Margaret Thatcher. The British prime minister had quickly rallied Parliament to declare war, and a task force carrying a well-armed and well-trained British force steamed south for the Falklands.

Supported by superior Royal Navy and Royal Air Force units, the British troops quickly retook the islands, capturing thousands of dispirited Argentine troops in a steady advance toward the capital city of Stanley.

Captain de Urquiza had refused to surrender. For almost a week, the troops he commanded had bravely defended a ridgeline above Stanley, thwarting the British drive on the port. When his men finally ran out of ammunition, the young officer had night-marched his soldiers across the island to a tiny port where they commandeered a civilian fishing smack and escaped to sea. A week later, they were picked up by an Argentine freighter.

De Urquiza emerged as one of the few Argentine heroes of the Falklands War, and promotions had followed rapidly through the next two decades. He was a full colonel at thirty-five, a brigadier before he was forty, Army Chief of Staff at forty-five.

During the years when de Urquiza was climbing the military ladder, a string of inept civilian governments

ruled in Buenos Aires. By 1998, inflation had soared to almost 200 percent a year, unemployment hovered near 22
percent, and the labor unions were staging continuous
strikes that crippled the country and worsened the economic situation.

Argentina's industrialists and major bankers increasingly viewed the military as the country's only stabilizing
force, and secretly urged the Army Chief of Staff to take
action. De Urquiza needed little encouragement. In June
1998, he staged a lightning coup d'état, replacing the fum-
bling civilian government with a three-man military
junta, himself at the head.

Within a year, inflation was down to under 10 percent,
unemployment had been cut in half and the trade unions
brought to heel. Under de Urquiza, the junta ruled with a
firm but benevolent hand that did not often touch the everyday life of the Argentines.

Given a choice between the inefficiency and economic
chaos of the inept politicians and the order and stability
of the junta, most Argentine citizens preferred that the
military remain in power. There was little discontent in
the country, and only a feeble organized opposition.

De Urquiza had closed his eyes again, and Maria studied his bulldog face. He was not a man a woman, or a
country, could love. He was too iron-willed, too lacking
in warmth and passion, to excite an emotional response in
others. Both Maria and Argentina saw him as a strong father who fed and clothed his children and never beat
them, but never hugged them, either.

Ordinary Argentines knew little about him personally,
and only a handful of his intimates were aware of his
poverty-stricken roots in Tierra del Fuego. Never having
had money, Ramon was tight with a peso. Despite his
protestation that he gave her a generous allowance, Maria
knew from talking with the mistresses of other powerful
men that he gave her far less than most.

He was saying something and she came back from her
musing. "I'm sorry, Ramon. What did you say?"

"I said I understand why you were curious. After all,
how many men wear their socks to bed?"

"I wouldn't know."

The general looked at her for a long moment. She wouldn't know. She'd been a virgin the first time they'd slept together, and as far as he knew, she had never had another man.

"You're a good girl, Maria."

"I'm not a girl. I'm almost twenty. I'm a woman."

"So you are," he said, thinking of how proud he was when he took her out to dinner, her luxuriant black hair done up smartly and her long, beautiful legs flashing through the slit of a form-fitting gown.

Sometimes he would let his gaze wander the restaurant as she walked, watching the faces of the men, the lust in their eyes and the way they wet their lips. At such times it was good to know that she was his, that when they were alone again, he would possess the body that other men could only fantasize about.

Still, sometimes he wondered how long he could keep her. He was thirty years older than she. And far from handsome, with his prizefighter's nose, balding pate, elephantine ears and overweight body. Not that he was without sex appeal. His position gave him that. Power, as the American statesman Henry Kissinger had said three decades before, was an aphrodisiac.

Certainly it was his high office that drew the beautiful girl to his bed. Maria had been eighteen when he'd met her at a reception for young officers. She was clinging to the arm of her fiancé, a young captain, when he spotted her across the room and arranged for an introduction.

De Urquiza had seen the hero worship in her eyes when she found herself shaking hands with the most powerful man in Argentina. He'd asked her to dance. A waltz. Every eye had been on them as he whirled her around the ballroom, her face flushed, her eyes shining up at him in adoration.

As the young captain stewed in impotent frustration, they'd stayed on the floor, sharing a second dance. De Urquiza discovered that she was an art student, convent-school-educated, and from a middle-class family.

The next day, he'd sent her two dozen roses and an invitation to dinner. A week later, her fiancé was suddenly and inexplicably assigned as the military attaché at the

Argentine Embassy in Canada. A month after that, Maria moved into the apartment de Urquiza found for her. He took her virginity that first night, and they'd been lovers ever since.

The general put out his cigar, swung his feet off the bed and patted a *rat-a-tat-tat* on his stomach. "I have to go. I have a busy afternoon."

Maria stood and put on a rose-colored silk robe as de Urquiza padded naked toward the bathroom. "You're going to make a deal for that nuclear submarine today, Ramon? You generals and your toys."

The general stopped in midstep and whirled, his beefy face flushed. "Nuclear submarine! What do you know about that?"

He was back across the room in three angry steps, grabbing Maria by her elbows. "What did you do, listen in on one of my phone conversations?"

Maria looked at him wide-eyed. She had never seen him so upset, and his fierce grip was hurting her. "I have never done that. And you know it. What is the matter with you?"

As his alarm ebbed, he realized that she was telling the truth. She was not the type to eavesdrop. Besides, he had never discussed the submarine over any phone, much less in a call from the apartment of his mistress.

"Maria, it's important," he said, loosening his iron hold. "How do you know about the submarine? Gossip? Did one of my officers' wives—"

"Ramon, I've told you before, you talk in your sleep. Night before last, you woke me up babbling about your precious submarine. I finally had to put a pillow over your head to shut you up."

"God in heaven!"

There was fear in his eyes now. She had never known him to be afraid before.

"Ramon, what is said here, even in your sleep, it goes no farther. You should know that by now."

He nodded, his mind far away. He wasn't worried about Maria talking. But what if he'd talked in his sleep elsewhere? In his barracks quarters, where he occasionally spent a night. Could someone passing in the hallway

have heard? Last month he'd been out in the field on biv-
ouac. He'd slept in a tent, sentries only yards away.

"Ramon?"

He patted her arm. "It's all right. I trust you," he said,
turning again for the bathroom. It was his habit to never
close the door, and a moment later she heard the sound of
his urine streaming into the toilet. When he came back,
his expression was still preoccupied.

"If you trust me, why do you look so worried?"

He walked over to the chaise longue, where he'd taken
off his uniform an hour before, and began getting
dressed. "Because your bed is not the only one in which I
pass my nights. Suppose someone else overheard me
talking in my sleep? Help me with this damn tie."

She came over and knotted the olive-drab tie. "I don't
know why, but you seem to talk in your sleep only after
we've made love. I wouldn't worry. Unless you are sleeping with another woman."

"You know better than that."

"It's such a big secret? This nuclear submarine?"

"Argentina has no bigger."

"What do you want it for, anyway? We have the largest
army in South America, you've said so yourself. And no
enemies, at least none bold enough to attack us."

The general walked over to the French doors that
opened onto a balcony. "Come here."

Maria crossed the room.

"What do you see?"

She looked out over the balcony at the modern, sky-
scraper-crowded city of Buenos Aires. One of the world's
busiest ports, the capital of Argentina sprawled along the
shore of the Rio de la Plata, a mouth-shaped arm of the
South Atlantic.

Buenos Aires was a wealthy, thriving metropolis, the
hub of a vast industrial complex that manufactured everything from automobiles to textiles, paper, chemicals
and clothing. Nearly nine million people lived in the city,
and its universities, churches, libraries, museums, science
centers and opera made it an international center of learning and culture.

"I see the Avenida Nueve de Julio," she said, looking

down at the world's widest boulevard. "And over there, Palermo Park, the cathedral, buildings, cars, shops, people."

"No, no," he said, pointing a finger upward. "Up there."

"What? The sky?"

"What's in the sky?"

"The sun. Is this a new game?"

"If you were in New York, Paris, Moscow, Beijing, what would you see?"

She was about to say "the same thing" when she remembered. "All those cities are in the northern hemisphere. I suppose I would see volcanic clouds."

"Exactly, Maria. And every country under those clouds—that is to say, every country north of the equator—is a potential enemy."

"I don't understand. Why would any of those countries want to attack Argentina?"

"Because they can no longer grow food and we can."

"So can every other country in the southern hemisphere."

"Maria, look at a map. Most of the large land masses and densely populated countries are in the northern hemisphere."

"Yes, but not all. What about Brazil? It is three times the size of Argentina. Why can't they grow food in Brazil?"

"They can, but only enough to feed their own people. Much of the agricultural land has been reclaimed from the jungle. The soil is too thin to grow crops for more than three or four seasons in a row."

"Africa, then. A third of the continent is in the southern hemisphere."

He shook his head. "There are hundreds of thousands of square miles they could farm, but the infrastructure is not there: the roads, irrigation systems, silos, barns. They have no tractors, no harvesters, no trained farm managers and agricultural workers."

"Australia?"

"Nine-tenths desert."

She saw where he was leading. "And we have the pampa."

"Yes, Maria, we have the pampa. It is the glory of Argentina. Two hundred and fifty thousand square miles of the most fertile land on earth. For over a century, the pampa has been the breadbasket of South America, exporting wheat, corn, dairy products and beef all over the world. Until R-Nine erupted last year, the pampa was second only to the U.S. Midwest in food production. Now, with the United States cold and sunless, the agriculture of the pampa is unsurpassed in all the world."

The general returned to the chaise longue and began pulling on his boots. "The infrastructure is already in place. We have the finest farmers in the world, most of them descendants of the original Italian, Spanish, French and German immigrants who began raising crops out there a hundred years ago. They know the soil, the weather, the best fertilizers and insecticides to use. The pampa is crisscrossed with railroads to bring the crops and animal products to Buenos Aires and La Plata for shipment abroad."

De Urquiza stood and buttoned his tunic. "We have modern granaries and meat-processing plants that are already being expanded. It is only a matter of putting more land under cultivation and enlarging our beef and dairy herds. Argentina will feed and clothe the north, and our exports will make us the richest nation on earth."

Maria stared across the room at a Picasso print on the far wall. "It is not only Argentina that will become wealthy, eh, Ramon?"

He followed her eyes. Her attention was not on the Picasso. Her mind was on the bundle of land deeds inside the small, titanium-walled safe behind the artwork.

"Yes, I've bought land. My position does not preclude me from investing in the future of our country."

"When you showed me the deeds, my eyes grew as big as eggs. Four million acres, Ramon! It must pay well, being head of the junta, to afford so much land."

"Don't be silly, I didn't pay cash. The junta has arranged certain trade and pricing agreements that will reap the large landowners huge profits over the coming years. In return, we have been granted loans and non-secured mortgages that allow us to buy land."

"It doesn't seem fair. I mean, you're using your position to make a fortune. Meanwhile, the slum dwellers are scavenging in the city dump and living in cardboard shacks with open sewers a yard from their doors."

De Urquiza's face twisted in rage. "How dare you say such a thing? My family was as poor as those scavengers. I wore the same rags once. I ate the same rotten potatoes. Now, when I have a chance to make a profit, why shouldn't I? The money won't come from our people. It will come from the rich Japanese and Americans and Europeans who will pay dearly for our food, just as we have always paid through our noses for their manufactured goods."

"You're getting upset."

"What do you expect when you imply that I am cheating the people? I've told you of the social programs I plan. In five years, there will be no more scavengers, no more slums, no more malnutrition. What is the harm if I make a few pesos at the same time I am improving the lot of my countrymen?"

He would make a lot more than "a few pesos," but she let it drop. "Will you be here for dinner?"

"No. I'm having dinner with my family."

The way he said it, he was making clear that his family, his wife and children, came first and that she, his mistress, was but a dalliance. Maria's face showed her hurt.

"I'll see you tomorrow then?"

"I don't know. My time is not my own these days. Ring for my car, will you?"

She phoned and told the attendant that the general was ready to leave. The garage was a block away. The large black Cadillac would be out front by the time de Urquiza emerged from the building.

The general picked up his high-peaked cap, the gold braid catching a glint of sunlight through the French doors. "I'll call you."

"I hate it when we fight."

He shrugged. "We don't usually. I suggest we not discuss the land deeds again."

"As you wish."

She could tell that he wasn't going to kiss her good-bye

as he always did, not this time. He was still mad. For a moment, she debated going to him, of forcing his kiss. Then her pride welled up and she caught herself.

He turned to the wall mirror next to the door and adjusted his cap on his bull head. "You know, now that I think of it, I shall probably be busy all week. Why don't you go to your mother's? The change of scenery would do you good."

"My mother thinks I'm a whore. Since living with you, I can never go there again."

"We are what we are," he said, then opened the door without looking at her and left.

For a long time, Maria stood rooted, listening to his footsteps descend the marble staircase outside. He had never said such a hurtful thing to her before. Perhaps he was getting tired of her. She sighed and went to the balcony to watch him drive away.

As always, there were motorcycle escorts in front and in back of his limousine. The guards saluted smartly as he came out of the building and entered the car. He had come a long way from the freezing foot of Tierra del Fuego. The boy who slept with his socks on in an icy hut had become the most powerful man in Argentina.

And soon, as the food of the pampas became ever more critical to the survival of the northern hemisphere, Ramon Saavedra de Urquiza would be the most powerful man in the world.

BIOSPHERE AMERICA,
PRINCETON, NEW JERSEY
•••••••,••••••••••••••

7:25 a.m.–April 15th

BEN MEADE TURNED ON the shower in the Biosphere America apartment he shared with Marjorie Glynn and stood facing away from the nozzle, letting the warm spray beat down on his tense and tired shoulders.

There was a waist-high window, three feet tall, built into the tile at the end of the shower, and he stared out through the slowly steaming glass. Because the bathroom jutted out at a right angle to the habitat, he had a clear view of the rain-forest ecosystem through the sloping glass wall of the biosphere.

For several minutes, he watched a flight of rainbow-hued macaws flit through the dark green jungle in the pyramid, darting among the lush foliage of orchids, banana plants and towering Brazil Nut trees.

Finally, feeling his muscles begin to relax, he turned and reached for the natural soap he used. He hated having any artificial scents on his body, just as he didn't like the constriction of rings or bracelets. He wore a watch only when he had to.

His clothes were of all-natural fibers, wool and cotton, but for his one concession to luxury—a pair of silk pajamas Marjorie had given him early in their relationship. Despite the fact that he was a multimillionaire, the suit he'd worn to the U.N. with the President yesterday was one of only three he owned.

He usually wore jeans or khakis, and his shirts and sweaters ran to earth colors. Clothes to him were meant to keep him warm and comfortable, not to present him like some damn peacock strutting its finery.

His preference for the natural extended to the people in his life. As chairman of Meade International, he regularly rubbed elbows with presidents and prime ministers, and he was on a first-name basis with the titans of finance and industry from Europe to Japan. He knew his way around Washington and the boardrooms of Wall Street, and he wasn't above using contacts and lobbyists if it furthered a cause he believed in.

Yet he preferred direct talk and simple, unpretentious men. His friends ran to scientists, field engineers and hands-on environmentalists, guileless men who struggled to pay the mortgage and took their kids fishing. Ben's best friend was Mel Sanderson, the gruff and good-natured captain of the Meade International research vessel, the *Abyss*.

As he finished rinsing off, he saw the bathroom door open through the frosted glass. It was Marjorie; no one else would walk in on him like this. He turned off the water and opened the stall door.

They'd been lovers for over a year now, but the sight of her after a week apart still sent a swift surge of excitement through him. Thirty-three-year-old Marjorie Glynn had the wholesome beauty he'd always been drawn to.

Her wavy auburn hair cascaded down to her shoulders, framing an oval face with healthy, glowing skin, wide-set green eyes, a strong but feminine nose with a freckled bridge, and full, sensual lips. As always, Marjorie looked every inch the English lady. She was wearing a beige cashmere suit, an off-white silk blouse and a designer scarf. A pair of tortoiseshell reading glasses hung from a beaded strand around her neck.

She carried her slim, five-foot, six-inch body with shoulders back, chin slightly tilted up, the carriage having been drilled into her at the exclusive English girls' school she'd been sent to at the age of eight. Yet there was also a tomboyishness about her: the way she laughed and ran and handled tools, and the way she looked in jeans with her hair pulled back in a ponytail.

"Hi. You just get in?" he asked.

"Ten minutes ago. I took the red-eye across."

"Hand me a towel, will you?"

She pulled a towel from a wall rack and gave it to him, her eyes traveling down over his naked body. For a moment, he thought he caught a flicker of desire in her face, a spark of sexuality she hadn't shown in a long time.

"I could turn the water back on if you'd care to join me. After all those hours on a plane, I bet you could use a warm, soapy back rub."

She looked past him into the shower stall, and he knew she was remembering their showers together. He'd soap her neck and back, then move down to her small, round bottom. She'd turn and he'd softly lather her firm breasts, her pink nipples swelling beneath his gentle touch. Her breath would quicken as he soaped slowly down her stomach to the soft triangle of auburn pubic hair over her Mound of Venus.

Then it was his turn. She'd take his unscented soap and lather his swelling erection and then move down between his legs. When he was thoroughly aroused, she'd kiss the tip of his nose, then turn around and bend forward, resting her head on a towel on the window ledge as he entered her from behind.

She always climaxed first. Then he'd come, holding her bottom close against him and, at the end, leaning forward over her, nibbling at her neck with small love bites.

"It's hardly my back you're interested in rubbing," she said finally, turning for the mirrored vanity across the bathroom. She grabbed a brush from the marbled top and began furiously brushing her hair.

"Problem?" Ben asked, feeling foolish and resentful at her rejection.

Marjorie whirled around, her face contorted in anger. "I'd barely put my bags down—thanks for meeting me at the airport, by the way—when I saw your memo on my desk."

"How could I meet you when I didn't know when you were arriving? What memo?"

"Your memo to the staff about my press tour tomorrow. I suppose everyone in the northern hemisphere except me knows that I'm to herd a mob of reporters through the biosphere. Typical. And why didn't you know when I was coming in? I left a message on your answering machine."

"I haven't listened to my messages today."

"Obviously."

"I faxed the memo to you."

"Really? Where?"

He looked at her. It was the first time she had ever directly questioned something he told her. They were in bigger trouble than he'd thought.

"I send it to the biosphere in Kent."

"Then it missed me by only three hundred miles. I was in Dublin. I flew back direct from Shannon."

"How was I supposed to know you were in Ireland?"

"By reading my itinerary. I left one for you."

Ben sighed and finished drying himself. It was strange. In the past he had felt natural with her and enjoyed being naked in front of her. Now he felt awkward and vulnerable, and he wrapped a towel around his middle.

"I didn't look at your itinerary. You told me you were going to London. I left it at that. I was busy."

"Yes, I saw your picture in the *Times* yesterday morning, tête-à-tête with the President at the U.N."

"What the hell's that supposed to mean, 'tête-à-tête'? You know damn well I don't like that political crap. The President asked me to speak to the third-world ambassadors. They still haven't grasped the fact that the climatic changes are long-term, that America can't grow the food to feed their populations any longer."

"You're such an authority on everything, why don't you hold the press tour? I'm sure the reporters would be far more interested in your sagacious view of the world today than they would be in my puny one."

Ben let out a long breath. "What the hell's happened to

us? You're not back five minutes and we're fighting."

He walked into the bedroom, opened the top drawer of his dresser, yanked out a pair of jockey shorts and put them on.

Marjorie followed him, her arms crossed tightly over her chest. "I wasn't the one who invited the press in. That's what started this."

"No, that's not what started this. It's been going on a long time. You don't get my fax, I don't read your itinerary. We're out of sync. The rhythm's gone. Have you noticed how often lately we fumble around trying to explain what we meant by something? Understanding used to be intuitive between us. Without you saying a word, I knew what you were thinking."

"And you don't anymore?"

"No. Unless you're pissed off at me. That's always written all over your face. Like now."

"Lovely. The only emotion you recognize in my face is 'pissed off.'"

"You're twisting things."

"It's our relationship that's bloody twisted, damn it. I don't know you anymore."

Ben stomped across to the wide closet they shared and jerked open the door. As he pulled out a shirt, the wire hanger snagged on one of her blouses and the silk garment tumbled to the floor.

"What are you doing? That's the only decent blouse I have left! Your bloody American cleaners have shredded every other top I own."

He sat down heavily on the bed that once was sanctuary to their physical hunger for each other, the bed on which they hadn't made love in over a month now. "Marjorie, I swear to God, this is driving me crazy."

She bent and picked up the blouse, hugging it to her breast. "I know."

"Sit down." He patted the bed beside him. "Let's talk."

"Let's have a tumble, you mean."

"That's not what I mean, but would that be so bad? We haven't made love in a long time."

"Four or five weeks, but who's counting?"

"Don't you miss it?"

"I'm too tired for sex these days."

"What about the intimacy? Just holding each other. Falling asleep in each others' arms."

"That's rather hard to do when most nights lately you seem to prefer the couch in your office."

"That's because most nights I can feel the tension, the animosity, the moment my head hits the pillow. I can't sleep next to someone with hostility coming out of her pores."

"You're the one who's hostile. Like now. Blaming everything on me. You're a bloody cad, do you know that about yourself, Benjamin Franklin Meade?"

"I'm not blaming everything on you, damn it. It's the workload you're carrying. You never have time for yourself, or for me, anymore. You've got to slacken off."

"And your way of helping me 'slacken off' is to schedule a bloody news tour for the morning after I return from a grueling week abroad?"

"All right, all right, my timing was bad. If you want me to, I'll cancel it."

"It's too late. By now, there'll be reporters and TV crews coming in from all over the country. If I call things off this late, they'll be rude and antagonistic when I do see them. I can't handle any more antipathy, thank you. The biosphere project has enough wolves at the door as it is."

"Look, I could call Charlotte, have her release a statement that you've come down with the flu or something. I'll tell you what; we could disappear for a week. Just you and me. Maybe fly down to Rio and relax on the beach."

She shook her head. "I prefer to just get the conference over with. And I certainly haven't time for a week in Rio."

"What you're really saying is that you don't have time for us," he said quietly.

Marjorie hesitated. For a moment, the tension seemed to seep out of her and her face lost its guarded look. He saw something in her eyes he hadn't seen in a long time: if not love, at least a longing for love, for what they'd lost.

"Ben, I don't want it this way, you know."

"You're working too hard, Marjorie. You can't let go, not of the smallest detail. This news-tour thing is a perfect example. It won't kill those reporters to wait."

"You don't understand."

"I'm trying very hard to."

"My genetic plant research has made tremendous progress. I'm at the seedling stage now. You'd think people would be gratified that I've gone so far in so little time." She shook her head wearily. "But they're not. I got a fax from Jay Stevens last week practically demanding that we plant the first crops outside."

Six months before, Jay Stevens, head of the National Science Foundation, had asked Marjorie to meet with him in Washington. She'd gone, expecting to talk about Biosphere America. Instead, Stevens had asked her to take on yet another gargantuan job, the creation of genetically altered food crops that could carry out photosynthesis in the weak, indirect sunlight that managed to filter through the volcanic clouds.

When she'd pointed out to him that her workload was already staggering, that she couldn't possibly head another project, the American scientists had reminded her that she was the world's preeminent molecular biologist and that her recent work in plant genetics was considered cutting-edge. No one else was in her league.

They'd gone back and forth for a while, with Marjorie remaining adamant that she didn't have the time to devote to the project. Then Stevens had brought out his clincher: a Foundation tape showing throngs of walking skeletons in Asia and the republics of the former Soviet Union, lands where crop failures had worsened an already desperate food crisis.

Despite the loss of direct sunlight, it was still warm enough to grow crops in those parts of the northern hemisphere that were near the equator. If only Marjorie could develop grains, beans and leafy vegetables that could survive without direct solar radiation.

She couldn't look at the tapes—at wailing mothers holding infants to milkless breasts, at benumbed fathers scratching out graves for their children with sharpened sticks—and not agree to at least try to help.

She had made amazing progress in the past six months. Yet manipulating genes and culturing plant tissue required countless hours of computer and lab work, and she now spent most of her days in the Intensive Agriculture Biome. The research work, coupled with the hours she continued to devote to Biosphere America, had left her hair-tempered and impatient.

"I'm sure Jay understands that you're doing all you can," Ben said. "Jesus, eighteen, twenty hours a day in the lab."

"I can't stop now, Ben. If I do, it will all unravel. Time's against me. It's not just Jay who's getting impatient; the politicians are all over my back wanting to see results. If I don't get my seedlings into the fields in Florida and start raising crops, I may lose my funding. As it is, a couple of negative stories in the press could undermine what credibility I still have. Damn it, I can't afford to offend those reporters. Can't you see that?"

"I see a very tired woman. A woman close to cracking. You've got three full-time jobs, for God's sake. You're doing plant-genetics research and building Biosphere America, and you're still flying to Europe every couple of weeks to supervise biosphere construction in the U.K. Can't you turn the day-to-day stuff in Britain over to someone else?"

Ben was referring to the crash biosphere-building program Marjorie headed up in England and Ireland. The British Isles had suffered a double blow from the mid-Atlantic volcanism. At the same time that the clouds of gases and ash had blocked out the warmth of the sun, the chain of volcanic peaks rising from the ocean floor had diverted the warm waters of the Gulf Stream from the British Isles.

For millennia past, the easterly winds had picked up heat from the Gulf Stream and carried warm air over England and Ireland. Now, with the tropical current no longer off her western shores, the British Isles suffered a further ten-degree-Fahrenheit drop in mean surface temperatures, plunging England and Ireland into a near Ice Age climate.

With the land surface becoming uninhabitable, British scientists had soon realized that they must create artificial environments wherein life could continue to exist. As Britain's leading biologist and zoologist, Marjorie Glynn was put in charge of the crash program to build glass-enclosed mini-Earths where people could live, work and raise crops.

She was prepared to build her biospheres all over the British Isles but for one critical shortfall: energy. The only possible power source for Biosphere Britannia was geothermal energy, and the preeminent international expert in that field was an American whom Marjorie had never met, Benjamin Franklin Meade.

Ben had answered Marjorie's call for help, and under his direction, a geothermal well was sunk into a huge reservoir of superheated water and steam beneath the seabed of North Channel, a narrow neck of the Irish Sea between Scotland and Ireland. The success at North Channel opened the way for Biospheres Britannia to be built in both England and Ireland, their cavernous interiors and powerful grow lights powered by the energy of the North Channel geothermal field the countries now shared.

Across the Atlantic, American scientists had resisted the tremendous cost of a national biosphere-building program for several months after the eruption of R-9, believing they could raise enough crops in the southern states to feed the country. The freezing spring and summer of the year 2000 had proved them disastrously wrong, and the past September, the National Science Foundation had asked Marjorie to build Biosphere America.

Ben was already scouring the country for geothermal fields with which to power the huge mini-Earths, and after all he had done for Britain, she could hardly say no. Marjorie had accepted the new challenge, flown to the United States and begun construction of the first Biosphere America at Princeton.

"I can't just step away from Biosphere Britannia, Ben, not yet. There've been construction delays, problems with bringing flora and fauna in from the southern hemisphere, political bickering between London and Dublin. If I left now, everything would come to a bloody, screeching halt."

Ben reached up and took her hands. "It's you who's going to come to a screeching halt, Marjorie. You're going to have a goddamn breakdown. All the signs are there."

Marjorie sighed. "I won't deny it. I can't sleep, can't eat. My nerves are shot. But I can't give it up, Ben. I can't not do everything I know how to do."

"Listen to me. The more exhausted you become, the more you're going to spin your wheels. Maybe the reason you can't get anywhere with your plant genetics is because your brain is too numb to assimilate facts. A week off could do you more good than a month in the lab."

"I can't take any time off. Please don't bring it up again," she snapped.

"I won't," he said bitterly, dropping her hands.

"The reporters will have questions tomorrow that you're better qualified to answer than I. Geological stuff. I'd appreciate your coming along on the tour."

"I'll be there."

"Perhaps . . . perhaps we could talk later in the week."

"You know we won't. This is as close as we've come to it in months."

"All I know is that I have a news tour that you've arranged and for which I must now get ready." She turned and left, pulling the door shut behind her.

For a moment, Ben stared at the closed door. Then he smashed his fist into the pillows, again and again.

SEVASTOPOL, UKRAINE
• •

2:45 p.m.–April 5th

ANATOLI DMYTROVYCH DEMYANOV WAS a merchant of death who peddled arms around the world with the relentless pursuit of an Amway salesman hawking laundry detergent.

As minister of defense for Ukraine, the now independent former Soviet Republic bordering Eastern Europe, he had taken the most marketable resource his country possessed—weapons of war inherited from the Soviet Army—and engaged in selling them to the highest bidder.

Tall, thin and urbane after decades as a diplomat in Western capitals, the sixty-two-year-old minister of defense had a reputation for driving a hard bargain. But then, he had a motivation far beyond the greed that drove most of the world's arms dealers. Anatoli Demyanov was turning guns into butter and a hundred other foods to keep the sixty million half-starved citizens of Ukraine alive.

Before the eruption of R-9 had plunged the northern hemisphere into a volcanic winter, the Ukrainian steppe had been one of the chief wheat-producing regions of

Europe and a major source of corn, rye, barley, potatoes and sugar beets. The surplus grain was exported, along with forest products, cement and petrochemicals, and Ukraine enjoyed a healthy trade balance with the rest of the world.

Then in February 2000, the terrible sunless cold had descended on the country and suddenly grain crops could no longer be raised on the freezing steppe. The forests were inaccessible beneath towering snowdrifts; limestone and clay for cement could not be dug from the frozen earth; and the oil that was once used to manufacture petrochemicals was now desperately needed to heat Ukrainian homes and factories.

Yet, if Ukraine had no natural resources that it could now trade, the government did have one product left to sell. While the country was still part of the Soviet Union, the central planners in Moscow had stockpiled over ten billion dollars' worth of munitions throughout the nation.

Demyanov recognized that selling the entire store at once would flood the arms market and drive prices down, and he had wisely restricted sales to five hundred million dollars a year. Yet with the coming of the Earth Winter, Demyanov's plans for slow and orderly arms sales vanished like the smoke billowing out of the country's millions of constantly burning fireplaces. Every ruble was now needed to feed the populace, and he began pursuing weapons' buyers in the southern hemisphere with a fierce determination.

For over a year, arms sales had been brisk. Angola purchased tanks and field-artillery pieces; Indonesia spent hundreds of millions on Mig jet fighters; Brazil lined up for land mines and napalm bombs; and insurgent groups from Borneo to Chile carted off millions of mortars and rifles.

Yet the store of arms the Soviets had abandoned in Ukrainian depots was finite, and by March 2001, the defense minister found himself with only one valuable weapon of war left to sell. It was a killing machine far more powerful than planes or guns, a weapon so uniquely lethal that it could change the balance of power among the nations of the southern hemisphere.

This weapon was the reason that Demyanov had come to Sevastopol, the Ukrainian port on the Black Sea. For many centuries, Sevastopol had been a thriving metropolis, a bustling harbor where ships unloaded goods from around the world. In years past, icebreakers from the Ukrainian Navy had kept the port open through the winter, but that was no longer possible. The Black Sea was layered with ten feet of ice, far too thick for icebreakers to penetrate.

Demyanov stared out at the ice floes through the filthy, frosted windows of the old Soviet Navy headquarters high on a rocky promontory two miles up the coast from the civilian port. The headquarters had been abandoned back in 1991 when Ukraine declared her independence and the Soviet Black Sea Fleet sailed away to Russian ports.

The door behind Demyanov opened and he turned as Leonid Zlenko, President of Ukraine, entered, trailed by two of his aides. At five-foot-six, Zlenko weighed almost two hundred and fifty pounds, and his round body looked even bulkier in his full-length, fur-collared coat. Like most Ukrainian men, he had grown a beard, not out of choice, but because razor blades were unobtainable. He looked more than ever like a bear.

"Greetings, Leonid Kirillovich," Demyanov said. "Did you have a good flight from Kiev?"

"No, it was miserable," Zlenko replied irritably, blowing into his gloves. "It was snowing when we landed and the damn plane skidded off the runway. I tell you, I saw my dead grandmother, bless her soul. We had to walk a mile to the terminal. Then we spent another hour driving around the damn port looking for this place. There's no one on the street to ask. Most of the signs are buried in the drifts." His voice went up an octave. "I don't even know what the fuck I'm doing here."

"You will shortly. But first I must ask that your aides leave us. Our business is top secret."

"What are you talking about? Pynzenyk and Gerts have been cleared at the highest level."

"I don't doubt it. Still, I prefer that we keep the matter between ourselves."

The two bearded deputies stared at Demyanov with open animosity. His clean-shaven face and hand-tailored English overcoat were infuriating reminders that the defense minister was the recipient of razor blades and clothes, and who knew what other gifts from the middlemen who brokered his arms deals?

Zlenko narrowed his black eyes at the defense minister. "You are a man of many secrets, Anatoli Dmytrovych. Sometimes I find you fascinating. At other times, your little games are a pain in the ass. Which will it be today?"

"That is for you to say."

Zlenko sighed and turned to his aides. "Wait in the car."

"You'll need one of us to take notes," Pynzenyk protested.

Demyanov shook his head. "No notes, nothing on paper."

"This is highly irregular," Gerts said nervously. The consummate bureaucrat, paper was as vital to his existence as blood.

Zlenko snorted. "You find that surprising, Gerts? Everything the minister of defense does is irregular. Go on, wait in the car."

The two men gave Demyanov a baleful glare, then turned and left the room.

Demyanov walked over to a table and opened his briefcase. "Coffee?" he asked, taking out a thermos. "It's a Brazilian blend. I just got it."

Zlenko's eyebrows arched. He hadn't had a real cup of coffee in six months. "I'm almost killed in a plane and you think you can make this up to me with a fucking cup of coffee?"

"When the coffee's this good, yes."

Despite his pique, Zlenko laughed. "You are the only man in Ukraine who could get away with dragging the president of the country to a deserted building on the Black Sea and then kicking his two top aides out the door. Pour me a cup. I'm freezing my balls off."

Demyanov smiled and filled their cups. Zlenko brought the steaming coffee up to his vodka-reddened nose and inhaled, a look of ecstasy spreading over his face. "God Almighty, it smells better than a hot woman."

"I wouldn't go that far."

"Of course not. You have coffee every day."

"I'll send you a couple of pounds."

"Do that. Now, what is this all about?"

"What I have to show you is several floors below. The elevator's not working; we'll have to take the stairs. If you will follow me, Mister President."

Zlenko sighed. "Let me finish my coffee at least."

Five minutes later, Demyanov picked up his briefcase and led Zlenko down the hall to a padlocked steel door, where he took out a large key ring. Inside, a stairwell descended through the dark interior of the building.

"Be careful going down, Leonid Kirillovich," Demyanov cautioned, pulling a flashlight from his briefcase. "The steps are icy in places."

The mildewed walls and rotting carpet treads gave off a rancid odor as they descended, and Zlenko wrinkled his nose in distaste. "How much farther? I have a heart condition, you know. I hate to think of climbing back up these stinking stairs."

"Six flights," Demyanov said, aware that the president's "heart condition" had been diagnosed as a shortness of breath due to overweight. It was a convenient excuse for Zlenko to stay home in bed when he had one of his frequent hangovers.

"But we came up only one floor to the office where I met you."

"The building stands on a cliff. We're going down through the rock to sea level."

"If I have a stroke going back up, they'll blame it on you, Anatoli Dmytrovych. Serve you right if they shot you."

"We don't shoot people in Ukraine anymore."

"With all the enemies you've made in Kiev, for you, they may bring back the old ways."

Ten minutes later, they reached the bottom of the stairwell and Demyanov led the way down a long, dark corridor. At the end of the passage, he stopped and unlocked a second steel door.

"What is this place?" Zlenko asked.

"A submarine pen," Demyanov told him, opening the door. "It was used by the Black Sea Fleet when Ukraine was still part of the Soviet Union."

Inside, the light from Demyanov's flashlight stabbed out into a pitch-black void. A cold wind blew in Zlenko's face; he shivered and closed the throat of his greatcoat. "There's a door open somewhere down here."

"The wind is coming through a tunnel leading to the sea. There's a grate at the entrance to keep people out, but of course it doesn't stop the wind. Stay here while I turn on the generator."

Zlenko remained motionless as Demyanov moved forward into the dark, his light revealing a forest of huge pipes as he passed. A moment later, the president heard a generator lanyard being pulled, once, twice. The motor roared to life, powering several banks of floodlights.

For a moment, the sudden glare blinded Zlenko. Then his eyes adjusted and he stared in astonishment at the vast rock cavern before him. Three hundred yards wide and almost a thousand yards long, the pen was divided into three rectangular submarine berths covered with ice. Large cranes loomed above the wharves beside each berth, their orange-painted towers reaching up toward the rough rock ceiling two hundred feet above.

The berths fed out to a wide, frozen channel that stretched through a distant, crescent-shaped opening in the face of the cliff. Zlenko guessed that it was the tunnel to the sea Demyanov had mentioned.

"Come over here, Leonid Kirillovich." Demyanov waved from the nearest wharf. Beside him, a portable gas generator chugged away, feeding electricity to a battery of floodlights set around the frozen berth.

As Zlenko approached, Demyanov took a small cellular phone from his briefcase and punched in a number. He exchanged several hushed words with someone, then broke the connection as Zlenko walked up.

The president cocked his head curiously. "Who the hell were you talking to? Down here, of all places."

"The chief engineer of the submarine *N. I. Bukharin*," Demyanov said, putting the phone back in his briefcase. "You remember the *Bukharin*?"

"Of course. It was the largest and most modern submarine in the Soviet Fleet. Named after N.I. Bukharin, the great Party intellectual and friend of Lenin."

Demyanov nodded. "Typhoon-class. Thirty thousand tons. Six hundred feet long, eighty-five feet wide. Nuclear-powered and nuclear-armed." He paused for effect. "I brought you here to see her."

Bewilderment played across Zlenko's fat face. "But the *Bukharin* sank in the Black Sea. When was it, ninety-one, ninety-two?"

"Ninety-one. Or so it was reported in *Izvestia*."

"Don't dance me around, Anatoli Dmytrovych. What is this all about?"

Demyanov flashed a Cheshire-cat grin. "The *Bukharin* didn't sink."

"Then where has she been?"

"In a place where no one could find her."

"You've been hiding a thirty-thousand-ton nuclear submarine for ten years?"

"Yes."

Zlenko threw back his head and howled. "I swear, I thought I had plumbed the depths of your intrigues, Anatoli Dmytrovych. I thought I knew all your schemes, all your secrets. But you were saving one, the biggest secret of them all."

Demyanov permitted himself a small smile. "There were several times when I came near to telling you." He shrugged. "But you know what they say: The lifespan of a secret is in direct proportion to the number of people who know it."

"How on earth did you do it?"

"Do you remember when we first declared our independence, what happened with the Black Sea Fleet?"

"Of course. The damn Russians sailed off with every warship."

"But not the *Bukharin*. She was here in this submarine pen having her reactor fuel replenished when negotiations over the fleet were finally concluded. You recall that after Chernobyl, the Soviets weren't permitted to so much as look at a nuclear reactor on Ukrainian soil without our permission. The request to change the reactor fuel came across my desk at the Defense Ministry. I knew at once that Ukraine had to have that ship."

"Why the hell did you want a submarine? Why not a destroyer or an aircraft carrier?"

"Because the Black Sea is only seven hundred and fifty miles long and three hundred and fifty miles wide. In such a relatively small area, land-based Russian aircraft could find and sink a surface vessel in less than a day."

Demyanov put a conspiratorial hand on Zlenko's arm. "But if the Black Sea is not large, it is deep . . . over seven thousand feet in places. A sub can cruise undetected along the bottom and strike from far beneath the waves."

"By 'strike,' you mean launch her missiles?"

"The missiles were the point. Why we had to have her. The *Bukharin* carries twenty-six SS-N-Twenty sea-launched ballistic missiles. They burn solid fuel and have a range of almost six thousand miles. And each carries eight MIRVs."

Zlenko shuddered. "Multiple independently targetable reentry vehicles. Monstrous weapons. As I recall, when the missiles near their destination, the MIRVs are designed to separate and detonate over eight separate targets."

Demyanov grew animated. "Exactly. Enough destructive power to wipe out every major city in Russia."

"Why on earth would we want to wipe out Russian cities? All we asked from Moscow ten years ago was our independence."

"Don't you see, Leonid Kirillovich? The *Bukharin* was our guarantee of independence. In those days, none of us knew if Moscow would accept our secession from the Soviet Union. If the Russians had sent troops across our borders, I would have let them know that we had the sub and that her missiles were targeted on Russian cities. They would have had to withdraw."

Zlenko clasped his hands behind his broad back and walked several paces down the wharf, then turned and strode back. "All right, I understand now why you did it. I'm not sure it would have been my way. Frankly, the thought of nuclear missiles whistling overhead scares the shit out of me. All the same, I suppose there's a certain mad logic in it. What I still don't know is *how* you did it."

"Some things are meant to be, Leonid Kirillovich. They are preordained. Do you believe that?"

Zlenko shrugged. "If you're asking if I believe in fate, yes, I suppose I do."

"Fate. That is what I felt when I saw the signature on that request from the *Bukharin* to change the reactor fuel."

"Who signed it?"

"A man named Viktor Rafailovich Lobov. For ten years, the Lobovs lived in the apartment below us in Kiev. I knew Viktor when he was a boy."

"Fate. Yes, I can see why you'd think that."

"Elena and I never had any children, you know," Demyanov said, the disappointment still there in his eyes after all these years.

"Viktor became a surrogate son. We took him on vacations when he was small, and later I'd send him a few rubles now and again when he was at Lenin's Komsomol School in Leningrad. An hour after I saw his signature on that form, I was on a plane to Sevastopol."

"And he agreed to help?"

Demyanov offered Zlenko a cigarette, then lit one for himself. "Not at first. The idea of seizing the *Bukharin* scared him so badly he threw up."

He exhaled a cloud of smoke and grinned. "Puked all over his shiny submariner's shoes. But we walked in the woods and talked. For hours. I explained why Ukraine had to have the *Bukharin*. Viktor was a patriot. In the end, he agreed. Really, he became more enthusiastic than I was. The *Bukharin*'s executive officer and three of her senior petty officers were also Ukrainian. Viktor talked them into staging a mutiny when the *Bukharin* returned to sea."

"I heard rumors there'd been a mutiny. But how on earth did five men steal a nuclear submarine?"

"I supplied them with guns and an antitank mine from our military stores. As the chief engineer, Viktor went on and off the sub several times a day for parts. It was a simple matter for him to smuggle the weapons aboard."

"Did they stage the mutiny here?" Zlenko looked around the cavernous space. "In this pen?"

Demyanov shook his head. "Too risky. If someone had

managed to sound an alarm, the Soviets could have shut the gates to the sea and trapped the sub in here. Besides, our plan hinged on the *Bukharin* being over very deep water when the mutineers seized control."

"Why was that so important, the deep water?"

"Because the whole idea was to make the Soviets think the mutineers had blown the *Bukharin* apart and that the debris had settled to the bottom. The deeper the water, the less chance that they could go down and search for the wreckage."

A thin smile of admiration came to Zlenko's face. "You thought of everything, Anatoli Dmytrovych."

Demyanov shrugged. "So we thought. Six hours after the *Bukharin* sailed, there was a mile of water beneath her keel. Viktor and his comrades armed themselves and took over the control room. They told the captain they were Ukrainian nationalists who intended to blow up the *Bukharin* and themselves with it."

"Why? I mean, what reason did they give the captain for such a suicide mission?"

"Patriotism. Viktor told the captain they were convinced that if the *Bukharin* were allowed to reach a Russian port, someday she would return to launch her missiles against Ukraine. Their lives meant nothing compared to the terrible death and destruction a nuclear submarine could rain down on their country."

Zlenko nodded his head. "Patriotism. Yes, that is something a Russian captain would understand."

"Oh, he understood, all right. But that didn't prevent him from arguing, threatening, pleading. In the end, Viktor put a pistol in his ear and forced him to bring the boat up. The captain and the Soviet crew were ordered into lifeboats and set adrift. Then the *Bukharin* dove again. On the way down, the mutineers stuffed the torpedo tubes with clothes, mattresses, books, lubricating oil. Anything that would rise to the surface. Then they shoved in the antitank mine with a one-minute detonator."

Comprehension flooded Zlenko's florid face. "When the mine blew, the mattresses and other debris floated to the surface. The Russians in the rafts would think the mutineers had carried out their threat to blow up the *Bukharin*."

"Yes, that was the plan we worked out."

"Clever."

"Too clever. I had checked the dimensions of the mine and it was small enough to fit through the torpedo tube. But we'd forgotten to figure in the detonator. It stuck out on one side, like a stem from an apple. When the mine was ejected, the detonator—we're pretty sure that's what it was—snagged on the outer door."

Demyanov studied the end of his cigarette, his mouth a hard line. "When the mine exploded, it blew in the hull of the forward torpedo room. The executive officer and two of the petty officers were sucked out into the sea."

"Three men. A pity." Zlenko took a deep drag on his cigarette. "But the *Bukharin* didn't sink."

"No. When the port bow blew in, watertight doors closed automatically throughout the sub. Only the forward torpedo room flooded. The vessel was badly damaged, but she was still seaworthy. Ironically, the accident was probably what convinced the Soviets that the *Bukharin* had blown up."

Zlenko squinted. "I don't understand."

"When their Navy launched a search, they found the dead mutineers floating in the sea," Demyanov said, sending his dying cigarette out over the frozen berth with a flick of his forefinger.

"From the condition of their bodies, there was no doubt that the men had died in an explosion at great depth. The Soviets could only assume that the bodies of the other mutineers were still trapped in the wreckage of the *Bukharin*, somewhere at the bottom of the sea."

Zlenko threw up his hands. "So finally, after ten years, I understand why the KGB came around with all those questions when the *Bukharin* sank. None of us in the government could figure out why the bastards were grilling us about a sunken submarine."

"They were fishing. Still not sure what had really happened. And scared. Gorbachev was in a panic that the West would find out. Can you imagine the reaction in Washington if they had discovered that one of our most powerful warships had been scuttled during a mutiny?"

"It would have made the Soviet Navy a laughingstock and undermined the credibility of the entire military."

"Not to mention the effect on the country. Gorbachev was holding the republics together by threads in those days. News of the mutiny would have emboldened the separatist movements from the Baltic to Siberia. That's why the investigation lasted only a week or ten days. Any longer and Moscow risked blowing the whole thing open."

Zlenko ground out his cigarette with the toe of his shoe. "Lucky for you, Anatoli Dmytrovych. If the KGB had really gotten their teeth into it, someone would have broken. You would have breathed your last against a wall."

Demyanov shook his head. "It wasn't luck. I knew the political realities. I was confident that if we could find a way to seize the *Bukharin*, in the end, Moscow could do nothing about it."

Zlenko laughed and clapped his gloved hands. "Someday the whole episode will become a folktale, do you know that? Schoolchildren will recite the story of how five Ukrainian sailors stole a nuclear submarine from the—"

Zlenko stopped in midsentence as a hissing roar began to build in the cavernous chamber, the ominous sound echoing off the rock walls hidden in the dark. The roar was coming from somewhere below him, vibrating the quay beneath his feet. He stared down at the cement in terror, certain the wharf was about to collapse.

Suddenly the ice in the berth beside the quay bulged upward and split along its center with an earsplitting *crack!* Zlenko gaped, frozen in fear, as the sail of an immense submarine rose up through the shattered ice, its black bulk streaked with peeling rivulets of rust.

The overweight president felt his heart beating wildly as terror coursed through him. The huge surge of adrenaline turned his muscles to mush, and his knees suddenly gave way, spilling him onto the cold concrete quay.

The screeching sound of metal grinding against ice grew deafening as the flat deck emerged. And still the mammoth sub kept rising, water and great slabs of ice cascading off her sides in avalanches of foam and broken floes.

Finally, mercifully, the sub stopped moving and the monstrous cacophony of sound died away, to be replaced by a steady hum that Zlenko could feel in his teeth. He realized suddenly that he'd been holding his breath and he gasped, drawing great gulps of air into his smoke-clogged lungs.

As his senses cleared, he became aware of Demyanov standing over him, the defense minister's face wreathed in worry. "Leonid Kirillovich, are you all right? You're as pale as a ghost."

A wave of fury swept over Zlenko and he struggled to his feet, his fists balled. "Why didn't you warn me, damn you! I have a heart condition. A heart condition! Are you trying to frighten me to death?"

Demyanov backed up, his palms pressed hard against Zlenko's heaving chest. "Leonid Kirillovich, please. Calm down. I swear to you, I didn't know the sub would come up that fast."

"I'm going to tear your head off, you infuriating old fop."

They both heard the shot at the same time, followed instantly by the ricochet of the bullet off the cement twelve inches from Zlenko's feet. The president whirled in the direction of the report.

The gun was in the hand of a thin, flat-faced man wearing an oilskin jacket and the peaked cap of a Soviet submarine officer. He was standing half out of an open hatch on the deck of the *Bukharin*.

"So, you would tear off Anatoli Demyanov's head?" the man asked, a mirthless grin hanging like wizened fruit on his pale face. "Try it. And the next bullet will be between your eyes."

"Who the hell are you?" Zlenko roared, too maddened now to be afraid.

Demyanov scurried around between the two. "It's Viktor. Viktor Lobov. Jesus God, what a stinking mess!"

"I don't care who he is, he has just tried to murder the president of Ukraine! He's dead. Dead, do you hear me?"

A derisive laugh came from Lobov. "I was declared

dead ten years ago. If you want to kill me again, you'll have to resurrect me first, like Christ."

"That's enough, Viktor," Demyanov said, fighting for his composure. "For God's sake, put that damn pistol away."

He smoothed back his ruffled silver hair with a trembling hand. "Leonid Kirillovich, please believe me. I had no idea that Viktor would surface that quickly. I thought I had time to warn you."

Lobov lowered the pistol into a holster at his waist. "Did the big bad submarine scare the poor man?"

"You fool!" Demyanov screamed. "Shut your imbecilic mouth before you ruin everything."

Zlenko stood staring across at Lobov, his hands on his hips. "So this is the vaunted Ukrainian hero who stole the *Bukharin*."

Lobov lit a cigarette. "Liberated the *Bukharin*," he said, blowing smoke through his nostrils like a snorting dragon.

Demyanov sighed. "I ask you to make allowances for Viktor Rafailovich. He has lived alone for many years. His manners have rusted, along with the *Bukharin*."

"You know what I think? I think he is crazy. And I am just as crazy to even be here."

Zlenko kicked his foot at the sub in a paroxysm of rage, almost losing his balance. "Just look at that rusting piece of shit! You dragged me all the way to this freezing hole in Sevastopol to see that?"

"The *Bukharin* is still one of the most formidable weapons of war on the planet," Demyanov said. "I grant you, she needs a coat of paint. But as you can see, Viktor has repaired the mine damage. And inside, the computers, the navigational equipment, the weapons systems, even the nuclear reactor—everything is like new."

"Why did he bother repairing the damn thing? We no longer need a nuclear submarine to threaten the Russians with. Since the climate changed, their military is so short of food and fuel and everything else that the pathetic bastards couldn't invade the Vatican."

"I do not intend to use the *Bukharin* for our defense. As you say, that need passed long ago."

"Then what the hell are you going to do with it?"

"The *Bukharin* is worth three billion American dollars. I plan to sell her."

Zlenko shook his head incredulously and stared off toward Lobov. "Three billion dollars! You are as mad as that fool!"

Demyanov straightened. "I have a firm offer from a foreign government. The documents are in my briefcase."

Zlenko rubbed his fat face in indecision, the flesh shifting like Jello beneath a spoon. "Three billion?"

"Three billion. Just think of all the food that will buy for our people!"

Zlenko stared hard at the immense black submarine. "All right," he said finally, shaking his head in disbelief that he was agreeing to this. "I'll give you ten minutes to show me the documents. Then I want the fuck out of this place."

Demyanov let out a relieved breath. "You won't be sorry," he said, turning and walking to a wheeled gangway several yards away. "Give me a hand with this, will you?"

Zlenko threw up his hands. "Now I'm a porter!" But he crossed the quay and bent his shoulder to the gangway next to Demyanov.

Lobov watched in disgust as the two out-of-shape men strained to push the walkway across the quay. Then he flipped his cigarette over the side and disappeared down the hatch.

When the gangway extended out over the sub, Demyanov started across. Zlenko followed, his hands gripping the guard chains as he stared down at the ice-choked water thirty feet below. The hatch was a tight fit for the overweight president, but finally he squeezed through and climbed down the ladder after Demyanov.

The gleaming interior of the *Bukharin* was in stark contrast to the sub's rusting hull, and Zlenko looked around the high-tech control room in wonder. Everywhere, glass gauge faces and computer screens twinkled like diamonds; along the ceiling, brass fittings and stainless-steel piping sparkled in the light. Beyond arrays of sonar equipment and reactor monitors, the white-painted bulkheads were as spotless as a hospital operating room.

"Didn't I tell you?" Demyanov grinned. "Like new."

Zlenko arched his eyebrows. "I must admit, it's a miraculous difference from the outside."

Lobov was leaning insouciantly against the periscope housing, his arms and feet crossed before him. "Miraculous!" he sneered. "As if the Virgin appeared and waved a wand. I've worked my ass off cleaning, oiling, painting, changing parts. A thousand times at least, I've pumped out the bilges. You're looking at ten years of sweat. Ten years!"

"You've done a remarkable job," Zlenko said grudgingly.

"Wait until you see the rest of it," Demyanov said. "Every inch of the vessel is in the same condition as when she sailed from Sevastopol a decade ago."

"I have no intention of crawling all over this boat," Zlenko said. "I agreed to give you ten minutes."

"Very well," Demyanov shrugged. "But at least have a glass of vodka in the wardroom while you look over the documents."

Zlenko grunted. "Vodka. That's the first sensible idea I've heard since I got here."

Lobov led the way aft to the spacious wardroom and took a bottle of vodka from a cabinet. He filled three glasses and handed drinks to Zlenko and Demyanov. "To the second life of the *Bukharin*."

The men clinked glasses and drained the vodka.

"Sit, sit," Demyanov said, sliding onto one of the two benches flanking the table. "Viktor, give us another."

Zlenko sat down opposite Demyanov as Lobov refilled their glasses. The president downed a second drink, then sat back against the bench, his anger waning as the vodka warmed him inside. He gave the chief engineer a reassessing look. "So, Lobov, you've been hiding the *Bukharin* in here for ten years. Incredible."

Lobov arched his eyebrows at Demyanov as he sat down next to him. "You didn't tell him?"

Demyanov shook his head. "No. I haven't had a chance."

Zlenko looked from one to the other. "Tell me what?"

Lobov lit a cigarette, savored the smoke for a moment, then exhaled toward the ceiling. "It would have been impossible to hide the *Bukharin* in here for so long. Boys exploring in the summer, lovers looking for a place to screw—inevitably someone would have wandered down here and seen her. I brought the boat in under the ice only ten months ago."

Zlenko stared at the chief engineer in disbelief. "Ten months ago! Then where was she for the nine years before that?"

Lobov grinned. "At the bottom of the Black Sea. Hidden from Soviet sonar in a submarine canyon four thousand feet down."

Zlenko stared hard at the man for a moment, then made a gesture of dismissal. "Impossible."

"Impossible, my ass." Lobov snatched the bottle off the table and splashed vodka in his glass. "I did it. Nine years I lived down there in the *Bukharin*."

Demyanov said, "The original plan was for the mutineers to stay submerged as long as the Soviet threat persisted, a year or so we thought. After that, Viktor and his comrades were to mothball the sub and surface through the escape hatch in the conning tower. If we needed the *Bukharin* later on, it would have been a simple matter for Viktor to go back down, reenter through the conning tower and reactivate the reactor and the other systems."

"The best laid plans of mice and men," Lobov said, dipping a callused finger in his vodka and licking the tip.

"The explosion in the torpedo room," Zlenko guessed.

"Yes." Demyanov nodded slowly. "When the mine blew, the explosion sprang a leak in the hull near the control room. The pumps had to be kept going continuously, which meant that Viktor and the surviving petty officer couldn't mothball the *Bukharin* after the Soviet threat passed. They had to either bring the sub into port for repairs or stay submerged and maintain the pumps."

Zlenko reached for the vodka bottle. "And you could hardly have brought the *Bukharin* into port," he said, pouring himself another brimming drink.

"Can you imagine the Russian reaction?" Demyanov asked. "Seizing the *Bukharin* was an act of war on the part of Ukraine. It's possible they would have launched an air strike on Kiev, or sent several divisions across the border."

Zlenko looked at Lobov. "Of course you did have a third alternative. You could have simply abandoned the *Bukharin* and left her to her watery fate at the bottom of the sea."

"Never!" Lobov said, his eyes fierce. "You politicians! What do you know about sailors and ships? The *Bukharin* is not simply a piece of seagoing machinery. She is a living entity, with a heart and a soul. To let her flood would be like letting a comrade drown. And that I would never have done."

Zlenko shook his head. "I can understand a sailor's loyalty to his ship. But, my God, nine years on the bottom of the Black Sea! It must have been like being in prison."

Lobov shrugged. "It was not as bad as you think. We had hundreds of movies and books on board. More important to me were all the technical manuals for the computers and the weapons systems. I studied everything, even the nuclear physics of the reactor. Really, most days it was like being back at the university."

"What did you do for food? Or air? You had to eat, you had to breathe."

"Neither was necessary in my case. Submariners are not like other men, you see. I entered a state of suspended animation. Like a frog that has burrowed into the mud under a winter pond."

Demyanov rolled his eyes. "Viktor had all the food and water he needed, Leonid Kirillovich. The *Bukharin* had just sailed from Sevastopol with a year's supply of provisions for a hundred and ten men. Viktor couldn't have eaten all that food in a lifetime."

"What about air?" Zlenko asked. "How the hell did you breathe down there for nine years?"

"You don't know much about modern submarines, do you?" Lobov asked, not bothering to hide his contempt for the overweight politician. "In a nuclear submarine, the oxygen is recycled. As long as you have power, you can breathe."

"Remember, the reactor fuel had just been replenished," Demyanov added. "The *Bukharin* had sufficient nuclear power to travel submerged at full speed for two years. Viktor was using only a tiny fraction of that energy. He could have stayed down there for fifty years."

Zlenko pushed his glass forward and Lobov poured him another drink. "What happened to the petty officer who survived the mine explosion with you?" the president asked.

The engineer exhaled a long stream of smoke and looked off into the distance. "His name was Vladimir Ioffee. He went mad the third year we were on the bottom. He shot himself. I put his body into the sea through one of the aft torpedo tubes."

"So for the past seven years, you have had no human contact," Zlenko said, beginning to understand why Lobov acted so strangely.

Lobov laughed his crazy laugh. "What, you don't consider Anatoli Dmytrovych human?"

Zlenko looked at the defense minister. "What the hell is he talking about now?"

Demyanov said, "Viktor and I were in contact every six months. Twice a year he would send an antenna up on a float and radio a message from the S.S. *Kotovsk.*"

Zlenko looked bewildered. "The S.S. *Kotovsk?*"

"A nonexistent fishing boat I registered in Sevastopol. On the radio, I played the part of Viktor's partner on shore, giving him fish prices, weather reports, that sort of thing. Of course we were using a code."

"And you kept this up for nine years?" Zlenko shook his head.

"Yes, until the Black Sea froze over last year and the Russian patrol vessels were forced into port. With the Russian sonar net no longer covering the sea, Viktor was able to bring the *Bukharin* in undetected under the ice."

Lobov tossed down a fourth drink, then rose unsteadily. "I've got to take a piss. After that, perhaps I'll take you out for a cruise. Maybe fire one of our missiles up through the ice, show you what the *Bukharin* can do."

Zlenko looked alarmed.

"He's joking," Demyanov said quickly. "The vodka is talking."

"Don't be so certain," Lobov said, a strange, wolfish grin on his drunken face. He turned and staggered out of the wardroom.

"He's lost his mind, you know that," Zlenko said.

Demyanov lowered his eyes. "Nine years at the bottom of the Black Sea. I doubt that any man would return from such an experience completely sane."

"Why didn't you order him to abandon the *Bukharin* after the Soviet threat passed?"

"I did. Many times. But he always refused. You must understand that alone down there, he formed a bond with the vessel. The *Bukharin* became a part of him. I don't know how many times he told me over the radio, 'The *Bukharin* is keeping me alive and I am keeping the *Bukharin* alive. Neither of us can exist apart.' "

"He really is mad, you know."

Demyanov avoided the president's eyes. "Perhaps. One might also consider him a soldier who wouldn't leave his post."

"Whatever he is, he makes me nervous with that damn pistol strapped around his middle."

"We'll get our business over with then, and I'll take you back."

"Yes, I'd prefer it."

Demyanov took a sheath of papers from his briefcase and shoved it across the wardroom table. "The documents are all in order. They require only your signature to complete the sale of the *Bukharin*. The three billion dollars will be deposited in a numbered account in Switzerland."

"You still haven't told me, Anatoli Dmytrovych. What nation would buy a nuclear submarine?"

"Since the eruption of R-Nine, there is only one country in the world with enough money. Argentina."

"Argentina! So that's why you had all those meetings with the junta leader last month. What's his name?"

"General Ramon Saavedra de Urquiza."

"Yes, de Urquiza. What the hell does he want with a nuclear submarine?"

"I didn't ask," Demyanov said, refilling their glasses. "If I knew, I don't think I could sleep at night."

CHESAPEAKE BAY, DELAWARE

6:45 a.m.–April 6th

IT WAS THE TIME when spring normally came to Chesapeake Bay, and the Canada geese were restless. The males in the twenty-thousand strong flock ran at each other in mock challenge, and the yearlings gathered marsh grass from beneath the snow, as if to build nests on the frozen lip of the bay.

In the midst of the flock, a large gander hopped about in agitation on its one leg, its bugle-like honks asserting its leadership over the geese around him.

The gander had lost its left leg and left eye to a blast from a hunter's shotgun two years before. The pellets had also ripped away half of its flight feathers, and it had fallen from the sky into the barnyard of a farm a quarter-mile from the marsh where the hunter had lain in wait.

Yet if the shotgun blast had been a stroke of terrible fortune, the landing place of the gander had been lucky indeed, for the farm was the home of a twelve-year-old boy who loved animals and dreamed of becoming a veterinarian.

The boy found the wounded gander and brought it into the house to tend. At first sight of the bird's missing leg and eye, and its pellet-ridden body, the boy's father had shaken his head sadly and told his son the gander was beyond saving. But the boy had insisted he must try, and try he did.

For several days, the gander lay in a straw-filled box near the big kitchen stove, barely moving. Every few hours, the boy would force open the bird's mouth and feed it a nourishing concoction of wheat germ, milk, vitamins and antibiotics.

Finally, on the fourth day after it had been wounded, the gander began to lift its head and show signs of recovering. The next day, the boy came down in the morning to find the goose trying to stand on its one remaining leg. The twelve-year-old lifted the wounded bird from the box and placed it on the floor, where the goose promptly fell over on his side.

All the rest of that day and the week that followed, the boy helped the gander learn to balance on one leg, and within ten days, the bird was hopping around the kitchen, its wings beating the air for stability.

"God, what a brave bird," the farmer said one morning as he watched the gander struggle across the kitchen floor.

His son's eyes lit up. "That's what we'll call it, Dad—Brave Bird."

His father smiled. "Brave Bird. It's a good name."

Slowly, Brave Bird's feathers grew back and the pellet wounds in his body healed. Then one morning just before Thanksgiving, the family awakened to the sound of Brave Bird honking and beating his wings, and when they came downstairs, the goose was flying around the kitchen.

"It's time to let Brave Bird go back to his own," the farmer said.

The boy's face had shown his hurt that the bird he had come to love must leave, but he knew his father was right. After breakfast, the youngster carried Brave Bird outside and stroked his neck and talked softly to the gander for a long time before placing him on the ground.

For a moment, Brave Bird looked quietly at the boy. Then he let out a loud bugle honk and took off, hopping madly on his one leg. After several strides, he was air-

borne, his great wings beating rhythmically as he rose
higher and higher into the air.

"Good-bye, Brave Bird," the boy called with tears in his
eyes as the gander became a speck against the winter-
gray sky.

Brave Bird had rejoined his flock on the shore of Chesapeake Bay. Life slowly returned to normal for the gander
as he passed December and January replacing the weight
he had lost with a steady diet of aquatic plants, grains and
an occasional fish or mollusk. Then came February and
the eruption of R-9, and the world of the geese changed
forever.

The birds' food supply disappeared beneath ice and
snow as the terrible sunless cold descended on North
America. By spring, a third of the flock had starved to
death. Despite the near-Arctic cold, Brave Bird's biological clock told him it was time to fly north, and in April,
the gander led his flock into the air for their yearly migration to Baffin Island, off the northeast coast of Canada.

Migrating birds have tiny compasses in their brains
that guide them by fixing on the magnetic lines of force
stretching from the north to the south magnetic poles.
This year, though, the eruption of R-9 had saturated the
air with iron particles that masked the earth's magnetic
field.

Soon after becoming airborne, Brave Bird began to
honk in frustration and fear, for he couldn't tell in which
direction north lay. Finally, after flying in circles for days,
the flock ended up passing the summer in western New
York State.

In the fall, the flock had again flown back and forth in
confusion, until instinct prompted Brave Bird to follow
the river valleys of the Delaware watershed south to
Chesapeake Bay.

Thousands of geese starved to death during the winter
that followed, and only a massive grain-feeding drive
by Maryland conservationists had saved the twenty-
thousand-strong core of the flock. And now it was April,
and time for the geese to try once more to reach the remembered rich feeding grounds of Baffin Island.

For the past week, Brave Bird had awakened in the

dark before dawn and noted the horizon to the east lighten to a dull pink as the sun rose behind the ash clouds. He knew from years past that if he flew with the rising sun on the side of his remaining eye, he would be heading north toward Baffin Island.

By mid-morning, the instinct to migrate had become overpowering, and Brave Bird's bugle-like honks echoed loudly across the frozen marsh, stirring the rest of the flock to their feet. The excited geese bobbed their jet-black heads and necks and waddled about honking and flapping their wings, their brown-topped cream bodies and black tails stark against the white snow.

Soon the *onk-or, onk-or* calls of individual birds had melded into a raucous cacophony that could be heard two miles away. As the din rose, Brave Bird spread his huge wings and began to hop over the snow on his one webbed foot.

As he took to the air, the other birds began to rise behind him. Within minutes, all twenty thousand geese in the flock were strung out in a huge V formation, a great feathered arrow shooting north.

Buenos Aires, Argentina
● ●

10:10 a.m.–April 6th

MARIA ECHEVERRIA WAS SLIPPING into her shoes to go shopping when she heard the soldier guarding her apartment vomit onto the tiles in the hallway outside.

She opened the door to find young Sergeant Martinez leaning weakly against the wall, his face white, his eyes bloodshot and watery.

"You're sick, Julio. Oh, you poor thing, come in, come in."

"No, Señorita." The sergeant gulped a breath as he wiped the vomit from his chin. "The general forbids it."

"Screw the general. I'll not have you standing out here suffering. Come in and lie down on the couch."

"I have to clean this up."

"I'll ring for the porter. Now come in here."

The young sergeant was too miserable to protest, and he allowed Maria to lead him into her living room. In the six months that he had been guarding the junta leader's mistress, Martinez had never been inside her apartment, and his eyes widened at the sight of the opulent Oriental rugs and Renaissance artwork.

She led him across to the couch. "Lie down," she insisted. "I'll get you some crackers. My mother always made me eat crackers when I was sick to my stomach. It absorbs the bile, you know."

"I shouldn't be in here," the sergeant said, careful not to get his boots on the maroon velour as he half-reclined against the plush cushions.

"Nonsense. If you're worried that I'll tell the general, don't be," she said, crossing to the kitchen. "Besides, I'm going shopping. You'll have the place to yourself."

"You can't go out without me. He'd have my stripes."

Maria came back with a box of saltines. "It'll be all right this once," she said, suddenly liking the idea of shopping without her omnipresent soldier shadow. She hadn't been out alone since she'd started living with Ramon fifteen months ago. It would be an adventure.

Martinez nibbled on a cracker. "I never get sick. I think it was the pastry that woman gave me when I came in this morning. It tasted funny."

"What woman?"

"I don't know. She was standing on the street outside your building when I came on duty. She said that she and her husband had opened a bakery around the corner and she was giving away free samples."

"A new bakery? Well, after what her pastry did to you, I'll never shop there."

"When I'm feeling better, I'm going to report her. Who should I report her to?"

Maria reached for her purse. "I don't know, Julio. There must be a bakery commissioner or something."

"I hope they put her out of business. Oh, shit. I'm going to be sick again."

"Wait!" Maria yelped, racing across the room for the wastebasket beside the general's mahogany desk. She made it back just in time to shove the basket under Julio's face as a stream of bile and crackers erupted from his mouth. "Do you want me to stay with you?" she asked.

The young soldier turned away in embarrassment. "No. I'd rather be miserable alone. Thank you."

"All right then." She patted his shoulder. "Rest. Eat more crackers if you can. I'll be back in an hour. I hope you're feeling better."

"Maybe I should sue her."

"It's a thought, Julio. I have my key. I'll let myself back in."

On the way out, Maria called the concierge and told her about the mess in the hall, then left the apartment and went down the two flights of marble stairs to the foyer.

The early morning Buenos Aires sun was already warm as she emerged from the building and walked briskly down the street. At the corner, she turned onto the Avenida de Corientes, her eyes searching the shop fronts on both sides of the street for the new bakery. She'd give them a piece of her mind for handing out bad pastry.

But there were no bakeries, and after three blocks, she decided that the young sergeant must have misunderstood where the new shop was. The intoxicating aromas of the open market down the boulevard wafted toward her, and she put the matter of the spoiled pastry out of her mind.

She could smell the mingled scents of freshly ground coffee and flowers and roasting meat as she neared the bustling stalls. An exuberance flooded through her as she realized that today she could float through the market like a bubble, free of the heavy encumbrance of the guard she had to drag around like an anchor. Shopping was going to be fun.

Maria bought a dozen short-stemmed roses, then a jar of wild honey, and some asparagus for dinner. She was always on a diet, and normally she resisted the temptation to snack at the market. But today she was feeling so free and heady that she threw caution to the wind and bought a shish kebab of teriyaki chicken and a rich café au lait.

She sat down at a table beside the food stall and put her shoulder bag on the checkered tablecloth. Feeling deliciously wicked, she sipped the coffee and pulled the succulent pieces of meat off the spit with her teeth. Several men gave her long, appraising looks as they passed by, staring openly at her bare legs beneath her short skirt.

She was in the mood to tease, and when two white-smocked butchers walked past carrying a side of beef, she recrossed her legs, deliberately giving them a brief glimpse of her panties. The man in back stumbled and lost his grip on the carcass, dropping the meat on the cobblestones.

"Asshole!" his partner swore. "Pay attention to what you're doing."

"You looked, too," the culprit grumbled as they hoisted the slab again and shouldered their way on through the crowd of shoppers.

Maria smiled to herself and sipped the coffee. It was a wonderful day to play games. Five minutes later, she was nibbling the last piece of chicken when a shadow fell across the table from behind her. She turned just in time to see a scruffy-looking man in cheap, wraparound sunglasses reach across the table and grab her bag.

"Bring that back!" she screamed, leaping to her feet as the thief darted away between the booths. "Stop him! He stole my bag!"

Before she could get out from behind the table, a tall man in a gray suit ran past her. "I'll get him!" he yelled over his shoulder, slicing into the throng after the thief.

Maria elbowed her way through the crowd after the two, weaving past the shoppers and vendors as the chase led toward the Avenida de Corientes. Out on the broad avenue, she could see the thief running down the sidewalk toward Palermo Park, the man in the suit hard on his heels. She took off her shoes and tore after them.

Halfway down the block, the purse-snatcher suddenly darted into an alley, the second man now close behind him. When Maria reached the entrance, she could hear grunts and cursing, and the thud of fists landing.

The two men continued to exchange blows as she timidly approached, her back against a brick wall and a hand at her throat. Then the well-dressed man landed a powerful punch and the robber went sprawling into several garbage cans, spilling the rancid-smelling refuse all over himself.

For a moment, the thief lay stunned amidst the flotsam of rotten fruit and eggshells. Then he collected himself and tore down the alley and out the other side. The gray-suited man relaxed his fighter's stance and ran a hand through his disheveled hair.

Then he bent and retrieved Maria's bag. "I believe this is yours," he said, his breath still labored.

Maria took the bag. "Thank you, Señor. You are very brave." And very handsome, she thought, appraising his dark blue eyes, square chin and thick, wavy brown hair. The general's bald pate turned her off, and if she didn't close her eyes when they made love, she couldn't climax.

"It was nothing."

"Look at what he did to your suit," she said, pointing at a torn lapel. "Please let me buy you a new one."

The gentleman smiled. "I bought it in London. Besides, it's only ripped at the seam and I have an excellent tailor. He'll stitch it as good as new."

"A reward then," she said, opening her purse.

"Money is neither a motivator nor a need of mine. Please, don't insult me."

"I'm sorry. I only wanted to express my gratitude."

"In that case, perhaps you'd share a coffee with me. I could ask no greater reward than the company of a beautiful woman."

"You are very gallant."

"Not at all. There's an excellent place down the street. The Café de la Platte. Their coffee is unsurpassed."

Maria was about to say no, as she'd had to say no to every such invitation from a man since moving in with Ramon. But this man had just fought a thief to retrieve her bag. And he was so handsome, and so obviously a gentleman. Besides, when would she ever be out alone again and have a chance like this?

"I'd like that," she said, putting her shoes back on.

"Wonderful." He offered her his arm. "My name is Oliver Alberdi."

"I am Maria Echeverria."

"Señorita or Señora?"

"Señorita."

"Wonderful again." He led her out of the alley and down the avenue. "Are you a student at the university?"

"How did you know?"

"You're not married, you're not at work. What else?"

"A mistress," Maria almost blurted.

Over coffee, he told her that he was an architect. He

had designed buildings all over the world, but since the volcanic winter had descended on the northern hemisphere, most of his work had been in South America. Nothing was being built north of the equator anymore.

She told him about her artwork, and over their second cappuccino, he asked her if she'd be interested in illustrating his architectural drawings. The prospect of actually having a commission thrilled her, and she instantly agreed. Then she realized that she'd have to find a way to do it without Ramon finding out. He would never approve of her working. Certainly not with a man such as Oliver.

They dallied in the café for an hour; then Maria looked at her watch and told him she had to go home. Oliver insisted on escorting her the six blocks to her apartment.

When they reached the entry to the building, Maria took out her key, searching for a reason not to invite him in. "I live with my father, and he's at his office. I'm afraid he wouldn't approve of my inviting a man up when he's not at home."

"Of course. Still, I want to see you again. You said you'd be interested in doing the illustrations?"

"Very."

"May I have your phone number?"

Maria felt a small wave of panic. If he called when Ramon was there, how would she explain it? "I'd rather call you. Father is very old-fashioned."

"I understand," Oliver said, taking a business card from an expensive leather billfold. "Please call me. And soon."

"I will."

"Promise?" he asked, taking her hand.

"Promise."

He bent and kissed her hand, and she was surprised at the flood of warmth that surged through her at the brief press of his lips against her skin. "Thank you again, Oliver. You were so brave to go after that thief. He might have killed you."

"He was nothing but a common purse snatcher. Besides, for you, I'd fight every desperado in Buenos Aires."

Maria smiled. "I'm glad I met you, Oliver."

He smiled back. "I'm glad I met you, too."

She tucked his card in her purse and let herself in, turning to wave to him through the glass as the door shut behind her. Then she hurried up the stairs.

He watched her go, admiring the shapely legs and the curve of the beautiful little behind. Then he walked briskly down the avenue and turned the corner. Halfway down the block, a white four-door Ford pulled to the curb beside him. He opened the door and got in.

From behind the wheel, the thief from the market grinned at him. "It went well?"

"Perfectly, Carlos. How's your jaw?"

Carlos brought his hand up to his chin and smiled ruefully. "Sore, you son of a bitch. Did you have to hit me that hard?"

"Sorry. It had to look good."

"I get clobbered and you get the girl. Story of my life. What name did you give her?"

"Oliver Alberdi."

"You used your real first name?"

"Yeah," Oliver Fleming said. "I've got to establish a relationship with Maria Echeverria. There will be intimate moments. I can be more myself, you know, more natural if she's calling me by my real name."

"You mean you couldn't get it up if she were whispering some other guy's name in your ear."

"Exactly."

"I'll buy that."

"How did Ilona get rid of the guard?"

"With a chocolate eclair."

"What?"

"She posed as a bakery worker giving away free samples. When the sergeant came on duty, she gave him an eclair laced with enough syrup of ipecac to make a horse puke. The poor bastard's probably still throwing up."

Oliver laughed. "Beautiful."

"We'd better get back to the safe house," Carlos said. "The director wanted to be notified immediately when you made contact."

"Jesus, this new guy's only been at the agency—what, a month?—and he's already got his nose in field operations. He'll be going through our expense reports next."

"He's a former Federal judge, an amateur. What do you expect?" Carlos said. "The first thing new directors want to be briefed on is the spy stuff. They all think they're going to be the next Alan Dulles."

"I hear that Madam President loves the clandestine shit, too. You wouldn't think a woman would be into it."

"Face it, Oliver. What we do is glamorous."

"I hope the accountants in Langley think my funding request is glamorous. I'm going to need a place to take her. An expensive place. Furnished. Silk sheets, silver service, a wine cellar, the whole nine yards. It's big bucks."

"Money's not going to be a problem. The boys on the South American desk have been trying to get close to de Urquiza for years. Now that you've made contact with the generalissimo's mistress, they'll open the purse strings wide."

Oliver brought his hand up to his nose. He could still smell Maria's expensive Parisian perfume. "Making contact was the easy part," he said. "Now I've got to become her lover."

BIOSPHERE AMERICA, PRINCETON, NEW JERSEY

●●●●●●●●●●●●●●●●●●●●●●●●●

11:05 a.m.–April 6th

THERE WERE TWO DOZEN REPORTERS and photographers in the compact Biosphere America auditorium as Ben Meade came in, threaded his way through the video cameras and climbed the three steps to the small stage.

Marjorie Glynn was sitting in one of the rows of folding chairs behind the podium, talking to Charlotte Taylor-Skeel, director of public relations for Biosphere America. Ben sat down and leaned forward toward the women.

"I had no idea that so many reporters would show up. This could turn into a circus."

"I won't let that happen, Ben." The attractive PR director smiled confidently, pushing a strand of curly blond hair off her forehead with a pencil.

"We can't have a mob like this wandering around the biosphere," Marjorie said worriedly. "If someone gets lost in the rain forest, we'll be looking for him for a week."

"I've thought of that," Charlotte said. "We'll pile them all into the Centipede and keep on the pathways."

The Centipede was the name the Biosphereans had given to the ten-car electric conveyance that rolled around the mini-Earth on a hundred fat, soft tires. The supple tires were designed to spread the weight of the vehicle and spare the biosphere's delicate soil and ground cover.

The PR director looked at her watch. "You two ready?"

"I hate this," Marjorie said.

"A necessary evil." Charlotte patted Marjorie's knee, then rose and crossed to the podium.

"May I have your attention, please?" she said into the microphone, then adjusted the volume and tried again. "Settle down, please."

Gradually the hubbub in the auditorium died away and the reporters turned their attention to the stage. The video cameramen focused their lenses on Charlotte without rolling their tapes, and the still photographers studied their light meters.

"Thank you all for coming. A few ground rules before we get started. No shouted questions, wait to be recognized, and when we go into the biosphere, I'll ask you all to keep together. After the news conference, there'll be an hour's break for lunch; then we'll take you on a tour of the biomes. Now I'd like to introduce the director of Biosphere America, Doctor Marjorie Glynn. Please keep your questions short."

The video cameras began to roll, and several still cameras flashed as Marjorie rose and took Charlotte's place at the podium. "Thank you, Charlotte. And thank you all for coming today. I'll try to answer all your queries, time permitting. I'll take the first question now."

Several hands shot up and Marjorie wondered for a moment who to recognize first. Then she spotted the gray-haired science editor of *The New York Times*. Charles Ickles had run several positive pieces about the biosphere. She decided she owed him a favor. "Yes, Mister Ickles?"

The tall, thin journalist smoothed the wrinkles from his pinstriped suit as he rose, his snow-white hair and deeply crevassed patrician face making him look older than his fifty-four years. He glanced down through his rimless glasses at the notes in his hand, then returned his gaze to Marjorie. "Doctor Glynn, your press releases refer to Biosphere America as a 'mini-Earth.' That's rather a presupposing title, isn't it, for what is essentially a huge greenhouse?''

Ben noticed Marjorie's back stiffen. She hated to have the biosphere referred to as a greenhouse. Ickles had turned out to be a poor first choice.

Marjorie gave the Timesman a forced smile. "The only similarity between a greenhouse and Biosphere America, Mister Ickles, is that both are enclosed in glass. A greenhouse is essentially a single ecosystem in which all the plants and insect species live under the same conditions of temperature and humidity. Nutrients and water must be brought in, and there is also an interchange of air, insects and pollen with the outside through doors and windows.''

Marjorie turned her gaze from Ickles to the full audience. She wanted to be sure everyone understood this. "In contrast, Biosphere America contains five separate biomes, or ecosystems, that duplicate the biological, geological and chemical cycles of Earth's biosphere—the vertical bands of sea, land and air in which life exists on this planet.

"The water and air inside are continuously recycled, and not a single insect or pollen spore goes in or out. If the biosphere were put down on the face of the moon, the life inside could exist indefinitely, constantly renewing itself. Biosphere America is called a mini-Earth, Mister Ickles, because that is exactly what it is—a miniature version of Earth itself.''

Marjorie nodded at a carefully coiffed, middle-aged woman wearing a dark gray wool suit in the second row. "Yes?''

"Carin Callisch of KQED public television in San Francisco, Doctor Glynn. As I understand it, there are already twenty million people living in the biospheres you've built in England and Ireland.''

"Closer to twenty-two million, actually. We expect to have most of the remaining population inside by the end of the year.''

"If I read Miss Taylor-Skeel's press releases correctly, you intend to move everyone in America into biospheres as well. Isn't your plan terribly high-risk? After all, you're talking about uprooting two hundred and fifty million people."

Ben rose and stood next to Marjorie at the podium. "Let's be clear about something; it's not Doctor Glynn's plan to move our population into the biospheres. The project was proposed by the President and passed by Congress. The National Science Foundation asked her to come over and direct our biosphere-building program because she virtually pioneered the concept. I might add that we're damn lucky to have her."

Marjorie mouthed a silent "Thank you" to Ben as he lightly touched her shoulder and sat down again.

A dozen hands rose among the reporters, and Marjorie pointed at a swarthy, dark-haired man wearing a cream-colored sports jacket over an open-necked, aquamarine shirt. "Yes?"

"Felipe Rodriguez, *Miami Herald*. Driving up this morning, I could see the biosphere from over five miles away. Can you give us some statistics? How big is the structure?"

"Of course. The main pyramid sheltering the five ecosystems is a mile long, three-quarters of a mile wide and eight hundred feet high. It encloses an area of roughly fourteen billion cubic feet. The human habitat, work areas and agricultural wing total another ten billion cubic feet."

Rodriguez let out a low whistle through his Chiclet teeth. "I've heard rumors that the biospheres are going to be built in the northern states first. That the people in my home state of Florida won't be able to move into your mini-Earths for perhaps two more years."

Marjorie's set smile wavered. "It is a physical impossibility to build all the biospheres at once. We have neither the skilled craftsmen nor the materials with which to do it . . . not to mention bringing in all the ecosystems. So we're going to build the biospheres in two phases. The initial phase will be built primarily in the northern and plains states, where the weather is more severe. We estimate that the first thousand biospheres will be completed by January of next year."

"So states like Florida take a back seat. When will you

get around to building the biospheres down south?"

Marjorie shifted uncomfortably. "The second phase will be completed in January, two thousand three. And it is not a matter of favoring one part of the country over another, Mister Rodriguez. It's simply that it's a great deal colder in states such as Minnesota and Wyoming than in Florida, or out on the West Coast. There's a far greater urgency to move people into the warm shelter of the biospheres in these areas."

Rodriguez sat down and Marjorie called on a tall young reporter with red hair and freckles.

"Sam Player, Passadumkeag, *Maine Weekly Express*."

The PR director leaned toward Ben. "Passadumkeag *Weekly Express*! My high-school paper had a larger circulation."

Ben threw her an exaggerated grimace. "I'm glad that's not you up there, Charlotte. You'd eat the poor boy alive."

Charlotte appraised the handsome twenty-something reporter. "Yum-yum."

"Yes, Mister Player," Marjorie said.

"I've been reading your fact sheet on these Intensive Agriculture Biomes you plan for each biosphere. Now, I was raised on a farm and I understand most of the principles you're proposing: crop rotation, hydroponics and all that. Still, a hundred thousand people is one hell of a lot of mouths to feed. Are you planning some sort of reduced diet for Americans?"

"I anticipate a normal caloric intake, Mister Player, although there will necessarily be a reduction in individual red-meat consumption. After all, we can't raise herds of cattle in the biospheres. Still, there will be meat on the menu, although the diet will primarily consist of grains, cereals, vegetables and fruit."

"What about jobs? We can't all be farmers."

"Of course not. The biospheres will be built around the major urban centers where the jobs are, and where we have some chance of keeping the roads clear of ice and snow. We hope to eventually convert much of the American economy to low-pollution light industry that can be carried on in structures attached to the biospheres."

Player scribbled in his note pad. "What sort of light industry are you talking about?"

"Computer design, genetic engineering, medical research, financial services, communications, and of course, intensive agriculture. In the future, heavy industry will best be left to the countries in the southern hemisphere. Indeed, many European, Asian and North American companies have already moved their factories south of the equator."

A flurry of hands shot up and Marjorie smiled at an old woman with piercing blue eyes and a latticework of wrinkles crevassing a face rich in character and strength.

"I'm Nel Forsythe, publisher of the *Des Moines Register*," the woman said, rising with the help of a knobby cane.

"Welcome to Biosphere America, Mrs. Forsythe," Marjorie said, seeing in the publisher her own grandmother seated in a rocking chair, knitting needles in her hands and a cat on her lap.

"Thank you, Doctor Glynn. I'm very pleased to be here. You mentioned five ecosystems. Would you kindly describe them?"

"Yes, of course. As you'll see shortly, Biosphere America contains a savanna, a marsh—actually, there are both fresh- and saltwater marshes—a desert, a tropical rain forest and a small ocean."

"Why all these different ecosystems?"

"Are you familiar with the Gaia theory, Mrs. Forsythe?"

"No, I must say I've never heard of it."

"Basically, the Gaia theory concerns the role of biota in maintaining a climatic heostasis."

"Say what?"

Coming so incongruously from the stooped octogenarian, the question convulsed the reporters and the auditorium erupted in laughter.

Even the tense Marjorie allowed herself a smile. "Forgive me, Mrs. Forsythe. I'm afraid I'm so used to talking to my fellow scientists day in and day out, I forget that our vernacular is hardly popular usage."

Behind Marjorie, Ben sat back glumly in his chair. "Day

in and day out" was right. Hell, she was so buried in her work that she couldn't even talk to people anymore without slipping into lab lingo.

"Gaia is the name of an ancient Greek goddess, the Earth Mother who brought forth the world and the human race from the gaping void. Back in seventy-nine, a rather deep thinker named J.E. Lovelock applied the name to his hypothesis that the entire planet is one living organism. The Gaia theory holds that plants, animals, the atmosphere and the earth's crust are all intricately connected in a three-billion-year biogeochemical balancing act that allows life to flourish on this planet."

There was a new energy in Marjorie's voice now, and Ben could tell that she was getting into her subject. Science was her life, and talking about it excited her. Far more than he had lately.

"Life exists on Earth because our atmosphere is an active part of our biosphere," Marjorie went on. "Three to four billion years ago, our atmosphere was primarily composed of carbon dioxide, much like Mars or Venus today. Then at some point, primitive bacteria appeared and began harnessing sunlight to synthesize organic carbon from carbon dioxide. This process freed oxygen into the atmosphere."

"You're describing photosynthesis," Mrs. Forsythe said.

"Exactly. Photosynthesizers are constantly removing gases from, and pumping gases back into, the atmosphere. At the same time, the oceans—and on a far slower scale, the tectonic cycles of the earth's crust—are also essential to the interchange of chemical elements that govern the growth, death and rebirth of all the life-forms on Earth."

"Most informative. Thank you, Doctor Glynn," the publisher said, slowly easing herself back into her seat.

"Not at all." Marjorie smiled, then pointed to a large, florid-faced man in a tan cotton suit at the end of one of the middle rows. "Yes, the gentleman on the aisle there."

"Beau Culpepper, Athens, *Georgia Daily Sentinel,* Doctor Glynn. I can see where the atmosphere and plants and we humans are all interrelated. I mean, we breathe the air

and eat plants and all that. I suppose I could even understand that part about the ocean being involved; it's water
and we're mostly made up of water. What I don't get is
how in God's creation the earth's crust comes into all this.
Rocks aren't alive."

"Oh, but they once were, Mister Culpepper, at least
sedimentary rocks."

"Sedimentary rocks?"

"Yes. The bulk of the carbonate minerals in these rocks
is the residue of once living organisms."

"But I don't see how this Gaia cycle continues. Once
somethin's dead and turned into rock, that's the end of
that, right?"

"Wrong. Imagine a carbon atom that was once part of a
plant and is now trapped in sedimentary rock beneath the
ocean. It may remain immobilized for a hundred million
years. Yet the sediment in which it lies doesn't remain stationary. It's moving almost imperceptibly atop one of the
tectonic plates that make up the earth's crust. Eventually
the sediment reaches a subduction zone."

Culpepper's eyes glazed over. "Subduction zone?"

Marjorie turned toward Ben. "This is your area, Doctor
Meade. Would you care to explain?"

Ben rose and again stood beside Marjorie at the podium. "The hard outer layer of the earth is called the
lithosphere, and you could best picture it as a cracked
eggshell. These cracks, or faults, divide the lithosphere
into seven major plates and at least twelve smaller plates,
each about sixty miles thick. In some areas, two plates
will grind past each other, causing earthquakes."

"Like the San Andreas fault out in California?" Culpepper suggested.

"That's a good example. Along the San Andreas fault,
the Pacific plate is moving northwest in relation to the
North American plate. However, in subduction zones, instead of moving past each other, one plate is forced down
beneath the other. As the descending plate dives down
into the increasingly hotter mantle, it melts into magma.
Much of that molten material is then erupted back to the
surface through volcanism."

"Thank you, Ben," Marjorie said as he returned to his

seat. "So you see, Mister Culpepper, over the approximately four-point-five-billion-year history of the Earth, that single carbon atom might have made twenty trips back and forth between sediment, ocean, soils, the atmosphere and life-forms, including humankind."

"So I could have atoms in my body that were once part of the earth's crust?"

"You undoubtedly do, Mister Culpepper."

"I told you that you had rocks in your head, Beau," a fresh-faced young reporter with blond spiked hair called out, sending another peal of laughter rippling through the auditorium.

Marjorie grinned. "Naturally, Biosphere America would have to exist for hundreds of millions of years before an entire biogeochemical cycle could take place. Yet even over days, weeks and months, the same Gaian principles apply. The biosphere's plant and animal life, its atmosphere, soil and ocean, are linked in a constant symbiosis without which our mini-Earth could not survive."

Marjorie glanced at her watch. "Before we get too far along, I'd like to ask Doctor Meade to answer any questions you might have about our energy sources. After all, light and heat are as critical to the biosphere's survival as the life cycles I've described. Ben?"

Ben rose and crossed to the podium as Marjorie sat down next to Charlotte.

"Fire away," he said to the reporters, adjusting the height of the microphone.

Several reporters waved their hands to be called, and he pointed to a pretty, dark-haired woman in her late twenties, with large black eyes and a Cupid's-bow mouth. When she rose, her blazer jacket opened to reveal large, round breasts beneath a red cashmere sweater.

"Wouldn't you know he'd call on her? Men!" Charlotte Taylor-Skeel whispered to Marjorie. Marjorie gave the PR director a tight smile, then bored her eyes into the back of Ben's head.

"Gretchen Mosbacher, *Chicago Sun Times.* Could you tell us what fuel you'll use to power the biospheres?"

"At present, we use natural gas. However, when we start building biospheres all over the country, the immense amount of energy they'll need will overwhelm our fossil-fuel supplies of gas, oil and coal. The answer here, as it was in Britain, is geothermal energy."

"Geothermal is a rather revolutionary energy source, isn't it, Doctor Meade?"

"Not really. We have evidence that Paleolithic peoples cooked meat over geothermal vents, and we know that the Romans designed elaborate baths around European hot springs."

"I meant as a source of electrical power."

"Once again, Miss Mosbacher, there's a history there. Icelanders have been using geothermal energy to power generators for several decades now, and there have been experimental projects in several other countries for many years."

"Airhead," Charlotte stage-whispered, loud enough for the young reporter to hear her.

The pretty woman glared at the PR director, her lips curled in a wounded pout.

Ben took pity. "You're right, though, Miss Mosbacher, if you mean a source of electrical power on the scale we're proposing. If we're successful in harnessing the incredible heat reserves that lie beneath the land, geothermal energy will replace fossil fuels within five years."

The reporter gave Ben a grateful smile. "What exactly is geothermal energy? I mean, how does it work?"

"As the name suggests, geothermal is simply heat energy trapped beneath the earth's crust in reservoirs of molten rock called magma. In many areas, particularly in the western states, magma has risen through faults and cracks in the rock to within five miles of the surface. In some places, such as Yellowstone Park out in Wyoming, it's only a mile or two down. Where the magma is near the surface, it increases the temperature of the crustal rock above it, and that in turn heats any ground water that's present."

"That's why there are geysers in Yellowstone?"

"Yes, geysers and hot springs are always an indication of a shallow magma source and the presence of super-heated water above it."

"And the superheated water is the source of your energy?"

"Not always. There are four types of geothermal systems: magma, hot dry rock, water-dominated, and vapor-dominated. Where we have magma or hot rock, we usually pump water down and then retrieve it as boiling water or steam. Whatever the system, the end product is steam that drives turbine generators, which in turn produce electrical energy."

"It sounds so simple."

"It sounds so simple," the PR director whispered mockingly to Marjorie.

Marjorie gave Charlotte a conspiratorial grin, but there was no mirth in the eyes that locked again on the back of Ben's head. She was wondering whether the pretty, dark-eyed reporter excited him. Was that why he'd called on her?

"Yes, I know it sounds easy, but it isn't," Ben said. "Even with the new laser drill we've developed, high temperatures and hard rock at depth can slow the drilling to a crawl. Then there's the problem of scrubbing the steam."

The young reporter flashed a perplexed smile. "Scrubbing the steam?"

"It's a process that removes most of the vaporized gases, metals and minerals before they strike the turbine blades and foul the machinery. Yes?" he said, pointing toward the rear of the auditorium. "The gentleman with the goatee in the back row."

"Peter Maxwell, KCBS, Seattle," the heavyset reporter said, adjusting a set of horn-rimmed glasses beneath Groucho Marx eyebrows. "These geothermal fields you intend to tap into across the country, are they pretty much the same everywhere?"

"God, no. They vary all over the place, depending on the local geology. Along the Gulf Coast, for instance, I know we'll run into geopressurized zones: porous sand aquifers sealed between impermeable layers of clay and shale."

Ben noticed several reporters exchange bewildered looks. "Picture a sponge bulging with water squeezed between two dinner plates. The pressure in these aquifers can reach over fifteen thousand pounds per square inch. When you drill into a strata under that much pressure, it's like puncturing a tire, except that superheated water jets out instead of air."

"It sounds dangerous."

"It is. On my first job on a geothermal rig, we hit a geopressurized zone and a valve blew out. The explosion decapitated two guys on the platform. Still, the riskiest wells are the ones tapping high-temperature reservoirs. The water coming up the drill pipe can reach sixteen hundred degrees Centigrade; that's sixteen times the boiling point. One mistake and you can be scalded to death in seconds."

The next question was addressed to Marjorie, and Ben sat down again. For the next half hour, the two alternated in answering questions, until finally, forty-five minutes after the news conference began, Charlotte stepped to the microphone and announced that it was time for lunch.

"We'll reconvene in an hour and start our tour in the Intensive Agriculture Biome," she said. Now, will you all just follow me to the dining hall."

"Oh, Doctor Meade, Doctor Meade." The wellendowed Gretchen Mosbacher was waving from the aisle. "Could I walk with you? I want to know more about your geothermal work."

Ben smiled and bounced down the steps from the stage. "Of course, Miss Mosbacher. I'm always glad to assist the fourth estate."

Charlotte leaned toward Marjorie as they led the other reporters toward the auditorium door. "He'd like to assist her all right, right out of her panties."

Marjorie dug her fists into the pockets of her skirt and lowered her head. "Do me a favor, Charlotte, and just shut up. Just plain shut up."

BIOSPHERE AMERICA,
PRINCETON, NEW JERSEY
•

1:25 p.m.–April 6th

A HANDSOME YOUNG BLOND Biospherean, wearing the orange coveralls of the biosphere's technical-support staff, crossed the dining hall where the reporters were having lunch and stopped beside the chair of Charlotte Taylor-Skeel.

"The Centipede's outside in the corridor, Ma'am."

The PR director looked up and smiled. "Thanks, Jimmy. Did you make sure the batteries are charged? My version of hell is being stuck somewhere out on the desert with a couple dozen blathering reporters."

Jimmy grinned. "Fully charged, Ma'am. Anything else?"

"No. I appreciate it."

"No sweat."

Charlotte watched the young staffer walk away, then sighed wistfully and shook her head. " 'Ma'am'! Do you believe it? Here I am with an insatiable urge to pinch his buns and he treats me like his mother."

"I'm sure," Marjorie said absently, idly pushing carrots around her plate with her fork and staring at something past Charlotte's left shoulder.

The PR director didn't have to turn around to know what was absorbing Marjorie's attention: Ben Meade and Gretchen Mosbacher had decided to have lunch together. Even though she was several tables away, Charlotte could hear the two laughing together.

She looked at Marjorie intently. "You haven't heard a word I've said for the past hour."

"I'm sure."

"Marjorie! Jesus!"

Marjorie started. "I'm sorry, Charlotte. What did you say?"

"You haven't touched your lunch. And it's time to start the tour. Do you want me to order a sandwich from the kitchen? You could eat it in the Centipede."

"No," Marjorie answered, her eyes traveling past Charlotte again. "I'm not hungry."

Charlotte stole a glance over her shoulder at Ben and the pretty reporter. "Don't let it get to you."

"They certainly seem to be enjoying each other's company."

"He's doing it deliberately, you know—trying to make you jealous."

"I'm not the jealous type. Certainly not of some big-bosomed bimbo."

"That's why you've been staring at them all through lunch?"

"One can hardly not look over. They're making more noise than ten other tables together."

"Marjorie, we're friends. What's going on between you and Ben?"

Marjorie put down her fork and sighed. "Nothing. That's just it."

"Bedroom problems?"

"Among others. Look, Charlotte, this is neither the time nor the place. I could use a shoulder to cry on, but later. All right?"

"Of course. You ready?"

"Yes. If I have to watch those two coo at each other a moment longer, I'll scream."

Charlotte rose and tapped the side of her water glass with a spoon. "Attention, please. We're ready to start the tour. There's a tram waiting outside to take us through the biosphere."

The reporters finished the last of their chocolate mousse and coffee and followed Charlotte and Marjorie toward the wide hallway that bisected the huge complex. As the group reached the hall, Charlotte directed them to seats in the ten-car Centipede.

As Mrs. Forsythe tottered out on her cane, Marjorie took her arm. "Let me help you," she smiled, guiding the elderly publisher toward a car in the middle of the tram. "It's rather awkward climbing in."

"Thank you, my dear. I can see why you call it the Centipede," the octogenarian said, glancing down at the rows of fat little tires beneath the vehicle.

While Marjorie was seating Mrs. Forsythe, Charlotte intercepted Ben Meade and Gretchen Mosbacher as they wandered out with the last of the group. "Ben, if you don't mind, I'd like you to drive."

"Sure."

"Oooh, could I sit up front with you?" Gretchen tugged on Ben's arm.

Charlotte gave her a hard smile. "That might be construed as favoritism by the other reporters, Miss Mosbacher. Please take a seat with the rest of the group."

Gretchen pouted prettily. "All right, if I must. See you later, Ben."

"Yes, you can finish telling me about that screenplay you're writing," he said, arching his eyebrows at Charlotte as Gretchen wiggled her way toward the rear of the tram. "Marjorie ask you to do that?"

"No. I did it all on my own." She leaned toward Ben's ear. "You prick."

"Jesus, all I did was have lunch with her."

"Bullshit. You were fantasizing about screwing her the entire time."

"You're a carnal woman, Charlotte."

"You got that right, sweetie. Now be a good boy and play bus driver."

Ben laughed and wandered forward to the first car. A moment later, Marjorie and Charlotte came up and took the seat behind him.

"Enjoy your lunch?" Marjorie gave him a mirthless smile.

"Look, Charlotte's already raked me over the coals. You'd think I was balling her brains out on top of the goddam table."

"I think that Miss Mosbacher is more of an under-the-table type, don't you? Down on the floor with the spilled french fries and the rest of the rancid flotsam."

Ben sighed and shook his head. "You two ready?"

"Any time," Marjorie said.

He looked past them and down the row of cars. "Hang on, everybody. Here we go."

Ben depressed the accelerator, and the electric tram hummed smoothly down the twenty-foot-wide hall, the reporters grinning like children riding in a miniature train at the amusement park.

Air Traffic Controller Joel Dinolt noticed the large blip appear on the Philadelphia airport long-distance radar screen at 1:45 P.M. The two-mile mass had a strange triangular shape and was moving due north above central New Jersey.

Dinolt assumed the formation to be a heavy snow squall blowing up from Chesapeake Bay and made a mental note to track its path. If the squall changed course and headed west toward Philadelphia, the snow could really hurt airport operations.

His attention was diverted while he talked down a 747 from Detroit. When he looked back at the long-distance radar six minutes later, the blip had moved north almost three miles. Whatever the mass was, it was traveling at approximately thirty miles an hour, far faster than the afternoon's winds would carry a snow squall.

He hit a series of keys on the computer board before him and ran a close-up. The screen showed that the mass was made of thousands of small, solid objects. As he stared at the V-shaped formation, he suddenly knew: of course, migrating ducks or geese. Geese probably, to judge by their size.

Dinolt was about to turn away when he noticed the altitude reading. The geese were flying at eight hundred feet, unusually low for a migrating flock. A vague feeling of apprehension came over him.

Birds had been doing screwy things ever since R-9 had erupted the winter before. In a normal year, the Philadelphia airport could expect no more than two dozen bird-plane collisions, but there had been over two hundred in the past twelve months. And almost every day, birds crashed into the tower glass, unnerving the controllers inside.

His supervisor said it was due to all that volcanic ash in the air. The fine particles lodged in the birds' eyes and blinded them. Screwed up their internal navigation systems, too, so the poor things didn't know where they were going.

Dinolt decided to check the position of the low-flying flock again later in his shift. If the geese were on a line heading for New York City, there could be a problem. There were a lot of tall buildings in Gotham.

A hundred yards along the corridor, the Centipede rounded a corner and Charlotte swiveled in her seat to face the reporters.

"Off to your left is the first of the sixteen human habitats that will be attached to the biosphere," she said, a touch of a tour director's breezy boredom in her voice. "There are individual apartments for each Biospherean, along with offices, workshops, medical labs, a media studio, a fully equipped gym, and a hundred-thousand-volume central library."

Marjorie pointed at a lush growth of fruit trees. "We also have a rather lovely plantation garden with bananas, avocados and figs," she said.

"Up ahead is the Intensive Agriculture Biome," Charlotte went on. "Just a reminder—please don't touch the plants or pet the animals."

Fifty yards down the corridor, a set of double glass doors appeared on the right. Ben leaned forward and pressed a remote-control button on the dash, and the doors slid open noiselessly.

As the Centipede passed through, the pungent odors of warm, moist earth, decaying vegetable matter and animal droppings wafted over the reporters.

"It smells like the farm I was raised on," CBS correspondent Peter Maxwell said.

"God Almighty, look at that," a video cameraman toward the front of the Centipede said, bringing his Beta-cam up to pan the immense space stretching into the distance. The vast biome measured a half-mile wide by three-quarters of a mile long, and was entirely enclosed in a glass canopy. The canopy rose straight up on the sides, then vaulted four hundred and fifty feet above their heads in a series of nine soaring arches.

"As you can see, the 'farm,' as we call it, is divided into two halves," Charlotte said as Ben turned the tram down a wide, sandy roadway that split the green fields. "On the left are the terraces where we grow most of the vegetables. On your right are the grain crops."

"What are those things up there?" Athens' *Sentinel* reporter Beau Culpepper asked, pointing toward rows of glass-faced half-globes hanging from the arches on long cords.

"Grow lights," Marjorie told him. "They replace the direct sunlight that's no longer reaching the earth in the northern hemisphere. Without the lights, plant life couldn't carry on photosynthesis."

A quarter-mile down the track, Charlotte turned to Marjorie. "Feel like answering some more questions?"

"Do I have a choice?"

"You could resign. Slit your throat. Better still, you could murder Ben."

"That third alternative is rather attractive, but I think I'll carry on with the press tour for now."

"Good idea. If you kill him now, you won't have time to savor the moment." She leaned toward Ben. "Stop up here, will you?" Ben nodded, and pulled the Centipede over next to a ripening field of wheat.

Marjorie stood up. "I'll take questions on our agriculture now."

A reporter in the third car back raised his hand.

"Yes?" Marjorie said.

"Steve Graziano, WKKZ, Chicago. So far, I've recognized wheat, soybeans, beans and peas. Can you tell us what other crops are grown in here?"

"We rotate a hundred and fifty cultivars, or varieties, of plants, Mister Graziano. The primary crops include rice, oats, peanuts, leafy greens, and vegetables like beets and carrots. We also grow fruits such as strawberries and honeydew melons."

"You Biosphereans eat well," Graziano grinned.

"And so shall the millions of your countrymen who will inhabit Biosphere America in the years to come."

For the next ten minutes, Marjorie answered questions on the crops around them. Then a short, burly reporter rose from his seat in the last car.

"You said there'd be meat on the menu, Doctor Glynn, but all I see are plants," he said, neglecting the recognition regimen the PR director had insisted on.

Charlotte frowned and started to protest, but Marjorie raised a restraining hand and shook her head. "That's all right, Charlotte. I think we can go a bit informal the rest of the way. The livestock pens are farther on. Ben, would you drive us down there?"

"Next stop, the pigpen," Ben said, starting the Centipede back down the sandy track.

Several of the media snickered.

"It is not a pigpen!" Marjorie bristled, hypersensitive to any disparaging remark about the biomes she'd built.

"All right," Ben said. "Next stop, Hog Hilton."

Marjorie fumed as the reporters behind her broke into laughter.

Twenty-five miles south of Biosphere America, Brave Bird led his flock north, the twenty thousand geese in the formation behind him honking mournfully as they passed over the snow-covered New Jersey countryside.

In a normal year, the great birds would be flying up the coast toward Canada, coming down at intervals to feed in the rich river estuaries and brackish marshes that lined the shore. The mid-April sun would be warm, the skies blue, and the land below bursting forth with the first flowers and grasses of spring.

But this was not a normal year. With the magnetic compass in his brain made useless by the iron particles in the air, Brave Bird could not navigate east to the coast, and even if he could, the frozen marshes offered the hungry geese nothing to eat.

The flock could not fly for long without food to energize the continuously working muscles in their wings and shoulders, and the old gander swept the ground below with his one good eye, searching for any sign of greenery. He saw nothing but frozen fields and woods, crisscrossed by roads dotted here and there with the noisy, smelly machines that carried humans around. He avoided leading the flock over houses and towns in their path, for the air above was thick with smoke from chimneys and furnace vents.

Then, just west of Lawrenceville, the flock flew into a pocket of snow flurries that obscured the earth beneath them. Brave Bird knew that to spot food below, he must fly lower, and the old gander gave a loud honk and led the flock down to four hundred feet.

Twenty-two miles ahead, the snow began to coat the eight-hundred-foot-high sides of Biosphere America.

As the tram passed through the Agriculture Biome, Marjorie pointed out long rows of hydroponic vegetables, their roots trailing into containers of nutrient solution, and scattered groves of papayas shading mounds covered with broccoli, sage and thyme.

Several hundred yards down the road, a cacophony of bleats, grunts, quacks, and cackles began to build in the distance, and a few moments later, Ben stopped the Centipede in front of the fenced animal pens.

"Oh, what adorable little piglets," a stout woman reporter gushed, leaning out of the Centipede to reach a hand toward the nearest of a herd of tiny pigs beyond the fence.

"No petting," Charlotte reminded her sharply. "You could transmit a disease."

"I beg your pardon," the woman huffed.

Marjorie smiled. "It's more likely you'd get a nip. They're not piglets, you see. They're mature Vietnamese potbellied pigs we raise for meat."

"Are those full-grown, too?" a photographer asked, pointing his camera toward several dozen small goats grazing in the neighboring enclosure.

"Yes, they're pygmy goats that supply our milk and cheese. Over to your right there are guinea fowl, a sort of ancestral chicken that thrives both on our farm and in the tropical rain forest."

The woman reporter screwed up her face. "You mean to say you eat chickens that have been foraging in the forest? Good Lord, they've probably been gobbling up bugs and snails and God knows what else."

Ben couldn't resist. "We eat a lot of the wild animals in the biosphere," he said. "Lizards, tortoises, blue-tongued skinks, and some of the tastiest snakes you ever smacked your lips over."

"Uuooo, how vile." The woman recoiled. "You don't really eat snakes, do you?"

"Can't get enough of them."

Marjorie rolled her eyes. "Actually, while we do harvest the biosphere animals when their populations get too high, most of our animal protein comes from pigs, fowl, and tilapia fish that we raise in special tanks. The tubs are down past the Insectary."

As Ben started the Centipede back down the road, Marjorie pointed toward an acre-sized screened enclosure just visible beyond a field of barley. "That's the Insectary," she said. "We have approximately two hundred and fifty insect species in the biosphere, including termites, ladybugs, praying mantis, ants, bees and butterflies."

"I would think bugs would be something you'd want to get rid of," a small, cherubic-faced woman in an aquamarine pants suit said. "Won't they eat the crops in here?"

"Not the insects we raise. On the contrary, species such as the praying mantis and the ladybugs eat the pests that would normally devour food plants. Bees, of course, are natural pollinators, and the termites recycle nutrients by eating and breaking down dead plant materials."

"What do the butterflies contribute?" the woman asked, her pen poised over her notebook.

"Beauty," Marjorie smiled. "It's quite enough."

A signpost anchored in a cement block appeared in the middle of the sandy track ahead, a large "Road Closed" notice tacked to the top. Ben stopped the Centipede, reached for the cellular phone on the dash and put through a call to the maintenance department.

A moment later, he frowned, hung up the phone and swiveled around in his seat. "Maintenance is digging a pipe trench across the road to the tilapia tanks," he said to Marjorie. "If you want to show them the fish, you'll have to hike through the fields."

Charlotte said, "We could skip it."

Marjorie shook her head. "No, I want the press to see the tilapia for themselves. There've been too many stories in the media that we Biospheans are strict vegetarians. I don't want the American people to think they'll have nothing to eat but corn and carrots when they start moving into the biospheres."

Charlotte shrugged. "It's your call. All right, everybody, we'll cross the oat field to the right. Mind your step. The rows were fertilized this morning."

"My goodness, I don't think I'm quite up to trekking through an oat field," Mrs. Forsythe said.

"I'll stay here with you," Ben volunteered.

Gretchen Mosbacher's face lit up and she opened her mouth to say something. Before she got a word out, Charlotte took her arm and steered her toward the gate. "Those fish are just going to thrill you to bits, Miss Mosbacher. What a treat for you."

Marjorie grinned and followed the two into the field as Ben moved back and sat down next to the elderly publisher.

"I want you to tell me all about your geothermal work, young man," Mrs. Forsythe said.

" 'Young man'! Mrs. Forsythe, you and I are going to get along just fine."

Halfway across the field, Beau Culpepper stopped and

kicked at a mound of earth beneath a cornstalk. "You said everything's recycled in here. What about the chemicals in the fertilizer? Some of that stuff doesn't break down, does it?"

"We don't use chemicals," Marjorie replied.

"What do you use?"

"Primarily sheep feces and urine, along with human waste."

Culpepper looked at her. "You're kidding. You don't really spread . . ."

"Shit? Yes, that's exactly what we use."

Several reporters surreptitiously examined the soles of their shoes.

Marjorie grinned. "We don't just come out here and defecate in the fields. The human waste goes into a marsh where microbes, plants, insects and frogs consume the sewage and break down the organic materials. The process leaves the water clean enough to irrigate the crops, yet still rich in the nutrients that plants need in order to grow."

The reporter from the *Miami Herald* sniffed the air. "There certainly isn't any odor," Felipe Rodriguez said. "Matter of fact, the air in here smells . . . I don't know . . . healthy or something."

"That's because it's being circulated through the ground beneath your feet," Marjorie said.

"The air comes out of the ground?"

"Yes. We call it a soil-bed reactor. The biosphere air is drawn down and then it percolates back up through the four-foot-thick beds of soil beneath the crops. Almost all airborne solvents and organics are gobbled up by soil microorganisms in the process, and the air emerges fresh and clean."

"There are the fish tanks up ahead," Charlotte said as the group emerged from the oat field.

"They look like huge pie pans," one of the reporters observed. "Why so shallow?"

"Because we grow rice in there as well," Marjorie said, leading the group up three steps to a wooden catwalk that circled the first seventy-five-foot-wide tub. "We keep

the water low enough for the stalks to break the surface
and reach the light."

"Where are the fish?" someone asked, squinting down
into the murky water. "All I see is a bunch of weeds floating around in there."

Marjorie frowned. "Those are hardly weeds. The tiny
ferns floating between the rice stalks are azolla, a plant
high in nitrogen. The tilapia eat the ferns, and we com-
post what's left and use it for fertilizer."

A ladybug landed on the water and instantly an eigh-
teen-inch tilapia appeared from the depths to snatch the
insect from among the delicate ferns. A dozen other
spiny-finned fish rose hungrily behind the first, searching
the surface for more bugs.

"They look like big carp," a still photographer said as
he snapped a picture. "Where do they come from?"

"They're a tropical fish from the inland lakes of
Africa," Marjorie told him. "We chose them because they
reproduce rapidly and their meat has an unusually high
percentage of protein."

For the next ten minutes, Marjorie answered questions
on aquaculture; then she and Charlotte led the reporters
back through the field to the Centipede. Ben was explaining something to Mrs. Forsythe, his hands animated as he
talked, and the octogenarian was looking at him with a
rapt expression. As the reporters climbed back into the
tram, he finished what he was saying, patted her hand affectionately, then went forward to the first car.

As Marjorie came up, the publisher reached out to take
her arm. "What a fascinating man," she said, nodding toward Ben. "I understand you two are engaged to be married."

"We're engaged, but I'm not sure that the relationship
will progress to marriage," Marjorie blurted out, immediately startled at the words. What had possessed her? She
turned toward the front of the tram and found Ben staring at her.

"I don't know why I said that," she offered limply, sliding guiltily into the seat behind him.

"What do you say we discuss it later, when we're

alone?'' he said angrily, jamming his foot down on the accelerator.

Charlotte was just climbing in beside Marjorie as the Centipede lurched forward. The PR director gave a yelp as she lost her balance and fell toward the open door. Marjorie lunged across the seat and pulled Charlotte back into the car. "Really, Ben! Must you be a cowboy?''

"I am a cowboy," Ben shot back over his shoulder. "Born and bred on a Wyoming ranch. Remember?''

Marjorie folded her arms across her chest and glared at the back of his head as the Centipede sped down the sandy track and out into the wide access hall.

"Flight Eight-oh-two from Phoenix, you're cleared to land on runway A-five left," Joel Dinolt said.

"Roger, Tower. A-five left. Thank you."

Dinolt glanced over at the long-distance radar. Things had been busy for the past half hour and he hadn't had a chance to check on the flight of geese. He swiveled in his chair and studied the delta-shaped blip.

The geese were now north of Trenton, New Jersey. There were a lot of radio and communications towers in the area, and he hit a series of computer keys, bringing up the location of every tower above three hundred feet. There were a half dozen, but none appeared to be directly ahead of the geese.

Still, there was something about the flight path of the big birds that made the radar operator uneasy. He worked the keyboard again, and a map overlay of northern New Jersey appeared on the screen. If the geese continued on their present course, they would pass Lawrenceville, then fly almost directly over Princeton.

Dinolt sat back in his chair and tapped his teeth with his fingernails. Princeton. There was something he should remember about Princeton.

Ben eased his foot off the accelerator and half-turned in his seat as the Centipede approached a twelve-foot-diameter circular door that completely filled the corridor ahead.

"We're coming up to the airlock leading into the biosphere," he said to the reporters riding behind. "Please don't stand up or reach your hands out when we're in the tunnel."

He swiveled around again and leaned forward to hit the remote-control button on the dash. Instantly, the door's fifteen-foot triangular panels withdrew into the rim and the tram entered a long tube lined with gleaming white tiles.

"Why do you need an airlock?" *The New York Times* reporter Charles Ickles asked.

"We keep the air pressure in the biosphere higher than the atmosphere outside," Marjorie said. "That allows us to maintain a higher oxygen content and prevents any volcanic ash or gases from getting in. If we should spring a leak, the positive pressure inside will make the air flow out rather than in and keep the biosphere's atmosphere pristine."

The tram reached the end of the long tube, and a second airtight door opened. Light suddenly flooded the tunnel, and the reporters squinted as the Centipede passed through into the cavernous enclosure beyond the door.

Ben stopped the tram and Marjorie turned in her seat to face the reporters. "Welcome to Biosphere America," she said.

The reporters stared in awestruck silence, transfixed by the immense glass cathedral of life before them. Sloping upward in three huge tiers, the mile-long walls of Biosphere America were made of thousands of huge triangles of glass, each ten feet high and ten feet across at its base.

"I feel like I'm inside an immense crystal," Gretchen Mosbacher said breathlessly, her eyes sweeping up the gleaming glass walls to the pyramid's apex eight hundred feet above them.

"This is what I've always imagined paradise looked like," Peter Maxwell said, staring at the profusion of exotic plants and animals that stretched in all directions.

The tram had stopped at the fringe of a vast savanna of knee-high green grass dotted here and there with groves of flowering acacia trees.

A warm breeze bathed their faces, bringing with it the intoxicating scents of wild orchids and jasmine, and the calls of distant songbirds.

"Are those deer?" Carin Callisch asked, pointing at a herd of tiny, dark brown animals grazing languidly in a shallow valley a quarter-mile away.

"Yes," Marjorie said. "They're pudus, the smallest of the New World deer. We brought them in from northern Peru to keep the savanna grasses clipped. At the same time, their droppings fertilize the soil."

A flight of red-and-green macaws dipped down toward the tram as if curious, then swooped back up as one and flew on toward the deep green foliage of the distant rain forest. The jungle rose from the savanna like a leafy wall, its towering trees and dense underbrush climbing the slope of a three hundred-foot hill.

At the fringe of the forest, a small river cascaded out of the trees and flowed through a steaming marsh studded with red mangrove trees. As the river cut through the swamp, it split into a delta of meandering waterways thick with flocks of feeding ducks.

Directly ahead across the savanna, the reporters could make out the blue waters of the biosphere's small ocean, its sparkling expanse taking up nearly a third of the mini-Earth's surface area.

"It's hard to imagine that man could create something like this," Passadumkeag *Express* reporter Sam Player said quietly.

"Man didn't create it, woman did," Charlotte said. "Specifically, Doctor Glynn."

Marjorie smiled. "Actually, I'm merely the architect of Biosphere America. Nature is the creator."

"God, you mean," Beau Culpepper said.

"God, nature, they're really the same, are they not?" Marjorie asked. "All you see before you exists somewhere on Earth. The only thing new is that I've brought the various ecosystems together in a confined area, whereas normally they're spread out around the world."

"But how did you manage to get all these plants and animals here to Princeton?" a tall, balding reporter with a thick French accent asked. "Mon Dieu, some of those trees in the rain forest must be over a hundred meters high."

"The American military," Ben said. "The President sent two aircraft carriers to the Caribbean to bring back thirty acres of rain forest from the Finca La Selva research station in Costa Rica."

Marjorie said, "Along with those huge trees you see, our biologists collected fifty-yard-wide mats of ground vegetation and soil. They rolled the mats up like rugs, with all the jungle-floor microbes, insects and snakes still inside. The Navy also brought back crates of animals indigenous to the region, and an entire mangrove swamp from the Florida Everglades."

"The Air Force pitched in, too," Ben said. "They built a temporary airport in the middle of the Serengeti Plain in Africa, then flew hundreds of missions with their big C-135 cargo planes. Each flight out carried a half-acre of savanna land. Within two months, they'd brought back this entire grassland you see around you."

"Ah, but what about that?" the Frenchman challenged, pointing toward the mini-sea shimmering in the distance. "How does one transport an ocean, even a small one?"

"A dozen supertankers were filled with Caribbean seawater and brought north to a dock in Perth Amboy," Ben said. "Then the main waterline between the port and Princeton was drained and the seawater pumped through the empty pipe into the biosphere ocean."

Marjorie added, "As soon as the sea was filled, the Corps of Engineers brought in a Caribbean sand beach and an offshore coral reef. We'll show them to you later."

The Frenchman shook his head in admiration. "In Europe, it's thought that American ingenuity is now second to the Japanese. But I do not agree."

"Not a chance," Ben said, then turned to Marjorie. "What do you want to show them first?"

"The desert, I think," she replied, stung by the edge of anger in his voice and the hard look in his eyes. She leaned forward across the back of his seat. "I said I was sorry."

"Why be sorry? The truth slipped out, and maybe it was time. Our relationship has been going down the tubes for the past six months."

Marjorie sat back and bit her lip as Ben put the Centipede in gear and they started across the grassland toward the distant sand dunes.

Air Traffic Control supervisor Craig Yamagi crossed the tower room and put his hand on the shoulder of Joel Dinolt. "Break-time, Joel."

Dinolt started. "Yeah. Thanks, Craig."

The supervisor cocked his head quizzically. "Why so jumpy? Something wrong?"

Dinolt rose and stretched, nodding toward the long-distance radar screen. "I don't know. It's probably nothing, but I've been tracking a formation of geese. There's something about their flight path that bothers me."

Yamagi leaned forward and scrutinized the screen. "Which direction are they flying?"

"North."

"So what's the problem? It's spring, or at least it would be in a normal year. Birds fly north in the spring."

"They're going to pass almost directly over Princeton."

"What? Are you worried they're going to dump goose shit all over some pretty co-ed up there?"

Dinolt laughed. "You're a big help, Craig."

"Go find a cup of coffee. You're getting spacey."

"Okay. You want anything downstairs? A doughnut?"

"Naw. I'm trying to lose weight."

Dinolt descended the circular stairs to the cafeteria in the base of the tower, poured a cup of coffee from the large urn in the corner and put a dollar in quarters into a vending machine for a cheese Danish.

As he sat down, another controller from his shift took the table next to him and flicked on a portable radio. "You mind?" he said to Dinolt. "I want to catch the two-o'clock news."

Dinolt shook his head no and nibbled listlessly at his

Danish as the news came on. The Argentine junta had just announced the second increase in grain prices in the past six months . . . cannibalism was reported rampant in the starving former republics of the Soviet Union . . . the Japanese economy continued its freefall as unsold cars and electronic appliances piled up in warehouses . . . the director of Biosphere America was conducting a press tour—

Dinolt dropped the Danish and sprang to his feet. Jesus God, Biosphere America! That was what he'd been trying to remember about Princeton. The biosphere was just west of the university up there. Directly in the flight path of the formation of geese. And the huge mini-Earth was eight hundred feet high!

The controller sprinted across the cafeteria and up the stairs to the control room. He almost knocked over the shift supervisor as he tore across to his radar. Still standing, he punched in a keyboard code and ordered a close-up of the Princeton area.

The screen before him flickered and a map overlay of the university town appeared, the image of the huge biosphere a half-mile off to the west. As he watched the radar, the radius swept the screen beneath the map like a second hand around a clock face, leaving behind the familiar triangular blip.

Dinolt sucked in his breath. The geese were on a direct heading for the towering glass mini-Earth. And they were now less than five miles away. "Holy shit!"

The shift supervisor came up and looked over his shoulder. "Problem?"

"Big fucking problem, Craig," Dinolt said, grabbing for the phone on the console before him. "Thousands of geese are about to fly through a glass wall eight hundred feet high."

The Centipede reached the edge of the biosphere's savanna and started across the desert, the vehicle's small wheels digging into the loose sand as Ben gunned it up the side of a steep dune. The reporters clung to the handrails before them as the Centipede careened over the top of the dune and bumped down the slope on the other side.

Marjorie leaned forward to Ben's shoulder. "Will you please slow down. You're going to have these people flying out the sides."

"I'm getting tired of playing tour guide."

"You organized the tour. Remember?"

"Yeah. I also suggested we cancel it and fly down to Rio. Remember?"

"It's getting worse, isn't it, Ben? We don't even communicate anymore without butting heads."

Before Ben could reply, a question came from one of the reporters behind them. "What are those plants up ahead there?" Sam Player asked as the Centipede started across a dried salt lake.

Marjorie composed herself and swiveled around in her seat. "Halophytes," she said. "Plants that can grow in salty soil."

She pointed toward the skirt of a basalt ridge to their right. "Those are boojum trees over there, and I think you all recognize the various cacti."

"Where'd all this come from?" Beau Culpepper asked in his slow, Southern drawl. "It doesn't exactly look like Arizona."

"No, we brought this ecosystem in from the Vizcaino coastal fog desert out in Baja, California."

"Whatsamatter, an American desert wasn't good enough?" Culpepper asked.

"Asshole," Ben muttered, loud enough for everyone on the tram to hear.

As Marjorie turned to answer Culpepper, she casually flung her right hand out and slapped the back of Ben's head. Everyone missed the move but Charlotte, who grinned.

"National origin had nothing to do with any of the ecosystems I chose, Mister Culpepper. I decided on this particular type of desert because its growth cycles dovetail perfectly with the other biomes in here."

"Why do you need all these ecosystems?" Gretchen Mosbacher asked. "I guess you could grow stuff on the savanna, and you could eat the fish in the ocean, but what good is a desert?"

"For one thing, a coastal fog desert such as this is a winter rainfall ecosystem. It remains dormant during the summer, when the other biomes are using carbon dioxide for rapid growth. Then each winter, when the plant life in the other ecosystems has become inactive, the desert flora spring to life, balancing the atmospheric carbon-dioxide levels in the biosphere. The desert also helps create the weather in here. Without these hot, dry sands, there wouldn't be any precipitation over the rain forest, and the plants there would soon wither away."

"You mean it rains in here?" Peter Maxwell asked. "This I gotta see."

"So you shall, Mister Maxwell. Ben, will you pull over and pass back the binoculars? Please."

Ben stopped the Centipede thirty feet from the edge of a large sand dune, then reached into the small storage shelf beneath the dash and handed back the glasses.

"Look up above the jungle," Marjorie said as Maxwell raised the binoculars to his eyes. "You'll see the clouds gathering now toward the apex of the biosphere."

"Well I'll be dammed," Maxwell said, focusing the glasses on the clouds forming several hundred feet above the distant rain forest.

"How the devil can clouds form in a closed environment like this?" Charles Ickles asked.

"It's a simple matter of physics, really," Marjorie said. "I designed the biosphere so that the floor line drops several hundred feet from the higher rain forest to the lower desert. The slope drives convection currents that pick up heat from the desert and carry the hot air over the ocean, where it absorbs moisture. Soon after, clouds form and accumulate above the forest."

"And you get rain?"

"Actually, before that happens, we must lend nature a hand." Marjorie pointed toward several huge metal canisters suspended above the jungle on thick cables. "Those big drums up there are condensers. They cool the moist air rising from the sea, and that causes the clouds to release their water content in the form of rain."

The cellular phone rang and Ben turned to pick up the receiver. "Centipede."

As he listened to the voice on the other end, his face suddenly paled and he jerked his head up to stare at the south wall. "You sure, Jack? Yeah, yeah, I understand. Call me back if they change course." Then he leaped out of the tram and ran back to snatch the binoculars out of Peter Maxwell's hands. There was a giant saguaro cactus blocking his line of sight and he darted over to the edge of the dune.

"What the hell!" Maxwell objected, following Ben across the sand.

"Ben, what on earth are you doing?" Marjorie jumped angrily out of her seat.

"Shut up, both of you," Ben said, sweeping the south wall with the glasses. For several long moments he could see nothing but the snow swirling around the mini-Earth.

Then the squall parted briefly and he spotted the first small, dark shapes just visible through the wind-whipped flakes beyond the glass. He refocused the binoculars. Geese! Thousands of them, Jack had said. And they were flying directly at the south wall!

Two miles south of Biosphere America, Brave Bird flew steadily on, the flock following his lead as they had for the past five seasons. With only one good eye and the air swirling with ash and snow, the old gander had virtually no chance to see the transparent glass wall that loomed ahead.

Still, Brave Bird sensed an ominous presence somewhere out in the worsening storm, and a terrible fear began to build in his brain. He knew, as all animals know, that he was in mortal danger. But he did not know how or from where death would come.

The huge gander honked mournfully and strained his one good eye ahead. What was out there?

* * *

Ben thrust the binoculars into Marjorie's hands. "You'd better take a look. Through the south wall there. About halfway up."

"Do you mind telling me what this is all about?"

"Look, dammit! Now!"

Marjorie was about to flare at Ben, but something in his face stopped her, and instead, she brought the binoculars up and focused through the glass to the south.

The geese were a little over a mile out now, and closing steadily. Marjorie stiffened.

"You're the zoologist," Ben said. "Will they veer off?"

"Will what veer off?" Peter Maxwell asked, his eyes following the direction of the binoculars.

Marjorie gnawed her lip for a moment; then she brought the glasses down. "I don't think they can see the biosphere."

"Why not? We can see them."

"For God's sake, use your head! The glass is transparent. They're looking right through it. All they can see is the snow on the other side of the pyramid."

Ben rolled his eyes. "Jesus!"

Carin Callisch and Beau Culpepper got out of the tram and crossed the sand to the edge of the dune, Charles Ickles a few steps behind them. "What's going on?" Callisch asked.

Ben said, "We'd better get everybody under cover. If those geese come through the wall, it's going to be raining glass knives in about two minutes."

"Raining knives?" Culpepper echoed. "What the hell are you talking about?"

"There's a formation of Canada geese flying directly at the biosphere," Marjorie said. "The birds are going to crash through the glass."

Culpepper paled. "Son of a bitch!"

"You've got to get us out of here," Charles Ickles said, panic in his voice.

Ben shook his head. "There's no time to drive the Centipede out. We've got to find cover around here." He said, his eyes searching the terrain.

Thirty yards from the bottom of the sand dune, a sandstone cliff, fifty feet high, jutted up out of the hardpan. At

the base of the precipice, a shoulder-high cavern ran back
into the rock for fifteen or twenty feet. It wasn't much, but
it would have to do.

"There," Ben pointed. "That cave. Everybody down
the slope. C'mon, move, move!"

For a moment, the four reporters hesitated, cowed by
the steep drop before them. "You want to die?" Ben
yelled. "Get the hell down to that cave!"

"He's right." Marjorie grabbed Callisch and Ickles and
rushed them forward toward the edge of the dune.
"Charlotte, help me."

The PR director reached for the arms of Culpepper and
Maxwell, yanking them with her over the lip of the steep
sand slope.

Ben ran back to the Centipede. "Everybody out!
C'mon, follow the others," he shouted.

Many in the group had overheard the exchange out on
the sand, and those who hadn't could read the fear in his
face. They erupted out of their seats and dashed for the
edge of the dune.

Most of the men tried to go down standing up, and one
by one, they lost their footing and began to tumble toward the foot of the dune. The women sat back on their
haunches and slid down the slope on their bottoms.

Everyone had evacuated the Centipede now except for
Mrs. Forsythe. The elderly publisher was still seated in
the middle of the tram, her hands folded placidly over the
head of her cane.

Ben looked at her in exasperation. "Mrs. Forsythe,
didn't you hear me? We have to get under cover."

"I could never get down that sand dune, Ben. Go on,
leave me. Perhaps my time has come."

"Not yet it hasn't." Ben leaned into the tram, swept the
octogenarian into his arms and began to run with her toward the edge of the dune.

"Put me down, Ben. We'll never make it."

"We'll make it."

Ben leaped forward down the slope, landing feet-first
in the soft sand. Mrs. Forsythe grunted at the impact and
almost pitched out of his arms.

"Hold on to my neck," he said, then leaped again.

This time the sand gave way when he landed and he rolled to one side to avoid going head over heels. Mrs. Forsythe hit the slope beside him, jarring her dentures out into the sand.

"My teeth!"

"Forget your teeth," he said, yanking her back across his lap.

They slid the rest of the way to the bottom. Then Ben picked her up again and started at a run for the cave ahead. The others were already inside.

"Hurry up, Ben," Marjorie yelled from the entrance, then brought the binoculars up and focused through the glass to the south. "Dear God," she breathed. The geese were no more than forty or fifty yards out. In seconds now, they'd smash into the glass. "Ben, for God's sake, run. Run!"

Two seconds before he died, Brave Bird saw the huge triangular panes of glass rising through the sky before him. Instantly, he raised his wings perpendicular to the ground, like the flaps on a plane slowing to land.

It was too late. The two ganders immediately behind him in the delta formation smashed into him and all three geese were propelled into the south wall of Biosphere America. The glass was tempered, strong enough to withstand hurricane winds. But it was not made to survive the impact of heavy geese flying at thirty miles per hour.

As the birds struck the first huge pane, glass exploded inward in a hundred pieces, leaving a border of razor-sharp shards embedded in the triangular frames. Brave Bird and the geese behind him were ripped to shreds, their beautiful brown-and-white bodies eviscerated.

Behind the leaders, the main body of geese began to strike the sloping wall, shattering glass panes inward as their V-shaped formation widened out.

Ben was ten yards from the safety of the cave when the geese began impacting the south wall. A cacophony of splintering glass and terrified honks echoed through the mini-Earth as dead and dying birds smashed through the glass into the cavernous interior of Biosphere America.

Glass and guts rained down in a nightmarish deluge. A falcon soaring over the desert looking for mice beat its wings frantically in a desperate attempt to escape the deadly hail from above. Too late. The falling glass caught the hunter two hundred feet above the ground, slicing the bird to ribbons in midair.

Ben was only steps from the entrance to the cave when the first glass shards began landing off to his right. An adrenal surge coursed through him, coiling the muscles in his legs. Without thinking, without knowing he would do it, he veered toward a knee-high boulder, sprang off the rock with his right foot and dove toward the cave, Mrs. Forsythe a deadweight in his arms.

The two landed on the sand floor just inside the entrance. The impact knocked the wind out of Ben and he lay gasping for air, still holding the frail publisher in his arms as the glass rained down outside.

Marjorie dropped into the sand beside them, her frightened eyes darting from one to the other. "Are you two all right?"

Ben nodded, still unable to speak.

Dazed but unhurt, Mrs. Forsythe blinked at Marjorie. "I've lost my teeth."

Out on the grasslands, the timid pudus panicked at the sounds of screaming geese and smashing glass. The entire herd took off at a run, racing madly north toward the sheltering cliffs and dunes of the desert.

The hail of glass caught them in mid-flight, slicing off ears, noses, eyes, heads. The wounded survivors lay bleating piteously thirty yards from the cave.

Four hundred feet above, the impact area widened out from the center as the trailing ends of the V formation exploded through the glass. A gaping wound fifty feet high and three hundred yards wide now punctured the south wall of Biosphere America.

Like air escaping from a punctured tire, the atmosphere of the mini-Earth was drawn out through the break by the lower pressure outside. The terrified reporters flattened themselves against the rock walls of the cave as a tornado of sand rose straight up from the desert outside.

The whirlwind began to tear debris from the other biomes, and huge mats of marsh grass and jungle foliage were sucked up through the shattered side of the pyramid.

As quickly as the tornado had started, the pressure inside began to equalize, and the outward rush of air died away. Now a freezing wind rushed in, sweeping down through the warm biosphere like an Arctic blast through Florida.

Marjorie rose from Ben's side and walked in a trance to the entrance of the cave, her hands reaching out as if to embrace the stricken biosphere.

Ben pushed to his feet and followed her. "We've got to get everyone back into the habitat. It'll be below zero in here within minutes."

Marjorie didn't answer. She was staring ashen-faced toward a wounded pudu limping toward them across the desert. "Look. He's still alive," she said, her voice strangely hollow.

As Ben turned to look, the tiny deer wobbled drunkenly, then collapsed into the glass-littered sand.

"He's finished, Marjorie," Ben said gently. "I'm sorry, but you've got to help me get these people out of here."

"I won't leave my animals," Marjorie said, then suddenly darted out of the cave toward the dying pudu.

"Get the reporters into the Centipede," Ben yelled at Charlotte, then tore after Marjorie. She had a head start and she was running across the sand with the speed of a woman possessed. A moment later, she reached the little deer and dropped to her knees, an agonized moan escaping her lips as she cradled the head of the dying animal on her lap.

As Ben ran up, Marjorie reached down and pulled a foot-long glass dagger from the neck of the tiny animal. Ben stopped in his tracks ten feet away, a sick dread prickling his skin. She'd been close to a breakdown already, and now the horrible tragedy of the last few minutes must have her teetering on the edge. He was afraid she'd use the glass dagger on herself.

"Marjorie, it's going to be all right," he said, holding

out his hands to her, willing her to drop the weapon and bury her head against his chest.

The pudu kicked convulsively, then went still. Marjorie softly stroked the tiny carcass, her tears raining on the bloodied hide. Then she rose and turned toward the savanna. "Everything's dead," she said.

Ben followed her gaze. Great swaths of bare ground striped the savanna where the winds had ripped away the grass. Beyond, the reeds and cattails of the marsh were flattened as if by a giant hand, and in the distant rain forest, a dozen towering Brazil Nut trees leaned over crazily.

"We can rebuild, replant the ecosystems," Ben said reassuringly. "I'll help you. I promise. Put down the glass, Marjorie. Please, just put it down."

Before she could answer, the wind changed direction, howling directly through the shattered south wall now, sweeping across the torn bodies of the geese impaled on the jagged edges of the window frames above. As the bodies of the birds trembled in the wind, the fatal wounds in their flesh opened wider and a fresh deluge of blood began to shower down over the desert.

For a long moment, Marjorie stared dumbly at the splatters on her arms and clothes. Then she looked up into the crimson rain, her eyes wide with horror. "Nooooo!" she screamed, wildly waving the glass dagger in the air as the blood of the geese coursed down her cheeks in red rivulets.

It was the moment Ben had been waiting for and he lunged for her hand holding the dagger, got a grip on her wrist and shook the long shard from her fingers. Then he folded her in his arms and rocked her gently back and forth. "It's all right, Baby," he said as she sobbed uncontrollably against his chest. "It's all right, it's all right."

A minute later, they heard the Centipede approaching. As the tram pulled up, Gretchen Mosbacher screamed in horror at the sight of the blood-covered couple, then fainted against the shoulder of Beau Culpepper. The rest of the reporters gaped at Ben and Marjorie in silent shock.

Charlotte leaped out from behind the steering wheel. "Are you hurt?"

Ben shook his head. "No wounds, but Marjorie's been badly traumatized. Help me get her into the tram."

Together, the two eased Marjorie into the middle of the front seat. "You drive," Ben said, keeping his arm around Marjorie. "Get us the hell out of here. Fast."

Charlotte jammed her foot down and the Centipede lurched across the desert. Behind the fleeing humans, the bitter-cold wind whistled through the five ecosystems. The first ice crystals formed in the marshes and the stagnant pools beneath the rain-forest canopy.

And one by one, the animals and plants in Biosphere America began to freeze to death.

BUENOS AIRES, ARGENTINA
• •

6:20 p.m.–April 7th

ARGENTINE COLONEL GENERAL RAMON Saavedra de Urquiza bent forward toward the gold-framed mirror in the
huge marble bathroom off his office and inserted the tips
of a tweezer into his left nostril.

He grunted and swore under his breath as he yanked
out a clump of wiry black strands. Hair was the bane of
his existence, for it sprouted all over his body like weeds
in an untilled field.

His nickname as a boy had been *el gorila*, the gorilla,
and he'd been deeply conscious of his hirsute appearance
ever since childhood. He barbered his right nostril, then
slicked back his jet-black hair, pleased as always by the
dignity his gray sideburns lent his beefy face. With a last
glance in the mirror, he straightened his gilded uniform
and walked through the open door to his office.

The two men seated before his immense mahogany
desk stiffened perceptibly in their chairs as he crossed the
room and lowered himself into his throne-like burgundy-
leather chair.

The bathroom was in the direct line of sight of where
the men sat, and de Urquiza was quite sure they had

glanced in as he performed his tonsorial chores, just as he had intended them to do. It was a matter of control. He wanted them to know that plucking hairs out of his nose took precedence over his meeting with them.

"Buenos dias, gentlemen," de Urquiza said, his tone neutral and perfunctory.

"Buenos dias," the two replied a split second apart, both men nervous at being summoned to this unscheduled audience with the junta leader. He had a habit of popping unpleasant surprises at these sudden meetings.

De Urquiza tented his fingers before his chest, lightly rubbing the tips together, then raised his eyes to the ceiling as though what he was about to say was of such weight that he must direct his words straight to God.

"I have called you here to ratify a decision I have reached," he said. "Effective immediately, we are going to raise the prices on our food exports by twenty-five percent—grains, meat, cooking oil, the lot."

Admirante Juan Bautista Secchi shifted uncomfortably in his chair. The heavyset, balding head of the Argentine Navy had a married sister living in Paris. He knew firsthand from her letters and phone calls that the cost of imported Argentine food was already severely straining the resources of people throughout Europe.

"Is that wise, General?" Secchi asked, immediately regretting he'd phrased the question in that way.

De Urquiza arched his eyebrows. "Wise?"

"I only meant that the cost of our agricultural products is already twice what is was before the Earth Winter descended on the north. Another increase will mean severe deprivations in the northern hemisphere, especially among the working people."

The third member of the junta, diminutive Air Force Brigadier General Alberto Cesar Moreno, nodded in agreement, his thin blond mustache looking incongruous on his boyish face. "It could mean mass starvation everywhere north of the equator."

"Nonsense," de Urquiza said, cutting an impatient hand through the air. "This idea that people can't afford food is only propaganda spread by the northern governments. Look at the import figures for Europe. Britain spends only twenty percent of her budget to bring in foreign foodstuffs, France around eighteen percent, Spain less than fifteen percent. And no more than a quarter of those monies are spent for buying Argentine products."

"Begging your pardon, General," Secchi said, "but you are quoting pre-Earth Winter figures. Since R-Nine blew, the nations of the north have been spending an average of over forty percent of their gross national product on imported food. And up to seventy-five percent of that is spent in Argentina."

De Urquiza arched his eyebrows. "Where do you get your numbers, Juan?"

"From the World Bank, General."

"And where do they get their figures?"

Secchi shrugged. "The individual nations report them."

"So, the import tallies come from the finance ministers, politicians whose main interest is in maintaining themselves and their fellow party members in office. They scream 'Argentina is bleeding us dry for food,' and we become a scapegoat for their mismanaged economies."

"I suppose there's some truth in that."

General Moreno came forward in his chair. "Whatever the foreign-import figures, we can expect an uproar at the United Nations if we announce food price hikes. They'll take our hide off in the Security Council."

De Urquiza made a gesture of dismissal. "No doubt they'll flay us with words. What does it matter? In the end, they'll all pay. They'll have to."

"I'm more concerned about the reaction in the United States," Secchi said carefully. "As you know, General, several of the more radical senators in Washington have demanded that the United States use military pressure to force us to lower our food prices. The Yanquis have the largest navy in the world. Suppose they were to impose a blockade? Or worse?"

De Urquiza's eyes smoldered. "A blockade is an act of aggression. If they dared such a tactic, we would sink their warships."

Secchi blanched. "I wish to go on record, General de

Urquiza: the Argentine Navy is no match for American warships. They are better armed and their crews better trained."

The junta head scowled at the naval chief. "You can stop pissing in your pants, Juan. I am well aware of the limitations of our Navy."

General Moreno said, "Should the Americans send a carrier force down here, our Air Force would be obliterated from the skies within the first forty-eight hours. The Yanqui planes are at least a generation ahead of ours in speed, armaments and electronics."

"You're pathetic, both of you," de Urquiza said. "If I left it up to you, you'd allow the Americans to sail up the Rio de la Plata and dictate policy to us with naval cannon pointed at the heart of Buenos Aires."

Secchi threw up his hands. "The reality is that the United States is a superpower, the only superpower left on earth. Militarily, Argentina is a distant second."

"We are the most powerful nation south of the equator," de Urquiza thundered. "Never forget that! We will not allow the Americans to dictate our national policy."

"And if they send their Navy to blockade our shores? How will we stop them?" Secchi challenged.

De Urquiza sat back in his ornate chair, a Cheshire-cat grin spreading over his face as he glanced down at the decoded communique that had arrived from Kiev that morning. The transfer of three billion dollars to Ukraine had been completed. The *Bukharin* would sail for Buenos Aires within two days.

"Have either of you ever heard of a Soviet nuclear submarine called the *Bukharin*?"

Admiral Secchi furrowed his brow. "Yes. A long time ago. She was a Soviet Typhoon-class nuclear submarine. Big as they come, six hundred feet bow to stern. Armed with Mark C wire-guided torpedoes and SS-N-Twenty sea-launched ballistic missiles."

"And if Argentina possessed a submarine such as the *Bukharin*," de Urquiza said, "do you believe that the Americans would still attempt a naval blockade?"

Secchi shrugged. "It's idle speculation, of course, but I believe they would be far more hesitant to risk their precious carriers if they knew our Navy had such a weapon. The wire-guided torpedoes aboard a Typhoon-class submarine are hard to defend against."

General Moreno's face became animated. "Never mind the goddam torpedoes, it's the missiles that class of sub carries that would scare the shit out of them. The SS-N-Twenty has a six-thousand-mile range. We could target any city in the United States from either the Atlantic or the Pacific. The Yanquis wouldn't dare screw with us."

"What is the point of all this?" Secchi asked, casting an annoyed glance at the enthusiastic Moreno. "The Argentine Navy has no such submarine."

"*Had* no such submarine, Admiral Secchi," de Urquiza said, his black eyes intense.

"I don't understand, General."

"I have purchased the *Bukharin*. She will sail for Buenos Aires within forty-eight hours."

Secchi's mouth fell open. "It is not possible. The *Bukharin* sank in the Black Sea a decade ago."

"Tell me, Secchi, do you believe in resurrection?"

"Do you mean the resurrection of Christ?"

"I mean the resurrection of a submarine. You see, gentlemen, the *Bukharin* has risen from the depths."

Newark Airport, New Jersey
• •

9:05 a.m.–April 8th

TRANSATLANTIC AIR TRAVEL HAD fallen off over 70 percent since the eruption of R-9 and there were only a handful of people in the British Airways VIP lounge as Ben and Marjorie waited for her flight to London.

"You feel like some breakfast?" Ben asked, nodding toward a groaning board set with fruit, pastries, and chafing dishes steaming with the aroma of sausages, eggs and fried potatoes.

"Just tea, thanks."

"You sure? We're practically the only people in here this morning. I hate to see all that food go to waste."

"A banana, then. That sedative the doctor gave me has my stomach doing cartwheels."

Ben shrugged and walked over to the sideboard. He loaded a plate with sausages and eggs for himself and brought back a cup of tea and a banana for Marjorie.

Marjorie sipped the tea and took several tentative bites of the banana.

"You all right?" Ben asked.

"A bit shaky still. Look, there's something I've got to say. I went bonkers on you in the biosphere after the geese hit." Marjorie slowly shook her head. "I still can't believe I went off the deep end like that. Really, Ben, I'm very ashamed."

Ben put down his plate and looked at her. "There you go again. What the hell do you have to be ashamed of? You were exhausted. At the end of your string. And suddenly there you are, covered with blood, an animal you loved dying in your arms and the biosphere being destroyed around you. No one, Marjorie, no one comes through something like that in one piece."

When the Centipede had reached the safety of the human habitat two days before, Ben had carried Marjorie to the infirmary. The biosphere physician had washed off the blood of the geese and given Marjorie a sedative and a vitamin supplement. Afterward, Ben took her back to their apartment, where she'd slept for almost thirty straight hours.

He'd sat in a chair beside her bed the entire time, leaving only twice to take phone calls from President Piziali and the chairman of the Joint Chiefs of Staff.

When Marjorie finally awoke, she'd been uncharacteristically subdued, and disinterested when Ben told her of the President's promise of immediate help to replace the destroyed ecosystems.

Still, although she said little, she had regained her composure and Ben no longer feared that she'd suffered a complete breakdown. She was one tough lady, albeit a lady who needed a long rest, and they'd agreed that she would fly home to England and spend the next few weeks at her parents' home in Scotland.

"I should have listened to you and taken some time off," Marjorie said. "I simply didn't realize I was that burned out."

"Let it go, Marjorie. The whole thing's history. Besides, I want to talk to you about something else."

"The biosphere?"

"No. The biosphere will be rebuilt. As I told you this morning, the chairman of the Joint Chiefs assured me that ships and planes are already on the way south to bring back new ecosystems. I want to talk about us."

Marjorie studied the swirl of steam rising from her tea. "I suppose we must."

"Tell me what you want, Marjorie. To break it off? If you're worried I'll be crushed, don't be. I'm a big boy. I'll survive."

Marjorie turned and looked at him, her eyes pained. "I'm not blaming you, Ben. I want that clear. But everything's gone so wrong between us. We can't seem to communicate."

"Did you ever stop to think it might be because we haven't had time to talk to each other in months?"

"Communication isn't just talking, Ben. What I meant was that we don't seem to link up on any level. We used to have clear channels to each other. Even apart, even across the sea, I could sense your mood. Whether you were happy or sad, angry or exultant. It was as if we had telepathy." She shrugged wearily. "But that's all gone."

"You loved me once, Marjorie. At least you said you did. Is that gone, too?"

She was silent for a long moment as she fought back the tears. "I don't know," she whispered finally.

Ben sighed deeply and sat back against the deep cushions of the couch. "You're right, of course. We're out of touch, have been for a long time. Even sitting here next to each other, it's awkward talking. More than awkward; it's goddamned painful."

"We can't go on like this, Ben. We'll end up hating each other."

"A clean break?"

"I think that's best. Don't you?"

He thought for a moment, then said, "Yeah, I guess I do."

Her face anguished, Marjorie slowly twisted Ben's engagement ring off her finger. "This ring's become a part of me. I'll feel rather naked without it," she said, taking his hand and putting the ring in his palm. "And quite alone."

Ben looked down at the ring. "I'll keep it. Maybe someday you'll—"

His words were interrupted by the crackle of the airport speaker. "British Airways flight five-fifteen to London now boarding at Gate Ten."

Marjorie put down the teacup and reached for her shoulder bag. "That's me."

Ben rose. "I'll walk with you to the gate."

"You don't have to."

"I know."

They had always held hands when they walked, and now as they started across the almost deserted terminal, Ben automatically reached for her fingers. At the last moment, he remembered and put his hand in his pocket.

Marjorie caught the gesture and bit her lip. "I'm going to feel awfully guilty lounging around in Scotland while you're working," she said, struggling to fill the void between them.

Ben stopped and put his hands on her shoulders. "Look, your DNA plant research is almost finished. Jay Stevens told me yesterday that he's started planting your first genetically altered crops in Florida. And you can't do any work in the biosphere until the new ecosystems arrive from the Caribbean and the southern hemisphere."

He took her elbow and they began walking again. "Besides, I prefer to keep busy. I'm going out to Wyoming to set up a geothermal drill site near Yellowstone. When I'm finished, I'll grab a week off at the ranch."

"I love your ranch," she said. "The week we spent there last summer was heaven."

"Heaven's eternal," he said, a trace of bitterness in his voice now. "What we had was just a blip on the screen."

They reached the gate and Marjorie handed her ticket to the attendant. "Take any seat you want," the bored woman said, handing Marjorie a boarding pass. "There are only eighteen passengers on your flight today."

"Thank you," Marjorie said.

Ben went with her to the entrance to the boarding tube. "I'll miss you," he said, taking her hands. "I'll miss you with my heart, my head, my eyes, my arms."

She couldn't stop the tears any longer; they welled up and ran down her cheeks. "It's for the best. You know that. I know that."

"At least . . ." Ben choked and looked away toward the

window, away into the snow falling gently on the tarmac outside. "At least leave the hall light on, will you?"

She cocked her head. "Hall light?"

"When I was a kid, I was afraid of the dark."

She forced a brave smile. "It's hard to imagine you afraid of anything, Ben."

"No, it's true. At night, when my mom tucked me in, my last words were always, 'Leave the hall light on.' I couldn't stand being alone in the dark."

Marjorie rose on tiptoe and kissed his cheek. "All right then, Ben. I'll leave the hall light on."

She turned and quickly walked down the tube. At the plane door, she looked back with a small wave, then disappeared down the shadowed aisle.

For several moments, Ben continued to stare at the empty doorway. Then he turned and strode out of the terminal and into the falling snow, his fist clenched tightly around the ring in his pocket as the cold flakes mingled with the hot tears running down his face.

THE WHITE HOUSE, WASHINGTON, D.C.
• • • • • • • • • • • • • • • • • • • •

2:50 p.m.–April 8th

PRESIDENT KATHLEEN PIZIALI ROSE from her desk and crossed the Oval Office as her appointments secretary ushered in U.N. Ambassador Larry Wiesler.

"Good to see you, Larry," she said, shaking hands warmly with the thirty-seven-year-old diplomat, then guiding him by the elbow toward a setting of chairs before the crackling fire. "How was the flight?"

"Delayed as usual, Madam President," the ambassador said. Wiesler was of medium height and boyishly thin, with intelligent hazel eyes and an aura of intense energy about him. He'd been a whiz-bang policy analyst on the Eastern European desk at the State Department before being tapped for the U.N. post.

"I don't know why they don't bring in more snow-removal equipment out at Dulles. We had to circle for an hour while they plowed the runway."

"We had a heavy snow squall this morning," the President said. "When I flew out to Chicago last week, the pilot told me there's been so much snow this winter that they've run out of places to pile the stuff. Please, have a seat."

Wiesler lowered himself into a wingback chair. "It's April, for God's sake. And still the blizzards keep coming. We might as well be living in Siberia."

"It's not quite that bad, Larry. From the satellite photos, Siberia's buried under thirty feet of snow. The intelligence boys tell me there isn't a road or rail line open from the Urals to the Sea of Japan."

Wiesler shook his head. "The Russian Government won't know until the snow melts this summer how many of their people have starved to death in the rural areas. But the estimates are in the millions."

"The weather may not be the only cause of starvation in the months to come," Piziali said. "I had a disturbing call from the French ambassador this morning. There are rumblings in Europe that the Argentines are about to raise food prices again. What's the word at the U.N.?"

"The talk in the halls is that they'll announce the new prices this afternoon. We're looking at a twenty-five-percent hike."

"So it's true."

"The bastards. Half the northern hemisphere is already on the brink of collapse. A twenty-five-percent price increase could mean mass starvation."

The President gazed into the fire. "We're not so far away from that scenario here in the States, Larry. We have sufficient reserves of grains, butter, milk and meat to take us through the next fourteen months. After that—" she shrugged "—God help us."

"Just wait until Congress hears about this." Wiesler shook his head. "Senator Crawford's already drumming up support for some sort of military action. He delivered a speech in Denver the other day demanding we send the Atlantic Fleet down there to blockade Argentine ports until they bring food prices down. Jesus, this will just send him over the edge."

The President's face hardened. "Crawford's a fool. The junta down there is made up of macho military officers. If the Atlantic Fleet appeared off Buenos Aires, they'd be bound to attack our ships. No, we must find some other way to deal with this."

"So you're ruling out military action?"

"For now. We'll try the diplomatic route first. If that doesn't work—" The President threw up her hands. "Well, I'll cross that bridge when I come to it."

"Then we've got to put pressure on the junta, Madam President. Today. Before they announce the price increases."

"I intend to. I've already summoned the Argentine ambassador. He'll be here in an hour. I want to know what the Secretary-General is going to do. Have you talked to him?"

"Yes, before I left for Washington. He plans to lodge a formal protest with Buenos Aires. He even brought up the possibility of expelling Argentina from the U.N.— assuming he can get the votes in the General Assembly."

"I'm thinking along those same lines, Larry. Withdraw our ambassador, sever all diplomatic ties. Judging by my last conversation with the prime minister in Ottawa, I'm confident that Canada will join us."

"What about Mexico?"

"Iffy. There's still enough sunlight reaching the Yucatan region in the south for them to grow food down there. They're not in the same bind we are. And they have cultural and linguistic ties to Argentina. I called Mexico City last week and pressed Mendoza to join Canada and us in a united North American position on the price hikes."

"Did he agree?"

"He didn't agree or disagree. He danced around the issue like Nureyev. The wimp should have been wearing tights and ballet slippers."

Wiesler grinned. "Any idea where Europe will go on this? If the European Community countries sever diplomatic ties, that could sting Buenos Aires good."

"There's a meeting of European Community foreign ministers in Brussels this week. I'm sending Rob Bonham over to talk to them about it."

A shadow crossed the President's face. "The hard reality is that the only way diplomatic pressure will work is if the countries of the northern hemisphere present a united front. Judging by my talks with the European heads of state, that's far from a sure thing. The French are going their own way, as usual. Spain and Portugal are dragging their feet, and Italy's on the fence. We can count on Britain and Germany, and probably the Scandinavian countries. Russia and the rest of the Eastern European countries are anybody's guess."

"What about Japan and China? They have just as big a stake in this as we do."

"I think we can rely on Chinese support, although they're importing most of their rice and fish from the southeast Asian countries, primarily Malaysia and Indonesia." The President shrugged. "Japan's a whole different ball game. I understand they're working out an import-export deal with Buenos Aires: Japanese farm machinery and communications equipment for Argentine grain and meat."

"Figures." Wiesler spat the word out. "The sons of bitches would make a trade deal with the devil."

"C'mon, Larry, we have no right to Japan-bash on this one. They're going down the tubes over there; new cars and trucks rusting on the docks, warehouses jammed with computers and electronics they can't sell. Half the country's subsisting on seaweed, for God's sake. They need Argentine grain, and Buenos Aires needs their tractors and trucks. It's a natural deal."

"Then why wasn't it a natural deal for us? We make tractors and harvesters and every other piece of farm equipment the Argentines could possibly use."

"This isn't a trade deal that just happened out of the blue. Back in the eighties and nineties, the Japanese established a network of farm-equipment dealerships and parts warehouses all over Argentina. They sowed the seeds of their deals years ago, and now they're reaping the rewards."

The President glanced toward her desk as the voice of her appointments secretary came over the intercom. "Director Jeung and Adviser Bonham are here, Madam President."

Piziali's brow furrowed quizzically. "I don't remember a meeting with Dan and Rob."

"They're not on your schedule, Madam President. However, they insist that the matter is urgent."

The President rose and smoothed her beige cashmere

suit. "All right, send them in." She turned to Wiesler. "Sorry, Larry. Sounds important."

"Would you like me to leave, Madam President?"

"No, no, stick around. If it's something not in your area, I'll kick you out."

The Oval Office door opened and National Security Adviser Rob Bonham walked in briskly, followed by C.I.A. Director Daniel Jeung. Bonham was tall and reed-thin, with dark eyes and razor-cut black hair framing a handsome, lantern-jawed face. Divorced several years earlier, the good-humored Bonham cut a wide swath through the unmarried female staff members of Congress.

Daniel Jeung, the first Chinese-American to head the intelligence agency, had been a computer-science whiz kid and still looked it with his boyish face, owl glasses and "gee whiz" reaction to events.

"Good morning, Madam President," Bonham said, managing, as always, to make his greeting of the chief executive sound slightly impious.

Piziali smiled. She liked the irreverent and witty Bonham, as much for his way of skewering stuffed shirts with his dry humor as for his considerable expertise in intelligence matters.

"Thank you for seeing us on such short notice, Madam President," Jeung said. Unlike Bonham, there was a note of adulation in the director's tone. Though he'd been head of the C.I.A. for almost a year now, he still couldn't get over the fact that at least once a week he found himself meeting with the President of the United States.

"I came over to talk to Rob about a piece of intelligence we picked up in Geneva. He thought we ought to run it by you," Jeung said, making it clear that barging in on the President was Bonham's idea.

"It's simply amazing what Dan's computers are able to ferret out," Bonham said. "Did you know that the prime minister of Bosnia is into computer porn? Dan found that out—discovered the guy had a whole CD ROM library of 'Debbie Does Dallas' stuff."

Jeung turned red. "Well, I mean, uh, that was hardly the focus of our intelligence gathering in Bosnia. Really,

Rob, I don't think the President is interested in that sort of thing."

Piziali laughed. "Relax, Dan. You two know Larry Wiesler."

Bonham extended his hand. "Larry. How's everything up at the International House of Nutcakes?"

Wiesler grinned. "Crazy as ever, Rob."

Jeung went to shake hands, then realized that he was still holding his briefcase in his right hand. Awkwardly, he switched hands and tried again. "Sorry to interrupt, Larry."

Wiesler waved a hand. "No problem, Dan. This eyes-only stuff?"

"Naw," Bonham said. "At least not yet it isn't."

"Sit down, you two," the President said, settling back in her chair.

The two men lowered themselves into the couch opposite the President.

"What have you got, Dan?" Piziali asked.

"Well, if you recall, about a month ago I told you we'd managed to tap into the Swiss banking network. We've been surfing through the numbered accounts for several weeks now."

"Jesus, you guys are looking at numbered accounts?" Wiesler asked. "Isn't that against international law?"

"It's also ungentlemanly," Bonham grinned. "Dan doesn't have any scruples at all."

Jeung's eyes widened behind his owl glasses. "Now just a minute here, Rob. I had your full concurrence on this. And the President's approval."

The President said, "In answer to your question, Larry, yes, it's illegal. Not to mention immoral. And a breach of faith with our friends, the Swiss. It's also normal intelligence-gathering practice; friends spy on friends. Did you know there are more Israeli agents in Washington than there are Chinese spies?"

Wiesler looked surprised. "No, I didn't."

"Fact of life," Bonham said. "Of course we've got agents in Jerusalem, too. And London, Paris, Berlin. Things happen so fast today, we often have to make policy decision on the fly. You can't do that without knowing how your allies will react."

"Let's get back on track here," the President said. "What accounts are we talking about, Dan?"

"Argentine. We were searching for evidence that the junta members in Buenos Aires are profiting personally from the past year's food price hikes."

"Dan's going to blackmail them," Bonham deadpanned.

Wiesler stared at the C.I.A. director. "He's kidding. Right?"

"I wouldn't use the word 'blackmail,'" Jeung said, flustered.

The President rolled her eyes. "Look at it his way, Larry. Evidence that the junta members are amassing huge private fortunes in Switzerland could be useful later as a means of pressuring them to keep prices down. If the people of Argentina learned that their vaunted leaders are siphoning money from the treasury, things could get hot for de Urquiza and his cohorts."

Wiesler sat back, slowly shaking his head.

"What did you find out, Dan?" the President asked.

"No personal accounts so far, at least not under the real names of the junta members. That's not to say they're not transferring pesos into the accounts of relatives or friends, or dummy corporations. It'll take us several more weeks to determine that."

The President folded her arms across her chest. "So?" she asked, meaning "What the hell's this meeting all about?"

"We came across an account labeled 'European Trading Contingency,' Madam President," Jeung said. "At first pass, it looked innocent enough. Then our people noticed that the account had some highly unusual activity in the past twenty-four hours."

"What's unusual?" Piziali asked.

"Yesterday the account held four point eight billion dollars."

"Nice piece of change, what?" Bonham asked wryly.

"Do you mind not interrupting me, Rob?" Jeung said,

annoyed that the insouciant Bonham was stealing his show.

"Sorry, Dan," Bonham said, his amused eyes making clear that he wasn't sorry at all.

Jeung looked back at the President. "Early this morning, a computer scan revealed that the account balance was down to one point eight billion."

The President whistled through her teeth, a trick she'd traded her teenage brother a baseball mitt to teach her thirty-five years before. "They spent three billion bucks in one day?"

Jeung nodded. "And what makes it all the more suspicious is that it was a single transaction. We traced the records back six months. The average expenditure during that time was for a hundred and twenty million. And most payments were far smaller."

"There's another thing," Bonham said, serious now. "Ninety-five percent of the payees for the past six months have been Western European countries or companies. The money was spent for German machine parts, British woolen goods, a French monorail system."

"And who was the payee in this case?" the President asked.

Jeung looked at the chief executive through his owl glasses. "Ukraine, Madam President."

"Ukraine!" Wiesler exclaimed. "What the hell does Ukraine have that's worth three billion dollars to Argentina?"

"That's the sixty-four-dollar question, Larry," Bonham said.

"What are Ukraine's chief exports?" the President asked.

"Cement, forest products and petrochemicals," Bonham said. "But they're exporting only a tenth of what they were before R-Nine erupted."

"And that only during the summer, when the sea ice melts and they can get freighters in and out of Odessa and Sevastopol," Jeung added.

"So what did the junta buy?" the President asked.

"It's got to be military hardware," Bonham said. "For that kind of dough, we're talking planes or ships."

"No way, Rob," Jeung said. "Five years ago, I would have agreed; Ukraine still had an arsenal of jet fighters and bombers, and the surface ships they got when they split the Black Sea Fleet with the Russians. But they sold all that stuff, much of it right back to Moscow. We know where every single plane and boat went."

"Maybe they held back a squadron of jet fighters or a couple of battleships," the President suggested.

"No, we have a mole in the Ukrainian leadership, near the top. He assures me that all their military hardware has already gone on the block."

"Then how does your mole explain this deal with Argentina?" the President asked.

"He's as mystified as we are. He was able to confirm the three-billion-dollar transfer from the Argentine account, but he has no idea of what the money was for."

Larry Wiesler came forward in his chair. "Remember, three or four years ago, when the Russians tried to sell a nuclear submarine to Indonesia?"

"We put the brakes on that deal," Bonham said. "President Clinton threatened to cut off all trade with Moscow."

"Yes, the deal fell through," Wiesler said. "But my point is, I think the Russians were expecting to get around three billion for the sub. Maybe the Ukrainians sold the junta a nuclear submarine."

Jeung shook his head. "They don't have one to sell. Back in the early nineties, the Soviets had a nuclear submarine based in Sevastopol, the *N.I. Bukharin*. But she sank in the Black Sea ten years ago."

"There's only one answer," Bonham said.

The President arched her eyebrows. "We're listening, Rob."

"Nuclear weapons. They don't have anything else the Argentines would want . . . at least nothing worth three billion bucks."

"Hold on a minute here," Wiesler said. "You're forgetting the START I Treaty signed by Bush and Gorbachev back in ninety-one. Under that agreement, Ukraine, Kazakhstan and Belarus were supposed to send the strategic nuclear warheads stored in their countries to Russia for dismantling."

"That was how the treaty was worded," the President said. "As it turned out, Belarus and Kazakhstan agreed to Start I, but Ukraine never ratified the pact."

"They did finally send several hundred warheads to the Russian nuclear-disassembly plant near Tomsk, in Siberia," Jeung said. "But we don't know the exact number of nuclear weapons they shipped."

"There were over twelve hundred warheads in Ukraine when the Soviet Union broke up," Bonham said. "If the Ukrainians kept only ten percent of those, that would leave a hundred and twenty nuclear weapons unaccounted for."

"What about the delivery systems?" the President asked. "What sort of missiles did the Soviets have in Ukraine?"

"Mostly short-range stuff aimed at Western Europe," Jeung said. "Although our reconnaissance satellites did identify at least ten sites that resembled the Soviet long-range missile complexes in central Asia."

"What's long-range?" the President asked.

"We're talking ICBM's," Jeung said. "Twelve-thousand-mile range."

A dark shadow crossed Bonham's face. "If the junta got ahold of those missiles, they could take out New York, Chicago, L.A., Washington."

"If the Argentines really did buy nuclear weapons from Ukraine, we may want to rethink before severing diplomatic ties," Wiesler said. "De Urquiza has already proven he's a megalomanic. You back him into a corner, he might do something nutso. It could be in our interest to keep the lines open."

The President rose and walked over to the windows facing the Rose Garden, her back to the room as she gazed out at the snow-covered grounds, deep in thought.

Finally, she turned back to the men. "So far, all we have is that the junta paid Ukraine three billion dollars for something. We could be way off base here. For all we know, it could be some long-term trade deal for forest products."

Bonham shook his head. "Three billion bucks' worth of trees? No way."

"All right, all right, maybe it's petrochemicals, or cement, or Ukrainian music boxes," the President said heatedly. "The fact is, Rob, we don't know, do we?"

Bonham conceded the point. "No, Madam President, we don't."

"Then I suggest we find out before we tear off in a panic." She turned to Jeung. "Have we got anyone on the inside in Buenos Aires?"

"No one high up. The three junta members make all the key decisions themselves. And they meet in secret session. There's no formal policy-making staff we can penetrate. The junta simply issues edicts."

Piziali threw up her hands. "Great."

"We've had a recent breakthrough though, Madam President. One of our people has managed to establish a relationship with Maria Echeverria."

"Who is Maria Echeverria?"

"De Urquiza's mistress."

"What sort of relationship? Is your man sleeping with her?"

"Not yet. And we can't really expect him to learn anything until he does. It's a fact of life that we glean far more intelligence from mistresses than we do from ministers."

"I'm aware of the realities." The President walked over to her desk and leaned forward, her hands pressing down hard on the polished top. "All right, Dan. Tell your boy in Buenos Aires to wine and dine Miss Echeverria. Tell him to buy her flowers, clothes, a beach-front condo. Whatever the hell it takes to get her between the sheets. I want to know what the Junta bought for three billion dollars."

SEVASTOPOL, UKRAINE
●●●●●●●●●●●●●●●●●●●●●●●●

12:40 p.m.–April 9th

"ARE YOU SURE YOU have enough men to sail her?" Anatoli Demyanov asked, casting a worried look at Viktor Lobov across the *Bukharin's* wardroom table. "After all, ten years ago she carried a hundred and ten officers and men."

"You worry like an old babushka," Lobov said, not bothering to look up from the charts spread out on the table before him. "I've told you twice already, twenty-one men are enough. We won't get much rest, I grant you, but it's only a ten-day voyage. When we reach Argentina, we'll all lie on some warm beach and sleep for a week."

Demyanov had been surprised at the ease with which Lobov had recruited a crew to take the submarine to Argentina. In less than four days, the officially appointed captain of the *Bukharin* had rounded up a chief engineer, four *michmanyy* (warrant officers), six *glavnyy starshini* (senior petty officers) and ten seamen. All had served aboard Soviet submarines during the eighties and early nineties.

Demyanov shook his head. "I don't know how you managed to get twenty-one volunteers so quickly."

"It was quite simple, Anatoli Dmytrovych. Over eight hundred Ukrainian veterans of the Soviet submarine fleet live right here in Sevastopol. Near the sea. Near their memories. They meet once a month to drink vodka and talk about the old days. I made a few phone calls and within a few days, I had more crewmen than I needed."

"Yes, but they must all have quite different lives now, with families, jobs, responsibilities. How did you get so many to drop everything and take off for South America?"

"They're ex-submariners, Anatoli, men who crave action and adventure. Most of them were working at boring jobs. They jumped at the chance to run beneath the waves again."

Lobov lit a cigarette from a pack on the table. "Of course, the twenty-five thousand dollars apiece the Argentines are paying them didn't exactly dampen their enthusiasm," he said, exhaling a cloud of smoke toward the low ceiling.

Demyanov frowned. The day the sale of the *Bukharin* was finalized, Viktor had slipped into the Argentine Consulate in Sevastopol to work out details of the delivery of the sub to Buenos Aires. When Viktor told him later of the amount the Argentines had agreed to pay the crew, Demyanov had felt his gut knot.

The onslaught of the Earth Winter the year before had brought 40 percent unemployment to Ukraine, and those who were working earned on average less than five thousand dollars a year. The sudden possession of a large amount of cash by a group of ex-submariners was bound to raise suspicions.

If the Americans found out about the sale of the *Bukharin* before the sub reached Argentina, they would undoubtedly do everything in their power to stop the deal, as they had squashed the sale of a Russian nuclear submarine to India the year before.

Demyanov found it infuriating that the U.S. could use its power to stop the "proliferation of arms" while its own huge defense contractors continued to sell planes, tanks and arms of all kinds all over the world.

Still, the reality was that the Americans gave his country nearly five hundred million dollars a year in foreign aid, and America was Ukraine's third largest trading partner after Russia and the European Community. If Washington got wind of the deal, the Piziali Administration might well cancel the aid package and slap on a trade embargo.

Yet if the sale remained secret long enough for the *Bukharin* to reach Buenos Aires, the Americans would be hard put to prove where the sub had come from, for the Argentine Navy planned a complete face-lift. The spherical bow would be extended to a sharp point, the flat missile deck rounded, and the towering sail heightened and angled toward the stern. The junta would then announce they had built the ship in Argentina from Soviet plans, just as they were now building Mirage fighters under license from French aircraft designers.

The Americans would undoubtedly be suspicious and launch an investigation. But it would be the Russians who would feel the American heat, for they had taken possession of every submarine in the former Soviet Fleet but the *Bukharin*. And the *Bukharin*, as far as the world knew, was lying on the bottom of the Black Sea.

Demyanov sat back against the wardroom bench and rubbed his tired eyes. Everything hinged on getting the *Bukharin* safely to Argentina. "I'm worried about security, Viktor," he said. "With so many now in on our secret, there's bound to be a leak."

"Not from the families of the crew. After all, a leak could prove dangerous to the very lives of their men."

Lobov was referring to the possibility that the *Bukharin* could be interdicted by an American or a NATO warship. The Americans often stopped and boarded ships they suspected of carrying illegal arms. Six months ago, they'd even had the audacity to search a Chinese vessel reportedly carrying missiles to Iraq.

A submarine would be more difficult for the Allies to stop, of course, but with dozens of antisub warships and planes in the Atlantic, not to mention their own killer subs, there was no question but that NATO forces could bring the *Bukharin* to the surface if they found her.

Demyanov drummed his fingers on the table. Even if

the *Bukharin* escaped detection by NATO, there were a hundred things that could go wrong on the voyage. "You're sure all the controls are working properly? Suppose a system breaks down."

"The controls are all replicated: navigation, rudder, dive planes, reactor controls. If anything goes down, we'll switch to the backup." Lobov pushed the bottle of vodka across the table. "Here, have a drink and stop worrying. You're beginning to get on my nerves."

"I don't want a goddamn drink. And I think you should lay off the vodka, too, Viktor. The voyage will be risky enough without a drunken captain at the helm."

Lobov looked up, his face set in the strange, wolfish grin that made the small hairs rise at the base of Demyanov's neck. "I don't get drunk, Anatoli Dmytrovych. To get drunk would be to lose control. And that I will never do."

Demyanov studied the younger man. It was true that he had never seen him drunk. But then, Lobov often said and did such peculiar things, how would he tell?

"Have you heard anything from your contact at the Turkish Consulate?" Lobov asked. "I must know if the Turks are monitoring the Bosporus."

The Bosporus was the narrow, twenty-mile strait separating Europe from Asian Turkey. The waterway fed south from the Black Sea into the Sea of Marmara. Beyond lay the Aegean Sea and the Greek Islands, then the broad expanse of the Mediterranean.

The Bosporus was one of the two choke points on the voyage; there the *Bukharin* would be in the most danger of detection by NATO antisubmarine forces. The other was the Strait of Gibraltar, where the Mediterranean met the Atlantic. Once safely past Gibraltar, Demyanov was confident that the sub faced little chance of discovery in the deep expanse of the South Atlantic.

Demyanov shook his head. "No, not yet."

"Goddammit! I must have that information before we depart. How many times do I have to tell you that?"

Demyanov bristled at the submariner's preemptive tone. Viktor had no respect for Demyanov's position as defense minister of Ukraine. But then, the man didn't give a damn about authority period. He was a rogue, a dangerous loner who operated by instinct.

Demyanov was about to reprimand the submarine captain when his eye went to the pistol Viktor always wore at his side. If the man had enough gall to take a shot at the president of Ukraine, he could have no compunction about using the weapon on a mere defense minister. Old friend or not.

Demyanov grabbed his briefcase from the bench beside him and rose. "I'll go call again. But even if the Turks are asleep, there's still Gibraltar. The British SOSUS post there is bound to be manned."

SOSUS was short for Sonar Surveillance System, a vast network of seafloor sonar receptors put in place by the U.S. and her NATO allies during the long years of the Cold War. Designed to track hostile ships and submarines, the seafloor sensors were tied to Navy shore stations by over thirty thousand miles of undersea cables.

"Don't worry about Gibraltar. I have a plan to get through. Just get me that information on the Bosporus." Lobov's eyes went back to his charts. "I'll be up as soon as I've finished plotting our course."

Demyanov was about to ask Lobov what his plan was, then thought better of it, turned and walked back through the control room. Chief Engineer Mykola Onopenko looked up from the bank of instruments he was checking and nodded to the defense minister. "It's quite amazing, Minister."

"I beg your pardon."

"The condition of these instruments after a decade under the sea. Like new. Every mechanical and electrical part in the vessel is in perfect working condition. I don't know how Captain Lobov managed it."

"He had nothing else to do down there all those years," Demyanov said, letting his pique at Lobov creep into his voice.

Onopenko threw him a reproving look and Demyanov felt a pang of shame. Give the devil his due, Viktor had kept the *Bukharin* in first-class condition. "I was joking," Demyanov said lamely. "The captain did a marvelous job."

"It's as if time stood still," Onopenko said, running a hand lovingly across the gleaming brass housing of the sonar set. "As if I were twenty-two again and about to set off on my first submarine voyage."

"But time hasn't stood still, has it, Onopenko? Ten years have passed. Let's hope you remember how to run all the systems," Demyanov said, leaving the chief engineer staring after him as he climbed the steel ladder to the deck.

Several banks of floodlights had turned the night-dark submarine pen into day, illuminating the freshly painted *Bukharin* and the quay beside her. Demyanov crossed the deck, dodging a seaman rolling a drum of machine oil toward the cargo hatch, then crossed the gangway to the wharf.

The quay was a beehive of activity. Two seamen wrestled with a freshwater hose, while near the stern, a *michman* supervised a work party loading smelly diesel fuel for the sub's auxiliary engine. Other crew members made round-trips between the cargo hatch and a supply truck crammed with fresh meat, eggs and vegetables. The crew of the *Bukharin* would not have to subsist on canned meats and dehydrated vegetables as Viktor Lobov had been forced to do during his lonely years at the bottom of the Black Sea.

Demyanov had provided the food as well as new uniforms, bedding and dozens of other supplies the *Bukharin* would need on her voyage to Argentina. The hardest thing to furnish had been the new reactor fuel. Demyanov had had to pay a fifty-thousand-dollar bribe to the manager of a nuclear power plant near Kiev to obtain the specific fuel he needed. A powerful plow-equipped truck had then taken sixty hours to bring the fuel south down the snow-covered highway to Sevastopol.

The defense minister walked off by himself into the shadows where he would be alone, then stopped beside a steel pillar and took the cellular phone from his briefcase.

He punched in a number and waited, frowning at the sight of several cases of vodka being carted aboard the *Bukharin*. If that goddamn Lobov got drunk and screwed up. . . .

"Consulate of the Republic of Turkey," a pleasant young female voice answered the phone.

"Naval attaché, please."

"May I tell Lieutenant Emin who's calling?"

"Yes, Orest Maksimovich with the Ukrainian Maritime Commission," Demyanov said, giving her the name of a mid-level commission member he knew. "He's expecting my call."

Turkey occupied the entire southern shore of the Black Sea, and several dozen boats from the large Ukrainian fishing fleet had been trapped in Turkish ports when the water froze over in the fall. A call from the Fisheries Commission to the Turkish naval attaché would not arouse suspicion.

"Hello, Orest. How are you?" Lieutenant Emin said over the phone.

"I'm good, Ferit, good. And you?"

"Bored out of my skull. There's little for a naval attaché to do when the goddamn sea is frozen over. I find myself watching American television shows half the day."

"Well, perhaps I can offer some relief for your boredom. The Commission is having a reception this Friday night and I've called to invite you to attend."

"That's very kind of you, Orest. Friday night, you say?"

"Yes. It wouldn't be a party without you."

"Without the caviar you expect me to bring, you mean," Emin laughed.

Demyanov chuckled appreciatively. The conversation was entirely for the benefit of anyone who might be listening to the cellular call—whether the ears belonged to a Turkish security officer at the consulate or a foreign intelligence agent.

"Have you invited the Bulgarians?" Emin asked. "Remember the last party? They brought along that secretary who got drunk and did a belly dance on the banquet table. What a night"

Both men laughed.

"Unfortunately, I think they sent her back to Bucharest the next day," Demyanov said. "The consul was furious."

"No sense of humor, those Bulgarians," Emin said.

"Well, then, can we expect you?" Demyanov asked.

The question was the one he and Emin had agreed on at a late-night meeting in the attaché's apartment two days earlier. When Demyanov asked whether the SOSUS station monitoring the Bosporus was being manned, the Turkish officer had been surprised at the question.

With the Bosporus frozen solid, surface ships couldn't pass through the strait until the ice broke up in late spring, and Emin felt certain that Ukraine possessed no submarines that might try to slip out beneath the floes.

Still, Emin had sold Turkish secrets before, and he knew better than to ask why Demyanov wanted the information. The defense minister was well known for his arms deals. Perhaps he intended to bring an icebreaker through with a cargo of munitions he didn't want NATO to know about.

Emin already knew that the SOSUS station was shut down during the winter months. As was true of every other nation in the northern hemisphere, the economy of Turkey had been devastated by the Earth Winter, forcing the country to slash her armed forces and close unneeded bases. The SOSUS station on the Bosporus wouldn't be reactivated until the following July at the earliest.

But the Turkish officer wasn't about to give away this information for free, and he'd boldly demanded twenty thousand dollars for the intelligence. Demyanov had agreed, with the proviso that Emin pass on the information within forty-eight hours.

"Let me just check my calendar. Friday, you said."

Demyanov could hear pages turning. Emin was obviously a method actor. "Yes, the day after tomorrow."

"It looks like my calendar is clear. I shall be delighted to come, Orest."

"Calendar is clear" was the code phrase meaning that the Turks had shut down the SOSUS station for the winter. Demyanov felt a weight lift from him, and this time he didn't have to fake the enthusiasm in his voice. "Wonderful, wonderful. I can't tell you how much this means to me, Ferit. I'll see you Friday, then."

"Until Friday, Orest."

Demyanov returned the phone to his briefcase and

walked back to the *Bukharin*. Lobov was standing on the gleaming black deck, talking to one of the *michmanyy*. He caught sight of Demyanov and crossed the gangway to meet him on the quay.

"Well?" Lobov asked.

"The Turks aren't manning the SOSUS station. The Bosporus is clear."

"Excellent!" Lobov exclaimed, then looked at his watch. "We sail in an hour."

For the next forty-five minutes, men scurried on and off the submarine carrying last-minute supplies and personal gear aboard. Lobov was everywhere at once, overseeing, cajoling, cursing. Demyanov sat on a packing crate on the wharf, quietly watching the activity.

Finally, everything was ready and the captain crossed the gangway to the quay and extended his hand to Demyanov. "So, it is time to say good-bye, Anatoli Dmytrovych."

The aging defense minister forgot his anger at the brisk submarine captain. Once again he saw before him the young neighbor boy he had grown to love as a son. "Take care of yourself, Viktor. And your men. You'll radio me how it's going?"

"Of course, but not until we reach the Atlantic. In the Mediterranean, it would be too easy for them to get a fix on our position."

"She's not a new boat. Don't push her, huh?"

Lobov put his hands on the older man's shoulders and brought his nose close to Demyanov's face. "I know her, Anatoli Dmytrovych, like a man knows a woman he's made love to for ten years. I will ask only what she can give."

"Good luck, then, Viktor."

"Luck is something a submariner can always use. I'll see you in a few weeks," Lobov said, then turned and crossed to the deck of the *Bukharin*. He ordered the gangway cleared away, then climbed a ladder to the tiny control station in the sail.

Demyanov watched as the captain barked an order to cast off the mooring lines. Then the sounds of the nuclear-powered engine changed tone and the huge bronze propellers at the stern began to churn the freezing water. Slowly, the sub moved away from the dock.

"Prepare to dive," Lobov's voice boomed across the water, sending the mooring party on deck scurrying toward a hatch. The deck clear, the *Bukharin* turned toward the ice-filled tunnel leading out to the Black Sea.

The captain waved at Demyanov for a last time, then disappeared through the hatch in the sail. A moment later, the sub began to angle down and the bow slid beneath the dark chop washing off the rock walls of the pen. Soon the deck was under water, and a hundred yards from the ice, the tip of the sail sank from sight.

For several minutes, Demyanov continued to stare at the wake left by the huge sub, a hard knot of fear eating at him like a cancer. He knew that the *Bukharin* was probably the most powerful weapon of war on earth, with enough destructive force in her nuclear arsenal to kill millions of people at the push of a button.

Demyanov shuddered. God have mercy, what had he unleashed upon the world?

YELLOWSTONE, WYOMING
●●●●●●●●●●●●●●●●●●●●●●●●●

9:10 a.m.–April 12th

BEN MEADE WAS BONE-TIRED after several sleepless nights of missing Marjorie, followed by a seven-hour jet-and-helicopter flight from New York to his Wyoming ranch the day before.

Still, he felt rejuvenated as he stared down from the Meade International helicopter at the rugged peaks and evergreen-carpeted valleys below. There was no place in the world he loved more than this wild and beautiful country where he made his home.

Ben had been born and raised thirty miles from Yellowstone Park. During the summer he turned twelve, he'd packed food and a change of clothes in a saddlebag and ridden his horse off to explore the wild backcountry around Yellowstone, disappearing into the wilderness for three days.

The trip had changed his life. He became fascinated by the steaming geysers, bubbling hot springs, and obsidian cliffs that rose from the slopes like walls of black glass. Riding home to the ranch, he made up his mind to become a geologist and learn all he could about the powerful subterranean forces that gave birth to the volcanic wonders around him.

In high school, he took every science course he could, and in his senior year, he won a full scholarship to study geology at Stanford University. After college, he went on to the Massachusetts Institute of Technology.

At M.I.T., his interest expanded to the other earth sciences, and after earning a Ph.D. in geology, he took masters degrees in climatology and oceanography. Six months out of M.I.T., he formed his own company, Meade International, now the world's leading private developer of geothermal energy.

When his parents tired of raising cattle and moved to Orange County, California, several years later, Ben bought the ranch and established his company headquarters there. In the years since, he'd built a state-of-the-art geological research facilities not far from the barn where he'd mucked out manure as a kid.

When he wasn't off at one of the dozens of Meade International geothermal sites around the world, he spent as much time as he could at the ranch. Research fascinated him, and when his mind grew weary after long stretches in the lab, he would mount his favorite palomino and renew his spirit with a ride into the rugged backcountry.

Often he would bury himself in a research project for weeks at a time, never leaving the ranch. Computer networks kept him in touch with his fellow geophysicists all over the world, and the lab's up-link to two GEOSAT satellites circling the globe let him scan geological formations on any continent with a quick set of keyboard commands.

Ben pulled a map from the backpack at his feet and studied the topography below, then leaned forward and tapped the pilot on the shoulder. "Set down in Meadow Valley, Frank. It's about ten miles east."

The pilot nodded. "You got it, Doctor Meade."

Ben sat back and turned to the large, florid-faced man in the seat beside him. "We'll be there in a few minutes," he said to Mel Sanderson.

Sanderson was Ben's best friend as well as captain of the Meade International research ship, the *Abyss*. The skipper was a barrel-chested man with a lion's mane of white hair, horn-rimmed glasses and a deep, booming voice.

"Meadow Valley, huh?" Sanderson said. "Sounds positively bucolic."

"It's very bucolic, Mel."

"I don't like the way you said that. You're not telling me something again."

Five minutes later, the pilot swiveled around and jabbed his finger downward. "Meadow Valley's coming up on the right. We'll be on the ground in a minute."

The two passengers turned to the window as the chopper lowered toward a narrow, three-mile-long valley. To the north, steaming hot springs and bubbling mud-pots pocked the deep snow like hot raisins in a tapioca pudding. The southern half of the valley was totally different. There, a large snow-free meadow filled the valley floor, its dark green grass in stark contrast to the white slopes around it.

"It's not possible," Sanderson said, looking at Ben in bewilderment. "Grass growing in the winter. And at this altitude."

"Anything's possible in nature, Mel."

"Yeah, but how? There must be a blizzard every week up here, yet that meadow doesn't have any snow on it at all."

"That's because the snow melts as soon as it hits the ground."

"I don't get it."

Ben handed a pair of binoculars to Mel. "Take a look at that big hot spring at the north end of the valley."

Mel squinted into the glasses. "The one with the little river running out of it?"

"Yes. Now follow the river south. About halfway down the valley, it splits into a delta of small creeks that fan out through the meadow. The warm water and the steam melt the snow and keep the grass green all year."

"I'll be damned," Sanderson said, focusing the binoculars on a dozen long-haired mountain goats grazing near the far slope. "It's like a little Garden of Eden down there."

"The southern part of the valley is," Ben said. "The northern end's more like a taste of hell."

As if to underscore Ben's words, a geyser suddenly erupted from the middle of the hot springs to the north, sending a plume of boiling water and steam three hundred feet into the freezing air.

Sanderson swung the glasses toward the geyser. "How often does that thing go off like that?" he asked worriedly.

"Two, three times a day," Ben said. "Depends on the pressure beneath it."

"I thought geysers erupted like clockwork."

Ben shook his head. "You're thinking of Old Faithful over in the park. You can almost set your watch by its eruptions. But Old Faithful's an anomaly; most geysers are fairly erratic."

"Erratic, huh? So you don't know when they're going to suddenly blow?"

"Right."

"How close are we going to get to that thing?"

"Right up to the edge of the hot springs. I need samples of the water and the gases coming out of that vent."

Sanderson threw up his hands. "Why is it, Ben, that every time I'm around you, my life expectancy drops? Last year you had me steaming the *Abyss* over an erupting volcano in the middle of the Atlantic. The year before that, we were dodging icebergs in Antarctica. Now you want me to risk getting my ass parboiled by a geyser."

"I thought you craved excitement."

"Dancing girls are exciting; geysers are dangerous. If you want, I could point out the specific differences."

"I get the idea."

"I would also like to remind you that you promised me a vacation. 'Come out to the ranch with me,' you said. 'We'll eat steaks, play poker and sleep 'til noon for a week.' Do you remember saying that?"

Ben laughed. "Relax, Mel. An hour down there, that's all. I promise. Then we'll fly over to the ranch and kick back."

"That's assuming we don't get turned into stew meat," Sanderson grumbled, staring down at the furiously steaming column of water jetting out of the earth below.

Ben leaned forward to the pilot. "Put us down on that ridge south of the hot springs, Frank."

"I don't want to get too close to that geyser, Doctor Meade," the pilot said. "If the spray washes over the chopper, it'll freeze against the cold metal and coat everything with a layer of ice."

"Don't worry, the hot water column will subside in a minute," Ben said.

Sanderson poked his beefy face between Ben and the pilot. "You sure he pays you enough to do this, Frank? Now'd be a good time to demand a raise."

The pilot grinned. "You kiddin' me, Mel? I'd do it for free. I haven't had this much fun since the Gulf War."

"Fun! You're as crazy as he is."

The pilot laughed and put the chopper into a steep bank to the right, sending Ben and Sanderson back against their seats. As Ben had predicted, the geyser subsided as the aircraft lowered, and a minute later, the ski-equipped helicopter settled softly onto a snow-covered ridge fifty yards below the hot springs.

As the sound of the motor died away, Ben picked up his backpack and opened the cabin door. "C'mon, Mel," he said. "The sooner we get finished here, the sooner you'll be gnawing on a thick T-bone."

Sanderson hefted his bulky frame from the seat and followed Ben out into the snow. A freezing wind blew at them from the direction of the geyser, and Mel wrinkled his nose at the odor in the air. "What the hell's that smell?"

"Sulfur dioxide seeping up from the volcanic vent," Ben said, taking two pairs of snowshoes from a storage locker beside the door. "Here, strap these beneath your boots."

"Tennis rackets? You want me to put tennis rackets on my feet?"

"If you tried to get around here in boots, you'd sink up to your ass in snow. Stop bitching and put the damn snowshoes on. We've got work to do."

"My, we're testy today."

"Mel!"

"All right, all right, I'll put the stupid things on," Mel said, taking the snowshoes from Ben. "Which way do they go?"

Ben sighed and helped Mel on with the snowshoes, then turned and started down the slope toward the hot springs.

Sanderson took his first step to follow and toppled over into a drift. Ben looked back and shook his head. "Slide one foot forward, then the other. You'll get the hang of it."

"I doubt it," Mel said. But after falling twice more, he finally mastered the shuffling gait and followed Ben down the slope.

Though the geyser had subsided into the hot springs at its base, Sanderson hung back as Ben walked up to the lip of the steaming pool. He watched nervously from ten feet away while Ben took out a thermometer and measured the temperature of the water, then jotted down the figures on a note pad. Ben next began filling a small glass bottle from the pool.

"What are you doing?" Mel asked.

"Taking water and vapor samples," Ben said, inverting a bell-shaped canister over a small steam vent. "The chemical composition will tell me how far down the magma source is."

Mel looked around at the dozens of hot springs, steam vents and bubbling mud-pots pocking the northern end of the valley. "Looks to me like the main chamber's about ten feet under our feet."

Ben laughed. "If it were that close to the surface, the magma would erupt through the rock like fire through paper. No, the chamber is two to three miles down."

"Then what makes the water and mud boil up in these pools around here?"

"In places, there are fractures in the rock, extending from the surface down to the chamber. Magma seeps up through the cracks, water seeps down, and where the two meet, the water boils."

Mel shook his head. "And to think that tourists travel thousands of miles to Yellowstone to see stuff like this. You ask me, you'd get the same kind of thrill goin' out and standing in the fast lane on the freeway."

Ben laughed and went back to work. For the next hour, he took samples from a dozen other geothermal pools scattered across the north end of the valley, labeling each bottle and storing them in his pack.

When he finished, he led Mel back up the slope toward the helicopter, stopping at a large rock outcropping that jutted out from the ridge like a turret from a castle wall. The winds had swept the outcropping free of snow, and Ben sat down on a ledge and took a sketch pad out of his pack. Mel dropped down beside him with a weary sigh.

"We'll build the geothermal plant as close to the hot springs as possible," Ben said, sketching out a rough site map on the pad. "That will leave most of the meadow open for the animals up here to graze."

"Seems a shame to plunk down a power plant in a beautiful place like this," Mel said reflectively. "All those damn steam pipes and high-voltage lines."

Ben stopped sketching and looked out over the valley. "You read my mind, Mel. I had to think long and hard before deciding to drill here. But in the final analysis, I had no choice. There's enough geothermal power under this valley to power biospheres in six high plains states. And at least the site's not in Yellowstone Park."

"Yeah, I guess—" Mel stopped in midsentence and jumped to his feet. "Look, look!" he said, pointing excitedly across the valley. "A herd of buffalo just came over that ridge. Damn, I've never seen any outside a zoo before."

"They're called bison," Ben said, his face softening as he gazed at the huge animals. "I used to ride up here when I was a kid and just sit under a tree and watch them for hours. I found out later that the bison have been coming here to feed on the grass for hundreds of thousands of winters. And they aren't the only life-form to benefit from the geothermal heat. A whole ecosystem thrives in the meadow. Mammals, birds, insects, plants."

"Kind of ironic, isn't it? Up here in the mountains, a flow of warm water from a geyser creates a Garden of Eden while the rest of the country is covered with ice and snow. Too bad we don't have a great big river of geothermal water flowing through our farm states."

"It would do a lot more good if we had a geothermal river flowing into the Arctic Sea, Mel."

"Why the Arctic Sea?"

"Because that's where the intense cold gripping the northern hemisphere is coming from. The sub-zero winds blowing south off the sea ice send temperatures plummeting all the way from northern Canada to the Gulf of Mexico."

"So the Arctic Sea ice is the reason winters are so damn cold in the northern hemisphere?"

Ben nodded. "If the polar region were free of sea ice, winter temperatures in the middle latitudes would rise eight or nine degrees. That's enough to almost completely reverse the cooling effect of the volcanic clouds from R-Nine."

A distant rumble began to build in the valley, and tons of ice suddenly sheared off a cliff on the opposite side of the river, plunging into the heated water below and sending a fountain of steaming spray out over the surrounding snow.

"I'm glad we weren't standing on the riverbank when that happened," Sanderson said.

"We would have gotten a little wet, Mel, that's all," Ben grinned, turning his attention back to his drawing.

As Ben sketched, Sanderson studied the sudden dam formed by the falling ice. "Those big slabs of ice that came down are backing up the river. The hot water's running off into that snow-covered field along the bank. You ought to see this, Ben. For some damn reason, all the bison are moving over toward that flooding field."

Ben looked up. "They know that within an hour or so, the thermal water will melt all the snow and ice and expose the grass underneath."

"How the hell do they know that?"

"Because the same thing's undoubtedly been happening at least once a week for the past hundred thousand winters. Steam rising from the river coalesces into thick slabs of ice on the face of the cliff. After building up for several days, the ice collapses into the river under its own weight and diverts the warm water out over the surrounding fields. As soon as the grass thaws out, the bison eat their fill.

"Then the geyser erupts and sends a sudden surge of superheated water down the river to melt away the ice dam. The water returns to its normal channel, and a snowstorm covers the field again. A few days later, another huge slab of ice falls into the river, and the cycle starts all over—"

Ben suddenly dropped his sketch pad into the snow and leaped to his feet. "Son of a bitch! Why didn't I think of that before? Jesus, the answer's right there in front of my dumb-ass eyes and I couldn't see it!"

"What the hell are you talking about?"

"I think I have a way to melt the Arctic Sea ice, Mel. C'mon, let's get back to the chopper. I've got to run some computer projections at the ranch."

"Melt the Arctic ice pack!" Mel said, scurrying up the snowy slope after Ben. "Are you nuts?"

"Could be, Mel. I'm either crazy or I've just found a way to change the weather of the world."

BUENOS AIRES, ARGENTINA
••••••••••••••••••••••••••

12:30 p.m.–April 12th

C.I.A. AGENT OLIVER FLEMING looked up from the port-
folio of sketches in his hands and smiled at Maria
Echeverria, sitting nervously on the couch beside him.
"These are absolutely wonderful. You have real talent,
Maria."

The beautiful nineteen-year-old beamed. "Do you really think so, Oliver? Some days I'll do a drawing and
think, 'It's not bad. Perhaps I can be an artist.' " Her eyes
fell away from his. "But most of the time, I look at my
work and think it's so klutzy that I just want to rip everything to pieces and give up."

"Nonsense. You're an artist. Creating beauty is in your
blood. Like winning races is in the blood of a great thor-
oughbred." He took her hands in his. "Promise me you'll
never again speak of abandoning your art."

Maria blushed, flustered by his praise and his touch. "I
promise."

Oliver withdrew his hands from hers. She was young,
and as skittish as a bird taking its first seeds from a feeder.
He would have to seduce her slowly or she would fly
away. He rose and crossed the sumptuously furnished

penthouse to a liquor cabinet built into the mahogany paneling on the far wall.

"We're going to celebrate your talent," he said, opening a small refrigerator. "I've been saving a special bottle of champagne for just such an occasion."

Maria stole a glance at her watch. It was barely past noon. An hour before, her bodyguard had dropped her off at the university for her usual Wednesday art class. She had walked into the building, then watched through a window to be sure Sergeant Martinez parked in his usual shady spot. She'd then come back out and taken a taxi to Oliver's apartment. The sergeant would be reading a cheap paperback in the front seat of the car, killing time until she finished class at two o'clock. She had time for champagne.

A deliciously wicked feeling coursed through her. A dozen times she had almost torn up the card Oliver had given her the day he'd fought the thief for her purse. But each time, something had stopped her. He was so handsome, so gallant. And he wanted to see her artwork.

Still, she had not called him until yesterday. Ramon had arrived at one o'clock, distracted and in more of a hurry than usual. She had spent the entire morning preparing a special poached salmon for lunch, but he was hungry for sex, not food, and he had ignored her beautifully set table and rushed her into the bedroom.

His foreplay was even briefer than usual, and she wasn't ready when he'd abruptly entered her. It had hurt. Afterward, he had fallen asleep for ten minutes, snoring loudly through his black-forested nostrils.

Maria had risen on an elbow and stared at him as he snored. For the first time, she saw not the strong and powerful junta leader who had swept her off her feet, but an overweight, balding, insensitive, fifty-year-old man.

She'd suddenly had an image of the charming and handsome stranger who'd fought for her purse the week before. She'd flopped back on the pillow wishing it were Oliver in bed beside her instead of the brutish Colonel General Ramon Saavedra de Urquiza.

When Ramon left a half hour later, she'd gone to the phone, hesitated for a minute, then called Oliver. He'd been delighted to hear from her, and anxious to see her artwork. It had thrilled her that he was interested in her as an artist, and when he'd asked her to bring her portfolio by his apartment, she'd instantly agreed.

"This is a lovely place, Oliver," Maria said, looking around the huge, expensively furnished living room. The penthouse was even larger than the opulent apartment Ramon had bought for her, and the walls were hung with works by several of Argentina's finest artists.

"Thank you," Oliver said, hunting through the cupboard for champagne glasses. He had been in the penthouse for less than a week and he didn't yet know where everything was.

Maria rose to study one of the dozen paintings on the walls. "This is an Ortea, isn't it? I love his work."

Oliver found the glasses and looked across the room. "An Ortea? Yes, yes it is," he said, not having the slightest clue as to who the artist might be. The paintings had been leased from the most expensive private gallery in Buenos Aires, and like everything else in the penthouse in the wealthy Recoleta section, they were costing the C.I.A. a fortune.

The accountants at the Agency's headquarters in Langley would scream when they got the bills, but he knew that his expenditures would be approved at the highest level. The Agency had been trying to get close to General de Urquiza ever since he'd seized power in Argentina three years before, and Maria Echeverria was their best shot yet.

He popped the champagne, filled the glasses and crossed the room. Maria was absorbed in the painting before her and didn't notice his approach. "I'd give all I possess to have you look at me that way."

She started. "What?"

"That painting brings rapture to your face. It makes me envious."

She smiled "Ortea's work has the power to mesmerize."

"Perhaps someday your paintings will cast just such a spell."

Maria laughed. "Oh, I'll never be as good as Ortea. I

couldn't even come close. Really, I'd be satisfied just to have a show."

"I know a couple of gallery owners. I'll see if I can arrange it."

Her eyes widened to saucers. "A show? You'd do that? For me?"

"No promises; I'll have to talk to my friends first. Meanwhile, here's to you and your wonderful talent, Maria."

They clinked glasses and sipped the champagne, their eyes locking over the crystal rims. Maria felt heady with the promise of a show of her own and the nearness of the handsome Oliver. The taste of the expensive champagne tingling her tongue capped the perfection of the moment, and a soft invitation came into her eyes.

With practiced ease, Oliver took the glass from her and put it down with his on a side table. He reached out and caressed her cheek with the tips of his fingers, then bent and gently kissed her lips. It was the most tender kiss Maria Echeverria had ever received, and she expected him to take her in his arms.

Instead, he stepped back, his face contrite. "Forgive me, Maria. I've been too forward."

Maria looked at him, wanting to tell him, *No, no, I want you to kiss me,* but she had neither the courage nor the words.

"You're so much like your art," he said. "Did you know that?"

"Like my art?"

"Beautiful and alive. A joie de vivre pours out through your skin like the passion of Ortea pours out through his paint."

To Maria's astonishment, Oliver did a pirouette before her, throwing his arms out as if to embrace the room. "You bring more beauty to my home than ten Orteas. Say you'll stay for dinner."

"I can't."

"Can't or won't?"

"Can't." She searched for an excuse. "I'm hosting a dinner party for my father."

"Tomorrow night, then."

Maria's mind raced. What was tomorrow? Thursday? Ramon always had dinner with his wife and children on Thursdays. Perhaps it was possible . . . if she could find a way to ditch her bodyguard.

It would be taking a terrible risk. Then the image of Oliver a moment ago flashed through her mind. She was sick to death of the dour General de Urquiza. She wanted to be with a young man—a man who did pirouettes.

"Very well. Tomorrow night, then."

"I'll make us a perfect dinner. Do you like lobster?"

"I adore lobster. But now I must go."

"So soon?"

"I'm late for an art class."

"I'll drive you."

"No, I've imposed on your hospitality enough. I'll take a taxi."

"It's impossible for you to impose on me."

Maria gathered her purse and portfolio from a chair. "You're very gallant, Oliver, but I'll take a taxi. And I'll take a taxi here tomorrow evening, too."

"You're a very independent young woman."

If only he knew, Maria thought. I am not independent at all. I am a kept woman, owned body and soul by the most powerful man in Argentina. But at least with Oliver, I can be myself. "What time shall I come?"

"At sunrise. We can have hors d'oeuvres for twelve hours."

Maria laughed. "Seven?"

"Seven would be wonderful. And don't dress up. There'll be just the two of us. We don't need airs."

She liked that. And it would make it easier for her to sneak away from her apartment.

"Thank you for your kind words about my artwork, Oliver. Your praise means a lot to me."

"It is I who should thank you for sharing your work with me. Really, you must have a show. I'll make those calls this afternoon."

He walked with her to the door. "Don't be late. The next thirty-one hours will be an eternity."

"What a romantic you are. Until tomorrow, good-bye."

"Good-bye, Maria."

The door closed behind her and Oliver returned to the living room and plopped down in a chair next to the phone. The smell of Maria's perfume lingered in the air, and for a moment he closed his eyes and rekindled the sight of her face and the touch of her hand.

Maria Echeverria was everything he'd ever wanted in a woman: beautiful, intelligent, artistic. It would be so easy to fall in love with her.

Then, like suddenly finding a spider in a bouquet of roses, he remembered that she was also the mistress of General Ramon Saavedra de Urquiza.

Oliver Alberdi sighed, picked up the phone and dialed the C.I.A. office in Buenos Aires.

CODY, WYOMING
••••••••••••••••••••

3:30 p.m.–April 12th

DICK JEROME WAS DRAGGING firewood back to the house on the kids' toboggan when he heard the sound of the helicopter approaching from the northwest.

A helicopter had passed over several hours before, but when he ran out of the house, the aircraft had been only a speck passing along the horizon to the north, too far for the occupants to see him on the ground.

This time, the helicopter sounded much closer, and when he looked up, he could see it coming in over the drifted pasture beyond the barn. His heart thumping wildly, Dick dropped the toboggan rope and plowed through the snow as fast as he could toward the middle of the farmyard.

A mile to the north, Mel Sanderson leaned toward the window and surveyed the snow-covered Wyoming countryside below. "How far's your ranch?" he asked Ben Meade, in the seat next to him.

Ben looked up from the calculation-covered note pad in front of him and glanced out the window at a familiar pine-forested hill. "About twenty, twenty-five miles. We'll be there in ten minutes or so."

"I haven't seen a plowed road anywhere down there. Must be a bitch getting supplies into your place."

"Nothing comes in by surface vehicle, Mel, not during the winter. I stocked up with frozen foods and canned goods before the blizzards started last fall. We also keep chickens for eggs and a half-dozen cows for milk and butter. Anything else we need is flown in by helicopter."

"You're lucky you can afford to stockpile food and send off a chopper any time you run out of something. Your neighbors out here must have tough going."

"The governor ordered everyone off the remote ranches in the state late last summer. My neighbors have all moved into Laramie or Cheyenne."

Sanderson suddenly caught a flicker of movement below and he craned closer to the window. "Not everyone's left, Ben. There's someone down there."

"What!" Ben leaned across Sanderson, his eyes sweeping the snow passing beneath them. "Where?"

"In that ranch yard ahead. See him? He's waving a coat or something. I think he wants us to set down."

Ben studied the half-buried ranch buildings below. "That's the Jerome spread, and I think that's Dick Jerome waving. I've known him and his wife, Diane, for years." He leaned forward, tapped the pilot on the shoulder and gestured toward the ground. "Take us down, Frank."

"Here?"

"Yeah. Set her down in front of that barn. Careful. The rancher's out in the yard."

The pilot turned to the window. "I see him. I hope he has enough sense to keep away until I turn the rotors off."

Exhilaration coursed through Dick Jerome as the helicopter circled once, then began to descend. He turned toward the house to shout for his family. No need. Diane was already standing at the open kitchen door, Jody and Emily peering out behind her billowing skirt.

A moment later, the helicopter landed, the whirling blades sending up a cloud of powdered snow. Ben zippered up his parka, opened the door and jumped down into a waist-high drift.

"Dick! Jesus, what the hell are you doing out here?" he said as the emaciated rancher struggled up to the helicopter.

"Ben, is that you? Oh, God, I didn't think anyone would come. I didn't think we'd live to see this day."

"I thought you moved into Laramie with Diane and the kids."

"I should have, Ben. God, I was such a fool. I thought we could make it through the winter on the ranch. But we ran out of food. If you hadn't come—" Dick broke into tears.

"Ben! Ben!" The woman's voice came from behind Dick. Ben looked across the yard as Diane Jerome pushed through the deep snow toward them, her coat hastily half buttoned.

"Get inside and warm up," Ben said, helping Dick into the helicopter. Then he started through the deep snow toward Diane. Thirty yards from the aircraft, the shivering woman fell into his arms.

"Ben, you don't know how I've prayed," she half-cried, half-laughed, against his shoulder. "How I've begged God to send someone." She pushed back and looked at him. "I should have known it would be you He sent. Ever since you went away to college, you always were the one we all looked up to, the one who could do anything."

"I was over in Meadow Valley on a geological survey," Ben said, embarrassed at her words. "I just happened to be flying back to the ranch this way. Dumb luck I found you."

"It wasn't luck, Ben," Diane said, her eyes feverish. "The hand of God pointed your way to us."

"Yeah, maybe. Look, are your girls in the house?"

"Yes. Frightened out of their wits. They've never seen a helicopter before."

The two turned as Mel Sanderson struggled through the snow from the helicopter. "Anybody need a hand?"

"Help Diane to the chopper, will you, Mel? I'll go get the kids."

Diane grabbed Ben's hands in a fierce grip that he

could feel through their gloves. "We'll never be able to thank you, Ben. Never ever."

"There's no thanks needed, Diane. Hell, we're neighbors. I'm just sorry I didn't know sooner that you were still out here. Do you want me to pack a bag for you when I'm in the house?"

Diane avoided his eyes. "I'd be ashamed to have you touch our clothes, Ben. I ran out of detergent two months ago. Everything's filthy. I don't think I'll ever get the smell out."

"Look, if you want, my pilot can fly you into Laramie in a day or two and you can buy new clothes. Meanwhile, I'm sure we can find something at the ranch for you and Dick and the kids to wear."

"Lord, how I've dreamed of clean clothes."

"What about personal stuff?"

"There's a metal file box in the cupboard near the stove; it has the kids' birth certificates, our mortgage papers, that sort of things. Could you bring it?"

"Sure. Now get into the chopper with Mel before you freeze to death," he said, starting across the snow toward the house.

Thirty yards away he could see the two girls peering out through the frosted glass, their faces small masks of wonder and fear. A minute later, he pushed open the door and stepped into the cluttered kitchen.

His heart ached at the sight of the small, cold room where the Jerome family had suffered through the winter. The kitchen reeked of unwashed bodies, wood smoke and the stench from the lean-to outhouse behind a tattered curtain. His eyes went to a small pile of dried grass and scraps of belt leather on a cutting board near the stove and he knew what they'd been eating.

From near the window, Jody and Emily looked at him with frightened saucer eyes, their tiny hands twisting nervously before them. They hadn't seen a single human being but their parents since the summer before.

"Hi, Jody. Hi, Emily. You remember me? My name's Ben and I live on a ranch near here."

The little girls continued to stare at him in silence.

"I've known your mom since she was just a little bigger

than you. You know, you guys look just like your mom
when she was little."

That brought an uncertain smile to the tense little faces.

"How would you guys like to ride in a helicopter? I'm
going to take you and your mom and dad to my house."
His eyes strayed to the grass on the drainboard. "I have
the best cook in the whole world at my ranch—I mean,
the best cook beside your mom. And you know what her
favorite thing is to cook?"

"What?" six-year-old Jody asked.

"Hamburgers and french fries. Do you guys like hamburgers and french fries?"

"I like cheeseburgers," Jody said.

"I like french fries," Emily said.

"Good, good." Ben turned toward the cupboard.
"Your mom said to bring the box with the important papers in it. Do you know where it is?"

Emily darted across to the cupboard and pulled out a
drawer at the level of her eyes. "It's in here."

Ben took out the box and stuffed it deep inside his
parka. "Okay, now is there anything you girls would like
to bring?"

"I want to bring Kevie," Emily said.

Ben smiled down at her. "Who's Kevie?"

In answer, she ran across and picked up her Cabbage
Patch doll from the bed. "This is Kevie."

"And I want to bring my doll, too," Jody said. "Her
name's Katie."

Ben laughed. "Okay. Now, is there anything else you
want to take along?"

"Yes," Emily said, kneeling to retrieve something from
under the bed. She straightened and held out a half-
chewed rubber bone. "This was our dog Sonny's favorite
toy. I want it to remind me of him."

Ben squatted beside the little girl. "What happened to
Sonny, Emily?"

"Daddy said the wolves got him," she said, her eyes
suddenly filling with tears.

"If he could have lived only another day, he would
have had food," Jody said, " 'cause the next morning,
Daddy found some stew meat in the barn."

Ben closed his eyes. The volcanic winter had become almost an abstraction to him, a matter of meteorological calculations, biosphere planning and conferences in Washington. His position and wealth had removed him from the everyday world, where the weather meant not scientific supposition, but intense suffering, a world where a father had to butcher his kids' dog to feed his family.

"You know what? I have two big dogs at my house. Jigs and Jedediah."

"What kind of dogs are they?" Jody asked.

"Jigs is a terrier, and Jedediah is an Irish setter."

"Sonny was a cockapoo," Emily said, a fresh torrent of tears streaking her cheeks. "He was the best dog in the whole world."

Ben knelt in front of Emily and took her small hands in his big ones. "I'm going to make you a special promise." He looked up at Jody. "Both of you. I'm going to get you another little cockapoo. A puppy. It may take me a while. You know, with the terrible weather we've been having, not many people are breeding dogs anymore. But I promise you I will find that puppy. And I'll bring him home to you."

"You will?" Emily said, hope lighting her eyes.

"I never break a promise," Ben said. "And until I find your new puppy, you can play with my dogs. Is that a deal?"

"Oh, yes." Jody clapped her hands. "We'll take real good care of your dogs, Ben."

Ben rose. "I know you will. Now get your coats on and we'll fly over to my place."

"Are we going to live with you, Ben?" Jody asked, snatching her snowsuit off the bed.

"You bet, Jody. I have a great big house with lots of extra rooms and plenty of food."

"Can you help me?" Emily said, one leg hopelessly backward in the snowsuit she'd retrieved from a nest of clothes and toys on the floor.

"She can't dress herself yet," Jody said, smugly slipping into her own snowsuit.

"Can to! I just can't get my snowsuit on."

"I'll be glad to help you." Ben smiled and sat the four-year-old on the bed. As he snugged her hands through the arms of the snowsuit, his heart melted at the touch of her soft skin and the scent of her sweet baby breath against his cheek.

He realized suddenly how big a void there was in his lonely life, how much he yearned for children of his own. He sighed. There wasn't much chance that he'd have a family in the foreseeable future, not since Marjorie had left him.

He finished zippering up Emily, then looked at the two little girls. It was going to be good to have kids around the ranch, even if they weren't his own.

"Okay, guys, let's go get those hamburgers," he said, picking up a child in each arm.

At the door, Jody looked back into the kitchen of the only home she had known. "Will we ever come home again, Ben?"

"Sure you will," Ben said with a confidence he didn't feel. "Next summer, when the snow melts."

As he carried the children across the snow toward the helicopter, Jody's question hammered in his head: "Will we ever come home again?"

For ranchers like the Jeromes, and for millions of other rural families across the country, the answer would depend on whether Ben Meade could change the climate of the northern hemisphere.

And to do that, he'd have to play God.

THE STRAIT OF GIBRALTAR
● ●

3:50 p.m.–April 15th

CAPTAIN VIKTOR LOBOV BENT toward the sonar scope and studied the image of the freighter working west through the Mediterranean waves. The ship was six hundred yards off the submerged bow of the *Bukharin* and moving toward the Strait of Gibraltar at fifteen knots.

Satisfied, Lobov turned toward his executive officer and barked an order. "Bring us up. Periscope depth."

"You are aware, Captain, that we are only ten miles out of Gibraltar?" Oleg Pynzenyk asked. "The British radar may spot us."

"Bring her up, damn you. That freighter off our bow is between us and the British radar tower. And if you question an order again, I'll relieve you."

Pynzenyk blanched. He had no doubt the captain would sack him. In the six days they had been at sea, the executive officer had come to the frightening realization that Lobov was unbalanced. The captain was capable of anything.

"Yes, sir," Pynzenyk said, turning to the helmsman. "Vent the main ballast tanks. Ten degrees up-angle on the diving planes. Level off at ninety feet."

The sound of compressed air forcing the water out of the tanks filled the control room, and a moment later, the *Bukharin* began to angle up toward the surface of the Mediterranean Sea.

Satisfied, Captain Lobov turned to the sonarman and tapped him on the shoulder. Evgeny Vasylyshn took off his earphones and looked up. "Yes, Captain?"

"What sort of traffic is coming through the Strait?"

"Four or five ships at least. Medium-sized freighters, I'd say, from the sound of their screws."

"No large tankers?"

"One, I think. A supertanker coming in from the west. But she's not in the Strait yet."

"How long before she's off Gibraltar?"

"If she maintains her present speed, I'd say about an hour."

Lobov looked at his watch. It was four o'clock. It would be dark in an hour. "Good. Let me know if she changes course or speed."

"Aye, Captain," the sonarman acknowledged, putting his earphones back on.

Executive Officer Pynzenyk glanced at the captain out of the corner of his eye. Why the hell was he so interested in a supertanker?

"Periscope depth," the helmsman announced several minutes later.

"Up-scope," Lobov ordered.

The hydraulic-pressured periscope hissed up through its casing, and Lobov bent to the eyepiece. It was dusk and everything looked gray: the ash-layered sky, the sea, the approaching shores of Spain and Morocco. The only color visible was the red of the rust rivulets streaking the freighter, now a half-mile distant across the choppy sea.

Lobov swung the scope toward the mountainous Rock of Gibraltar, guarding the Strait ahead like a monstrous medieval castle. In the British naval base at the foot of the Rock, he could see a Royal Navy frigate and several gunboats tied up. He could detect no activity aboard the vessels, and he turned the periscope to the foreboding face of the Jurassic limestone cliffs beyond.

Gibraltar had been a British fortress since 1704, and

Lobov knew that the Rock was honeycombed with gun emplacements and tunnels used to transport men and ammunition. The Rock was virtually impregnable, and from its heights the British maintained a continuous watch over the strategic mouth of the Mediterranean.

As Lobov panned up the cliffs, he spotted several of the myriad caves concealing guns. To do any damage, an attacking ship or plane would have to put a shell directly in the mouth of a cave, a daunting piece of marksmanship.

Lobov could see the British radar towers at the top of the Rock, their large, basketlike dishes turning to scan the surrounding air and sea. The radar posed no real threat to the *Bukharin*'s passage through the Strait, for the submarine could simply steam out to the Atlantic submerged.

The real enemy was the satellite ground station that Lobov could see just below the radar towers. He knew from Russian naval intelligence briefings a decade before that the satellite installation was an up-and-down link to SOSUS sound receptors implanted in the seabed below the Strait.

The sonar surveillance system recorded the engine noises of every vessel going in or out of the Mediterranean. There was no escaping the SOSUS ears. Unless. Lobov closed his eyes, his face still pressed against the headpiece. Unless there was enough noise in the sea to confuse the listening devices, like a radio in a bugged room turned up full blast to mask a clandestine conversation.

The captain straightened. "Down-scope," he ordered the helmsman. "Take us down to three hundred feet. Rudder hard a port."

The helmsman looked at Lobov quizzically. "Hard a port? You wish to circle, Captain?"

"Yes. For the next hour."

Behind Lobov's back, the executive officer and the helmsman exchanged nervous glances. Obviously, the captain intended to lie in wait for the supertanker. And both of them suddenly knew why.

Several times during the next forty-five minutes, Lobov crossed the control room to ask the sonarman for the location of the supertanker coming in from the west. Finally, at four forty-five, he ordered the helmsman to bring the *Bukharin* back up to periscope depth.

Then he turned to his executive officer. "Load the bow torpedo tubes."

Pynzenyk felt the hair rise on the back of his neck. The crazy bastard was going to do it; he was going to blow that supertanker out of the water to mask the *Bukharin*'s escape from the Mediterranean.

The officer had run his own trucking company during the ten years the *Bukharin* was on the bottom of the Black Sea. He was used to making his own decisions. He had signed on to deliver the *Bukharin* to Buenos Aires, not to murder God knew how many seamen aboard an un-armed tanker.

"No, Captain, I will not give the order."

Lobov didn't hesitate. In one swift movement, the pistol was out of the holster at his side and pointed at Pynzenyk. "You are under arrest for disobeying a direct order."

The others in the control room stared at the scene in shocked disbelief, the only sounds the hum of the machinery around them and the muted wash of seawater passing along the hull.

"You're mad," Pynzenyk said. "If you sink that tanker, every navy on the planet will be hunting for us."

"Hunting for what? A ghost? As far as the world knows, the *Bukharin* went to the bottom ten years ago."

Pynzenyk stared at the captain, debating whether to rush him. Lobov read his eyes and brought the pistol up. "You have children, Oleg. Don't make me kill you."

Pynzenyk's heart froze. His daughter was sixteen, a beautiful and bright girl. Volodymyr, his son, was only nine. Both of them needed a father. He swallowed the bile rising in his throat and sagged where he stood, the fight gone out of him.

"Zhulinsky!" the captain barked.

The junior officer of the watch jumped. "Yes, sir."

"Take this man to the wardroom. Lock him in and post a sentry outside."

Zhulinsky hesitated, his heart thumping wildly. Sink-

ing an unarmed tanker was a monstrous moral outrage
that would make him a party to murder.

"Now!" Lobov roared.

The pistol in the captain's hand decided the junior officer. He had no desire to be a murderer, but even less to be
a martyr. He leaped forward and took Pynzenyk by the
elbow. For a moment, the two men made sad eye contact;
then the executive officer shrugged and started toward
the aft hatchway, Zhulinsky at his side.

Lobov holstered his pistol and looked at his chief engineer. "You are now fire-control officer, Mykola. You
heard the order; carry it out."

"Yes, Captain," Onopenko said. A mid-level bureaucrat since Ukraine gained her independence, he was used
to following orders. And after a decade in a stifling office,
he craved action as a prisoner craves sex. He would let the
captain worry about the morality of sinking an unarmed
tanker.

Onopenko picked up the phone and ordered Mark C
wire-guided torpedoes loaded into two of the six bow torpedo tubes. A moment later, he hung up and turned to
the captain. "Torpedoes being loaded, sir."

"Search forward," Lobov ordered the sonarman.

The sonarman didn't need to be told what the target
was; everyone in the control room now knew they were
hunting the supertanker coming in from the west.

Greek Captain Constantine Papadopoulos sucked on his
pipe as he stood out on the wing bridge of the S.S. *Polyanthus*, contemplating the Rock of Gibraltar passing on his
port bow.

He had been skippering supertankers for twelve years
now, the past four as captain of the *Polyanthus*. At four
hundred thousand tons, the ship was huge, and hard to
maneuver when fully loaded with six million barrels of
crude oil, as she was now.

Still, it was a straight shot across the Mediterranean to
the refinery at Piraeus, the port serving Athens. As always, docking would be tricky, but until then, he could
relax.

Chilled by the wind off the freezing sea, Papadopoulos walked back into the warm bridge and clapped his first officer on the back. "They won't know you at home in Thessaloniki," he grinned at George Spandidakis. "You're as brown as a Fiji Islander."

The first officer laughed. "I couldn't get enough of the sun in Venezuela. I spent half my leave just lying on the beach soaking up the rays. I'll tell you, Captain, the Venezuelans don't know how lucky they are to live south of the equator."

Papadopoulos blew out a puff of pipe smoke. "Ironic, isn't it? The Earth Winter that has brought such suffering in the north has created riches in South America. Venezuela alone has quadrupled her oil exports."

"All the countries in South America are booming," Spandidakis said. "But none like Argentina. I read in the Caracas paper that Buenos Aires is now exporting a hundred billion dollars' worth of food a year from the pampas."

Papadopoulos gazed through the bridge windows at the rapidly darkening sea, his face thoughtful. "Truth be told, it gives me the jitters to think of all that money flowing into a country controlled by a military dictatorship. From what I hear, the junta in Buenos Aires is using the lion's share of that foreign currency to buy armaments—planes, tanks, God knows what else."

God, and the captain of the rogue submarine circling in the depths five miles east of the *Polyanthus*.

"Range?" Viktor Lobov asked.

"Range eighty-nine hundred yards, sir," the sonarman reported. "The tanker will be off Gibraltar in five or six minutes."

Lobov turned to the helmsman. It was time to stop circling, time to close on the four-hundred-thousand-ton quarry ahead. "Steer one eight zero, helm."

"One eight zero, sir," the helmsman repeated, turning the brass wheel.

* * *

"The scuttlebutt is that we'll be heading for Stockholm on the next run," First Officer Spandidakis said. "You hear anything from the home office?"

Captain Papadopoulos scoffed. "No, but it sure as hell won't be Stockholm. Whoever started the rumor hasn't looked at a calendar lately. The sea ice around Scandinavia won't melt until late June. The only way into Stockholm is by air. If I had to bet, I'd say Barcelona or Marseille."

"I hope it's Marseille," Spandidakis grinned. "My girlfriend wants one of those little French nighties. You know, those sheer lace things you can see through."

"She wants one, or you want her to want one?" the captain asked, and they shared a knowing laugh.

"Range?" Viktor Lobov asked.

"Range seventy-seven hundred yards, Captain," the sonarman said.

"Enter target data," Lobov ordered the fire-control officer. "Fire torpedoes at sixty-five hundred yards."

The fingers of Mykola Onopenko flew across the keyboard as he fed the range figures into the computer. "Torpedoes one and two targeted, sir."

"Prepare to fire."

"Flooding torpedo tubes," Onopenko said, flipping switches on the console before him.

"Open outer torpedo-tube doors," Lobov ordered.

"Opening outer torpedo doors," Onopenko confirmed, a tremor in his voice now.

"Range seventy-six hundred yards," the fire-control officer said. "Two minutes to target range."

The men in the control room of the *Bukharin* stole surreptitious looks at each other, a terrible fear in their faces. They were not afraid for themselves. They were afraid for the men they were about to murder.

Only Lobov showed no feeling. His flat eyes were as devoid of emotion as the passionless orbs of a wolf stalking a rabbit dinner. "Prepare to fire," he said.

* * *

"Did I show you the Indian doll I got for my granddaughter, Katrina?" Captain Papadopoulos asked.

The first officer shook his head. "No. Where'd you buy it? In Caracas?"

Papadopoulos made a face. "Not likely. The dolls in the city are all made in some factory—machine stitching on the clothes, the faces spray-painted. I went out in the country and found an Indian village. I'll show you the doll at dinner. The face is carved from a jungle tree, or maybe from a big nut. Who knows? And the hair is real, probably from some little girl like Katrina."

Spandidakis smiled. "You've got a good heart, Captain, trekking out to the jungle for a doll."

Papadopoulos made a deprecating gesture. "Ah, I did it for the reward."

"Reward?"

"Katrina's smile when I give her the doll. Like a sunrise. I can see it already."

The sweat was pouring down the cheeks of the firing officer now. "Range sixty-six hundred yards."

Lobov's fingers absently caressed the butt of his holstered pistol. His touch was loving.

"Sixty-five fifty . . . sixty-five twenty-five . . . target in range."

"Fire one and two," Lobov ordered.

"Firing one," Mykola Onopenko said. "Firing two."

The *Bukharin* shuddered as twin blasts of compressed air sent the wire-guided torpedoes into the sea.

"What's for dinner?" First Officer Spandidakis asked. "Not lamb stew again. I swear, one more dish of that and I'll start bleating."

"No, the cook told me this morning he's preparing frietas."

"Frietas! That stupid Zoitakis doesn't know how to prepare frietas. The bastard can barely cook Greek food."

Papadopoulos shrugged. "He says he learned the dish in Caracas."

Spandidakis groaned. "He's going to give the whole ship diarrhea again. Just like on the last voyage."

Before Papadopoulos could respond, the bridge phone buzzed and he walked across to the communications panel. He jabbed at the speaker-phone button. "Yes?"

"Captain, I'm reading two high-speed screws coming toward us off our port bow," the sonar operator reported from his soundproof cubicle two decks below.

"Probably British patrol boats out of Gibraltar," Papadopoulos said, reaching for a set of binoculars on the top of the console.

"The sounds are too deep to be coming from surface craft, Captain."

Papadopoulos scanned the sea to port. It was too dark now to see anything beyond a hundred yards. "Are you sure they're headed for us?"

"Direct bearing, Captain. About twenty-four-hundred yards out now."

"How deep are the screws?"

"About forty feet, sir."

Spandidakis crossed the bridge to the captain's side. "Did he say forty feet? Jesus, that sounds like torpedoes."

Papadopoulos flushed. "Who the hell would fire torpedoes at us?"

Spandidakis shrugged. "You tell me what those screws are then."

The captain chewed hard on his pipe stem. "Perhaps it's some sort of British Navy war games. Raise Gibraltar immediately, George. Ask them what the hell's going on."

"Range two thousand yards," the sonarman said. "They're coming right at us, Captain."

Spandidakis yanked the ship-to-shore radio receiver off the communications console. "S.S. *Polyanthus* to British Navy headquarters, Gibraltar. Come in please."

"Torpedo-target range nineteen hundred yards," the *Bukharin*'s warrant officer said. "Closing speed forty-five knots. Estimated time to target, ninety seconds."

Lobov nodded and turned toward Junior Officer Zhulinsky at the helm. "Rudder amidships. When I give the order, I want you to take us down fast."

"Yes, Captain."

Royal Navy Bos'n Mate Percy Whitetower lowered his pants and settled onto the toilet seat, a copy of the latest issue of *Punch* in his hand. He had the evening watch on the radio and by the rules, he should have asked for a relief operator before he left his post for the W.C.

But the rules book had been abandoned two years before, when the economic deprivations of the Earth Winter had forced the British to pare their military down to a skeleton force. Now the Royal Navy was far too short-handed to afford a relief operator. The unofficial policy on trips to the privy was to switch on the tape recorder, then answer any messages when the operator returned from the W.C.

Whitetower opened the issue of *Punch* and began reading a satirical feature on the Royal Family. He'd be in the privy only five minutes. What was the harm?

"S.S. *Polyanthus* to Royal Navy headquarters, Gibraltar," Spandidakis said for the fifth time. He waited for a couple of seconds, then looked at the captain in exasperation. "I can't get through to anyone at Gibraltar, sir. A recording keeps intercepting my calls."

"Torpedo range fourteen hundred yards, Captain," the frightened voice of the supertanker's sonarman said.

Captain Papadopoulos spun toward the helmsman. "Turn ninety degrees to port. Bring her about. Now!"

The helmsman spun the wheel frantically.

"Target aspect changing. Getting smaller," the *Bukharin*'s sonarman reported. "She's turning, Captain."

"Correct for changing aspect," Lobov coolly commanded his fire-control supervisor.

Mykola Onopenko entered the new sonar data into the computer. In less than a tenth of a second, the computer sent a new target solution down the insulated wire to the two Mark C torpedoes, now only six hundred yards from the starboard side of the *Polyanthus*.

"Torpedoes retargeted, sir," Onopenko said.

Lobov nodded to himself. Even if the captain of the supertanker made a ninety-degree turn, his ship was far too large and slow to maneuver out of the path of the torpedoes cutting toward her at forty-five miles an hour.

Lobov looked at his watch. Thirty seconds to go.

First Officer Spandidakis slammed down the radiophone, his face a mask of maddened frustration. "It's no good, Captain. I'm still getting that damn recording."

"Hit the abandon-ship alarm," Papadopoulos ordered.

The first officer spun around and jammed his finger into the alarm button on the console. Instantly, a shrill clarion sounded through the massive supertanker and seconds later, the first crew members began running out onto the deck from their duty stations.

"Screws two hundred yards out, Captain," the sonarman reported over the bridge speaker.

Papadopoulos tore over to the bridge windows and scanned the football-field-sized deck below. Perhaps a dozen crew members had reached the lifeboat stations and were tearing the tarpaulin covers from the small craft. He knew that the engine-room crew and the other seamen working five and six decks below would never make it up in time.

"A hundred yards out, Captain," the sonarman said, his voice breaking now.

"Where will they hit us?" Papadopoulos asked.

"Starboard side. Near the stern."

"Who would do this?" Papadopoulos screamed. "What madman would do this?"

Viktor Lobov watched the second hand circle his watch face: ten seconds, nine, eight. "Up-scope," he ordered. The periscope hissed up through its greased casing and he leaned his brow against the headpiece. Four seconds, three, two . . . .

Captain Constantine Papadopoulos knew he was about to die. He stared across the bridge at First Officer George Spandidakis, who looked back in speechless horror. George was only twenty-nine. He'd never been married, never had a child. And now he never would.

Papadopoulos closed his eyes and saw the faces of his family. It tore at him that he would never again feel his wife Mariana's embrace, never kiss his daughter or hug his son.

And little Katrina. He would never give his granddaughter the doll he'd bought for her in Venezuela. The last image Constantine Papadopoulos had on earth was the face of his granddaughter as the two Mark C torpedoes exploded against the hull of the *Polyanthus*, instantly igniting the six million barrels of light crude oil in the belly of the ship.

The explosion that followed flung the massive vessel straight up out of the water. The supertanker came down stern-first, her entire length now engulfed in a cocoon of roaring flames and oily black smoke. Below decks, a dozen crewmen who'd survived the explosion were roasted alive as flames spread through the vessel in seconds.

The torpedo hits had ripped open a huge hole below the waterline, and the *Polyanthus* began to sink stern first, towering columns of hissing steam and smoke jetting skyward as the rising waters met the inferno aboard.

Captain Viktor Lobov's face was impassive as he watched the fiercely burning supertanker. The ship was sinking rapidly; that was all that mattered. If he timed it right, the *Bukharin* would pass beneath the hulk as the tanker plunged toward the bottom in a cacophony of sounds.

"Down-scope," Lobov ordered. The red light in the control room gave his face an eerie, diabolic cast as he turned to the helmsman. "Take her down to four hundred feet. Full speed ahead."

As the *Bukharin* angled toward the bottom, the last few feet of the supertanker's bow slid beneath the waves and the *Polyanthus* began to break apart. Countless noisy bubbles and the horrendous sounds of metal twisting and snapping deafened the SOSUS listening post implanted in the floor of the Strait of Gibraltar.

With the death rattle of the *Polyanthus* masking her passage, the *Bukharin* sliced through the depths undetected, like an invisible presence passing through a crowded room.

Like a ghost.

WASHINGTON, D.C.
• •

9:25 a.m.–April 16th

BEN MEADE FINISHED THE last of his calculations on the
laptop before him as the Meade International Lear Jet
lowered toward Dulles Airport outside Washington.

He ejected the floppy disk and pressed the call button
for the stewardess. "Get me a printout, will you please,
Abby. Just stick it in my briefcase."

"Certainly, Doctor Meade," the thirty-five-year-old
woman said with a perfunctory smile. Abby was having a
hard time convincing her boyfriend to marry her, and her
biological clock was ticking loudly in her ear. Men were
not her favorite life-form these days.

"Anything else, Doctor?"

"Yes. Shake Mel awake, will you? We'll be landing in a
few minutes."

"The last time I woke Captain Sanderson, he flung out
an arm and knocked a dinner tray out of my hands. The
food splashed all over me. I spent the rest of the flight
walking up and down the aisle with roast-beef gravy
squishing out of my shoes."

Ben laughed. "Tell you what. Stand back about five feet

and yell this." He beckoned her head down and whispered the phrase.

Abby grinned and straightened. "I couldn't yell that."

"Go on. I guarantee it'll get him up."

Abby warmed to the idea. "All right, I'll try it." She backed up the aisle several feet, then grinned at Ben and tossed back her head. "Shore patrol!" she yelled as loud as she could.

In the middle of a snore, Mel Sanderson's eyes popped open and he levitated half out of his seat "Run for it, men!" he shouted. "Out the back way!"

The sound of Ben and Abby's laughter snapped him back to reality; he rubbed his eyes and stared angrily across the aisle at Ben. "You son of a bitch, that's the third time you've used that 'shore patrol' bit on me. I never should have told you that story."

"What story?" Abby asked.

Ben grinned. "When Mel was still in the Navy, he and a couple of buddies got out of hand at a topless joint in San Diego and the owner called the shore patrol. To hear Mel tell it, their escape out a back window was one of the most daring feats in the history of topless dancing."

Mel threw an embarrassed look at Abby. "As I keep telling Ben, it was not a topless joint. I happen to be a great aficionado of nude interpretive ballet."

"Are you really?" Abby grinned, arching her eyebrows at Ben.

Mel sighed. "Could we get off this subject?" He gave Abby a pleading look. "I'd like a cup of coffee, please."

"Right away, Captain," the stewardess laughed, and turned up the aisle toward the galley.

"I'll never be able to look her in the eye again," Mel moaned, glaring at Ben. "I'll get you for this, you know. It's only a matter of time."

Ben laughed. "Hey, it worked, didn't it? You're wide awake. Most of the time, you're still comatose half an hour after your eyes open."

Mel yawned. "I may be awake, but I'm still tired."

"You're always tired."

"Maybe if you didn't run me like a goddamn sled dog, I'd be able to recharge my batteries once in a while."

"You can rest up on the *Abyss* while you're provisioning in Miami. I want the ship stocked with enough food and supplies to stay at sea for at least six months."

Sanderson threw up his hands. "Hold on a minute, just hold on. When you told me about this plan of yours to melt the Arctic Sea ice . . . what the hell do you call it?"

"The Arctic Alteration, Mel."

"Whatever. You told me you wanted me to sail to Bremerhaven and pick up a cargo of heat-exchange engines. That right?"

"Right. You have to be in Bremerhaven in two weeks. That should give you enough time to load the Spreckles engines I ordered, then come back across the Atlantic and pick me up in Newfoundland a month from now."

"How many engines am I loading in Bremerhaven?"

"Three hundred."

Mel whistled. "I remember talking to the Spreckles chief engineer when he came down to inspect the engines we were using in Antarctica last year. He told me they only produce about fifty a month. You must have bought their entire goddamn stock."

"Their stock plus next month's production run."

"How the hell did you get the Spreckles people to sell you every engine they had?"

"Actually, it was rather easy once I bought the company."

"You *bought* Spreckles? When?"

"About six o'clock last night."

Mel shook his head slowly. "Spreckles is a good-sized multinational. You must have laid out a lot of dough on that deal."

"About a hundred fifty mil."

"That's a big piece of change, Ben, even for you. How the hell do you know you didn't buy a pig in a poke?"

"I had my finance guys check it out. Spreckles is a solid outfit. Besides, I expect to get my investment back from the U.S. Treasury."

"Suppose Washington balks."

"Then I own a German company that makes heat-exchange engines. Look, I needed every engine Spreckles had, and the only way I could guarantee that was to buy the company."

"I'll say this about you, Ben, you never were one to shrink from taking big chances. You buy a hundred-and-fifty-million-dollar company and then risk most of its assets on the wildest scheme you've ever come up with."

"The Arctic Alteration may be unorthodox, Mel, but I wouldn't call it a wild scheme. Over the next three weeks, a dozen of the best minds in science will be flying out to the ranch to help work out the details."

"You're talking about those oceanographers you spent half the night calling?"

"And climatologists and glaciologists. We'll be working out ocean currents, marine temperature fluctuations, the rate of iceberg calving in the Labrador basin and a hundred other details. Nothing will be left to chance."

"When you're through with your research, you're going to be flying directly to Saint John's?"

Ben turned to the window and stared down at the snowbound Virginia countryside passing beneath the plane. "No, I'm going to fly over to Scotland first. I should be in and out in twenty-four hours."

"Marjorie?"

"Yeah."

"You want some advice from a man who knows something about women?"

"No. And I don't want any advice from you, either."

"Very funny. You're making a mistake, you know."

"I make a lot of them. One more won't tip the scales."

"She called me to say good-bye the night before she left. We talked for a long while."

"About what?"

"About how your relationship has fallen apart. She said she doesn't know you anymore. And that you don't know her."

"I'd say that's pretty close to the truth."

"She also said that she needs time to work things out—how she feels about you, where her life is going. If you'll listen to me, you'll stay out of her hair. Give her the time she needs. Skip Scotland."

"I'm going to be out in the middle of the goddamn

ocean for the next six months, Mel. I want to say good-bye, that's all."

"You ask me, it's a dumb move."

"I didn't ask you," Ben said angrily.

"All right, all right. Jesus, you don't have to bite my head off. I just don't want to see you screw things up any worse than they already are."

"Could we drop it, Mel? We'll be landing in a few minutes. There're some things we need to talk about."

Five minutes later, the Lear Jet touched down at snow-bound Dulles International Airport and rolled to a stop in front of the V.I.P. terminal. As the jet's fold-out door hummed down, a White House limousine crossed the tarmac and stopped several yards from the plane.

A tall, thirty-something White House aide with long, dark brown hair and a small gold ring piercing his right earlobe stepped from the back of the limo and extended his hand as Ben came down the steps.

"Tom Howard, science adviser to President Piziali," the aide said. "Welcome to Washington, Doctor Meade."

"Thank you," Ben said. He'd heard of Howard. The young science adviser had begun his meteoric career by inventing a new interactive video-editing system while still a freshman at San Jose State ten years ago.

After graduation, he'd earned a dual reputation as a brilliant digital-electronics theorist and an equally adept ladies' man. It was rumored that the boyishly handsome Howard had slept with half of the single women in Silicon Valley.

"Is my meeting with the President set up?" Ben asked.

"For nine o'clock," Howard said. He glanced at his watch. "We'd better hurry. We have just over an hour, and the road into Washington is a bear."

As Ben bent to enter the limousine, Mel Sanderson popped his head out the door of the Lear. "Do yourself a favor, Ben. Don't go to Scotland." Ben frowned and followed Howard into the back of the limo.

Leaving the airport, the White House car had to cut around several snowslides that had toppled off the towering snowbanks on each side of the highway. "I see what you mean about the road," Ben said.

Howard gazed out the window. "The snow-removal crews have given up trying to cart the stuff away. It's like trying to empty the ocean with a pail. For the past couple of months, they've just been plowing the snowbanks higher and higher. Half the time, the piles collapse back onto the road as soon as the plow goes by."

The limo pulled out to pass a large new snowmobile ahead and Ben craned to the window for a closer look. "Damn, that thing's as roomy as a car."

Howard looked back through the rear window. "It's one of the new Ford snow sedans. All of the Big Three in Detroit are putting them out now."

"I spent the first few months of the Earth Winter in the U.K.," Ben said. "You should have seen the homemade snowmobiles over there. They used every kind of technology from tread drives to old airplane engines mounted behind."

"There's a whole snowmobile cottage industry thriving in the U.S. now, too, Doctor Meade. I saw a White House study the other day that estimates four million Americans are employed full- or part-time either manufacturing snowmobiles or supplying parts. Most of them in small, family-sized operations."

"There are a lot of little companies making coal stoves now, too," Ben said. "Especially out in the West where I live. There are Mom-and-Pop forges all over the coal-fields in Colorado."

"Everyone's an entrepreneur today," Howard chuckled.

"Thank God for that," Ben said, settling back into the deep velour seat. "Individuals can adapt to change far faster than governments or industries can. And if we're going to survive the Earth Winter, we've got to change things fast."

SAN FRANCISCO, CALIFORNIA
• •

10:00 a.m.–April 16th

THE FOG HAD STOPPED rolling into San Francisco the year
before as the ash-shrouded sun and plunging temperatures changed weather patterns along the central California coast.

In place of the fog, a haze of hate hung over the Bay
Area as rapidly escalating unemployment and dissipating social services pitted the established population
against a tidal wave of Chinese immigrants.

The onslaught of the Earth Winter the year before had
decimated supplies of food and fuel throughout China.
Millions shivered in poorly insulated urban apartments
and rural huts, most of them existing on less than eight
hundred calories a day as government rations of rice,
vegetables and fish became smaller with each passing
month.

Since the day the sun disappeared from the skies of the
northern hemisphere, over three million Chinese had
crossed the Vietnamese border and trekked south on foot,
headed for the warmer countries near the equator. The
mass migration put an intolerable burden on the housing
and food resources of Southeast Asia, forcing Vietnam

and Cambodia to close their borders in October 2000. A month later, Thailand, Burma, Malaysia and Indonesia also forbade any further migration from the north.

A quarter-million wealthy Chinese had immigrated to the warm countries of South America. But the lack of large, sheltering Chinese settlements below the equator discouraged a mass migration from China to the southern hemisphere.

Yet millions of Chinese had relatives in the United States, where long-established and vibrant Chinese communities meant that the new arrivals could live among people who spoke the language and had the customs they'd known at home.

For the people living in southern China, it was also relatively easy to get to America. Over the past decade, a well-entrenched human-smuggling syndicate had brought tens of thousands of Chinese citizens from Fujian Province to the United States. The ring had begun operations in the mid-eighties, using old, rusting freighters to carry illegal immigrants from ports north of Hong Kong across the Pacific to safe landing areas along the California coast.

The smugglers soon became more brazen, landing shiploads of illegal immigrants in San Francisco Bay and on Long Island, New York. The American public was outraged, and the resulting government antismuggling measures forced the ring to move its operations to Guatemala. The syndicate flourished in Central America, bribing public officials in a dozen countries to look the other way while it established smuggling routes into the U.S. through Mexico and the Caribbean.

The syndicate was controlled by Taiwanese with ties to the notorious Fuk Ching, or "Young Fujianese," a violent gang of native-born Chinese. Typically, the Fuk Ching would hold newly arrived immigrants in custody until their families paid smuggling fees of as much as thirty thousand dollars.

During the 1990s, over two thousand Chinese aliens were smuggled into the United States each month. Then R-9 erupted in February 2000, and within weeks, the number of immigrants doubled, then doubled again.

Still, the flow of Chinese across the Pacific did not reach flood stage until Washington announced the building of Biosphere America. Tales of the wondrous glass-enclosed mini-Earths that could feed and shelter hundreds of millions of people spread like wildfire through the villages of China.

The biosphere's Intensive Agriculture Biomes would need rice and soybean farmers, the stories said, and the light industries planned for the mini-Earths would create millions of other jobs.

Within a month of the announcement of Biosphere America, over thirty thousand Chinese a week were boarding tramp steamers and hastily converted fishing boats bound for the Americas. Many of the smuggling ships landed immigrants in Central America to be trans-shipped through the Caribbean to destinations in the central and eastern United States. But the majority of the filthy and overcrowded vessels put their human cargo ashore along the West Coast, and over the past six months, almost half a million Chinese had found their way to the Bay Area.

The Chinese community took in tens of thousands of their fellows, but the sheer number of recent arrivals soon overwhelmed their resources, and most of the immigrants had no choice but to turn to the Bay Area's social-service agencies.

Family aid organizations, food-stamp programs and medical services were flooded with ten times the number of cases they were set up to handle. Families received first priority, and single Chinese men—adrift, cold and hungry—roamed San Francisco in daily search of food and shelter.

At the same time that the tide of illegal immigrants was reaching its crest, jobs in the Bay Area were rapidly disappearing as central California's computer, biotech and agribusinesses suffered the economic effects of the Earth Winter. Unemployment had reached a staggering 32 percent, and almost every day, another company announced new layoffs and job losses. The shrinking economy forced San Francisco and other Bay Area cities to levy emergency taxes to pay for the burgeoning costs of feeding and sheltering a homeless population that had been doubled by the swelling tide of Chinese immigrants.

A deep resentment simmered just beneath the surface of the Bay Area's non-Chinese communities. Increasingly vocal right-wing groups fanned the flames of hatred, painting the illegal aliens as a horde of locusts that was devouring central California's shrinking resources of food, fuel, housing and public funds.

The spark that ignited the tinder was a brazen pre-dawn murder at the corner of Broadway and Columbus, a block east of Chinatown. Sixty-one-year-old Bodega Bay fisherman Al Smith had driven his pickup fifty miles south to San Francisco to sell the two hundred pounds of salmon he'd caught off the coast the day before.

The corner was the turf of the Fuk Ching gang. In recent years, the Fuk Ching had branched out from human smuggling to prostitution, drug dealing, extortion and strong-arm robberies, and the dozen gang members standing on the corner took an immediate interest in the fisherman's cargo.

Two Fuk Ching slipped behind the truck as it idled at the light and flipped up the tarp covering the bed. At the sight of the open boxes of freshly caught salmon, the men signaled their comrades, and instantly a stolen Buick roared into the intersection to block the truck.

While the fisherman honked his horn at the car in his path, a dozen Fuk Ching began emptying the boxes of salmon. Feeling the truck rock, Smith turned to stare in horror at the Chinese stealing his hard-caught fish.

The old fisherman snatched a tire iron from under his seat and leaped out to confront the thieves. He never had a chance. Four Fuk Ching surrounded him, and he gasped in shock and pain as a knife slid from a sleeve and into his back. Sixty-one-year-old Al Smith died on the pavement as the last of his salmon disappeared from his truck.

A store owner on his way to work witnessed the robbery and called the police. Within minutes, two squad cars arrived. The cops took a report from the store owner and several bystanders, and an all-points bulletin went out for the Chinese gang members.

Radio and TV news stations routinely monitored the
police radio, and within an hour, the story of the robbery
and murder was on every local TV and radio morning
news show. By 8:00 A.M., most of the Bay Area knew that
a gang of Chinese had murdered a local fisherman and
stolen his catch.

Even more than the murder, the theft of precious food
incensed the citizens of San Francisco. Food was life itself,
and now the hated Chinese immigrants were not only
draining the supplies of relief agencies, they were stealing
from ordinary citizens.

A mob of unemployed and hate-filled whites, blacks
and Latinos began to gather at the site of the robbery,
grabbing and beating any Chinese foolish enough to ven-
ture out of Chinatown. By 10:00 A.M., the crowd had
swelled to almost twenty thousand. Half of the San Francisco police force stood along Broadway between the mob
and Chinatown, and for almost an hour, they were able to
keep the rioters in check.

Then a Chinese housewife in an apartment half a block
from Broadway opened her kitchen window to air out the
smell of the sea bass she was cooking for her family's
lunch. Within minutes, the unmistakable odor of frying
fish had wafted across Broadway to the crowd.

"Smell that!" an unemployed dockworker shouted.
"The fucking Chinks are eating that poor dead bastard's
fish!"

"They're eating my babies' food!" a black mother with
two children and four cans of beans at home yelled out.

A furious roar went up from the mob, maddened at the
thought that the despised aliens were eating the stolen
food, food meant for them. The angry crowd suddenly
became a riotous mob as thousands surged forward
across Broadway, taking the police by surprise and breaking through their lines in a dozen places.

The rioters stormed up Grant Street, driving several
hundred terrified Chinese immigrants before them.
Along the way, knots of men and women broke off from
the main body of the mob to smash store windows and
loot liquor, food and weapons.

At the corner of Grant and Jackson, the rioters came

upon a rickshaw stand where in warmer times tourists had boarded the two-wheeled carriages to be pulled around Chinatown by men dressed in traditional coolie garb.

A dozen rickshaws were confiscated by the mob and quickly filled with loot from shops plundered along the way. Live-television camera crews followed the rioters through the streets, broadcasting pictures of the pillaging.

The televised shots of the booty proved too much for thousands of out-of-work residents of the impoverished Tenderloin and Mission Districts. Hard-drinking men who hadn't had a beer in months, and mothers tormented by empty larders, watched their neighbors carrying off liquor and food and streamed out of their homes to join in the plunder.

The new arrivals pressed into Chinatown from the south, trapping the Chinese immigrants fleeing the mob advancing from Broadway to the north. With no place left to go, almost a thousand exhausted immigrants sought refuge in one-block-long Merchant Street, between Kearny and Montgomery.

Both entrances to the short street were quickly closed off by the pincer grip of the two mobs. For several moments, the rioters and the terrified immigrants eyed each other, indecision and fear rippling through the two groups like eddies through a turbulent sea.

"Just look at them clothes. They're all aliens," a taxi driver who hadn't had gas for his cab in three months yelled out, pointing at the baggy pants, sandals and Chinese-style coats worn by the trapped immigrants.

"They're supposed to be deported," another rioter screamed. "The goddamn government's supposed to ship 'em back to China."

"If the government won't deport 'em, we'll do it ourselves!" a woman yelled out.

"Yeah, send 'em back to China," a fourth voice joined the chorus.

"Throw 'em in the Bay and let 'em swim home!" yet another rioter echoed, bringing a roar of approval from the mob.

Now whipped to a frenzy, rioters streamed into Merchant Street from both sides, descending on the half-starved and frail Chinese like vultures on wounded prey. Several dozen of the immigrants managed to escape, leaping through glass windows and scampering up fire escapes. But over three hundred fell into the merciless clutches of the mob.

"Throw 'em in the Bay!" the cry went up again, and the rest of the rioters screamed their approval. "To the Bay, to the Bay!"

Dozens of terrified Chinese were piled into the stolen rickshaws and pulled down Montgomery Street by teams of drunken, laughing men. Hundreds of other captives were yanked along by their hair, leaving trails of blood as their flimsy sandals came off and their feet were flayed to the bone by cobblestones and curbs.

As the mob dragged their captives along, a terrible chant rose from thousands of throats and echoed off the brick fronts of the buildings along the way.

"Chinks back to China,
    Throw the bastards in the Bay.
Chinks back to China,
    Throw the bastards in the Bay."

When the chanting army of vengeful men and women reached Broadway, it turned to the right, toward the Embarcadero. Suddenly the terrified Chinese captives could smell the salt air and feel the freezing wind coming off the Golden Gate.

In sobbing Mandarin, they beseeched their Chinese gods to save them. But their gods were not in this place. There was only hatred here, and closer with every step, the cold waters of San Francisco Bay.

THE WHITE HOUSE,
WASHINGTON, D.C.
• • • • • • • • • • • • • • • • • • •

11:00 a.m.–April 16th

AN HOUR AFTER LEAVING Dulles Airport, the limo carrying Ben Meade and National Science Adviser Tom Howard turned off Pennsylvania Avenue and rolled up to a security checkpoint at the south gate of the White House.

As the limo came to a stop, Ben noticed several heavily armed members of the Executive Protection Service, the uniformed arm of the Secret Service, going in and out of a large guardhouse that hadn't been there on his last visit. On top of the fortified building, sandbags were piled around what looked like a machine-gun emplacement.

"You guys have sure beefed up security," he said to Howard.

"Had to," the science adviser said, lowering the electric window next to him. "That 'Rally for Food' a couple of months ago got out of hand and a couple of hundred militants went over the fence. They got right up to the White House doors before the guards could stop them. Scared the shit out of the Secret Service."

Howard handed their I.D.s out to an EPS guard, who checked their credentials against an arrivals list, then waved them through. Five minutes later, Ben and Howard were ushered into the Cabinet Room.

Presidential Appointments Secretary Megan Humpal met them just inside the door. "Good morning, Ben," Humpal said, looking every bit the Vassar graduate in her burnt-orange crewneck sweater, herringbone-tweed skirt and cordovan penny loafers.

"How are you, Megan?" Ben smiled, shaking hands with the attractive, bright-eyed aide. Twice during the recent Senate Appropriations Committee hearings on funding Biosphere America, Ben had requested last-minute meetings with the President, and Humpal had gone out of her way to squeeze him into the frenetic Oval Office schedule.

"I still owe you a dinner at Le Trec," Ben grinned.

"Yes, you do, and I'm not forgetting it," Humpal said, meaning every word. There were few single women in Washington who would turn down a date with the ruggedly handsome and wealthy Ben Meade.

"I'm afraid the President's running late," Humpal said. "There's some sort of trouble in San Francisco and she's been on the horn with the mayor for the past twenty minutes."

"I've had a lot of trouble in San Francisco," Howard deadpanned. "Blond trouble, redhead trouble, brunette trouble."

Humpal rolled her eyes. "Bachelors! I'd hate to think of what you two talked about on the way in from the airport."

"Science," Ben said. He raised a hand, palm out. "Honest."

"Yes, I bet. Tom, your secretary said to tell you there are several urgent calls on your voice mail."

"Urgent, my ass. It's probably the usual congressmen wanting me to arrange tours of the Johnson Space Center for their constituents. I'll see you in a few minutes, Ben."

"Thanks for meeting me at the airport, Tom."

"Come say hello," Humpal said, leading Ben toward a knot of Administration officials standing at the foot of the conference table. "I think you know most of the people here. Admiral Mike Mathisen, chairman of the Joint Chiefs of Staff; National Security Adviser Bonham; Director Jeung from the C.I.A. and Senator Hollis Crawford, chairman of the Senate Armed Services Committee."

Ben shook hands and exchanged a few words with each of the men in turn. As he was greeting Senator Crawford, he heard a familiar voice boom out behind him.

"Ben. Jesus, it's good to see you." Ben turned as National Science Foundation Director Jay Stevens strode across the room and grabbed his hands.

"How are you, Jay?" Ben asked. He had worked with Stevens on several geothermal projects, and the Foundation director had been an invaluable ally during the planning phase of Biosphere America.

"I understand you've already started reconstruction of the biosphere in Princeton," Stevens said, steering Ben away from the others by the elbow. "Hard to believe that a flock of geese could cause damage like that."

"They're big birds, Jay, and about twenty thousand of them came through the glass."

"How long do you figure it will take before the biosphere's operational again?"

Ben shrugged. "Rebuilding the physical structure shouldn't take more than a few weeks; it's only a matter of reglazing the south wall. But most of the plants and animals inside froze to death. The President has authorized all the transport planes and ships we need for bringing new species in, but it will still take a couple of months at least before the ecosystems are viable again."

"I hear that Marjorie took it pretty hard."

"She was stressed out even before it happened, Jay. When the geese crashed through that glass, she snapped. I warned her it was coming—that she was working too hard, taking on too many responsibilities."

Stevens frowned. "I blame myself for a lot of the burden she was carrying. Jesus, I was calling her three or four times a week, demanding progress reports on the genetic plant engineering project."

Ben looked away. When Stevens had first asked Marjorie to take on the assignment, Ben had advised her to turn him down. He pointed out that she was already overburdened with work on Biosphere America.

She'd countered with the argument that while the bio-spheres could feed Americans, there would be no food for export to the tens of millions of starving people in Europe, Africa and Asia. It was an argument Ben couldn't refute, and in the end, Marjorie had undertaken the job. Ben didn't blame Stevens; the National Science Foundation director had asked for help in a humanitarian cause.

"You were only doing your job, Jay. Marjorie under-stood that. She knew how important the work was."

Stevens leaned forward and lowered his voice. "How is she, Ben?"

Ben sighed. "I haven't talked to her since she flew home to Scotland to rest about a week ago. She's probably still pretty rocky."

He put his hand on the director's arm. "But I know Marjorie. She's a strong woman. Give her a chance to re-charge her batteries, and she'll be back. She just needs a little time without people like you and me making de-mands every time she turns around."

Senator Crawford wandered over to the two men, his fingers splayed across his pin-striped vest as if to hold in his considerable paunch. The white-haired, sixty-five-year-old Georgia senator had gained the chair of the Sen-ate Armed Services Committee through seniority.

Most liberals and moderates in Congress had opposed his appointment, for Crawford was a sabre-rattling hawk who believed the U.S. should maintain her military might at full strength despite the economic realities of the Earth Winter. The southern-born senator was also a dyed-in-the-wool Creationist with a vocal distrust of any science that didn't march in lockstep with the Book of Genesis.

"I'm not entirely clear why we're all here, Doctor Meade," Crawford said, his Georgia accent as thick as the mud of the Okefenokee Swamp where he'd been raised by a bible-quoting mother and an alligator-poaching fa-ther. "I hear you want to play God and change the cli-mate."

Ben bristled. "I'm just a scientist, Senator Crawford. There's nothing celestial about my plan to try to raise temperatures in the northern hemisphere."

"Your plan may not be celestial, Ben, but I'm sure it's

inspired." The voice of Kathy Piziali came from behind him. The men turned toward the door as the President of the United States crossed the Cabinet Room. Like the seasoned politician she was, she shook hands with each of the men present.

"Please sit down, gentlemen," she said, her intelligent green eyes troubled. "I'm sorry to keep you waiting, but I'm afraid we have a rather explosive situation out in San Francisco. A mob has attacked Chinatown. Several hundred immigrants were apparently dragged down to the Bay and thrown off the wharf. There are reports of mass drownings."

Senator Crawford shook his head gravely. "I warned this would happen, said as much right on the Senate floor. It comes of that bleedin'-heart Mayor Alioto offering sanctuary to all them damn immigrants floodin' in from China. There's barely enough food to feed our American citizens out there, and she issues an open invitation for every rice eater west of Hawaii to sidle up to the public trough. It's no wonder the good citizens of San Francisco have taken to riotin'."

" 'Good citizens' don't drown helpless immigrants," the President said angrily.

"The people have been driven to it, Madam President. The Central Valley out there used to grow the most bountiful crops in the world. Now, with the cold, they can't raise a stalk of corn. And most of the year, the passes through the High Sierra are blocked with snow. It's impossible to get food trucks through from the east. How do you expect people to react when a half-million hungry Chinese descend on 'em? Folks are scared out of their wits they're all goin' to starve to death out there."

"I understand the fear in California, but you can't blame the poor immigrants," Ben said quietly. "Even in the most remote villages of China, people have heard of Biosphere America. They know that the thousands of mini-Earths we're building will provide food and shelter for hundreds of millions of people."

"Why can't the Chinese build their own damn biospheres?" Senator Crawford asked.

Ben shook his head. "They don't have the money, the

resources or the technical expertise. No, the only way to stem the tide of immigrants flooding this country is to give the people of China hope that conditions in their homeland will change. And that means reversing the effects of the Earth Winter."

Ben turned to President Piziali. "That's why I'm here, Madam President. I believe I may have a way to raise temperatures in the northern hemisphere enough to allow the cultivation of crops again in the higher latitudes. I call the plan the Arctic Alteration."

"Are you talking about dissipating the sulfate aerosols in the atmosphere, Ben?" Tom Howard asked. "Bringing back the sun?"

"No, Tom, I'm afraid that's not possible. The climatologists at our lab in Wyoming are researching ways to scrub the aerosols out of the atmosphere, but they're years away from a breakthrough. For now, we have to assume the worst-case scenario—that normal solar radiation won't return north of the equator for at least fifteen years."

"I'm afraid you've lost me, Ben," the President said. "How do we grow crops without sunlight?"

"My fianc—" Ben stopped in mid-word. Marjorie wasn't his fiancée, not anymore. "My colleague, Doctor Marjorie Glynn, is developing genetically altered food plants that can grow in the weak sunlight reaching the northern hemisphere."

"Doctor Glynn has made tremendous progress," Jay Stevens said. "We've recently finished planting the first seedlings she's developed. We hope that in a few months we'll have several million acres sown with vegetables and grains that can carry out photosynthesis in indirect solar radiation."

"The Lord God gave us wheat and corn and all the other crops we eat," Senator Crawford objected. "It's an abomination to mutate the natural plants He's created. Besides, over the past two years, the Argentines have tripled their production of grains and meats. Let them worry about feedin' the starvin' masses."

"That's a debatable viewpoint, Senator," Security Adviser Bonham said. "Yes, the pampas can feed the world, but at what cost? The junta in Buenos Aires has doubled its prices for food over the past year. The entire world trade balance is shifting. The U.S., Europe and Japan are fast becoming net importers, while Argentina has become the leading exporter nation.''

The President fixed Senator Crawford with a pointed stare. ''What concerns me, Hollis, is what the junta is doing with all that foreign exchange flooding into Buenos Aires. From the C.I.A. reports Dan has been bringing to the Oval Office, they're spending billions on armaments.''

Admiral Mathisen tented his fingers, the tips brushing his lower lip thoughtfully. ''If the junta continues building up its armed forces at the present pace, in three or four years the Argentine Army and Navy will be bigger and better-equipped than any military power on earth save the U.S. The junta will have the power to exert awesome pressure, not only in South America, but around the world.''

Ben said, ''The decimation of our food production is only one of our problems. The Earth Winter has made it all but impossible to harvest forest products, to work surface mines, or drill for oil and natural gas.''

''Whoa, hold on a minute here, Doctor Meade,'' Senator Crawford said. ''I thought these geothermal wells you're sinkin' all over the country were going to supply all the energy we need.''

''Most of the geothermal energy we're now developing will be used to heat and power the biospheres,'' Ben said. ''It will be a couple of years before we can move all our people and industries inside. In the interim, we'll still need fossil fuels to supply power to homes, office buildings and factories outside.''

''We'll also need fuel for surface vehicles and planes,'' Jay Stevens said.

Ben nodded. ''Yes, for at least another decade.''

''Won't our future cars and vehicles use electric motors?'' Rob Bonham asked. ''Hell, I just bought one of the new battery-powered Pontiac snow sedans myself.''

''Electric motors are fine for personal vehicles,'' Tom Howard said. ''But today's batteries can't store enough electricity to power large, long-range trucks and heavy equipment like snowplows."

"And there's no electric motor on the horizon that's even close to meeting the power needs for aircraft," Jay Stevens added.

"There are several other reasons I'm proposing climate alteration," Ben said. "They range from the danger of changing sea levels as Arctic ice captures more and more ocean water, to the weather-caused deterioration of our road and rail arteries. I've spelled it all out in a position paper that our research people will make available later this week. For the moment, though, I want to touch on a prime concern, and that's the effect of the Earth Winter on the ecosystems in the northern hemisphere."

"You mean the plants and animals being killed by the cold," the President said.

"Yes, Madam President. They're irreplaceable. Once a species goes extinct, there's no bringing it back. Plants and animals can survive a precipitous temperature drop for a year or two, but not the fifteen years or more of intense cold we now face."

"Doctor Meade is absolutely right," Jay Stevens said. "Foundation studies indicate that we could lose forty to fifty percent of the plant and animal species indigenous to the northern hemisphere—everything from butterflies to fish, mammals, flowering plants and hardwood trees. The list is almost endless."

"It was my understanding that we could freeze plant tissue and animal semen and ova," the President said, "and regenerate species later in the lab."

"That works with specific species, Madam President," Ben said, "but we're talking about dozens of ecosystems with thousands of different plants and animals. At most, we might be able to regenerate twenty or thirty percent of the species. And we'd have to keep those in controlled environments such as zoos and botanical gardens because the ecosystems where they once lived would no longer be viable."

"The myriad life-forms in an ecosystem are woven together like threads through cloth," Tom Howard said.

"When you start losing individual species, the fabric weakens and finally tears apart."

Ben said, "If we don't do something to reverse the effects of the Earth Winter, when the sun returns in fifteen years, our environment will have been irreversibly altered. Our children will live in a different world, a world where less than half the plants and animals still exist."

There was a long silence around the table. Finally, the President came forward in her chair, her face glum. "If there's any chance to warm the climate, I believe we must try."

The men around the table nodded in silent agreement.

"It only remains, Ben, for you to tell us how the Arctic Alteration will work," the President said. "How do you propose to raise temperatures in the northern hemisphere?"

All along the Embarcadero, the cold waters of San Francisco Bay were littered with the ice-encrusted bodies of almost three hundred drowned Chinese.

Several news helicopters hovered just offshore, their searchlights and cameras pointed down at the carpet of carnage undulating on the surface of the Bay. The cameras broadcast the scene to a numbed worldwide audience, bringing a flood of outraged calls into City Hall.

The Chinese government in Beijing threatened to break off diplomatic relations, and newscasters throughout Asia and Europe cited the massacre of the immigrants as yet one more evidence of America's racist, violence-prone society.

Mayor Angela Alioto's office could do little more than assure callers that the California National Guard would be in the city within an hour to restore order. Meanwhile, local authorities were powerless. Draconian budget cuts had slashed the police force in half, and the remaining twelve hundred cops had no hope of controlling the mob of twenty thousand, many of whom were drunk on looted liquor and armed with stolen guns.

When the military reinforcements arrived, the mob would be dispersed and mass arrests made, the mayor promised. Until then, the best the outnumbered police could do was to set up defensive positions around the financial district and City Hall.

While the police waited nervously several blocks away, the rioters paused in their rampage, satiated for the moment by the murderous revenge they had wreaked on the hated Chinese immigrants.

For a mile along the Embarcadero, thousands huddled around fires, burning wood ripped from nearby buildings and boats. Like soldiers encamped on a victorious battleground, the men exchanged tales of personal bravado as they passed around bottles of purloined liquor.

Yet if the fires of hate had died down, they had not gone out. The flames flared again when Mayor Alioto held an ill-conceived news conference to announce that she would shortly put an end to mob rule in the city. When the National Guard arrived, she told the assembled reporters, the soldiers and police would round up the rioters and throw them in prison. The ringleaders, she promised, would go to the gas chamber at San Quentin.

Sitting before a fire in the midst of the mob encampment, a laid-off bellhop from the Hyatt Regency listened to the news conference with a stolen radio to his ear. The mayor's threats of prison and the gas chamber incensed the hotel worker, and he leaped to his feet, waving the radio in an angry hand.

"The mayor says she's gonna put us all in prison. Give us the gas chamber."

"That bitch, Alioto," burly Golden Gate Bridge tolltaker Max Logan yelled. "First she gives our food to the Chinks, and now she wants to gas us like common killers."

"She's a dirty Chink-lover," an unemployed ironworker with rotten teeth and a week's growth of beard screamed out. "We ought to throw her in the Bay with her slant-eyed buddies."

"Yeah, yeah, throw her in the Bay," a dozen more men yelled.

Suddenly the mob came alive again. Like a school of fish that suddenly turns as one, the rioters coalesced and wheeled in a body toward Market Street. The terrible chanting began again, the words now aimed at Mayor Alioto.

> "Send the Chink-lovers to China,
> Throw the mayor in the Bay.
> Send the Chink lovers to China,
> Throw the mayor in the Bay."

At a hastily erected police barricade at the intersection of Fifth Street and Market, the sound of the approaching mob sent a chill down the spine of S.F.P.D. Police Lieutenant Russell Morita.

A ten-year veteran of the force, Morita had heard the reports of the drownings and the looting of gun shops and liquor stores. The prospect of trying to stop a drunken mob armed with Uzis and high-powered hunting rifles terrified the thirty-one-year-old Morita. As the rioters approached down Market Street, he wondered, sick-at-heart, whether he'd ever see his wife and young son again.

Morita waited until the mob was a hundred yards away, then cleared his dry throat and reached for a bullhorn. "This is Lieutenant Morita of the San Francisco Police Department. By direction of Mayor Angela Alioto, you are hereby ordered to disperse. I repeat, disperse immediately."

A maddened roar went up from the mob as the front rank came to a sudden stop, forcing the mass of rioters behind to bunch up like a wave building before a beach. For a moment, the mob milled about in confusion. Then the toll-taker leading the riot took another swig from the vodka bottle in his hand and advanced with drunken bravado toward the police line.

"It's the mayor and the rest of the Chink-lovers that's gotta disperse," Max Logan screamed. "Disperse 'em back to China."

"Throw 'em all in the Bay!" the rioters behind him yelled.

The blood was pounding so hard in Morita's temples that he thought the arteries would burst. "The mayor has

ordered you to disperse," he repeated into the bullhorn.
"Clear Market Street immediately."

Logan drained the last of the vodka. "You cops clear
out!" he yelled back, throwing the bottle toward the police line.

The bottle shattered against the top of the barricade,
sending a razor-sharp shard slicing through the cheek of
a twenty-two-year-old police-academy rookie. The young
cop screamed and collapsed to the pavement, his gloved
hands unable to stop the river of blood streaming from
his face.

"Jesus, put him in a car!" Morita yelled. "Get him to
Saint Francis."

As a sergeant helped the rookie toward a patrol car,
Morita turned back to the mob. The front rank of rioters
was now less than fifty feet away. "This is your last warning. Disperse by order of Mayor Alioto."

"Fuck the mayor," the drunken toll-taker roared, starting toward the barricade again. "We're goin' throw her in
the Bay with her Chink friends."

"Yeah, yeah, throw her in the Bay," a dozen voices
echoed.

Morita spun toward his officers. He had less than a
hundred men. And there were thousands coming at him.
His only hope was to take out the leaders. Maybe the
shock would panic the mob behind and put it to flight.
"When they come, aim at the ones in front," he ordered
his men. "Get ready."

"C'mon, they can't stop us!" Logan screamed, running
toward the barricade. Behind him, the mob surged forward.

"Fire!" Captain Morita ordered.

Market Street erupted in a cacophony of gunfire and
the screams of wounded men as the police fusillade
mowed down the front rank of rioters like a scythe
through wheat.

The mob fell back in shock, trampling the wounded in
its headlong flight. The retreat was brief. Sporadic shots
rang out from the rioters, building steadily to a drumbeat
of gunfire as automatic weapons opened up at the police.

Then one of the rioters yanked a length of rubber heater

hose from a nearby car and began siphoning gasoline from the vehicle's tank. Eager men crowded around him, filling empty liquor bottles with fuel and stuffing pieces of gas-soaked cloth into the necks for fuses. A moment later, the first flaming Molotov cocktail arced toward the police line, smashing into the pavement ten feet away and spraying the barricade with flaming gasoline.

A hail of bottle bombs followed, exploding among the terrified police beyond the barricade. A dozen cops screamed in agony as their uniform coats caught fire and the spreading flames seared the flesh from faces and hands.

At the same time, the withering gunfire from the mob increased. Sergeant Morita took a bullet through his throat and sank slowly to the pavement, his eyes staring in blank disbelief. His last thought before he died was of the wife and son he would never see again.

Decimated by the firebombs and bullets of the mob, the surviving cops broke and fled back up Market Street, dragging their burned and wounded comrades with them.

On the pavement, toll-taker Max Logan groaned and rolled over on his back. He had taken bullets through his side and left knee, but the liquor and fury boiling through him deadened the pain.

"Help me up!" he screamed.

Two comrades pulled him to his feet and yelled for others to bring up one of the stolen rickshaws. As he was hoisted into the wooden conveyance, he could feel the blood flowing from his side and knee. He knew he was going to die in the street, and he knew who to blame: Angela Alioto, who'd brought on the riot with her decree of asylum for the filthy slant-eyes. And now her cops had shot him. Before he died, he'd make the Wop bitch pay for what she'd done.

"We've got the cops on the run!" Logan yelled with ebbing strength. "Now let's go get that Chink-lovin' mayor!"

"To City Hall!" a rioter yelled back.

"Yeah, yeah, to City Hall!" a dozen voices joined in.

A roar went up from the mob as several men grabbed

the tugs of the toll-taker's rickshaw and started forward at a trot. The rest of the mob followed behind, its chant audible all through the freezing streets of downtown San Francisco.

> "Send the Chink-lovers to China,
> Throw the mayor in the Bay.
> Send the Chink-lovers to China
> Throw the mayor in the Bay."

Ben Meade felt the adrenaline surge through him as the President and her advisers waited for him to tell them how he proposed to alter the climate. This was it. The moment of truth. He would be putting his reputation on the line, maybe his future as a geophysicist. He'd better be right.

"The Arctic Alteration is a plan to melt the polar sea ice, Madam President."

There was a collective gasp of astonishment around the table. Jay Stevens coughed gently and forced a sympathetic smile. "Ben, I don't think there's any doubt that when it comes to the earth sciences, you're the man. I believe everyone here would agree."

They all nodded, except for Senator Crawford, who scowled skeptically, and President Piziali, who regarded Ben with a noncommittal half-smile.

"But this, the melting of the Arctic Sea ice." Stevens shook his head. "God Almighty, you're talking about tens of thousands of square miles of ice. I just don't know that mankind possesses the power to pull off something like that."

"No, mankind doesn't possess the power," Ben said, "but nature does."

"And what is that power, Ben?" the President asked.

"The Gulf Stream, Madam President—the warm-water current that rises in the Caribbean and flows north along the East Coast. The Gulf Stream is virtually a river in the sea, a huge current a hundred miles wide and a thousand feet deep. A river carrying warm, tropical water directly from the Caribbean Sea to the North Atlantic, transferring heat from the equatorial regions to the higher latitudes. I intend to divert the Gulf Stream north into the Arctic basin."

Admiral Mathisen came forward in his chair. "I don't understand, Ben. When R-Nine rose from the sea floor, it formed an island directly in the path of the Gulf Stream. The volcano and the other seamounts rising out there are forcing the current to the southeast, away from the North Atlantic."

"That's true," Ben said. "But R-Nine and her sister peaks intercept the Gulf Stream hundreds of miles to the east of where I intend to divert the current."

Ben turned to the President. "If we can pull this off, Madam President, if we can turn the flow of the Gulf Stream northwest into the Arctic and melt the ice pack, it will raise temperatures in the northern hemisphere as much as nine or ten degrees Fahrenheit."

Jay Stevens came half out of his chair. "Nine or ten degrees! That's a big enough rise to almost completely reverse the effects of the Earth Winter!"

C.I.A. Director Jeung shifted uneasily in his chair. "If you melt the Arctic ice cap, Doctor Meade, won't that raise the level of the oceans?"

"I'm not proposing to melt the ice on land, Director Jeung. That would indeed raise sea levels, because the water now trapped in glaciers would flow off into the oceans. My plan is to melt the sea ice in the Arctic basin, and that will have no effect on ocean levels because the ice is already displacing water in the sea."

"What I don't understand is how melting the Arctic Sea ice will raise temperatures in the U.S.," the President said. "After all, the Arctic is over two thousand miles to the north."

"The Arctic ice pack affects the U.S. climate in two major ways," Ben said. "If you look at a map, you'll notice that there are no major mountain ranges stretching east-west. The Appalachians, the Rockies and the Sierra run north to south. That means there are no physical land barriers to stop the cold, heavy air that forms over the Arctic ice pack from spreading south across the plains all the way to the Gulf of Mexico."

"The same thing's true in Europe and northern Asia," Jay Stevens said. "East-west mountain ranges such as the Alps and the Himalayas act as natural barriers to the southward flow of Arctic cold. But the vast land masses north of those mountains are wide open to freezing air blowing down from the pole."

"Exactly," Ben said. "So the larger the Arctic ice pack, the colder the weather in most of the northern hemisphere."

"You said the ice pack affected our climate in two ways, Ben," the President said. "What's the other?"

"The circumpolar vortex, Madam President."

Senator Crawford's eyes glazed over. "The circumpolar what?"

"Vortex, Senator. In layman's terms, the jet stream. You could think of the circumpolar vortex as a great river of air blowing from west to east high up in the stratosphere, six to twenty miles above the earth. The vortex tends to follow the edge of the sea ice. In years when the pack shrinks north toward the pole, the circumpolar winds follow, blowing in a tight circle around the Arctic. Climatic zones to the south expand northward, and temperate regions such as the U.S. have mild weather, with no great extremes of temperature or rainfall."

"So the smaller the Arctic ice pack, the better our weather," Director Jeung said.

"There are short-term exceptions, of course," Ben said, "but as a general rule, yes, that's the case."

"And what happens when the ice pack expands?" the President asked.

"The vortex weakens, and local high-pressure systems form, Madam President. These high-pressure systems block the winds and force rain-bearing, low-pressure systems to take extreme zigzags north or south. The result is droughts in some areas and floods in others."

Stevens shifted uneasily in his chair. "Ben, there's no question that melting the polar sea ice would raise temperatures in the northern hemisphere."

"And stabilize rain patterns," Tom Howard said.

Stevens nodded. "Yes, the meteorological data supports all that. It's the means you're proposing that I have a problem with. Good God, how the hell do you change the course of the Gulf Stream? As you said yourself, Ben, the current's over a hundred miles wide. Even if you could build a dam out there in the North Atlantic, the thing would have to be thousands of feet high to reach the surface from the ocean floor."

"I'm going to build a dam all right, Jay, but it won't be made of concrete and steel, and it won't have to stretch down to the seabed. I intend to divert the Gulf Stream into the Arctic with a dam made of icebergs."

San Francisco Mayor Angela Alioto sat at her desk frozen in fear. Five minutes before, her young aide, Kimberly Gutlaven, had burst into her office with the ominous news that the Chinatown mob had broken through the last police line guarding City Hall.

"They're in the building, Angela," Kimberly said, her terrified eyes as big as saucers. "There are cops in the lobby and maybe a dozen in the hall outside, but they won't be able to hold back the mob for long."

The mayor's eyes darted nervously to her watch. "The National Guard should be here in an hour or so."

"An hour! Jesus, Angela, we don't have an hour. We need help now. Now!"

The two women could hear the ominous chanting of the drunken rioters in the plaza below:

> "Send the Chink-lovers to China,
> Throw the mayor in the Bay.
> Send the Chink-lovers to China,
> Throw the mayor in the Bay."

"I'm not going to let them take you," Kimberly said, pulling a small, twenty-two-caliber pistol from her handbag.

The mayor rolled her eyes. "Kimberly, for God's sake, put that thing away. The most you could do would be to wound a few of them. The others would kill you for it."

"I don't care." Kimberly was crying now. "I won't let them take you."

Both women jerked their eyes toward the door at the sound of gunshots and screams in the hallway outside.

"Get in the bathroom, Kimberly. Lock the door and keep quiet. They're after me. Maybe I can reason with them."

"Reason with a mob?"

The mayor shot out of her chair at the sound of pounding on the door. "Get in the bathroom, dammit. Now!"

"Angela . . ."

"Now!"

The young aide threw her arms around the mayor. "God keep you, Angela," she sobbed, then turned and fled to the bathroom, locking the door behind her.

A moment later, the blade of a fire ax splintered the top panel of the door, and Mayor Alioto felt her knees weaken. *Oh, God, please don't let them kill me with an ax!*

As she stared transfixed at the door, the panel burst apart and a hand reached in to flick open the lock. Then they were in the office, a dozen unkempt men with stubbled faces and red-rimmed eyes, several of them splattered with the blood of the cops they'd killed on their march to City Hall.

The stench of unwashed bodies and liquor fumes was overpowering, and Alioto began to tremble. "Halt!" she screamed, her voice sounding as if she were hearing it from far away.

The rioters paused, staring at the tiny woman in disbelief at her audacious command.

"You'll go to prison for this!"

"You're the only one that's goin' anywhere, Angela," an unemployed dockworker sneered. "You're goin' for a swim in the Bay."

The thought of being thrown into the freezing waters of the Bay all but paralyzed Alioto. Yet she came from a long line of gutsy Italians, and from deep inside, she summoned up the courage to confront the rioters.

"Go home, all of you. The National Guard is on the way. They have orders to shoot rioters on sight. Do you want to die? If you don't care about yourselves, think of your families. Who'll feed your children?"

"It sure as hell won't be you, will it, Angela?" a taxi driver who hadn't worked in six months screamed in fury. "You're givin' all our food away to the Chinks."

"The Chinese immigrants have as much right to our food as we do," Alioto said.

"They're illegal aliens," a Mexican fieldworker screamed in a thick Spanish accent.

"It doesn't matter whether they're here legally or not," the mayor shot back. "They're human beings. They're our brothers and sisters."

"Yeah? Well, you're goin' for a swim with your 'brothers and sisters,' " a bricklayer yelled.

"Throw the bitch in the Bay," a carpenter echoed.

A dozen hands reached for the mayor and she was hoisted into the air above the mob. Hand over hand, the drunken rioters passed her out through the door. Hard, dirt-caked fingers ripped at her clothes as she was borne down the stairwell like a crumb of bread over an army of ants.

A tumultuous roar went up from the mob in front of City Hall as the half-naked mayor was carried through the front entrance and down the stone steps.

"Bring up one of them rickshaws!" someone yelled. Laughing and shouting, a knot of rioters emptied the nearest rickshaw of its cargo of liquor and weapons and brought it through the crowd to the steps. The terrified woman was thrown into the wooden carriage as a dozen men fought for a place between the wooden tugs.

"To the Bay, to the Bay!" the call went up, and the rickshaw jerked forward down Market Street toward the Embarcadero, two thousand drunken men shouting and firing weapons into the air as they followed in the carriage's wake.

Huddled in a corner of the swaying rickshaw, a freezing and terrified Angela Alioto crossed herself and began to pray.

"Icebergs!" Senator Crawford laughed out loud. "You want to build a dam out of icebergs? Madam President,

I've got better things to do than sit here and listen to this crazy bullshit Doctor Meade's tryin' to pass off as science."

Crawford began to rise from the table, only to pause midway as the voice of the President cut the air like a whip.

"Sit down and shut up, Hollis," Piziali said, not bothering to hide her displeasure. "Ben, please continue."

"An iceberg dam is entirely feasible," Ben said as a sputtering Senator Crawford lowered himself back into his chair. "The iceberg season in the North Atlantic lasts roughly from February to October. Large bergs have been calving off the Greenland glaciers for several weeks now, and most of that ice is being carried south through the Labrador Sea by local currents."

"Doctor Meade's absolutely right," Mike Mathisen said. "Every spring, the Navy sets up an iceberg watch in the North Atlantic. Some of those bergs are the size of cities, hundreds of feet high and a couple of miles across."

Ben said, "The key thing to remember about icebergs is that only one-ninth of their total mass projects above the water. So a berg visible for a hundred and twenty-five feet actually descends a thousand feet into the sea below."

"A thousand feet!" Tom Howard exclaimed, suddenly full of life. "That's deep enough to divert even the bottom flow of the Gulf Stream."

Ben nodded. "Of course it will take more than one iceberg. I estimate we'll need seventy-five or more large bergs averaging two miles across. My plan is to lash the ice together into a hundred-and-fifty-mile dam spanning the path of the Gulf Stream off Newfoundland."

Admiral Mathisen stared at Ben, his granite-slab face impassive beneath a mantle of iron-gray hair. "I can't fault the theory behind your plan, Doctor Meade," the admiral said. "But I want to know more about the logistics. For starters, how do you intend to move these icebergs to the dam site?"

"Nature will do a lot of the work for us. The Greenland Current is already carrying dozens of big bergs down into the Atlantic. Once they're far enough south, we can tow them the rest of the way to the Gulf Stream with either Navy or civilian vessels."

The self-disciplined flag officer arched his eyebrows. "The sea off Newfoundland is several thousand feet deep. How do you propose to anchor the bergs to the sea-floor?"

"I hadn't planned on anchoring the dam. I'll keep the ice in place with the new Spreckles engines developed in Germany four years ago."

Tom Howard's face lit up with cognition. "Heat-exchange engines! Damn, they'll work like a charm in the Gulf Stream."

The non-scientists around the table looked at each other in perplexity. "What is a 'Spreckles engine,' Ben?" the President asked.

"It's a chemical-mechanical motor powered by an ex-change of heat, Madam President. We used them in Ant-arctica a couple of years ago to move icebergs away from our geothermal drill platforms."

The President shook her head in wonder. "Engines for icebergs! How on earth do they work?"

"The first step is to carve out engine rooms in the bergs below the waterline. The Spreckles engines are then in-stalled, with the drive shafts extending out through the ice to seventy-five-foot propellers."

"What's the power source?" Rob Bonham asked.

"I'm coming to that," Ben said. "Once the engines are in place, cylinders of liquid Freon are stored in the ice around the engine room. The Freon is then pumped under high pressure into heat exchangers submerged in the sea. As the liquid Freon leaves the sub-zero ice and hits the warmer sea water, it turns into a gas, expands rapidly and spins turbines that drive the propellers. The Freon is then recycled into liquid form and used again and again."

"The Spreckles engines will operate at maximum effi-ciency in the Gulf Stream," Howard said confidently, his face animated.

"And why is that?" the President asked.

"Because the tropical waters in the Gulf current are so much warmer than the ice, Madam President. The liquid

Freon will practically flash into gas and spin those propellers like bats out of hell."

"Thank you for that scientific explanation, Tom," the President said, drawing a burst of laughter from the men around the table.

"Ben, how many Spreckles engines will you need to keep the dam from drifting out of the Gulf Stream?" Jay Stevens asked.

"I did a preliminary computer analysis yesterday," Ben said. "If the numbers are right, we should be able to keep the dam stationary in the current by using two engines for every mile of ice."

"Then if the dam is a hundred and fifty miles across, you'll need three hundred of these Spreckles engines," Director Jeung said. "Are that many available?"

"The company had two hundred in stock. They've agreed to run three shifts at their plant to have another hundred ready in three weeks."

Ben turned to the President. "To get my hands on those engines, I had to buy the Spreckles company. I expect the government to assume the cost of the engines and guarantee that I'll recoup my investment when this is all over."

"Have your finance people get in touch with my Congressional liaison staff, Ben," Piziali said. "We'll move it through the Senate Appropriations Committee as quickly as—"

The President stopped in midsentence as Domestic Affairs Adviser Lisa Benson burst through the door and ran across the room, her face a mask of shock and disbelief.

"Lisa, what on earth's the matter?" the President asked, alarmed by her aide's ashen skin and frightened eyes.

"A National Guard officer just called from San Francisco, Madam President. By the time their troops reached the city, the mob had broken through the police lines at City Hall and dragged Mayor Alioto out of her office. They . . ." Lisa began to sob.

The President reached up and put a hand on the woman's shoulder. "Calm down, Lisa. Calm down and tell me what happened."

"They threw Angela Alioto into the Bay."

Piziali shot to her feet. "Dear God! Did anyone help her? Did they get her out?"

"She's dead, Madam President. Drowned. The National Guard just recovered her body from the water. Oh God, oh God, what a horrible way to die!"

A communal gasp went up from the men around the table.

The President shuddered, her face a mask of revulsion. "Three hundred Chinese murdered by the mob. And now Angela Alioto. I thought the food riots the past few months were bad. But this. This is anarchy."

"It's only the beginning," Ben said.

The President sighed deeply. "I'm afraid you're right, Ben. As food and fuel reserves dwindle, immigrants and the public officials who support them will become targets for murderous mobs all over the country."

"Surely you're bein' an alarmist, Madam President," Senator Crawford said. "I mean, the situation in San Francisco was an aberration; half a million illegal aliens crowded into a city already runnin' out of food. We don't have that lethal combination in our other cities."

"But we will, Senator, and soon," Piziali said. She turned to Admiral Mathisen. "How many immigrant ships out of China would you estimate are headed for the United States at this moment?"

The flag officer frowned and scratched his lantern jaw. "The count goes up every time one of our surveillance satellites sends back reconnaissance photos. As we sit here, there are at least three hundred suspect vessels sailing east from China. We estimate that each one of them carries upward of a thousand immigrants."

"Did that register with you, Senator?" the President asked. "Three hundred ships headed this way with hundreds of thousands of desperate immigrants aboard. And they're only the vanguard. If the Earth Winter drags on, we can expect a human tide across the Atlantic as well— tens of millions of refugees from the Balkans and the former Soviet Republics."

"If that happens, we'll call out the Army," Crawford

said belligerently. "Round the damn aliens up and deport 'em."

Ben shook his head. "As fast as you deport them, others will take their place. They'll have no choice. The biospheres here, and those in the U.K., will be the only oases of life in the northern hemisphere. We don't have the resources to build enough biospheres to take them all in. It will be a case of us or them, and the carnage in San Francisco will be repeated ten thousandfold, because the only way to keep the immigrants out will be to kill them."

For a long moment, there was a somber silence around the table. The President sat motionless, her eyes closed. Then slowly, almost imperceptibly, she shook her head. "No. The American people will not survive at the price of massacring countless innocent immigrants."

She looked across at Ben. "The Arctic Alteration is our only hope. Tell me what you need from Washington."

"On the diplomatic front, it's vital that we have the cooperation of Canada and Russia. Their northern lands border the Arctic, and both nations have the highly skilled experts we'll need. Over the next several weeks, I'll be working out the details of the project at my ranch in Wyoming. It's important that Canadian and Russian scientists join in the planning phases."

"I'll call Prime Minister Stuart and President Yakov. I believe I can guarantee their cooperation."

"It's also vital that we have the support of the Navy and Coast Guard, Madam President. I want as many large ships as possible deployed north to tow icebergs down from the Labrador basin."

Piziali turned to Admiral Mathisen. "Are you prepared to commit your ships, Mike?"

"Fully, Madam President. I'll have the Atlantic Fleet provisioned and headed north within a week."

"There remains the matter of announcing the project to the media," the President said. "The press will want specifics: facts, figures, timetables. When will you have all that worked out, Ben?"

"In two weeks, Madam President."

Domestic Affairs Adviser Lisa Benson leaned toward the President. "You're scheduled to make a major policy speech on immigration in two weeks, Madam President. Since the Arctic Alteration will directly affect immigration, that might be a good time to announce the plan."

President Piziali nodded. "That's an excellent suggestion, Lisa. Have the speechwriters go to work on it."

The President looked back at Ben. "You'll have everything you need from Washington—diplomatic support, ships, men, money. The rest is up to you. Give us back our climate, Ben. Give us back our hope."

Rio De La Plata, Ten Miles off the Argentine Coast
••••••••••••••••••••••••••••••

3:00 a.m.–April 25th

THE ARGENTINE NAVY HELICOPTER skimmed south above the dark waters of the Rio de la Plata, Pilot Hernando Roca searching the surface below for the signal lights he had been told would flash from the submarine coming in from the sea.

Roca was nervous. He had suddenly been assigned to the mission only an hour before, after having been awakened at 2:00 A.M. by the duty officer at the General San Martin Navy Base, thirty miles south of Buenos Aires.

He had been told only that he would rendezvous with a submarine somewhere in the fifty-mile-wide mouth of the Rio de la Plata. When the sub was located, he was to land on its deck and let off the San Martin harbormaster and the two other passengers seated in the cabin behind him.

There was nothing unusual about landing the harbormaster on the deck of an incoming vessel, even a submarine's. Roca had done it a dozen times before. But he was mystified by the presence of the other two men on the flight.

One was a translator from the Foreign Ministry, a nervous little man in a cheap, food-stained suit. The other was Admirante Juan Bautista Secchi. Why the hell was the chief of staff of the Argentine Navy going out on the River de la Plata in the middle of the night to meet a submarine?

Roca felt a tap on his arm and looked sideways at his copilot.

"There." The copilot pointed at the radar screen. "At the two o'clock position ahead. I think that's it."

Roca studied the blip on the green scope. The calibration marks on the sides of the screen told him that the object in the river ahead was at least six hundred feet long. "It's too big to be a sub. A freighter probably."

The copilot shook his head. "Can't be. It's too low in the water."

Roca shrugged. "Give them the recognition signal. One long, three short, two long."

The copilot reached forward to the toggle switch controlling the powerful searchlight mounted on the belly of the Blackhawk and flashed the signal. Instantly, the correct sequence came back: two long, one short, two long.

Roca shook his head. "She can't be one of ours. There isn't a sub in the fleet even close to that size."

The copilot's face suddenly lit with cognition. "Quay number five! I'll bet you a month's pay that's where she's going."

"Five? You mean the one they're roofing over?"

"Yes. Suddenly, two weeks ago, construction workers show up one morning and start crawling over the place like ants. Three shifts going around the clock. In ten days, they had a shed over the whole thing."

Roca was puzzled. Why roof over a quay unless you want to hide something that might be spotted from the air by overflying planes or reconnaissance satellites? Perhaps his copilot was right. Perhaps it was the mysterious submarine heading in from the South Atlantic that the junta meant to keep secret. What the hell was going on?

The pilot really didn't want to know. Those who learned the secrets of the junta had a way of disappearing. It was far better to play dumb.

"I'd better tell the admiral," he said to the copilot. "Take the controls."

The copilot nodded, and Roca took off his headset and went aft to where Admiral Secchi sat looking out the window on the left of the cabin. Translator Julio Pena occupied the middle seat, his nervous hands picking at a piece of dried egg yolk on his lapel. To the right, Harbormaster Manuel Marmol stared down at the black water below, his splotchy face and watery eyes testimony to his off-duty consumption of a quart of gin a day.

Roca bent toward the admiral, shouting to make himself heard above the noise of the engine and the whirling rotors. "We've made contact with the submarine, sir. She's about two miles ahead."

The white-haired admiral nodded. "Put down on her bow deck. As soon as we're inside the sail, lift off and head directly back to the base. No lights, no radio. Understand?"

"Yes, sir."

"And remember, Captain, you're not to file a flight plan. This mission never happened."

"I understand, Admiral."

"Good. I won't forget your discretion."

As the pilot went forward again, Admiral Secchi leaned toward the harbormaster, his nose wrinkling in distaste at the body odor of the translator between them. "I want to be in the dry dock before dawn, Manuel."

Marmol nodded. "We'll have the tide behind us," he said, thinking that he could be sitting in Maria's Cantina hoisting his first by nine o'clock. "There won't be a problem."

"Good." Secchi straightened, suddenly irritated by the jittery translator beside him. "What's the matter with you? You're as nervous as a goddamn cat."

"I'm worried," Julio Pena confessed in a high-pitched, squeaky voice. "I may not understand all the terms."

Secchi's dark eyes narrowed. "I thought you spoke fluent Ukrainian."

"I do. My mother was from Kiev. It's not that. I'm worried about the technical language. I'm not in the submarine service, you know."

"All I want you to do is to translate the conversation between the captain and myself. We're not going to be talking about the reactor."

"Reactor?"

"It's a nuclear submarine."

The little man's eyes bulged with alarm. "Jesus, no one told me that!"

"Oh, for God's sake, relax. You'll be aboard for only a couple of hours. Then you can go back and hide in your damn cubbyhole at the Foreign Ministry."

"I have my own office," Pena protested feebly as he sank back in his seat.

Five minutes later, the three men in the cabin felt the Blackhawk begin its descent. The pilot flicked on a searchlight and they could suddenly see the huge submarine below them as it plowed slowly up the dark river at five knots.

They heard the Blackhawk's engine change tone as Captain Roca slowed to match speed with the sub. A moment later, they were down, landing on the wide deck with a gentle bump.

As soon as the Blackhawk landed, three men ran forward from a door at the base of the sub's towering black sail. As the Argentines climbed out, a seaman linked arms with each, quickly guiding the three across the pitching deck to a door in the sail.

The moment the men were safely inside, the Blackhawk lifted off, its whirling blades whipping up the water below as it headed back up the dark river toward the naval base.

One of the seamen said something in Ukrainian and descended the ladder into the bowels of the sub. Secchi shot an inquiring look at the translator.

"He said to follow him down to the control room," Pena said.

Secchi nodded and climbed down the ladder, the harbormaster close behind him. Pena hesitated. He had claustrophobia. The helicopter flight had been horrible. And now he was about to be trapped inside a submarine. He forced back the panic rising in his gut and started down, his sweating hands clutching each rung of the ladder with a death grip.

The lights in the control room were dimmed, standard procedure for a sub on the surface, but for a circle of light from a gooseneck lamp above a chart table near the center of the room. Beyond the illuminated table, the three Argentines could see only scattered banks of red, green, orange and yellow control buttons glowing through the murk like protruding insect eyes.

They sensed more than saw the shadowy forms of men sitting or standing at their stations. For several long moments, the Ukrainian submariners made no move to welcome the visitors. Silent and uneasy at the base of the ladder, the Argentines could feel a strained tension in the sub as their eyes adjusted to the dim light.

Finally, a thin man with strange, flat eyes and the insignia of a Ukrainian submarine captain on his shoulder boards stepped forward into the pool of light. "I am Captain First Rank Viktor Lobov, commander of the *Bukharin*," he said in Ukrainian.

Pena cleared his throat nervously and translated.

Admiral Secchi smiled and offered his hand. "I am Admiral Juan Bautista Secchi, Navy Chief of Staff. Welcome to Argentina, Captain."

Lobov regarded the admiral with the eye of a moray eel, then reluctantly shook the outstretched hand. "You are fifteen minutes late, Admiral. We were to rendezvous at four A.M. precisely."

Secchi bristled. Who the hell did this Ukrainian captain think he was, reprimanding the chief of staff of the Argentine Navy? Then he remembered his last phone conversation with Anatoli Demyanov. The Ukrainian minister of defense had cautioned that Lobov "could be difficult at times."

The admiral swallowed his pique. It was vital to have the cooperation of this man if the Argentine Navy was to learn how to operate the complex systems aboard the submarine.

"Did you have a good voyage, Captain?"

"Uneventful," Lobov replied, bringing an involuntary guffaw from one of the crewmen.

"What did the captain say?" Secchi asked as Lobov turned to glare at the offender.

Pena shrugged. "He said the voyage was uneventful."

Secchi searched Lobov's face as the captain turned back. Obviously, something had happened at sea. What? He made a mental note to pursue the answer later, then jerked a thumb at the harbormaster next to him."

"This is Señor Manuel Marmol. He is the best harbormaster in the southern hemisphere. If you will be good enough to introduce him to your helmsman, we can proceed upriver."

The translator repeated the admiral's words in Ukrainian, and the captain nodded curtly and led the way across the room to the sub's brass helm. "This is Junior Officer Zhulinsky," Lobov said. "He is the best helmsman in the northern hemisphere."

Admiral Secchi cocked an eye at the captain. Had he repeated his praise of the harbormaster to mock him, or was it a gentle joke? Lobov's expressionless face told him nothing.

"Zhulinsky has been practicing his Spanish," the captain said. "He will be able to follow your harbormaster's instructions even without the need of your interpreter. Show them, Zhulinsky."

The young officer blushed. "Really, I know only a few dozen words, Captain."

"Show them," Lobov commanded, his voice no longer teasing. "Say something."

"Right full rudder," Zhulinsky said in heavily accented but passable Spanish. "Come left ten degrees, come right twenty degrees. Slow ahead. All stop."

"Splendid," Admiral Secchi said. "Your helmsman's fluency will allow my interpreter to accompany us on a tour of the vessel."

When Pena had translated, Secchi turned to the harbormaster. "Go up on the bridge and get us started upriver. Three-quarters speed. We don't have a lot of time."

"Yes, Admiral," Marmol said, turning for the ladder that led back up through the sail to the bridge.

Lobov's eyes followed the harbormaster. "Where is that man going?"

"The admiral has sent him up to the bridge," Pena told him in Ukrainian.

Lobov stiffened. "I give the orders aboard this boat, Admiral. That has been agreed to by our governments. I remain in command until I have trained an Argentine crew to sail the *Bukharin*."

Pena translated Lobov's angry words.

"I did not mean to usurp your authority, Captain," Secchi said pleasantly. "I am only interested in getting the *Bukharin* under cover before the sun rises. An American reconnaissance satellite passes over each morning just after seven."

The translation mollified Lobov and he nodded curtly. "Just so we understand each other." He turned to the helmsman "Open the phone line to the bridge. The navigation of the *Bukharin* is now in the hands of the harbormaster. Follow his instructions."

"Yes, Captain," Zhulinsky said, putting on a headset.

Secchi rubbed his palms together, as if the matter were settled. "Now, Captain Lobov, I would like to inspect the boat."

For a long moment, the Ukrainian stared at Secchi, indecision playing across his face. Finally, he shrugged. "I suppose you have that right, Admiral. You bought her, didn't you?" he said, then wheeled and strode briskly across the control room toward an aft companionway.

Secchi shook his head imperceptibly and followed the captain, Pena trailing reluctantly behind.

For the next forty-five minutes, Captain Lobov led the two Argentines through the entire length of the submarine. He showed them the galley, the reactor room, the crew's quarters, the tiny infirmary, the engine and torpedo rooms, and a dozen other spaces.

Secchi was astonished at Lobov's intimate knowledge of the vessel. Most good submarine skippers know their boats thoroughly and have a comprehensive understanding of the various operating systems aboard—but Lobov's familiarity with the *Bukharin* went far beyond mere technical competence.

The Ukrainian knew where every wire led, what every pipe and conduit carried, what every metal screw and bolt secured. In the reactor room, the captain explained the operation of the power plant with the easy familiarity of a nuclear physicist, and as they toured the other compartments, he displayed an equally profound knowledge of every mechanical, electronic and hydraulic system on board.

There was a fervent passion in the captain's voice as he talked about the *Bukharin*, and when he was describing a piece of machinery, his hands stroked the metal parts as another man might caress his lover's breasts.

Secchi realized uneasily that to Lobov, the submarine was not merely a command, a boat he took to sea. No, to him, the *Bukharin* was a living entity, a majestic metal being imbued with courage and character, and a soul.

As Lobov led the way back toward the control room, Secchi noticed an armed guard standing beside a closed door. Curious, he asked, "What's in there?"

Lobov stopped and turned around, his dark eyes hooded. "It's the wardroom."

"You keep the wardroom guarded?"

"There's a prisoner inside. A mutineer."

"You had a mutiny on board?"

"Yes, off Gibraltar. It was only one individual. My executive officer, Pynzenyk."

Secchi digested that. The executive officer was second in command on submarines. It was likely that the "mutiny" had been the officer's refusal to carry out one of Lobov's orders. What order?

"What are you going to do with him?"

Lobov patted the holstered pistol at his side. "I am going to shoot him."

Secchi was unpleasantly startled. "Shoot him? For disobeying an order? Such things are done only in wartime."

"Just so. At the time I gave the order, we were at battle stations."

Secchi's brow furrowed. What the hell was the man talking about? Then, like a hammer blow to the head, it hit him. Gibraltar! That supertanker that had been blown out of the water ten days before! His officers had talked about little else for days.

The British divers that had gone down to inspect the

wreck had reported two gaping wounds along the starboard side of the *Polyanthus*, near her stern. And the plates had been blown inward!

There were three possible explanations. The first was that the supertanker had been torpedoed. This was quickly ruled out after a NATO computer check showed that no submarines or surface vessels armed with torpedoes were within two hundred miles of Gibraltar at the time.

The second scenario was that unknown terrorists had attached time-delayed explosives charges to the hull when the *Polyanthus* was in port in Venezuela. This prospect was also quickly dismissed, for there was neither a terrorist movement in Venezuela nor a logical motive for attacking a Greek tanker.

The third possibility was that the *Polyanthus* had struck a pair of drifting mines, and this was considered the most likely explanation. The Mediterranean had been strewn with millions of mines during World War II, and even after fifty-five years, a dozen or more popped to the surface each year as their anchor chains rusted away. It was a logical theory, and the world had accepted it.

Now Secchi knew the truth. The *Bukharin* had sent that tanker to the bottom. The old admiral's heart pounded as he realized that within hours, the renegade submarine would be berthed in the midst of the largest naval base in Argentina.

The sheep had invited a wolf into the fold! If Viktor Lobov was insane enough to sink an unarmed tanker and send two dozen innocent seamen to their death, surely he was capable of further murderous acts.

The Ukrainian captain had only to give the order and the sub's Mark C wire-guided torpedoes could sink every naval vessel in General San Martin harbor. Far worse, the *Bukharin*'s 26 SS-N-20 ballistic missiles were capable of reducing Buenos Aires and every other city in the country to piles of radioactive dust.

The blood drained from Secchi's face. God help them, Argentina was at the mercy of a madman.

NEAR DUNDEE, SCOTLAND
••••••••••••••••••••••••••

6:20 p.m.–April 30th

BEN MEADE STRETCHED OUT his long legs and sank back wearily against the plush leather seat as the Bentley snow sedan moved down the drifted country road twenty miles west of Dundee, Scotland.

"You look tired, Ben," the handsome, graying man behind the wheel said in a thick Scottish brogue.

Ben looked across at Marjorie's father, the muted lights from the dash revealing concern on the kindly, sixty-four-year-old patrician face, and let out a long sigh.

"I am tired, Lord Glynn. For the past three weeks, I've spent eighteen hours a day on research. And now I have jet lag on top of that."

"Really, you must call me John."

"John, then."

"I hope you can stay with us for a time. We're well off the beaten track out here, you know, and with the snow and cold, we get few visitors. I know you're anxious to get started on the Arctic Alteration you've been telling me about, but by the look of you, you could do with a bit of rest."

"It's a tempting offer, but I'm afraid I can stay for only a day. I have to fly across to Newfoundland tomorrow to meet our research ship there, then leave immediately for the dam site in the Gulf Stream."

Lord Glynn downshifted as the snow sedan climbed a hill, the tread drive behind kicking up twin rooster tails of powdered snow. "Really, you're as bad as my daughter; both of you are gluttons for work."

"How is she? I've been worried."

Lord Glynn pursed his lips. "When she first got home, she was quite done in. Underweight, dark circles under her eyes, her nerves all a tatters. I must say, she gave her mother and me a frightful scare."

"Is she doing better now?"

"Yes, thank God. I give all the credit to Freddy."

Ben smiled. Marjorie had often talked about her "best friend" Freddy, the golden retriever her parents had given her on her eighteenth birthday.

"What really concerned me was that she wouldn't talk about what happened at the biosphere," Ben said. "She kept it all inside."

Lord Glynn nodded. "I know what you mean. She hardly said a word to us those first days. Her mother and I resolved to simply wait it out, to let her come around in her own good time."

He smiled. "But old Freddy wouldn't have a bit of it. He followed her everywhere she went, kept nudging her for attention. At first, she only petted him silently. Then, a couple of days after she got home, I passed the solarium and heard her talking away. I peeped in and there she was, curled up in a wicker couch with Freddy beside her, telling him all her troubles. I didn't want to eavesdrop, of course, so I tiptoed away. That night at dinner, she was almost her old self, though there's still a sadness in her eyes. Sometimes it hurts me to look at her."

"She's been through a lot."

"I take it you two are on the shoals. Mind, I don't mean to pry."

Ben stared into the snowflakes swirling in the Bentley's headlights. "She broke off our engagement. I can't say I blame her. The past few months, I don't know, we just seem to have drifted apart. Neither one of us wanted it to happen. I know I didn't."

"If I know my daughter, Ben, she didn't want it to happen either. She's missed you."

"Did she tell you that?"

"Not in so many words. But the signs are all there—your picture on her nightstand, the way she stands before the window rubbing her bare ring finger and staring out on the verge of tears. Several times she's gone to the phone and asked for the overseas operator, then hesitated, her face all gone to mush, and finally put the receiver down again. One needn't be clairvoyant to know it was you she wanted to call."

"But she didn't."

"No. My daughter's a proud and stubborn woman, Ben. And I think perhaps you've hurt her."

Ben's jaw tightened. "I have. I hope you'll believe that I didn't do it intentionally."

"We never hurt our loved ones intentionally, do we? Still, it's the oversight that cuts the deepest—the words of caring not spoken, the embrace not delivered, the commitment taken for granted."

"You're a wise man, John."

Lord Glynn guffawed. "If I were wise, I wouldn't have committed those same sins with Lady Glynn. And more than once."

"Did she ever leave you?"

"No, she wreaks revenge in quite another way, unique perhaps in the annals of the relations between the sexes."

The nobleman turned and grinned at Ben. "She smashes porcelain vases over my head. Done it a dozen times since we've been married."

Ben laughed. "You're kidding."

"God's truth. Brings me to my senses rather quickly."

"Isn't she afraid she'll hurt you? Or kill you?"

"No danger of that. The vases are of the most delicate porcelain. Thin as eggshells. You wouldn't believe what they cost. But you see, that's part of my punishment. She marches right out, buys another and deducts the cost from the household account. Instead of beef for dinner, I end up being fed fish and chips for a month."

Ben grinned. "I never would have thought Lady Glynn capable of such calculated vengeance."

"Right! She's a woman, isn't she? We men strut about thinking we rule the roost. Bloody tripe. It's the women who steer us where they want with their subtle guiles."

The Bentley topped the hill, and Lord Glynn shifted into fourth again. "Almost home. Thank God for these new snow sedans. The country roads out here aren't plowed more than once a week. Wouldn't have a prayer of getting about in a wheeled vehicle."

"The biosphere in Dundee's been finished for several months," Ben said. "I'm surprised that you and Lady Glynn haven't moved there."

An anguished look came over John Glynn's face, the worry lines deepening into dark crevasses beside his mouth. "I'm afraid that's not possible for us."

"Is it something you'd rather not talk about?" Ben asked quietly.

"Actually, I intended to bring up the subject. I told Marjorie I wanted to drive in alone to pick you up so we could have a man-to-man talk. The real reason was that I didn't want her to hear what I must tell you." There were tears running down Lord Glynn's face now. "My wife has terminal cancer. Her lungs. It's the bloody cigarettes, of course. She smoked for forty years."

"I'm terribly sorry, John. Is there any chance . . ."

"None. The doctors give her three months."

"You're not going to tell Marjorie?"

"Her mother's adamant that we don't. Not yet. She doesn't want a cloud darkening these last days she'll have with Marjorie. The doctors tell us that at the end, in the last few weeks, Lady Glynn won't be able to get out of bed. We'll tell Marjorie then."

"Goddammit, John. Goddammit all to hell!"

"Yes, Ben. Goddammit all to hell."

"There must be something I can do. Just name it."

"When the time comes, you can be there for Marjorie. She'll need you."

"I'll be there, John. I promise."

"Thank you. You should know that we told Marjorie we'd be moving into the biosphere as soon as we can settle our affairs. Closing down an estate like Glennheather isn't quite as simple as moving out of an apartment in Glasglow. We have over fifty tenant families to see to, and all the farm animals as well."

"What are you using for fuel? It must cost a fortune to heat the main house. Not to mention your tenants' homes."

"No real problem there. We have coal on the land. Surface deposit. Our tenants can take all they want. As for the main house, we've closed all the rooms but our personal apartments."

The headlights revealed two tall granite columns by the side of the road ahead, and Lord Glynn swung the Bentley in past massive wrought-iron gates half buried in the high snowbanks.

"Well, here we are," he said as the snow sedan started up the long, oak-flanked drive.

"I'd forgotten how big Glennheather is," Ben said, peering through the falling snow at the stately manor house ahead. "And how beautiful."

A wide, Doric-columned portico extended out over the drive, flanked by an imposing granite facade inset with large, leaded-glass windows. Set back on each side, the manor's four-story wings rose to a steep mansard roof. The Bentley's headlights washed over the mansion, and Ben could see the Scottish royal arms above the front door, and beside it, the Glynn family shield.

As Lord Glynn shut off the engine, the door opened and Marjorie came down the wide steps to the snow-covered drive, a white-haired butler following behind.

"Hello, Ben," she smiled, embracing him as he got out of the car. Her hug was warm but tentative, and she kissed his cheek instead of his lips.

Ben felt vaguely cheated, and foolish that he'd nurtured illusions of a passionate reunion. He'd dreamed of taking her in his arms and kissing her, of feeling her cheek next to his as he told her how sorry he was. And how much he loved her. Shit!

He forced a smile. "I've missed you," he said, trusting himself with no more than a friendly tone.

"Oh, I doubt that." She laughed with a bit too much

gaiety, a trace more abandoned than was her usual self.
"You've been much too busy to think about me. There've
been endless stories in the *Times* about all those mysterious scientific conferences you've been having out at the
ranch."

"If I said I missed you," Ben said, the smile steely now,
"then I missed you."

"Yes, Ben, of course." Marjorie smiled politely.

For a long moment, they looked at each other in mutual
despair, helpless to make contact, to bridge the deep pit
that yawned between them. They couldn't even say hello
without the words getting twisted, the meanings sideways somewhere between them.

"May I take your bag, sir?" the butler asked from the
bottom of the icy steps, a thick wool shawl covering his
bony seventy-eight-year-old shoulders.

"I can get it, Malcolm," Ben said, not wanting to burden the elderly servant he'd come to like during his visit
to Glennheather during the previous spring.

"If it's all the same, Doctor Meade, it is my job," Malcolm said, his white-whiskered chin jutting pugnaciously
into the cold wind. "And I have been doing it without as-
sistance for some fifty-seven years now."

"Of course, Malcolm. It's only that there are ten or
twelve rather thick research studies in my suitcase. It
must weight a hundred pounds."

"It won't be a problem, Ben," Lord Glynn said, opening
the trunk. "Go on in before you catch your death."

"Come along," Marjorie said. "Mother's waiting in the
library."

Ben shrugged and followed Marjorie up the steps. At
the top, he stole a glance over his shoulder and spotted
Lord Glynn hefting one end of his bag while Malcolm
struggled with the other.

"Stubborn people, you Scots," he said to Marjorie as
they went in the door.

"Just realizing that, are you?" Marjorie said, only half
teasing.

As Marjorie led the way across the cavernous main
hall, Ben glanced up at the wide marble stairway leading
to the floors above. Portraits of past lords and ladies of

Glennheather lined the walls beside the stairs, their visages stern in the light of an immense, multitiered crystal chandelier suspended thirty feet above the floor.

The hall was as big as the barn on his ranch, Ben mused as he followed Marjorie toward a set of tall oak doors to the right of the stairs. Marjorie tapped lightly, then led Ben into the library where he'd spent several fascinating hours on his last visit, discovering first editions of Bacon, Byron and Dickens.

Lady Glynn was seated in a lemon-colored wingback chair before the fireplace. Behind her, a wood fire crackled, sending shadows dancing out across the room's large Persian rug. As Ben neared, he was shocked at how much she had aged.

On his first visit to Glennheather, Ben had marveled at the vitality and joy that played in Lady Glynn's deep blue eyes, sparkling from a face still youthful despite her sixty-two years. Now her eyes were sad and frightened, and sunken into purple pouches of fatigue. He could see the cancer pain in the deep lines etching her cheeks and the way her shoulders were hunched forward toward her chest.

"Hello, Ben." Lady Glynn forced a smile. "It's wonderful to see you."

"And you, Lady Glynn. I hope my sudden visit hasn't put you out."

"Not a bit. We love having you. And besides, you're part of the family, or will be soon."

Marjorie frowned and took a sudden interest in a book from the shelves behind her mother.

"Please do sit down, Ben. Will you have a sherry?"

"No, thank you," Ben said, though he'd love a drink right now. The problem was that if he had one, he'd want a dozen more, throwing drinks down until he passed out. He'd admitted to himself several years earlier that he was an alcoholic. It had crept up on him. At first, he'd used booze to relax, to get to sleep after eighteen-hour days in the lab, marathon sessions that left him exhausted, yet still keyed up when he went to bed.

Then his marriage had fallen apart, shattered by the discovery of his wife in bed with his brother. He'd almost killed them both, then almost killed himself drinking to forget. He'd let his work slip, and Meade International had lost several lucrative geothermal contracts.

Finally, Mel Sanderson came out to the ranch, poured every bottle of liquor in the house down the sink and forced Ben to sit down and listen to him. The sea captain hadn't pulled any punches. Ben was drinking himself to death, throwing his life away. And Meade International was quickly going down the tubes.

At the time, Ben didn't give a shit about himself. In his months-long alcoholic haze, the betrayal by his wife and only brother had left him with little purpose in living. But he did care about the people who worked for him and about the geothermal research that had consumed him since he was a boy. He'd pulled himself together, dried out and put his company back on track.

Alcohol was the only real chink in his armor, the only thing that really scared him. That and the thought of losing Marjorie.

"Coffee, then?" Lady Glynn asked.

"Coffee would be great," Ben smiled.

Lady Glynn glanced up at her daughter. "Marjorie, be a dear and bring in the coffee cart."

"Yes, Mother."

"Oh, and some of that pound cake Molly baked this morning. It's simply divine, Ben. You must try it."

"It sounds delicious, Lady Glynn," Ben said as Marjorie headed for the kitchen.

As the door closed behind her daughter, Lady Glynn reached for Ben's hands. "If I weren't so glad to see you, I'd give you a proper scolding. I've already delivered a lecture to Marjorie."

"Let me guess; the whole time you were lecturing, she was standing there with her arms folded over her chest and her foot tapping the floor."

Lady Glynn laughed. "I thought she'd wear out the rug. I take it she does the same when you tell her something she doesn't want to hear."

"Every time. The drawbridge goes up and she's in her castle keep, impervious to my siege of words. Drives me nuts."

"You, of course, are quite open to constructive criticism, Ben."

"Hell, no. I'm as pigheaded as Marjorie. Probably worse."

"The problem is that you each have such a strong personality. I suppose you've had to have, to climb to the top of your profession as you both did. Still, that characteristic can play havoc on personal relationships. You both must learn that a lasting relationship requires constant compromise."

"I think we do know that. It's putting it into practice that seems to be our problem."

Lady Glynn sat back in her chair and appraised him with an eagle eye. "You must ask yourself what is more important to you: pride or love."

"Must they be mutually exclusive?"

"No, but one must be tempered if the other is to survive. End of lecture."

Ben smiled. "Marjorie has a wise and wonderful mother."

"She will have a wise and wonderful husband if you two ever manage to come down off your high horses."

The library door opened and Marjorie wheeled in the coffee cart, followed by her father.

"I've put you in the room next to Marjorie's in the east wing, Ben," Lord Glynn said, settling into the chair beside his wife. "It's the only part of the house we're heating these days. We turn the furnace off at nine, but I'll have Malcolm lay a coal fire in the grate."

"Thank you, John," Ben said.

Marjorie poured coffee from a silver pot. "You must tell us what you've been up to, Ben," she said, handing him a steaming cup. "The press has been full of wild speculation that you have some plan to raise temperatures in the northern hemisphere."

"The plan is called the Arctic Alteration," Ben said, sipping his coffee.

"He told me all about it on the way home," Lord Glynn said. "Simply inspired!"

"Actually, the inspiration came from nature," Ben smiled. "I was watching warm geothermal water melt the ice covering a mountain meadow out near Yellowstone. Suddenly it occurred to me that if we were able to divert the Gulf Stream north into the Arctic, the warm tropical waters would melt the sea ice up there."

"And what would be the purpose of melting the ice, Ben?" Lady Glynn asked, taking a steaming cup of coffee from Marjorie.

"The less pack ice in the Arctic, the warmer the climate in the northern hemisphere. We expect the warming trend to begin late next fall. In three or four years, when most of the sea ice has melted, temperatures will have risen as much as ten degrees Fahrenheit."

"What did you say!" Marjorie exclaimed, her hand stopping in midair as she extended a cup of coffee to her father.

"I said that we hope to raise temperatures by ten degrees."

Marjorie's hand began to shake and Lord Glynn reached for the spilling cup. "Here, let me take that."

"Ten degrees Fahrenheit! That's enough of a climb that we could grow crops again."

"That's the idea," Ben said.

For a moment, there was life in Marjorie's face again, the same vivacity Ben had seen there on the day he'd first met her and she'd led him on a tour of Biosphere Britannia. He could still vividly remember the ardor in her eyes and the passion in her voice as she'd introduced him to the life-forms in the vast mini-Earth. But now, as quickly as it had come, the animation disappeared and her eyes dulled again.

"What you're proposing is only half the solution, isn't it? It will be useless unless I can develop new strains of genetically altered crops."

"Marjorie, you've already created wheat and corn strains that can photosynthesize the weak sunlight coming through the sulfate cover. Hell, Jay Stevens has already planted millions of acres in Florida with those seedlings you developed. I told you that before you flew home. Remember?"

"What I remember is that I still haven't succeeded with rice or leafy vegetables, not to mention a half-dozen vital grains beside wheat that are desperately needed."

"Both the President and I are confident that you'll succeed with the other plant families," Ben said.

"The President and I are confident," Marjorie echoed irritably. "Really, Ben, I don't think you have the foggiest idea of how much work remains to be done. Plant genetics is not a science that lends itself to pell-mell research. There's a lot more involved than just splicing genes. Every time I come up with a new strain, I have to wait for the maturation process. I can't just snap my fingers and have plants sprout up."

"I don't think I suggested you could," Ben said tersely. "I know your work takes time."

Lady Glynn feigned surprise as she looked across the library at the three-hundred-year-old grandfather clock ticking away near a bank of leaded windows. "Just look at the hour," she said, reaching for her cane. "John, it's time we were off to bed."

"Quite right, my dear," Lord Glynn said, rising to help his wife from her chair.

"I'm glad you're here, Ben." Lady Glynn patted Ben's hands affectionately, then turned and kissed Marjorie on the cheek.

"We'll see you at breakfast," Lord Glynn smiled.

The door closed behind the elderly couple and for a long moment, Marjorie and Ben stared at each other in silence.

"I suppose it was a mistake to come," Ben said finally. "Mel advised me not to. But I'll be out in the middle of the Gulf Stream on an iceberg for the next six months. I didn't want to leave without seeing you again."

Marjorie sighed. "Perhaps it's best you'll be gone for so long. And to such an inaccessible place. I need time alone, Ben. I've told you that."

"And I respect how you feel. I'm not here to try to talk you into anything, to commit to anything. I simply wanted to see you. To make sure you were all right."

"I can't say that I've staged a miraculous recovery. I'm still rather depressed. And frankly, the thought of dealing with people again sets my teeth on edge. But I'm on the mend. I truly think I am."

"You look better."

"You'd say that whether I did or not."

"No, really. When we said good-bye at the airport, you looked like a hunted animal. Now, I don't know, your face is different. Tranquil." He grinned. "Well, maybe half tranquil."

"It's Glennheather. It's my refuge, the one place I feel safe. Here, with my parents, and the servants I've known since I was a child. And Freddy, of course."

"You used to tell me there was another place you felt safe," he said. "Remember?"

Her face softened. "Yes. In your arms. It was a safe place once. A good warm and loving place."

"When the time's right, Marjorie, when your anger and fear ebb and you're ready to trust again, my arms will still be there for you."

"I can't tell you when that time will come," she said sadly. "Or even that it will come at all."

Ben closed his eyes, numbed by her words.

Marjorie felt a spasm of guilt at the pain in his face. "I don't mean to hurt you, Ben. Jesus God, that's the last thing on earth I want to do. Please say you believe me."

"I believe you, Marjorie. You're incapable of insensitivity, much less of malice."

"Perhaps it's simply the wrong time for us. Or it's not right at all. I don't pretend to know. All I know is that I need a man who's there for me all the time, not just on the fly between meetings with the President and research projects out in the middle of the bloody sea."

"It's not just distance that matters in a relationship, Marjorie," Ben said defensively. "You might have been physically present, but your mind was always a million miles away. Every time I tried to talk to you, I could see in your eyes that your mind was on plant genetics or biosphere construction, or the feeding habits of some exotic animal in one of the biomes."

"Guilty, as charged," she said. "But that's the whole point, isn't it? For both of us, our work comes before all else."

"Your mother believes we're each too proud, too used to getting our own way."

"Gave you her 'What's the matter with you children?' lecture, did she?"

"She made sense to me."

"Oh, I know. She's right about a lot of it. Still, there's more to the breach between us than simple pride. Good God, Ben, with millions of lives depending on our work, maybe having a personal life is a selfish luxury neither one of us can afford."

"All of which leaves us where?"

"Right where we are. Sitting here at arm's length, lovers who've become strangers."

"I wish we'd never met," Ben said flatly. "All we've managed to do is make each other miserable."

"There were good times, Ben. You mustn't forget them. Those first months we were together—God, your very presence used to intoxicate me. Literally. Did I ever tell you that?"

He shook his head, his eyes studying his hands. "No."

"Oh, yes. Apart, I would count the minutes until I'd see you again. Then when finally you'd walk into the room or come down the boarding ramp from a plane, I'd get all heady at the sight of you. Really. Being near you always made me feel like I'd just downed a bottle of champagne."

"If you meant to twist the knife, you've succeeded."

"You've just told me that I wasn't capable of malice."

"Why are you telling me all this?"

"Because I want you to know that I don't take what we had together lightly. I was in love with you, and it was the most wonderful thing that ever happened in my life."

"You said you *were* in love. Past tense. You don't love me anymore?"

Marjorie's hands twisted in her lap, her face a mask of frustration and pain. "It's not that I've fallen out of love with you, Ben. It's just that I don't know if I can go on paying the price your love extracts. The emotional anguish that seems to follow as night follows day. God! I loved being in love with you. The exhilaration. But then comes the pain of your distractions, your absences, the feeling that I'm second to your obsession with your work."

"What do you want me to do, Marjorie?" Ben asked quietly. "Give up my research? Sell off Meade International and hang around the house in a robe and slippers?"

"Of course not. That's not you, not the Ben I would want."

"Who is the Ben you would want?"

"A Ben absorbed with his work, but not obsessed by it. And, yes, I know, I'm guilty of that same obsession."

Ben's frustration boiled over. "We're going back and forth, back and forth. Jesus, do we have to carve this stuff in stone? We both know what the goddamn problems are between us. Now what do we do to make things right?"

"We must have faith, Ben," she said, reaching for his hand. "And patience. We're on separate paths, and there's no turning back for either of us. We must complete our journeys alone, come full circle to where we started."

He brought her hand to his lips and kissed her fingers one by one. "I'll be gone for a long time, Marjorie. There'll be temptations—for me, for you."

"I know."

"How do we handle that?"

"I can't say it wouldn't wound me to find that you'd slept with another woman, as I'm sure it would hurt you if I made love with another man. Still, I don't expect you to become a monk."

"There's still tonight."

Indecision and reluctance played across her face. "No. I don't think it would be wise for us to sleep together again. Not yet. We'd end up saying things we shouldn't, making promises the future might not allow us to keep."

Ben relinquished her hand and rose. "You've always been a wise woman, Marjorie. Unfortunately, at the moment, I need something more than wisdom."

"I'm sorry, Ben. I'm sorry for all of this."

"Yeah. Look, I'm beat. I'd better turn in."

"I hope you sleep well."

"Knowing you're sleeping in the next room? I don't think so."

For a moment, Marjorie almost went to him. She wanted him as much as he wanted her, although he would never believe that. She wanted desperately to be held, to make love, to spend the night in that safe place within his arms. But she wasn't ready for any of that again. Not yet.

"Goodnight, Ben," she said in a small voice.

For a long moment, the two looked at each other, a cloying sadness enveloping them like a thick mist off the moors.

"Goodnight, Marjorie," Ben said finally, then turned and left the library.

For several minutes, Marjorie sat motionless, vaguely aware of the crackling of the fire in the hearth and the ticking of the grandfather clock. Then anguish and hopelessness welled up within her like a storm-fed spring bubbling up through a fissure in the ground. Alone in the vast medieval library, she brought the fingertips he had kissed up to her lips.

"Oh, Ben," she sobbed, "why can't you understand?"

It was snowing when Marjorie came downstairs the next morning. Ben was already seated at the breakfast table with her parents, the three turned toward the windows and obviously talking about the storm.

"Good morning," Lord Glynn greeted her, rising with Ben as Marjorie joined them.

"Good morning," Marjorie said, kissing both her parents. There was an awkward moment as she wondered whether she should kiss Ben, too. His body language told her that a kiss wouldn't be appropriate, and she took her seat.

"We were just trying to convince Ben to stay over a day or two longer," her father said. "The BBC's predicting six inches of snow today. I doubt they'll plow the runways at Dundee before the storm stops."

"The undercarriage of my plane is designed for a ski attachment," Ben said. "I've already called the pilot and told him to put the skis on. There won't be any problem taking off."

"Always prepared, aren't you, Ben?" Marjorie said, an

edge of sarcasm she hadn't intended creeping into her voice. "Like the Boy Scouts."

"Simple necessity, Marjorie," Ben said stiffly. "Without the ski attachment, I couldn't land on the ranch runway half the time during the winter."

He turned to John Glynn. "If you can get me to the airport, I can get out all right."

"No problem there. The Bentley's made it through worse storms than this."

Lady Glynn reached for a small silver bell on the table. "What would you like for breakfast, dear?" she asked Marjorie, ringing for the servant.

"Just coffee, thanks."

"Really, Marjorie," Lady Glynn said as the maid appeared. "You must have something, a soft-boiled egg at least."

"I'm not hungry, Mother." Marjorie looked up at Maggie. "Just coffee, Maggie."

"Your mum's right. You ought to eat something hot," Maggie said. "I've got a pot of porridge on."

Without warning, Marjorie slammed both palms down on the white tablecloth, sending orange juice sloshing up over the rim of Ben's glass. "Stop it, all of you! All I want is a bloody cup of coffee. I'm not a child, you know."

There was a strained silence at the table as Maggie shrugged and turned back to the kitchen.

Lord Glynn cleared his throat. "Ben, I'm afraid we should be off. Getting to the airport will take some time."

"I'm all packed and ready to go."

"I'll send Malcolm up for your bag."

Lady Glynn pushed back her chair. "I know how terrible that airline food is, Ben. I'm going to have cook make you a lunch."

"He's not flying on an airline, Mother," Marjorie said. "He has his own plane." She looked across at Ben. "With his own gourmet galley, as I recall."

"We do have a galley aboard, Lady Glynn," Ben smiled. "And Marjorie's right. The food's rather good."

"It's still that microwave fare, is it not?" Lady Glynn asked.

"That's true."

"I thought as much. I think you could do with a basket of watercress sandwiches and a plate of sliced beef. And some fruit. How does that sound?"

"It sounds wonderful, thank you."

"We really must get cracking," John Glynn said, taking his wife's arm.

Ben and Marjorie sat in silence as Marjorie's parents walked toward the kitchen. Finally, Ben tossed his napkin on the table and turned to face Marjorie. "Are you coming to the airport?"

For a long moment, she stared at the ribbon of cream swirling around in her coffee cup. Then she sighed and looked at him. "No, I'm not."

"I see."

"No, I don't think you do see. I don't think you've ever seen."

"What's that supposed to mean?"

"That we've spent half our time together saying good-bye at airports. It's so bloody public, so bloody impersonal. I won't ever do it again."

"I can't say that I blame you."

"I'm going to cry when you're gone. I won't do that in front of a mob of strangers."

"I'm going to cry, too."

"I don't believe that. I've never seen you cry."

"I cried after we said good-bye at the airport."

"You waited until I was gone so you could keep up the strong male front. Is that it?"

"What do you want from me? I was brought up on a ranch. Men don't cry in public out on the range. Shit, women don't cry in public out on the range."

Despite herself, Marjorie laughed. Then she turned serious. "I'll miss you, Ben. God, it's going to be awful, thinking of you out in the middle of the sea on a bloody iceberg."

"I'm not looking forward to it. May I call you, at least?"

"Yes. But let me make the first call. In a week or two weeks, a month. I need a bit more time to pull it all together."

Ben thought of Marjorie's screaming fit over the porridge a moment ago and nodded. She did need more time. "All right. I don't know yet what sort of communications we'll have out there. Call Mel on the *Abyss*. He'll tell you how to reach me."

Marjorie smiled wistfully. "Reaching you has always been my greatest challenge, Ben."

"I need to hold you before I go, Marjorie. I need to feel you against me. I want to take that with me."

"I need that too, Ben."

They rose together and fell into each other's arms. Marjorie clung to him, her fingers digging into his back, while Ben stroked her hair and pressed his lips against her forehead.

She brought her lips up and they kissed, hungrily and long, drinking each other in against the long separation to come.

"It's like a wound that won't heal, isn't it, Ben? We're together for a day, a week, and the wound starts to close. Our relationship glows a healthy pink. Then you have to leave, or I have to leave, and the wound gapes open again. Sometimes, most of the time lately, I don't think the wound will ever close."

"I love you," he whispered against her ear.

"Ben—"

He held up a restraining hand. "No, I don't expect you to say it back. Your emotions are on hold. I understand that. I'm willing to have that faith you talked about last night. I'll wait for you."

She hugged him. "Thank you, Ben."

They heard the pantry door open behind them and they turned together as Marjorie's parents crossed the dining room, a wicker picnic basket in Lady Glynn's hand.

"Here we are, Ben," she said. "Sandwiches, cold cuts and fruit. I've put in some of Molly's pound cake as well."

"Thank you, Lady Glynn," Ben said, bending to kiss her sunken cheek. For a moment, their eyes locked. Both knew that the cancer would kill her within months and that this was probably the last time they would see each other.

Ben took her thin hands. "I want you to know how much you mean to me, Lady Glynn. You're a very special person and I will miss you beyond telling."

Lady Glynn's eyes glistened. "And I will miss you, Ben. God bless you."

"And you."

There was a discreet cough from the doorway. "Doctor Meade's things are all in the Bentley, your lordship," Malcolm said in his thick Scottish brogue, his wrinkled face barely visible behind a thick plaid muffler.

"Right. Thank you, Malcolm," John Glynn said. "Well then, we'd best be off, Ben."

The four walked together through the soaring entrance hall. As they reached the front door, Ben turned to Marjorie and her mother.

"It's below zero out there. I'll say good-bye to you here."

Lady Glynn rose on tiptoe and kissed his cheek. "Good-bye, Ben. Do be careful out there on the ice."

"I will. You take care of yourself, too."

"I'll call," Marjorie said.

"I'll be waiting," Ben told her, bending to kiss her lightly on her lips. He squeezed her hands. "Forget about the work, about us, about everything but yourself. I need you whole again."

Lord Glynn opened the huge oak door, and Ben followed him out. He paused for a moment under the stone archway and looked back with a wave at Marjorie and her mother. Then he turned and went down the icy granite steps to the Bentley.

As Malcolm closed the door, Marjorie whirled and ran across the hall into the library, cutting past the fireplace to the large leaded-glass window overlooking the drive.

She pressed her nose against the cold glass and watched the Bentley start off through the snow, her fingers fluttering in a last wave. Ben Meade was the source of her greatest happiness, and of her greatest pain. She couldn't live with him, and she couldn't live without him.

As the car grew smaller in the snow-covered distance, her terrible depression suddenly returned, and for a horrifying moment, she wondered whether she really wanted to live at all.

BUENOS AIRES
• • • • • • • • • • • • • •

4:25 p.m.–May 1st

OLIVER FLEMING SMILED ACROSS the rim of his wine glass at Maria Echeverria. This was the third time she had been to his home since their lobster dinner eighteen days before.

The entire time, Oliver had remained a gentleman, showering her with romantic attention that was more courtly than passionate. Their only physical contact had been their hands, which seemed to find each other with some frequency, and a kiss on the cheek when their visits ended.

Tonight would be different, Oliver told himself as his eyes found Maria's. Tonight, he knew, they would make love.

Maria had come to treasure her stolen hours with Oliver. He praised her paintings, and asked her opinion on a wide range of art. Best of all, after the long months with the dour Ramon, Oliver made her laugh. She found she could be herself with him, for he was as young-hearted and playful as she.

"I see that look in your eyes," Oliver grinned. "You

want to ask me something, but you don't know how. Right?"

Maria laughed. "You know me too well, Oliver."

"What is it?"

"Well, it's just that you said you had a surprise for me."

"And you're dying to know what it is."

"Well, I wouldn't say 'dying.'" Maria took a long sip of wine to show how incurious she was.

"I've arranged a show of your work."

"A show?" she sputtered, sending a spray of Bordeaux over the front of her blouse and the white carpet at her feet. "You've arranged a show?"

Oliver grinned. "At the Galleria de Montez. How much of your artwork is framed?"

"God, I don't know. About half of it, I think. I've been so discouraged about it that I haven't framed anything for over a year. When is it, Oliver?"

"The sixteenth, just over two weeks from now. I suggest that you find a good frame-maker as soon as possible."

"I will, first thing tomorrow." Maria suddenly felt the wine dribbling from her chin and saw the burgundy spots on her blouse. "Oh, God. Look at what I've done." Her eyes went to the spotted carpet. "Your beautiful carpet! Oh, Oliver, forgive me. Get me a cloth. I'll clean it up. What a klutz I am."

The handsome C.I.A. agent laughed. "Please don't worry about it, Maria. The carpet needed cleaning anyway. But you should probably soak your blouse. It looks expensive."

Maria looked down. The blouse *was* expensive. But that wasn't what bothered her. Her maid always took her things to the cleaners. And her maid worked for Ramon. She might wonder how Maria had gotten wine stains on a blouse she'd worn to an art lecture. She might tell Ramon.

A helpless-little-girl look came over Maria's face. "What am I going to do? I can't sit here in my brassiere."

"You can wear one of my shirts. Come into the bedroom and change."

"Oh, Oliver, you must think me such an imbecile."

"Nonsense, it was my fault," he grinned. "I shouldn't

have sprung the news on you when you had a mouthful of wine. Come along."

Maria followed him toward the bedroom. "I remember that my mother told me to pour boiling water on wine stains. I think you have to pour the water from high up."

Oliver opened the door to the bedroom. "We'll try it," he said, leading her across the room to his dresser.

"You'll find shirts in the middle drawer. Take any one you want. I'll go blot up the wine on the carpet and start the water boiling."

He cupped her chin and bent to kiss the tip of her nose. "And stop worrying. It's a small thing, a very small thing."

Maria looked up at him, gratitude in her eyes. "Thank you, Oliver." He smiled and left the bedroom, closing the door behind him.

Maria looked around the sumptuous room as she unbuttoned her blouse. There was a large mirror on the wall behind the bed, and several oil paintings on the walls. A thick Oriental rug covered the wall-to-wall carpeting at the foot of the bed, and there was one of those Nordic Track ski exercise machines near the large floor-to-ceiling window.

Maria took off her blouse. "Oh, no!" The wine had seeped through and spotted her brassiere. It was the pink-silk bra Ramon had bought her the last time he was in Paris, and it was his favorite. He always insisted she wear it when they were playing their "doctor undresses his patient" sex game.

She sighed and reached back to unsnap the band. She would have to soak the bra, too. Naked from the waist up, she opened the middle drawer of Oliver's dresser. Three stacks of starched dress shirts were lined up neatly inside, each folded within a white paper band. She picked a light blue one with a button-down collar.

The shirt was several sizes too big, and she rolled up the cuffs to her elbows and buttoned the front. Then she smoothed back her hair and went into the adjoining bathroom. Oliver's razor and shaving cream were on the vanity next to the sink. A comb and monogrammed hairbrush sat to one side, below a set of thick maroon hand towels.

There was a bottle of Old Spice after-shave lotion next to the razor; she picked it up and unscrewed the top. It smelled like Oliver, clean and musky. Ramon wore an expensive cologne with a sweetly cloying odor that always struck her as more like a woman's perfume than a man's lotion.

Maria scrubbed the wine residue from her chin and neck and used Oliver's brush to fix her hair. Then she looked at her reflection in the mirror and frowned at how unfeminine she looked in the tentlike shirt. On impulse, she undid the top button, exposing the V of her breasts.

It helped, but only a little. She arched her eyebrows at herself in the mirror. "Leave it to you to screw up a perfect evening. You clumsy idiot!" she muttered.

With a resigned sigh, she picked up her blouse and bra and opened the door to the living room. Oliver was in the kitchen, a kettle of boiling water steaming on the stove beside him.

He smiled across the room. "The hot water's all ready."

Maria crossed to the kitchen and put the clothes in the sink. "I'm afraid the wine soaked through to my brassiere," she said, blushing. "It's imported from Paris."

"From Paris. Really? Well then, all the more reason to get the stains out. You said to pour the water from high up?"

"That's what my mother told me." She shrugged. "But I've never tried it. I've never been so stupid as to spill wine all over myself before."

"Maria, if I had a peso for every minor accident I've ever had, I'd be the richest man in Argentina. Let's try to get the stain out."

Oliver spread the blouse out in the sink and poured the boiling water directly down on the wine splotches. The discoloration began to disappear and he grinned at Maria. "Your mother was right; it works."

"My mother was right about a lot of things," Maria said wistfully, remembering her mother's warning not to become involved with Ramon.

When the stains were gone from the blouse, Oliver

wrung out the garment and put it on the countertop. Then he spread out the brassiere and tilted the kettle over the spotted cups.

Maria's face reddened again. "I can't believe I'm standing here while you launder my underwear. God!"

Oliver laughed. "It gives me a chance to show you how domestic I am."

In truth, far from feeling benignly domestic, the thought that only moments before, the delicate silk bra in the sink before him had encased Maria's perfect breasts stirred Oliver's already overactive libido.

"There, the stains are out," he said a moment later, willing himself not to think about her breasts. "Now to dry your things."

"Do you have a dryer?"

"No. But I have an oven."

"You invite me to dinner and end up cooking my bra." She began to laugh uncontrollably and fell against Oliver's chest at the thought of Ramon's favorite bra baking away in the oven.

Oliver began to laugh with her, his arms circling her shoulders. It *was* funny. More than that, it was the sort of intimately insane moment that usually comes only to couples who have been together for a long time. He suddenly felt very close to Maria.

"Do you prefer your bras rare or well done?"

Maria broke into a fresh peal of laughter. "Rare, please. Every time I overcook my underwear, it dries out and gets all scratchy." They laughed again. The moment wasn't what either of them had planned, but in a crazy, warm way, it was perfect.

Finally, their laughter ebbed, evolving into an easy, lighthearted feeling as they stood holding each other. Oliver stroked her hair, then reached down and lifted her chin.

"It's funny how this whole silly thing has made me feel close to you, Maria. I feel that we've known each other for a long time. We're comfortable with each other already. Do you feel that way, too?"

Maria's eyes shone. He'd put her feelings into words. "Yes, Oliver, I do."

For a long, electric moment, they stared into each other's eyes, hovering on the edge of the kiss they both knew was coming. Then Oliver brought his mouth down to hers. The kiss started slowly, tenderly, their lips barely touching. Maria ran the tip of her tongue along his lower lip. Then his tongue gently probed her mouth, and her teeth came down to hold his tongue captive for a moment. When she released him, his tongue eased in to explore the soft place behind her bottom teeth.

Maria arched her back, and Oliver could feel the firm roundness of her breasts pressing against him through the cotton shirt. He reached down and gently stroked her bottom, cupping the rounded cheeks in his hands. In response, Maria brought her hips in against his, the mounded V between her legs molding against his swelling erection.

Her hands were in his hair now, entwined in the thick strands, pressing his head down toward hers. His fingers explored the line of her temples, the lobes of her ears, her neck.

Maria had never known a kiss like this, so full of passion, yet so soft and gentle. Ramon always mashed his mouth on hers, thrusting in his thick, rough tongue the way he thrust his penis into her vagina. Ramon's kisses were one-sided statements of male supremacy and animal power; Oliver's kiss was a gentle and sensuous invitation.

Oliver nibbled at her earlobe. "I want to make love to you, Maria," he breathed.

For a terrible moment, Maria was afraid. Not of Oliver, but of the irrevocable step she would take if she gave herself to him. What would Ramon do if he found out? People had disappeared for offenses far less severe.

Then Oliver kissed her again, his lips soft and passionate and inviting on hers. Suddenly she didn't care what happened later. "Oh, Oliver, I want you too," she murmured, melding her mouth to his.

They shared another long kiss; then he picked her up and carried her to the bedroom. He stood her beside the bed and knelt before her, his fingers going to the top button of the shirt.

He undid the buttons slowly and opened the shirt, the breath rushing from him in a gasp at the sight of her full round breasts. "Oh, Maria, you're beautiful, so very beautiful," he whispered, leaning forward to kiss her hardening nipples.

Maria arched her back, reaching down to press his head against her. She could feel her desire rising like a tide now, and the wet warmth between her legs.

"Hurry, Oliver, hurry."

He slid the blouse off her shoulders. Then his hands went to her waist and he eased her skirt down over her hips and thighs. Maria stepped out of the skirt, naked now but for her panties.

Oliver's mouth went to her tiny navel. His tongue circled the soft cavity, flicking inside; then he brought his lips down to kiss her Mound of Venus and he kissed it through the silk.

The room swam around Maria as she felt him slide her panties down to her ankles and then kiss his way softly back up to her lips.

"Now it's my turn." She unbuttoned his shirt and peeled it off his shoulders. Next, she unbuckled his belt and pulled down the zipper. His trousers fell around his ankles and he kicked off his loafers and the bunched pants.

Then Maria knelt before him and eased his shorts down over his hips. Her hand went to his erection and she stroked him gently. Oliver moaned, his breath coming in quick gasps now. His hands reached down for her, and their naked bodies melded against each other as they kissed. Their lips still joined, they lay back on the bed, their arousal building yet again as their hands explored the newness of each other's body.

Both were warm and wet and ready now, and he entered her, then eased his chest down over her soft breasts and nuzzled her neck. Maria's arms circled his neck. She had never climaxed when she made love to Ramon, but now, in the arms of this passionate but gentle man, she could feel the moment coming.

"When, Maria? Tell me when," he whispered, feeling the urgency in her thrusting hips.

"Now, Oliver, now!" she cried, digging her nails into his back.

They came together, a shared ecstasy enveloping them, shutting out the room, the light, everything in the world but themselves. Then it was over, the tidal wave past, and Oliver rolled onto the sheet beside her.

"Oh, Oliver, never, never before has it been like this for me," Maria sighed, running her fingers over his smooth chest. "I think I'm falling in love with you."

He rose on one elbow and looked at her. The tenderness and trust in her face was almost more than he could bear. "I'm falling in love with you, too, Maria," he smiled, meaning it, but aching in his heart.

God, if she knew that their meeting had not been an accident, that he'd been paid to make love to her. C.I.A. operatives often seduced women in foreign countries, women with information the Agency needed. The normal modus operandi for agents like him was to glean all the intelligence the women possessed, then disappear, leaving them to uncertain fates.

Oliver could not do that to Maria. Yet, he had a vital job to do. General Ramon Saavedra de Urquiza was a military dictator, a man obsessed with power and money. And Maria was his mistress. She undoubtedly had information that Washington could use to influence, perhaps even to control, the ruthless de Urquiza. Oliver would have to lie, scheme, maneuver her into telling him the secret things she knew about the man.

He leaned forward and gently kissed her cheek. She smiled at him, then snuggled her head against his shoulder.

He would have to betray Maria's trust. But he would not betray Maria. When the job was over, he would take her with him.

ABOARD AIR FORCE ONE
•••••••••••••••••••••••••••••

6:35 p.m.–May 1st

THE PRESIDENT OF THE United States was lying naked in her husband's arms thirty thousand feet over western Nebraska when the phone suddenly buzzed.

"Goddammit!" Rob Piziali swore as he came up on one elbow on the bed in the presidential cabin aboard Air Force One. "Can't they even leave us alone when we're making love, for God's sake!"

Kathy Piziali kissed her husband's cheek and reached for her robe at the foot of the bed. "Whoever it is, I'll get rid of him." She smiled and ran her hand down Rob's naked chest. "Don't lose the mood."

"I've already lost the mood."

"Then I'll help you find it again."

"Jesus, Kathy, when you told me you wanted to run for president, I knew that if you won, we'd have to give up a big chunk of our privacy. But the last few months have been worse than I ever imagined. Every time we're alone, the damn phone rings or some presidential aide comes banging on our door. It's like living in a fishbowl."

"Patience, Rob," Kathy said, swinging her legs off the

bed and reaching for the phone. "It'll ease up. I promise you that."

"In a pig's ass," Rob said grumpily. He got up and stomped toward the small bathroom. "I'm going to take a shower. A cold shower."

The President sighed and hit the intercom button. "What is it, Lisa? Dammit, I told you not to disturb us."

"I'm sorry, Madam President, but I just got a call from Mark Crager at *The Washington Post.* He wanted me to confirm a story he's doing on Ben Meade's Arctic Alteration. Apparently there's been a leak."

The President's face was suddenly an angry mask. "Goddammit, if I find out who gave it to Crager, he's out on his ass. I can't run a government if every time I turn around, some son of a bitch is feeding the details of White House meetings to the press."

"The *Post* will publish its evening edition in about ninety minutes, Madam President. I suggest we issue a statement before the paper hits the streets."

The President threw back her head and stared at the close ceiling, her bare foot tapping the carpeted floor in frustration. It was a good thing Rob was taking a cold shower; their lovemaking was over for today. "All right, tell the media people aboard that I'll have an announcement in twenty minutes."

"Yes, Madam President."

"When we get back to the White House, I'm going to have Kim Haddy launch an internal investigation. I want to know who gave this to Crager. I mean what I say; whoever leaked the Arctic Alteration is in real trouble."

The President slammed down the phone and sat thinking, the muted sound of the shower coming from behind the bathroom door. Poor Rob. He was right; they did live in a fishbowl. It wasn't fair to him.

They might both be fifty years old, but contrary to what she'd always assumed when she was younger, their sex drive hadn't diminished. In fact, since the boys had gone off to college several years ago, their desire for each other had been rekindled.

The past few years had been like a long second honeymoon, and if they didn't make love quite as often—God, they'd been like minks that first year—their sex life had been compensated by an intimate knowledge of what turned each other on and a loving desire to give each other pleasure.

She'd make this afternoon up to Rob. Later. Right now she had to figure out what to say to the press. Ben Meade's Arctic Alteration had to be carefully explained to the public or there was danger of panic on the one hand and unrealistic hopes on the other.

The threat of public misconception was why it was so important that the President announce the details of the project rather than risk Mark Crager or someone else in the media getting the story wrong.

The President had already briefed the Congressional leadership on the Arctic Alteration and been astounded at how many Congressmen had immediately assumed the seas would rise when the warm waters of the Gulf Stream started melting the ice pack. She knew she would have to address that issue at once. She would also have to rein in unreasonable expectations that the Arctic Alteration would raise temperatures overnight.

She heard the shower stop, and a minute later, a towel-draped Rob opened the bathroom door.

Kathy rose from the bed and threw her arms around her husband. "I'm sorry, Rob. Affairs of state."

"Your affairs of state are knocking the hell out of our marital affairs. When you became president, I didn't think it meant I had to become celibate."

She reached around and slid her hand up under his towel. "Tonight I'll make it up to you. We'll have a candlelight dinner. A bottle of good wine. Romance."

"Promise?"

"Promise. I'll make it a night you'll remember."

"Is this an indecent proposal, Madam President?"

"It is."

"Then I accept."

"I thought you might." She kissed him on the cheek and turned to her dresser. "I have to go out there and hold a news conference. Dammit."

"What's going on?"

"Some bastard leaked the Arctic Alteration to Mark

Crager. He's got a piece coming out in this evening's *Post*."

"You were going to announce Ben Meade's plan at the dinner in San Francisco tonight anyway. So what's the big deal? You don't want Crager to steal your thunder?"

"It's not that, Rob," she said, pulling on a pair of powder-blue panties. "What I'm afraid of is that Crager will skewer the facts. If people get the wrong perception of the project, we'll be forced onto the defensive. I don't want that. I want to be proactive all the way."

"Anything I can do to help?"

"Yes," Kathy said, putting on her brassiere. "Fasten me in back, will you?"

Fifteen minutes later, the President emerged from the bedroom to find three media pool reporters and several photographers clustered around Press Secretary Robert Burnett.

She put on her presidential face and walked down the aisle, pausing to squeeze the hands of several important campaign-fund contributors who'd been rewarded with a highly coveted trip aboard Air Force One.

Burnett caught sight of the President approaching and turned toward the reporters. "Okay, cool it, you guys. Quiet down. The President has an announcement to make."

"Can I tape this?" ABC videographer Mike Brown asked as several photographers snapped pictures.

Burnett shook his head. "You know the rules, Mike. Only still pictures aboard Air Force One."

One after the other, the President made eye contact with each of the three reporters. "I'm giving you guys a scoop, a big one. In return, I want you to listen to my statement carefully and report the facts as I give them to you. It's absolutely vital that you get the story right. If you misquote me and the public comes away with the wrong idea of what we're planning to do, the country's in trouble. I think you'll understand when you hear what I have to say. Now, are we agreed on the ground rules?"

"No editorializing, is that the idea, Madam President?" Skip Garvin of the *Nashville Banner* asked.

"That's the deal, Skip. You three get an exclusive, I get a straight news piece."

Garvin looked at his colleagues, who nodded agreement. "All right, Madam President," Garvin said. "We'll play it your way."

The President smiled and sat down on the arm of an aisle seat. "I don't have to tell anyone here what terrible suffering and deprivation the Earth Winter has inflicted on the northern hemisphere," she began. "Thousands of people have starved or frozen to death here at home. In Eastern Europe and Asia, the death toll is in the millions."

"The Earth Winter also led to that massacre of Chinese aliens in San Francisco last month," Wall Street Journal correspondent Alicia McCoy said. "That's why we're flying out there, isn't it? So you can announce new measures to curb immigration."

"Certainly my statement will impact immigration, Alicia," Piziali said. "At least I hope it will. But the issue I intend to address is not that of illegal aliens but the hostile climate that's forced so many of these unfortunate people to flee their homeland."

One of the still photographers snapped a picture and the President frowned, distracted by the flash. Press Secretary Burnett read her face. "Okay, guys, let's hold the pictures until the President's finished her announcement."

Piziali flashed Burnett a grateful look, then quietly studied her hands for a moment to regain her concentration. "We have a plan to restore normal temperatures to the northern hemisphere," she said, keeping her voice carefully modulated. She was announcing a scientific project, not some breakthrough dishwashing detergent, and it was important she avoid any histrionics.

"The project is called the Arctic Alteration, and it was proposed by Doctor Benjamin Meade. I believe most of you are familiar with Doctor Meade's work."

"Meade's supposed to be some sort of geothermal genius," Alicia McCoy said.

"Ben Meade is perhaps the foremost geophysicist on the planet," the President said, "which is why I have such faith in his proposed Arctic Alteration."

"Just exactly what is the Arctic Alteration, Madam President?" Moe Daniels, the distinguished black Washington bureau chief for CNN asked.

"It's a plan to melt the Arctic ice pack," the President said, bringing a murmur of astonishment from the reporters. "Assuming that Doctor Meade's calculations are correct, if we can free the Arctic of sea ice, temperatures will return to the pre-Earth Winter range within three or four years."

For the next ten minutes, the President outlined the plan, and gradually the reporters' initial skepticism gave way to a cautious credence. Piziali made a special point of explaining that there was no danger of a sea-level rise. The warm waters of the Gulf Stream would melt only the sea ice that was already displacing ocean water. The land glaciers would remain intact.

"Why did you decide to announce the Arctic Alteration in San Francisco, Madam President?" Skip Garvin asked when the President finished her explanation.

"The Bay Area is the focal point of our immigration problems, the destination for hundreds of thousands of illegal aliens fleeing China," the President said. "My speech tonight will emphasize the point that the Arctic Alteration will soon warm the climate and that living conditions in Asia will return to near normal. There will no longer be any need for immigrants to seek refuge in the United States."

Alicia McCoy poised a pencil above her note pad. "You said living conditions will return to near normal, Madam President. Yet, if I understand your explanation of the Arctic Alteration, the project will have no effect on the loss of direct sunlight in the northern hemisphere."

"That's true, Alicia. The clouds of volcanic gases that are deflecting solar radiation back into space will take fifteen years or more to dissipate, whether or not we succeed in melting the ice pack."

"So the weather in China may be warmer, but they still won't be able to grow food crops without the sun. Won't the threat of starvation continue to send hordes of Chinese immigrants fleeing to the U.S.?"

"Part of my speech tonight will deal directly with the

food shortages in the northern hemisphere," the President said. "We have already planted new sub-species of wheat and corn in Florida, genetically altered crops that can photosynthesize the weak sunlight coming through the sulfate clouds. When those crops mature, we'll begin distributing the seeds they produce to China and the other nations north of the equator."

"Chinese agriculture is set up to grow rice, Madam President," Garvin said, "The country is covered with rice paddies, not wheat fields."

"We're aware of that. Genetically altered wheat and corn are only the first of the new food crops being developed by Doctor Marjorie Glynn, director of Biosphere America. I'm told that within the next year, Doctor Glynn hopes to synthesize new rice strains and leafy vegetables that can also grow under present sun conditions."

"Madam President, it seems to me that you're betting all your chips on one throw of the dice," Moe Daniels said. "If the Arctic Alteration fails and the Earth Winter drags on, people throughout the northern hemisphere will lose faith in the ability of either government or science to alleviate their suffering. Such a collapse of faith could lead to anarchy, a lawless every-man-for-himself mentality. Have you considered this possibility?"

"Yes, Moe, I've considered the consequences if the Arctic Alteration fails. I've also faced the certainty that if we don't at least try, this country will turn into an armed enclave besieged by millions of desperate immigrants."

The President leaned toward the white-haired Daniels, her eyes boring into his. "The Arctic Alteration is a tremendous risk. A hundred things could go wrong. We've known that from the start. But goddammit, Moe, if we don't give the people of the northern hemisphere hope that the problems can be solved, the San Francisco massacre will be only a taste of the carnage to come."

BUENOS AIRES
• • • • • • • • • • • • • •

6:50 p.m.–May 1st

ADMIRANTE JUAN BAUTISTA SECCHI wrinkled his nose in distaste as the smoke from the huge Cuban cigar in the hand of Colonel General Ramon Saavedra de Urquiza wafted toward him across the junta leader's office.

Secchi had asthma, and smoke was highly irritating to his congested lungs. He had asked de Urquiza several times not to smoke when he was present, but the general persisted in lighting up his twenty-dollar Havanas when the admiral was in the room. It was typical of the contempt with which de Urquiza treated his fellow members of the junta, and everyone else in Argentina.

The telephone call summoning Secchi to the palace had come when he was in the middle of an important meeting, desperately trying to mollify the bruised egos of the Argentine members of the crew of the *Bukharin*.

The intransigent Ukrainian Captain Lobov had been treating the Argentine sailors like children, telling them they knew nothing about submarines. He regularly countermanded the orders of their officers, and at one point had even demanded that the Argentine crew learn Ukrainian.

The training schedule was in shreds, and Secchi needed every hour to keep the operation going. Yet when he'd asked de Urquiza to excuse him from the meeting, the junta leader had insisted that it was more important for him to come to the palace and watch President Piziali's speech on television.

"Do you know what the President will announce in San Francisco?" Secchi asked de Urquiza, reaching into his jacket pocket for the small asthma inhaler he always carried.

The bull-like general twirled the cigar in his fingers. "Our ambassador in Washington said it will be a major initiative on climate alteration. He doesn't know the specifics."

"Climate alteration?" the third man present, Air Force Brigadier General Alberto Cesar Moreno echoed, crossing one short leg over another. "What do you suppose that means?"

"I have no idea," de Urquiza said. "But anything having to do with the climate affects crop growth, and crop growth affects Argentina. I wanted you both here in the event we have to react to whatever President Piziali announces."

Secchi and Moreno exchanged wry looks. Any decision would be made by de Urquiza alone; they were but rubber stamps.

De Urquiza glanced at his watch in irritation. "What's taking so long?" he asked the English language interpreter standing next to the sixteen-screen video wall across the office. "I thought the President was supposed to speak at eight o'clock."

"The newscaster just said she'll be on in a minute, General de Urquiza," the translator said. He pointed at the changing scene on the wall. "Yes, you see, they're cutting to her now."

The screens flickered, and the three members of the junta sat back in their chairs as the President of the United States appeared on television.

"Good evening, my fellow Americans," she said.

"She's a beautiful woman," de Urquiza commented, speaking over the interpreter's Spanish translation.

"Perhaps you could arrange a summit meeting with her," General Moreno leered. "Someplace romantic."

The three men shared a lascivious laugh.

"What did she just say?" de Urquiza asked the interpreter.

"That the Earth Winter has brought terrible privations to the northern hemisphere."

"The calamities are too numerous to list," the President went on, the interpreter repeating her words in Spanish after each sentence.

"Every country north of the equator is running perilously low on food and fuel. The nations of North America, Europe and Asia are now forced to import most of their food, at a continuously mounting cost. Argentina, in particular, has taken advantage of the situation to raise the prices of food exports to unconscionable levels."

De Urquiza bristled at this. "The goddamn bitch! Does she expect us to give our food away?"

"Social upheaval on an international scale has followed on the heels of the shortages," Piziali said. "There have been mass migrations of people out of nations where food is scarce toward countries with food reserves. Tens of millions have migrated into central Europe from the Balkan states and Russia. At the same time, the United States has become the destination for millions of Chinese fleeing the deprivations of their homeland."

"The Chinese are eating the Yanquis out of house and home," General Moreno said, a sneer on his wizened little face.

"The massacre of Chinese immigrants here in San Francisco was one of the most shameful events in American history," the President said. "Such lawlessness will not be tolerated. I have instructed the Federal Bureau of Investigation to hunt down and arrest the leaders of the mob. I promise you, these racist murderers will be prosecuted to the fullest extent of the law."

"She's spouting rhetoric," de Urquiza scoffed when he heard the translation. "America is a violent society. Every Yanqui over the age of five has a fucking gun. You watch; they'll be shooting down Chinese like rats in another couple of months."

"At the same time," Piziali continued, "I recognize the massive strain that the arrival of hundreds of thousands of immigrants places on a region such as the Bay Area, where food is already in short supply."

De Urquiza gestured with his cigar at the video wall. "You think it's bad now, Madam President, just wait a year. You'll pay our prices for food or your people will be eating the bark off trees."

The interpreter was sweating now, racing to translate the American President's words between the asides of the three junta members.

"There are some in Washington who call for the use of force to keep the immigrants out," the President said. "They propose patrolling our borders with ships and tanks, and troops with orders to shoot aliens on sight."

"She's talking about that Neanderthal from the state of Georgia, what's his name?" de Urquiza said.

"Senator Crawford," Admiral Secchi told him.

"Yes, Crawford. Can you imagine the assholes who would vote a man like that into office? I'll tell you, the American people get exactly the politicians they deserve."

Admiral Secchi looked at de Urquiza in wry amusement. What balls the junta leader had, denigrating a democratic process, however flawed, when he hadn't allowed any elections in Argentina for the past three years.

"Fortifying our borders is not rational policy," the President said. "It is a draconian measure that guarantees the death of innocent people, people whose only sin is their instinct for survival. Yet clearly something must be done to stem the unchecked flow of aliens across our borders. The answer, my fellow Americans, is not to arm our borders, but to alter our climate. To bring back the mild springs and warm summers we knew before the eruption of R-Nine."

"She's crazy," General Moreno said, his eyes wide with disbelief. "There's no way man can alter the climate."

"Shut up and listen," de Urquiza growled.

"This evening it gives me great joy to announce a plan to raise mean temperatures in the northern hemisphere as much as ten degrees Fahrenheit. The plan is called the

Arctic Alteration and it will allow us to warm the climate enough to cultivate the genetically engineered food crops now being developed."

"What are these genetically engineered crops she's talking about?" de Urquiza demanded.

"Our consul in Miami told me last week that they were planting new strains of wheat and corn in Florida," Secchi said. "Genetically altered crops able to synthesize the weak sunlight reaching the northern hemisphere through the ash clouds."

"Son of a bitch!" the general swore, jamming his cigar back in his mouth.

The camera began to pull back slowly to reveal a large map on an easel next to the podium.

"The Arctic Alteration was developed by Doctor Benjamin Meade, our nation's preeminent geothermal scientist. Most of you are familiar with Doctor Meade's work on Biosphere America."

The President picked up a pointer from the easel tray and set the tip against the white area of the map north of Canada. "This is the Arctic basin," she began, "and this is the Gulf Stream."

Five minutes into the President's explanation of the Arctic Alteration, Admiral Secchi suddenly paled. As a naval officer, he had a working knowledge of oceanography, and it had abruptly occurred to him where the President was leading.

"Jesus Christ!" he blurted out.

De Urquiza snapped his head toward Secchi. "What?"

"They're going to melt the Arctic Sea ice."

"What!"

"Listen," Secchi pointed at the video wall.

The camera focused on the President again. She was saying, "The Gulf Stream is over a hundred miles wide and a thousand feet deep. It carries an incalculable amount of thermal energy, enough heat to melt the polar floes were it to be diverted north into the ice fields. The Arctic Alteration proposes a way to accomplish that."

The three junta members sat in stunned silence as the President further detailed Ben Meade's plan. Admiral Secchi frowned as she revealed that the Canadian and

Russian fleets would assist American ships in towing icebergs south from the coast of Greenland.

The President ended her speech with optimism that the North American climate would begin warming by year's end, and return to pre-Earth Winter conditions within four years.

"Shut the damn thing off and get out," General de Urquiza ordered the interpreter as Piziali began to take questions from the reporters present in San Francisco.

As the interpreter closed the door behind him, the junta leader rose from his chair and walked to the large floor-to-ceiling windows looking out over the lush flowerbeds and deep green lawns of the palace.

"What are the chances that this Arctic Alteration will succeed?" he asked, his back to Secchi and Moreno.

"I think it's all a ruse," Moreno said. "A red herring to stop the Chinese immigrants from pouring into America. The Arctic ice pack is immense—hundreds of thousands of square miles. I don't see how they could possibly melt all that ice."

"And you, Admiral Secchi?" de Urquiza asked, watching a gardener prune a rosebush. "What do you think?"

"I believe the Arctic Alteration is entirely feasible. A combined fleet of American, Canadian and Russian ships is more than sufficient to tow all the icebergs they need south to the anticipated dam site."

"Let us assume they can divert the Gulf Stream into the Arctic basin. Does the current carry enough thermal energy to do what they propose, to melt the sea ice?"

Secchi nodded at the general's back. "Without question. The Gulf Stream is huge, bigger than all the rivers on earth combined. Once that immense volume of warm water reaches the Arctic, it will begin melting several hundred square miles of ice floes per day."

De Urquiza turned to face the two. "The President claims that the Arctic Alteration will allow them to grow food again in North America. If they succeed, in a few years, the Americans and Canadians will once again be raising bumper crops and huge beef herds. They'll flood the world with cheap wheat, corn and meat. The markets for our products will vanish overnight."

"We've invested tens of billions of pesos in our agricultural infrastructure," General Moreno observed. "If our markets disappear, it will bankrupt the nation."

"That must not happen," de Urquiza growled, his voice low and ominous. "Our agricultural exports have made Argentina one of the most powerful countries on earth. I will not allow our nation to slide once again into the backwater of world commerce."

Admiral Secchi shrugged. "I don't see what we can do."

"I would have thought the solution would have been obvious to a naval officer, Secchi," de Urquiza said, his eyes hooded.

"General?"

"The key to the Arctic Alteration is that iceberg dam. Destroy the dam and the Gulf Stream will continue flowing toward the mid-Atlantic, a thousand miles south of the sea ice."

Admiral Secchi paled. "If we send our forces north to destroy the ice dam, I promise you that American retaliation will be swift. They'll destroy our naval and air forces within hours. They might even declare war on Argentina."

"The Americans will not declare war on us, Admiral, for the simple reason that they won't be able to prove that Argentina launched the attack."

"What are you talking about?"

"I do not intend to send out planes or ships," de Urquiza said. "There will be no attacking force the Americans can identify."

Secchi threw up his hands. "Then how will we destroy the dam?"

"With a weapon of war the world does not know we possess."

Secchi came slowly to his feet. "The *Bukharin!*" he breathed.

"I suggest you accelerate your training schedule, Admiral," de Urquiza said, blowing a great cloud of smoke toward the ceiling. "Very soon now, the *Bukharin* will start north for the ice."

NORTH ATLANTIC, 250 MILES
OFF THE NEWFOUNDLAND COAST
••••••••••••••••••••••••••••••

2:20 p.m.–May 3rd

BEN MEADE FOCUSED HIS binoculars and swept the immense iceberg rising from the fog-layered waters of the Gulf Stream five miles off the starboard bow of the research vessel *Abyss*.

A strong westerly wind was blowing out from Newfoundland two hundred miles to the west, sweeping the fog off the upper reaches of the ice, and Ben could make out most of the features of the glistening white behemoth.

The western half of the two-mile-long berg was an almost completely flat plateau, its white surface stretching back from a ring of ice cliffs that dropped a hundred feet to the surrounding sea.

To the east, a jagged ice peak rose at least four hundred feet above the plateau. Ben inched the glasses slowly to the right and spotted a huge, harpoon-like iron spike embedded in the face of one of the cliffs.

A thick steel cable was spliced to the end of the spike, and he followed the taut wire across the choppy sea to the stern of a U.S. Navy destroyer, barely visible in the fog a mile south of the berg.

Ben could make out two other destroyers flanking the

stern of the first vessel, both of them trailing cables attached to the ice behind them. He knew from radio traffic that the destroyers were towing the berg toward its position in the dam. In twenty-four hours, the white behemoth would be part of a 150-mile-long frozen barrier cutting across the path of the Gulf Stream.

Ben felt a hand on his shoulder and lowered his glasses as Captain Mel Sanderson joined him at the rail. "Big son of a bitch," Sanderson said, jutting his granite jaw toward the distant berg. "Those Navy destroyers must be steaming at full power to pull that thing. I can almost hear the rivets popping."

Ben grinned. "There's going to be rivets popping out of the *Abyss* if you don't snug her up to that berg real careful like."

"May I remind you, my good Doctor Meade, that when I entered your employ, there was no mention of docking this vessel against an iceberg? It is not something a captain is called upon to do every day."

"I have total faith in your seamanship, Mel."

"More than I have, apparently. This little maneuver you're insisting on scares the shit out of me."

"You know, I'm glad to hear that. The very fear of failure will keep you alert. Razor sharp. You have to make your shortcomings work for you. I keep telling you that."

"I don't know how I managed to muddle through life before I met you, Ben. Your wisdom, your intuition, your willingness to take chances—these things have made an indelible impression on me."

"I had no idea."

"Oh, yes. They've also given me ulcers and ruined my sex life."

"I can understand the ulcers, Mel. You've been a nervous son of a bitch since the day you came to work with me."

"I rest my case."

"But how the hell have I ruined your sex life?"

"Let me count the ways. Last year you insisted we anchor in the middle of the Atlantic for three months, waiting for R-Nine to erupt. In case you hadn't noticed, it's a little hard to make love when there isn't a woman within two thousand miles."

"A few months at sea could hardly screw up your sex life, Mel. Assuming you actually had a sex life."

"I'm not finished. Before R-Nine, you had me down in Antarctica for an entire year. That followed the nine months we spent sinking geothermal wells off Siberia."

"You had shore leave in all those places."

"Shore leave? You call freezing my ass off on a pile of ice-covered rocks 'shore leave'? Shit, the places you drag me, the only females around have either feathers or flippers."

"What about the three days you spent in Bremerhaven loading the Spreckles engines aboard the *Abyss*? You can't tell me you didn't find some female company in those topless joints you always head for."

"I keep telling you, they are not topless joints; they are nocturnal centers of nude interpretive dancing."

"Right."

"Besides, I never got off the damn ship. Those Spreckles technicians were loading engines so fast I barely had time for meals, much less for recreation. That goddamn German efficiency is as hard on my sex life as your 'shore leave.' "

A sharp sound like a loud rifle shot suddenly crackled through the freezing air from the direction of the berg.

Mel whirled toward the ice. "What the hell was that?"

Ben pointed toward the eastern edge of the monstrous slab. "Part of the cliff is calving off. Probably undermined by the waves." He brought his glasses up. "Big chunk. Couple of hundred yards across, at least."

"Wonderful. Suppose a huge slab like that comes down when I'm docking the *Abyss* against those cliffs?"

"I'm not worried. Both the ship and you are fully insured. Incidentally, I am your beneficiary, am I not?"

"I assume that your levity stems from the fact that you will not be aboard while I'm docking."

"It does," Ben said, sweeping the binoculars across the sea toward the three Navy ships off their starboard side.

"I thought so."

"If I'm not mistaken, here comes my ride now," Ben

said, focusing on a helicopter lifting off its pad on the stern of the lead destroyer.

Sanderson looked at his watch. "Ten-fifteen. Right on time. Those Navy boys do things right."

"I hope they've done their excavations on the berg with the same efficiency."

"I glanced at your plans before I faxed them off," Sanderson said. "Looked like the same layout as the base we used on that berg in Antarctica."

Ben brought his glasses down. "Same concept, only on a larger scale. There'll be an Operations Center, sleeping quarters, kitchen, rec area, all that. And spaces for the Spreckles engines at sea level, of course, along with access tunnels down from the top of the ice."

A worried look came over Sanderson's face. "You watch your ass out on that berg, Ben. Remember those two roughnecks who slipped off the ice into the sea in Antarctica last year? If they hadn't been wearing immersion suits, hypothermia would have killed them in about five minutes."

Ben smiled fondly at the old sea dog. "I'll be careful, Mel."

"Yeah, I bet. I know you. You'll be wandering around with your head full of calculations and plans, not watching what you're doing. At least wear an immersion suit."

Ben frowned. "The damn things are too bulky. Besides, I'll be in the Operations Center most of the time."

"But not all of the time. If Marjorie were here, she'd make you wear one."

"Knock it off, Mel. Marjorie's a long way from here, and I don't mean just in miles."

"I take it your trip to Scotland didn't change anything."

Ben blew out a long breath. "No. She wants time to think over where life is taking her. Part of it's the workload she's been carrying; it's killing her. Mostly, though, she's unsure of where our relationship is going."

"What about you?"

"I love her. What the hell else can I tell you?"

The two men looked up at the sound of the Sea Stallion approaching across the whitecapped sea.

"I'd better get back to the landing pad," Ben said. "All my gear packed?"

"Yeah. Rich Kaneko packed everything on your list—both of your personal computers and a cellular videophone, all three with satellite uplinks. Plus a couple of boxes of research materials, mostly CDs and floppies. There's also a crate stenciled 'Hydrothermal.' I don't know what the fuck you've got in there."

"Equipment to monitor temperatures in the Gulf Stream."

"You did forget one thing."

Ben ran down a mental checklist of his equipment. "What?"

"Clean clothes. You do intend to change once in a while, don't you? Or would you prefer to slowly ripen, like a wedge of Limburger cheese?"

"Thanks, Mother Mel," Ben shouted above the sound of the Sea Stallion lowering toward the *Abyss*.

"Remember what I told ya," Mel shouted back. "Be careful. No shortcuts along the edge of the ice. One slip and you're frozen like a box of Mrs. Paul's."

Ben clapped the captain on the shoulder, then turned and started down the bridge ladder to the main deck as the Sea Stallion settled on the pad. Machinist Mate Rich Kaneko was loading the last box onto the helicopter when Ben came up.

"Everything's aboard, Ben," Kaneko yelled over the sound of the rotors, one hand holding his cap against the powerful downdraft from the whirling blades.

"Thanks, Rich."

"Tell those Navy guys on the ice there'll be a poker game the night we dock."

Ben laughed and bent toward Kaneko's ear. "How many kids have you sent through college so far on your poker winnings?"

"Five. I have one girl left to go. I figure about two hundred more all-night games ought to get her through Berkeley."

"I'll tell 'em," Ben shouted, accepting a hand-up from the cabin crewman aboard the chopper. The crewman strapped Ben into a seat, then handed him a headset with a throat mike dangling from one side.

"You ready to go, Doctor Meade?" a voice crackled through the earphones.

Ben glanced forward to the pilot, who was half-turned in his seat, and used the throat mike. "Let's do it, Lieutenant."

The young officer gave a thumbs-up and turned back to the controls. A moment later, the whine of the engines rose to a crescendo and the Sea Stallion lifted off, angling forward as it cleared the stern of the *Abyss* and headed toward the towering berg.

Ben glanced down at the waves of the North Atlantic. Chunks of ice the size of cars were bobbing in the three-foot chop. Mel was right; five minutes in those waters and he'd be as lifeless as a fish stick.

The chopper rose quickly to three hundred feet, and Ben switched his attention to the monstrous slab of ice ahead. As the chopper neared, the towering cliffs looked even more forbidding, the sheer ice walls streaked in places with rivulets of dirt and stones captured when the berg was part of a glacier scraping across the rocky ground of Greenland.

The chopper passed over the edge of the berg two hundred feet above the cliffs, then veered to the left and circled down toward the plateau Ben had spotted from the *Abyss*. Now he could see several hastily erected Quonsets and a large fuel dump piled high with barrels of oil and lubricants.

A communications tower soared at least two hundred feet above the Quonsets, and Ben wondered how many helicopter trips it had taken to ferry the tower sections across from the supply ships.

As they neared the base, he could make out a half-dozen tread-driven Sno-Cats moving over the plateau, most of them pulling trailers laden with tools and supplies. Here and there, knots of men were busy outside, their moist breath coalescing into small clouds of ice crystals as they worked.

Ben thumbed his throat mike. "You Navy boys have been busy out here," he said to the chopper crew.

The pilot swiveled in his seat and grinned. "We've been going day and night since the destroyers took the berg in tow ten days ago."

"It's been more like two and a half weeks," the cabin crewman seated next to Ben said. "Counting a three-day stretch loading supplies around the clock in Norfolk, then another week steaming up here."

"I'm going to put us down, Doctor Meade," the pilot said. "Hang on. There's a pretty good crosswind on the ice. Landing gets a little rough sometimes."

Ben nodded and gripped the arms of his seat as the Sea Stallion lowered toward the pad. Just as the pilot had predicted, the helicopter was buffeted by strong winds whipping across the ice from the open Atlantic, and Ben was relieved when he felt the craft touch down.

"Thanks, Lieutenant," he said.

"Good luck, sir," the pilot said as the crewman opened the door, letting in a blast of Arctic air.

Ben unbuckled his harness and pulled the hood of his fur-lined parka over his head. Then he dug his gloves out of a pocket and helped the crewman unload his boxes of equipment onto the snowy pad.

As they lowered the last crate, the crewman pointed toward a Sno-Cat waiting at the edge of the pad, its idling engine sending up a cloud of white exhaust.

"There's your ride, sir."

"Thanks," Ben said, then turned and dashed for the vehicle in a half crouch as the Sea Stallion took off again in a whirl of snow.

A tall Navy officer with deep blue eyes and a three-week growth of red beard climbed out of the Sno-Cat and extended his gloved hand as Ben ran up.

"Welcome to Ice Base Alpha, Doctor Meade. I'm Captain Todd Thorson, base commander."

Ben shook hands. "Good to meet you, Captain." He looked around. "It's hard to believe you've set up out here so quickly. You even have the communications tower up."

"When the chairman of the Joint Chiefs of Staff issues a direct order to build a base fast, it tends to get everyone's attention," Thorson grinned. "We've got the highest priority on manpower and supplies."

"How's the excavation going?"

"We're thirty-six hours ahead of schedule. Those laser gouges you sent us are working great. Ten of them were flown in a week ago, and we already have the Operations Center and half the tunnels dug."

Ben jerked his thumb at the crates he'd brought with him. "I'd like to get my equipment up and running as soon as possible. You have power in the Operations Center yet?"

"The command hub's got juice. We're still running cables to some of the other areas."

Thorson turned and waved to two Seabees sitting in the backseat of the Sno-Cat. "Shiffer, Bornschlegel, get Doctor Meade's gear into the Cat."

After the two manhandled the crates and Ben's bag into the bed of the Sno-Cat, Ben and Thorson climbed into the front seat and the captain started the hybrid vehicle toward the ice peak dominating the eastern end of the two-mile-long berg.

"You know, Doctor Meade, I've done my share of digging," Thorson said as the Sno-Cat bounced over the rutted track across the ice. "I've supervised the construction of tunnels and bomb shelters, but this is the first time I've ever built a base inside an iceberg."

"Setting up operations in the heart of the berg will give us access to the engine rooms down at sea level," Ben said. "We'll also be in out of the wind and snow. One good blizzard out here and those Quonsets of yours will be buried up to their stovepipes."

"Hell, it makes perfect sense," Thorson grinned. "Just never thought of doing something like this before. You're an ingenious man, Doctor Meade.

Ben shook his head. "Actually, I stole the idea."

"Stole it? From who?"

"The Eskimos. They've been sheltering from the wind and snow in ice igloos for about ten thousand years now."

The Sno-Cat began to climb a snow-covered escarpment leading up toward the ice peak ahead, the tracked drives behind slipping several times on the slick surface. As they went up, the featureless face of the berg changed quickly to a jumble of jagged ice hillocks cut by crevasses and yawning gorges.

Ben took in the vibrant shades of blue and green streaking the frozen cliffs as the vehicle climbed the floor of a narrow canyon leading up the slope. Then minutes later, the cat labored over a last ridge and stopped in front of the mouth of a twenty-foot-high tunnel cut into the white face of the cliff before them.

Thorson got out and walked over to an insulated hut with a motor pool insignia on the door and two Sno-Cats idling outside. He spoke to the guard for several moments, then nodded and rejoined Ben. "An electric cart will be out to pick us up in a minute," he said.

Ben surveyed the tunnel, noting the perfectly cylindrical shape of the entrance. "Your boys are pretty handy with those lasers. This tunnel has to be within inches of the specs I faxed out."

"Within half an inch, actually," Thorson said, climbing out of the Sno-Cat. "Those laser gouges are so precise that the Seabees needed only a couple of days' practice on a cliff down below and they were cutting the ice like surgeons."

As Ben got out of the Sno-Cat, an electric cart hummed out of the tunnel and stopped beside them. A grizzled chief bos'n mate hefted himself out, threw Thorson a half-hearted salute and stood appraising Ben.

"You Meade?"

Ben grinned. "I'm Meade."

"Kowslowski. I run Alpha."

Captain Thorson came up. "What Chief Kowslowski means is that he's in charge of the work crews up here."

"I like your lasers, Meade," Kowslowski said, ignoring the officer. "They burn through ice like a hot poker through butter."

"That's Doctor Meade, Kowslowski," Thorson said, annoyed now.

Ben waved a hand. " 'Meade's' all right. I don't care what the chief calls me, as long as he gets the job done."

"We'll get the job done, me and my Seabees. Shit, we're halfway there."

"Captain Thorson tells me that the Operations Center is finished," Ben said.

"Main chamber, yeah. We're still workin' on the sleeping quarters, galley, rec center." The chief scowled at Thorson. "Rec center! I suppose you're gonna put Ping-Pong tables and a fuckin' Coke machine in there, Captain."

Thorson grinned at Ben. "The chief would prefer we set up a brothel with a bar. Isn't that right, Chief?"

"Hell, yes! Ship in some hookers and beer. My Seabees aren't fuckin' Boy Scouts. They got hair on their chests and balls like bulls."

Ben laughed. "I don't think I can do anything about the hookers, Chief. But maybe I can get some beer flown in—for off-duty consumption, of course."

"You know, Meade, I think I'm gonna like you."

Thorson frowned. "If you're quite through arranging your leisure activities, Chief, Doctor Meade would like a tour of the Operations Center."

"That's what I'm here for," Kowslowski said, glancing at Ben's gear on the back of the Sno-Cat. "That your stuff, Meade?"

"That's it, Chief."

Kowslowski nodded and walked around to the bed of the Sno-Cat. In one motion, he bent his shoulder to the level of the bed, hefted the largest crate against his neck and straightened with a grunt.

"Jesus, let me give you a hand with that," Ben said, starting toward the chief.

"Don't need a hand," Kowslowski told him, crossing to the electric cart. He unloaded the crate into the cargo space, then went back and retrieved the second box and Ben's bag.

"As you can see," Thorson said wryly, "the chief is a man of great physical prowess."

"I work out every day. Beats the piss out of Ping-Pong." Kowslowski plopped the box and Ben's bag down next to the crate and climbed in behind the wheel.

"Let's go," he said, pulling a fat, half-chewed cigar out

of a breast pocket. "It's colder than a witch's tit out here."

Ben grinned and climbed into the seat beside him while Thorson got in back.

"Hang on," Kowslowski said, wheeling the cart in a tight circle that almost sent Thorson careening out the side. "I ain't no Sunday driver."

"Slow this damn thing down," Thorson yelled angrily as the cart sped through the tunnel entrance.

"Right, Captain," Kowslowski said, picking up speed as the vehicle traveled into the heart of the berg. Above them, the lights in the roof of the tunnel flashed by like lamps above an interstate.

A hundred yards into the tunnel, the chief slowed the cart, and Ben could see a pool of light ahead. A moment later, the cart emerged into a vast chamber carved out of the heart of the ice mountain.

The Operations Center was a circular chamber three hundred feet in diameter with several tunnels pocking the curving walls. Ben craned his neck and looked up at the glistening-white ceiling arching a hundred and sixty feet above the chamber floor.

The sound of an amplified voice echoed off the ice walls, and Ben looked over to where a noncom with an electric bullhorn was directing a work party laying thick transmission cables. In other areas of the chamber, men were setting up equipment and storing supplies. A half-dozen electric carts crisscrossed the Center, their cargo beds loaded with drums of fuel oil and crates of machine parts.

"Busy place," Ben said.

"Goin' twenty-four hours a day," the chief nodded. "Got to if we're goin' to meet that goddamn killer schedule you set up, Meade."

Captain Thorson leaned forward from the backseat. "What would you like to see first, Ben?"

"The command hub. That's where I'll be spending most of my time."

"You got it," the chief said, gunning the cart forward over several plastic-sheathed power lines. As they crossed the cavernous space, the aroma of food cooking wafted out from one of the side tunnels.

"Smells like we're havin' lasagna for lunch," the chief said. He pointed toward a line of men headed for a tunnel entrance to their right. "The galley and mess hall are down there. Meade, you as hungry as me?"

"I'll tell you what," Ben said. "Give the captain and me ten minutes in the command hub, then we'll go get something to eat. That work for you, Chief?"

"That'll work just fine."

Ben swiveled in his seat. "All right with you, Captain?"

Thorson shrugged. "Why ask me? I lost control the minute I got in this damn cart."

In the front seat, Kowslowski grinned and chewed his cigar.

A minute later, the chief stopped the cart in front of a wheel-shaped enclosure raised several feet above the center of the chamber. A thick trunk line of electric wires snaked toward the cell from the generator room down a nearby tunnel. A ring of high-wattage lamps shone down from posts set along the perimeter of the hub.

Obviously primed to reassert control, Captain Thorson leaped from the cart before it had come to a complete stop. "You might as well wait here, Chief," he said. "I'll brief Doctor Meade on the operation."

Kowslowski shrugged. "Suits me. I don't understand that computer shit anyway."

Ben got out and stood with his hands on his hips surveying the command hub. "All my equipment arrive from Wyoming okay?"

Thorson took his cap off and ran a hand through his red hair. "Sixteen crates, so far. The choppers have been ferrying loads over from the *Abraham Lincoln* for the past week."

"I've brought along my research on CD-ROMs. I'll need the data read into the mainframe as soon as possible," Ben said.

"I'll have the programmers take care of it while we're having lunch." Thorson put his cap back on and started up the five steps leading to the command hub. "C'mon up and take a look around."

Ben followed the officer up the steps, pausing at the top

to appraise the place where he'd spend most of his working hours in the months to come.

He had designed the twenty-five-foot–diameter command hub for maximum efficiency and ease of operation. Except for the stairway he'd just climbed, the hub was a continuous circle of computer screens and keyboards, systems monitors, communications equipment and circuit boards crammed with toggle switches and different-colored control buttons.

No matter where he would be working in the hub, every piece of equipment would be within a few steps. If a critical situation arose, he could evaluate the incoming data and react within seconds.

Ice was unpredictable on land, let alone at sea, and with over a hundred and fifty miles of huge bergs lashed together, buffeted by storms and melting below from the tropical waters of the Gulf Stream, he knew he had to be ready for anything.

"What do you say we start with the communications systems?" Thorson asked.

Ben nodded and turned toward the array of phones, speakers and computer monitors beside the officer.

"You have voice, videophone, fax and direct computer links to anyplace in the world."

Ben thrust his chin toward the bank of computers. "What about my data bank in Wyoming? We hooked up yet?"

"We patched through yesterday. You're also on-line with the Department of Defense computer system through Internet."

Ben spotted a dialless bright-red phone, conspicuous among the predominantly neutral-colored communications gear. "That what I think it is?"

Thorson arched his eyebrows. "You bet it is. Direct line to the White House. The President's science adviser— what the hell's his name?"

"Howard. Tom Howard."

"Yes, Howard. He ordered it installed a couple of days ago. Said President Piziali wanted instant access to you."

"I work well with the President, but I know from experience that her staff tends to micro-manage any projects involving the White House. I'm not about to sit still for any bureaucratic meddling."

"Brave words, Doctor Meade, but you know the realities as well as I do. Funding, personnel, supplies, all our mother's milk flows from the big tit in Washington. We piss off Mom and we're suckin' air."

"They need us, too, Captain. If our efforts here succeed, the worst effects of the Earth Winter will steadily lessen."

"And if we fail, Doctor Meade? What then?"

"Chaos, Captain. Starvation, anarchy, war—everywhere north of the equator."

"Including the U.S.?"

"Including the U.S."

"Hey, what's takin' so long?" the gruff voice of Chief Kowslowski bellowed from the cart below. "I'm goin' to eat the goddamn seat out of this thing in about five seconds."

"We'll be there in a couple of minutes, Chief," Thorson yelled down. He turned back to Ben. "I want to show you the satellite coverage before lunch."

Ben followed Thorson across the hub to where a video wall of nine television screens rose from the curving console. Two keyboards and a host of switches and dials were built into the countertop before the screens.

"A SEASAT went into geostationary orbit over the Gulf Stream last night," Thorson said. "We linked up and started getting pictures about seven this morning."

Ben stared at the screens. "My design didn't call for a video wall."

Thorson grinned. "I know. It's a little something extra that the technicians put in for you. When you're looking at ten thousand square miles of ocean, you need a big picture."

Ben smiled. "I like it."

"Wait'll you see the satellite shot," Thorson said, leaning forward to type a command into the keyboard. The screens began to flicker, and a moment later, a panoramic view of the North Atlantic from a hundred and twenty-five miles up appeared on the video wall.

Ben whistled at the sight of the vast tableau of sea and

ice. "Jesus! I didn't think we could get resolution like that through the ash clouds."

"You're looking at a composite of two images, radar and infrared. The computer combines the signals, then enhances the image."

"Beautiful! Just look at the Gulf Stream," Ben said, pointing toward the infrared image of the huge current cleaving the sea around them. "Like a big red tongue licking across the Atlantic."

"What do oceanographers call it? A river in the sea?"

"A river bigger than all the rest of the rivers on earth combined," Ben said.

Thorson pointed at the wall. "There's the coast of Newfoundland on the far left. And here we are in the center right. If you look closely, you can see the red heat signature the satellite's picking up from the Quonsets down on the plateau."

Ben narrowed his eyes at a formation of small, elliptical-shaped infrared images near the top of the video wall. "Are those ships?"

"Damn right! You're looking at a combined American-Canadian-Russian fleet, sixty ships altogether. Those radar images behind them are bergs being towed down from the Labrador basin."

Ben studied the wall. "How long before the fleet arrives at Ice Base Alpha?"

"I'd estimate four days, depending on crosscurrents and sea conditions."

"Once the bergs are towed into place, I figure it should take us about a week to string cables and lash the ice together."

"Sounds right," Thorson nodded. "Assuming a blizzard doesn't blow up."

Ben leaned toward the image of the Gulf Stream, his palms flat on the console top. "In ten days, the ice dam will be in place and the Gulf Stream will begin diverting northwest toward the Arctic."

He straightened and turned to look out over the busy Operations Center. "With hard work and a little luck, we're going to pull it off, Captain," he said, triumph in his eyes now.

BUENOS AIRES, ARGENTINA
●●●●●●●●●●●●●●●●●●●●●●●●●●●●●●

3:15 p.m.–May 3rd

CAPTAIN VIKTOR LOBOV WORE an unpressed work uniform splotched with oil, and his cap sat at a jaunty angle as he followed Admiral Juan Secchi across the marble-floored office of General Ramon de Urquiza.

Behind the two officers, Foreign Ministry translator Julio Pena trailed along, his nervous eyes flitting about the ornate office in awe. He had never been in the presidential palace before, much less in the office of General de Urquiza himself.

The junta leader looked up from the paperwork before him, his eyebrows arching at Lobov's unkempt appearance. "Sit down, gentlemen," he said, not bothering to rise or to shake hands with his visitors.

"Captain Lobov was repairing a bilge pump when we received word that you wished to see us," Secchi explained limply, at once furious at the Ukrainian for refusing to wear a dress uniform and embarrassed that an officer under his command would appear at the presidential palace in such disheveled attire.

"Do you always wear your cap indoors?" de Urquiza stared at Lobov, his face stony.

Pena translated the general's question into Ukrainian.

"Always," Lobov said, his wolfish eyes glaring back at the Argentine leader.

The normally placid Secchi exploded. "You're in the presence of the supreme leader of Argentina! Take the goddamn thing off at once!"

Lobov's jaw tightened as Pena translated. "Tell Admiral Secchi I will remove my cap for only one purpose, and that will be to shove it up his ass."

"I . . . I can't tell him that," Pena stuttered in Ukrainian, his eyes bulging in alarm.

"Tell him, you fat little fuck, or when we get back to the shipyard, I'll have you skinned."

"What the hell did he say?" Secchi demanded.

"Stop!" de Urquiza flared. "Can't you see what he's doing, Secchi? He's deliberately trying to provoke us to anger, to reduce the situation to two sides having an argument instead of an officer obeying a command from his superiors. This is how he's managed to gain control of the training of our submarine crew."

"Lobov doesn't control the training," Secchi protested.

"No? Whose schedule are you on, yours or his?"

"There have been delays, I admit that. But there is the language barrier, the unfamiliarity of the Soviet systems, other problems."

"There is only one problem, and he is sitting before us. Let him have his little victory. What does it matter?"

Secchi shrugged. "As you wish."

"Tell the captain he may keep his cap on," de Urquiza said. "Tell him I find the etiquette of the Ukrainian Navy most interesting, as opposed to the protocol of a more traditional navy like Argentina's."

Not sure whether he'd just been insulted, Lobov stared back blankly at the junta leader.

"Now, if we may get on with the meeting," de Urquiza said. "We are here to discuss a vital mission for the *Bukharin*. Ask him how long he thinks it will take to finish training the Argentine crew."

"I don't know why you don't direct that question to me, General de Urquiza," Secchi said in a huff as Pena translated the question into Ukrainian. "After all, the *Bukharin* is under my command."

The junta leader regarded Secchi with a fish eye. "No, my dear Admiral, you are not in command of the *Bukharin*. Captain Lobov has never relinquished that to you."

Secchi bristled, but before he could object, de Urquiza turned his attention back to Pena.

"Well?"

"He said that training our Argentine sailors to run the *Bukharin* is like teaching a bear to ride a bicycle; it will take weeks, perhaps months, and all his patience."

De Urquiza grinned, but his eyes were hard and mirthless. "Yes, I remember the Soviet circuses. Bears riding bicycles, bears dancing, bears, bears, bears. The Russians could teach them to do anything. However, we are speaking now of sailors, not bears. Naturally, I expect better results. The training in port is to be finished in ten days. Any further instruction will have to take place at sea. Tell him that."

As Pena translated, Lobov stiffened in his chair and gave a one-word reply.

"He's says that's impossible," Pena translated.

"That's his favorite word, impossible," Secchi said. "Every time I set a schedule, he says it's impossible."

De Urquiza pursed his thick lips thoughtfully. "When I was a boy in Tierra del Fuego, my father had a mule with a mind of its own. One day, halfway back from town with a load of firewood, the animal suddenly sat down in the middle of the road. My father beat him bloody, but the mule wouldn't budge."

The junta leader's jowly face softened as he remembered. "My father stormed home and sent me back to fetch the wood. Naturally, I didn't want to carry the load home myself, and I had an idea. I brought a couple of apples with me. I gave one to the mule, then walked down the road several paces and held out the other. To have another apple, the mule had to get up. He did, and I led him home with the wood. Let's see if Captain Lobov likes apples."

De Urquiza turned back to the translator. "Tell the captain that in ten days, the *Bukharin* will sail for the North

Atlantic on a top-secret voyage of great importance to Argentina. Tell him that if he is willing to continue the crew training at sea, I will put him in command of the mission."

Secchi came half out of his chair. "Put him in command! The man is half mad!"

"So was my father's mule, but he could carry wood."

"Jesus Christ, he's not even an Argentinian. We can't send our only nuclear submarine to sea with a foreigner in command."

"Nations have employed mercenaries since the first army took the field," de Urquiza said mildly. He thrust his jaw toward Lobov. "Translate my proposal to the captain."

Secchi threw up his hands. "I'll have no part of this."

Lobov didn't have to know Spanish to understand that the furious Secchi was against giving him command of the *Bukharin*. It made the junta leader's offer all the sweeter.

"Tell General de Urquiza that I accept his terms," he said to Pena, his emotionless face masking the exhilaration raging inside him. He was to take the *Bukharin* to sea again!

De Urquiza nodded. "Done. Ask him if he is familiar with the Atlantic off Newfoundland, the area of the Gulf Stream."

Pena translated, then listened to Lobov's reply. "He says the *Bukharin* often operated in those waters when he was in the Soviet Navy," Pena said. "The complex marine acoustics up there would make it difficult for any American ASW subs in the area to detect or track the *Bukharin*."

De Urquiza spread his beefy fingers flat on his desk and sat back in his chair. "Excellent. Instruct the captain to make all necessary preparations and chart a course north. The *Bukharin* sails in ten days. That is all, gentlemen."

Pena translated and the three visitors rose to leave. For a moment, Secchi lingered, debating whether he should try once more to change de Urquiza's mind. Then he let out a sigh of resignation and turned to follow the other men out.

As they walked down the long marble hall leading from the presidential office, Secchi stared at the back of Lobov's head. What was going on in that fathomless brain, that half-mad mind that would once more control one of the most powerful weapons of war on earth?

THE WHITE HOUSE,
WASHINGTON, D.C.
••••••••••••••••••••

5:20 a.m.–May 5th

PRESIDENT PIZIALI'S FACE WAS still puffy with sleep as she exited the elevator three flights below the Oval Office and walked down the corridor toward the White House Situation Room.

A half hour earlier, National Security Adviser Rob Bonham had awakened her from a sound sleep and requested a highly unusual 5:00 A.M. meeting of the National Security Council. There was growing evidence, Bonham told her, that there had been a serious violation of the International Arms Treaty.

As the President strode into the Situation Room, her green eyes took in the somber faces of the men who rose from the diamond-shaped table in the center of the windowless chamber. Bonham was already there, as were C.I.A. Director Dan Jeung, Secretary of Defense Martin Mune and Admiral Mike Mathisen, chairman of the Joint Chiefs of Staff.

"Good morning, gentlemen," Piziali said, crossing to her place at the table. "Is there any coffee around here? I'm not awake yet."

"I'll get you a cup, Madam President," Bonham offered, going to the sideboard. "Anyone else?"

"I could use some," Mune said.

"Not me," Jeung said. "I have enough adrenaline pumping through me already without adding caffeine."

"Mike?"

The stern-visaged chief of staff merely stared back at Bonham and shook his head.

"All right, what's going on?" the President asked as Bonham brought the coffee over. "All I've been told so far is that there's been a serious violation of the International Arms Treaty."

" 'Serious' is hardly the word for it, Madam President," Mune said. "This could shift the balance of power in the entire southern hemisphere. We must take some sort of action immediately."

"I want to emphasize that everything we have so far is circumstantial, Madam President," Jeung said. "We don't have a smoking gun."

"Bullshit!" Admiral Mathisen said angrily. "It all fits together. The deal went down, and you know it, Dan."

"Goddammit!" The President rattled her coffee cup angrily on the tabletop. "What are you all talking about? What's happened?"

"It appears that Ukraine has sold a nuclear submarine to Argentina, Madam President," Jeung said. "As you know, when the International Arms Treaty was amended back in ninety-eight, it specifically forbid the sale of nuclear-missile submarines from one nation to another."

The President stared at the C.I.A. director for a long moment. "Dan, I want to remind you that early last month, you came into the Oval Office with evidence that Argentina had just made a three-billion-dollar payment to Ukraine. Do you remember? Do you remember Larry Wiesler suggesting that the money went for the purchase of a submarine?"

"I remember, Madam President, but you must understand that—"

"What I understand is that you utterly decimated Larry's idea," Piziali flared. "You insisted that Ukraine did not have a submarine to sell."

"Madam President, at the time, our only evidence was

an unusually large cash transfer. It could have been payment for almost anything: manufactured goods, raw materials, chemicals, military hardware."

"But you now believe that Larry was right, that the money went to buy a goddamn nuclear-missile submarine? I assume that you have some new intelligence to confirm this."

"We don't have hard evidence, Madam President, satellite photos, that sort of thing. What we do have are a lot of little pieces to the puzzle that, taken together, suggest a submarine sale."

"Lay it out for me, Dan."

The C.I.A. director took off his owl glasses and began to clean the lenses with his handkerchief. "In Ukraine, the office of the deputy prime minister is responsible for fuel and energy. We've had a mole in the ministry ever since the Chernobyl disaster. Not long after we uncovered that Argentine payment, our mole reported that a truckload of uranium fuel elements was shipped south to Sevastopol. We routinely track the movement of uranium around the world because of its potential use in nuclear weapons. However, this particular shipment didn't set off any alarm bells because it was in-country, and Ukraine hasn't shown any inclination to develop nuclear bombs."

"I saw the report," Rob Bonham said, "and in Dan's defense, I didn't suspect anything out of the ordinary either. For one thing, Ukraine has a commercial nuclear-power plant outside Sevastopol. Both my analysts and I assumed that the fuel elements were headed there."

"As did the Agency," Jeung said. "In any case, the report was routinely filed away. Then, earlier this week, our consul-general in Sevastopol was approached by the Turkish naval attaché in the city, a lieutenant by the name of Ferit Emin. Emin wanted to peddle a piece of intelligence he had on Ukraine."

The President cocked her head quizzically. "Does this happen often in intelligence gathering, Dan? Somebody just wanders in out of the blue with some secret to sell?"

"These days, it's not uncommon, Madam President. Especially in Eastern Europe. The Earth Winter has left tens

of millions out of work. Selling intelligence is one way to
make a few fast bucks."

Bonham frowned. "C'mon, Dan. You're making it
sound like Emin is some hard-luck guy just trying to feed
his family."

The national security adviser turned to the President.
"Various U.S. intelligence agencies have been dealing
with this character on and off for several years, Madam
President. Emin's an intelligence whore. Totally amoral.
He'll sell information to the highest bidder, regardless of
nationality, ideology or the end use of the information."

"Not exactly a Boy Scout," the President said wryly.

"He's a slime ball, Madam President," Jeung said. "But
the fact is, his information has always been accurate in the
past. Our consul in Sevastopol knew that, and he paid
Emin the five thousand dollars he wanted."

"And what did the consul buy for five thousand dollars, Dan?"

Jeung took a deep breath. "Emin claims that about a
month ago, he had a clandestine meeting with Anatoli
Demyanov."

The President's eyebrows arched. "Demyanov? The
defense minister of Ukraine?"

"Yes, Madam President. It seems that Demyanov was
willing to pay handsomely—Emin wouldn't say how
much—to find out if the Turks were operating the SOSUS
post on the Bosporus during the winter."

"Why would Demyanov want to know about the
SOSUS post?" Piziali asked.

Admiral Mathisen's face was stony. "The Bosporus and
the Black Sea are both frozen solid, Madam President.
Surface warships can't get through until late spring. The
only goddamn reason Demyanov could possibly want to
know if the SOSUS were operational was if he planned to
send a sub out under the ice."

The President stared back at Mathisen. "Well? Is the
SOSUS operational?"

"No, goddammit! Like the rest of the northern hemisphere, the Turkish economy has been decimated.
They've mustered out ninety percent of their armed
forces and closed most of their bases. The Turks still oper-

ate the SOSUS post during the summer months, but they close it down in the winter to save on manpower and fuel. They claim that with the Strait frozen over, the SOSUS isn't needed anyway."

"Why hasn't the U.S. or some other NATO nation gone in there and taken over the SOSUS operation?" The President asked.

Mathisen shrugged. "It was a matter of not wanting to embarrass the Turks. I'm not saying that losing our listening post on the Bosporus didn't make Atlantic Fleet headquarters a little nervous. But frankly, with the Russian Black Sea ports frozen solid, and no ship traffic going in or out during the winter, we didn't see any crying need to monitor the Strait ourselves."

Dan Jeung took a handkerchief from his coat pocket and wiped the sheen of sweat from his forehead. "Naturally, this new intelligence from Emin changed the way we were looking at the situation. We got back in touch with our mole in the deputy prime minister's office and had him track down the grade of the fuel that was trucked into Sevastopol."

The C.I.A. director hesitated, his face glum. "A few hours ago, our control officer at the embassy in Kiev met with the mole. Immediately afterward, he sent me a coded cable. The fuel was highly enriched uranium 235, around ninety-percent pure. As soon as I heard that, I asked Rob to call this meeting."

The President continued to stare at Jeung. "I don't know the first thing about uranium, Dan. Help me out here. What does purity have to do with it?"

"Well, as an example, the fuel used in a commercial nuclear plant runs two- to five-percent pure. The uranium in a nuclear weapon is ninety-five-percent pure."

Admiral Mathisen brought his palms down hard on the tabletop, rattling the coffee cups. "There is only one reactor that specifically uses ninety-percent pure U-235, Madam President, and that is the power plant aboard a nuclear sub."

Piziali sank slowly back in her chair, an pained expression on her face. "Quite obviously, gentlemen, Ukraine has sold a nuclear submarine to Argentina. The question is, where did the sub come from in the first place?"

Admiral Mathisen ran a hand through his thinning hair. "They sure as hell didn't buy it from another nation, Madam President. Before I came over here, I had Norfolk run a computer check on all non-NATO nuclear subs. There are only a couple of dozen worldwide, and we know precisely where every one of those boats are, even those at sea."

"Is it possible that the Ukrainians built a new submarine?" Piziali asked.

"No, Madam President, it is not," Martin Mune said. "They simply don't possess the technology. The scientists and engineers who built the Soviet submarine fleet were primarily Russians. And the boats were built in Russian yards. Ukraine doesn't have a shipbuilding industry, much less one sophisticated enough to construct a nuclear submarine."

The President shook her head. "Am I missing something here? If they didn't buy it and they didn't build it, where the hell did it come from? The thing didn't just materialize out of thin air!"

"I think it's the *Bukharin*," Admiral Mathisen said.

"Impossible!" Rob Bonham exclaimed. "That boat sank in the Black Sea ten years ago."

Mathisen shifted his weight, wincing as a bolt of pain shot up his spine from his arthritic hips. "So the Soviets said. But we never sent a search sub into the Black Sea to verify the wreckage."

"That's pretty farfetched, Mike," Bonham said. "For one thing, the *Bukharin* hasn't been sighted in ten years. And neither our SOSUS array nor any of our ASW subs have picked up her acoustical signature since ninety-one."

"All that only means she hasn't been to sea. The bastards could have had her stashed somewhere."

"Hold on a minute," Jeung said. "Mike might be onto something here. When the U-235 stuff came in, I went back and looked at the Agency files on the Black Sea Fleet. It seems that when the *Bukharin* went down, the KGB launched an intensive investigation. They had agents crawling all over Sevastopol. It was highly unusual for them to be sticking their noses into what was essentially a navy matter. According to our records, there were rumors at the time that a handful of Ukrainian crewmen aboard had mutinied and scuttled the sub."

"There are two possibilities," Mathisen said. "One, the Ukrainian crewmen mutinied all right, but instead of scuttling the boat, they staged the sinking and then sailed the sub to Ukraine and hid it somewhere along the coast."

"I don't know, Mike." Martin Mune shook his head dubiously. "Ten years! You gotta figure someone would have leaked the information."

"What's the second possibility, Mike?" the President asked.

"Suppose they did scuttle her ten years ago. Assuming the crewmen made it out, they would have known exactly where the sub was. They could have gone out with a salvage vessel and brought her back up."

Mune said, "After ten years on the bottom? She would have been a useless hulk, a six-hundred-foot tube of rusty rivets and peeling plates."

"Goddammit, Martin!" Mathisen exploded. "If it's not the *Bukharin*, you tell me what sub we're talking about here!"

"All right, calm down, Mike," the President said. "Let's assume for the moment we can I.D. the specific sub later on. What I want to know is where the submarine is now."

"It's somewhere in the Mediterranean," Bonham said confidently. "Got to be."

"Why do you assume that, Rob?" the President asked.

"Because there are only two ways out of that body of water, Madam President: the Suez Canal and the Strait of Gibraltar. Obviously, they're not going to calmly sail a six-hundred-foot nuclear submarine through the system of locks at Suez for all the world to see. And Gibraltar's wired like a circuit board: SOSUS, sonar-equipped patrol boats, you name it. There's no way a sub could slip through undetected."

"It doesn't make sense," the President said. "Why would Argentina purchase a nuclear submarine from

Ukraine if they can't get the boat out of the Mediterranean?"

"Maybe they plan to cut it up into several sections and ship it out aboard a couple of freighters," Mune suggested.

Admiral Mathisen shook his head. "No way. If she were a conventional vessel, yeah, they might try that. But a sub's different. She's got to be able to take immense pressures during deep dives. If you cut one apart and then re-weld it, you're taking a terrible chance that one of the new rivets will pop or a seam will burst. No, once a sub's built, you never, but never, play around with the integrity of the hull."

Bonham tapped the tabletop with a pencil. "Suppose that instead of cutting her up, you disguise her."

"How the hell do you disguise a nuclear submarine?" Mune asked.

"You could weld a fake deck and superstructure over the sub and make her look like a freighter. Give her a smokestack, portholes, the whole nine yards. Then sail her out through Gibraltar on the surface with no one the wiser."

"That would require a shipyard somewhere in the Mediterranean," the President pointed out.

"I've thought of that," Bonham said, warming to the subject. "Remember Aristotle Onassis? Married Jackie Kennedy back in the sixties. He was born a Greek, but he became an Argentine citizen. His shipping empire used Greek ships and crews, but it was based in Buenos Aires. And the Argentine-Greek connection still exists. Suppose the junta arranged for the sub to be transformed into a Greek freighter or a big tanker?"

"Jesus Christ!" Admiral Mathisen said suddenly, his face turning pale. "That Greek tanker!"

The others stared at him.

"What is it, Mike?" the President asked.

The white-haired admiral let out a long, weary breath. "That sub's not in the Mediterranean, Madam President. She's escaped to sea. Odds are she's in Argentina by now."

"What are you talking about?" Jeung asked. "The

SOSUS listening post at Gibraltar hasn't picked up any unidentified sub."

"Any of you remember that Greek supertanker that blew apart off Gibraltar last month?" Mathisen asked.

"Yeah, she hit a couple of World War II mines that had drifted into the sea-lanes," Jeung said.

"That's pure nonsense," Mathisen scowled. "I didn't believe that explanation when the British came up with it. Those old mines didn't have the explosive power to inflict the damage that tanker sustained. Any of you see the photographs of the wreck the British submersible brought up? I did. The *Polyanthus* had two holes in her the size of freight cars."

The admiral shook his head. "No, mines didn't sink the *Polyanthus*. She was sent to the bottom by that Ukrainian sub."

"Jesus, Mike, what the hell are you talking about?" Bonham asked, his eyes as big as saucers. "Why in God's name would the Ukrainians want to sink an unarmed Greek tanker?"

"To mask their escape from the Mediterranean," Mathisen said bluntly.

"I'm not sure I understand, Mike," the President said. "How would sinking a ship help the sub escape?"

"The explosion and the sounds of the ship breaking apart deafened the SOSUS at Gibraltar for at least an hour, Madam President. That's long enough for a sub to slip through the Strait undetected."

For a long moment, the President and the others stared wordlessly at the chairman of the Joint Chiefs.

"You realize what you're suggesting, Mike?" the President said finally. "Twenty Greek seamen died when the *Polyanthus* went down."

"That's right, Madam President. And so far, the captain of that sub has only used his torpedoes. If it's the *Bukharin*, he's also got twenty SS-N-Twenty sea-launched ballistic missiles aboard. Those weapons carry multiple nuclear warheads."

Rob Bonham's mouth worked like a landed fish. "Son of a bitch! Those things have a range of six thousand miles."

Mathisen stared hard at Bonham. "That's right, Rob, and a man who's killed twenty innocent people in cold blood would have no compunction about killing twenty million more."

The admiral turned to the President. "We've got to find the *Bukharin*, Madam President. If we don't, the Argentine junta will have a nuclear sword to hang over our heads. And given their history, the bastards won't hesitate to use it."

GLENNHEATHER MANOR, SCOTLAND
• •

9:05 a.m.–May 6th

MARJORIE GLYNN WAS BOILING water for tea, watching the steam from the kettle waft up to shudder the leaves of the dried garlic ropes hanging from the iron pothooks above the huge old Glennheather kitchen stove, when the solution to her plant-genetics research was suddenly there in her mind.

At once, she saw it, and was amazed that she hadn't seen it before. The answer was simultaneously simple and complex.

She had been able to alter the DNA structure of several strains of wheat and corn to the point where the plants were able to carry on photosynthesis in the weak sunlight filtering through the volcanic clouds over the northern hemisphere.

Yet, despite the apparent success of the crops the National Science Foundation had planted in Florida, she had been doubtful that the new strains of corn and wheat would thrive farther north in the farming regions of the U.S., Europe and Asia, where the sunlight filtering through the clouds was far weaker. She was also uncertain that she could alter the DNA of chlorophyll-rich leafy vegetables enough that they could carry on photosynthesis under the Earth Winter conditions.

And now, suddenly, the steam rising from the kettle had reminded her of a seafloor geothermal site Ben had videotaped from his submersible, *Yellowstone*. Five hundred miles off the coast of Ecuador, he'd discovered a "black smoker," a hot spring jetting up through the seafloor. The spring was emitting sulfide-laden water heated to over six hundred and fifty degrees Fahrenheit by a magma source below.

Far more remarkable than the hot springs shown in the video was the oasis of life surrounding the vent: a profusion of giant clams, crabs, tube worms and other organisms surviving far from the light of the sun.

Unlike virtually all other life on earth, the animals and plants surrounding the hot springs were neither directly nor indirectly dependent on photosynthesis. Instead, in a process known as chemosynthesis, they fed on the chemicals rising from the mantle. As a life-support strategy, chemosynthesis was far simpler than photosynthesis, and biologists now believed that ocean-floor hot springs were most likely the origin of life on earth.

As she stood in the kitchen, snatches of DNA research raced through Marjorie's mind like the careening cars of an out-of-control freight train. Could it be possible to graft genes from a chemosynthetic life-form to a photosynthetic species?

Marjorie shuddered at the enormity of the inspiration that had materialized so suddenly. She knew at once, even as the star-burst of the idea burned brilliantly, that what she must do would invoke great costs, and threaten great careers. Learned scientists, their life's work threatened by the proposal, would fight her tooth and nail to discredit the theory. If there were some basic flaw in the concept that she was blind to, her cannibalistic colleagues would ridicule her, possibly even ruin her.

But! But if she were right, she would stand the whole field of agronomic genetics on its collective head. The hypothesis was untested; as far as she knew, it had never even been postulated.

From somewhere at the edge of the potpourri of ideas

simmering in her brain, she could smell the garlic bulbs as they softened and grew pungent from the warm steam. The aroma had wafted out to the dining room, drawing a curious Lady Glynn to the kitchen door.

"Marjorie, dear, what on earth are you cooking in here? The dining room smells like an Italian restaurant."

Marjorie turned and smiled at her mother. It was a bittersweet smile, for she had cornered her evasive father two days before and grilled him about her mother's obvious weight loss and haggard appearance. With tears streaming down his face, her father had finally told Marjorie of her mother's cancer and the doctor's prognosis that Lady Glynn had only a few months to live.

"Mother, what are you doing up? You should be resting in bed until noon, at least."

"Nonsense. I'm not an invalid. What's that garlic smell?"

Marjorie pointed at the stove. "It's only the teakettle steam loosing the aroma of the bulbs."

"Well, it's quite put me off from my sausage and eggs," Lady Glynn laughed. "I suddenly have this craving for clams oreganato."

"I could make it for lunch."

"I don't know if we have any clams."

"There's a tin in the cupboard. I saw it the other day when I was looking for powdered sugar, which we're out of, by the way."

Lady Glynn sighed. "Lord, we have little but the basics in the cupboard now. The last time I was in the market, it reminded me of that trip your father and I took to Hungary back in the seventies; nothing on the shelves but lard and pigs' knuckles and the like. The sort of things only the oddest people eat."

"Yes," Marjorie said, her face still alight with her new sense of direction. "Food is a terrible problem these days."

Lady Glynn cocked her head at her daughter's happy expression. "Here, what's going on in that busy mind of yours?"

Marjorie laughed and gave her mother a hug. "You've always been able to read me, haven't you?"

"Well, I did give birth to you, and most mothers understand their children rather thoroughly. You'll realize that someday, when you have your own children."

"Assuming that day ever comes," Marjorie said wistfully.

Lady Glynn patted her daughter's hand. "It will come, never fear. I have seen the love that's there between you and Ben."

"Mother—"

"No, I know what you're going to say. You two are on the rocks. It will pass, as did the unhappy times between your father and me. Life isn't perfect, Marjorie, nor are we poor humans who are passing through it. We all have faults and fears that muddle up our lives."

Lady Glynn took her daughter's hands. "There are times when we must simply endure, as you must do now. If you have faith in the love you and Ben share, it will all come right in the end. Trust me."

"I do trust you, Mother. You are the wisest person I've ever known."

"I think you're wildly exaggerating, but I thank you nonetheless. Now tell me what you were thinking about when I came in. By the look of you, you're mulling over some wonderful idea."

"It's terribly technical, Mother. I'm not sure you'd understand the scientific terms."

"I've followed your work for a long time, my dear, and I do read a few things beyond the *Gardening Club Journal*, you know."

Marjorie laughed. "All right, then. I'll fix us some tea and tell you all about it. I warn you, though—if I see your eyes begin to glaze over, I'll immediately stop."

For the next half hour, Marjorie told her mother of the inspiration she'd had. Lady Glynn listened quietly, asking only occasional questions, silently enjoying the animation that had returned to her daughter's face. Finally, Marjorie sat back in her chair and ran a hand through her hair. "Well, what do you think? Am I on to something, or have I taken a flight of fancy?"

"I'm certainly not a scientist, and you were right that some of your technical terms are beyond me. That said, I haven't followed your work all these years without learning a few things about microbiology. It seems to me that it all comes down to whether or not you can successfully transfer the properties of chemosynthetic cells to photosynthetic plants."

"That's it in a nutshell, Mother. If I can do that, we could raise plants that derive their energy from sulfides we could add to the soil. That would drastically reduce the amount of sunlight the plants need and allow us to raise food crops even in the higher northern latitudes, where the volcanic gases are the thickest."

Lady Glynn's eyes glowed. "What a mind you have, Marjorie. I'm so proud of you."

"Thank you, Mother. But I'm a long way from producing chemosynthetic crops."

"What's your first step?"

"I have to get samples of the life-forms around those seafloor vents I told you about." Marjorie's face suddenly took on a faraway look. "The last time I was in a submersible, Ben and I dove to the floor of the Irish Sea. It was only last year, but it seems a lifetime ago now."

"At the risk of sounding like a scheming woman, it sounds to me like a very logical reason for spending some time with Ben. I imagine it would be quite cozy in a submersible alone at the bottom of the sea with him."

"Mother, really!"

"Only a thought, my dear."

Marjorie laughed. "Right. Actually, the *Yosemite* would be just perfect for retrieving the specimens I need. It has all sorts of retractable arms that can reach out and grab things off the seafloor."

"May I make a suggestion?"

"You're going to make it whether I say yes or no."

"That's what mothers are for. Now, why don't you call Ben, then pack a bag and catch the next plane over?"

"No, Mother, I can't leave you. Not now."

"Not while I'm dying, you mean."

"That's not what I was going to say."

"I know it isn't, but that's what's in your mind. Let me tell you something, Marjorie. There are two of us dying in this house; I'm dying of cancer and you're slowly dying

of a broken heart. I can't do anything about the cancer
that's killing me, but you can put a stop to the thing that's
killing you."

"I'll go in a month or two perhaps."

"Listen to me, Marjorie. Go back to your work, go back
to your life." Lady Glynn reached across the table and
laid her hand against her daughter's face. "Go back to
Ben."

"If I went, you'd call and tell me if things get . . . well,
if . . ."

"If I think the end's near, I'll call. I promise you I will.
But for heaven's sake, don't dwell on it. I don't. The doctors tell me I have several months."

"Several months! As if that were very long."

"You're wrong, Marjorie. It's a long time. It's strange
about time. Every minute is precious to me now, so I
spend my minutes far more wisely than I used to. I experience more now, I take in more in an hour than I used to in a
week."

"I'm not sure I understand."

"A good example is that Persian rug in the library. I've
been walking on it for over forty years, ever since I came
to Glennheather as a bride. Yet I never really looked at it,
never realized what intricate patterns and changing
shapes it has. Did you know that it has over fifty differ-
ent-hued threads?"

Marjorie smiled. "No, I'm afraid I've never paid it that
much attention."

"There, you see. I hadn't either until a couple of weeks
ago. I suddenly looked down and realized what a work of
art I'd been traipsing over for the past four decades. It's
the same with the beauty of the woods, the feel of the
wind on my face, the warm, pungent smell of the animals
in the barn. I'm really sensing everything around me for
the first time, discovering the world I've lived in all my
life. There's much more for me to experience, for me to
do."

Marjorie stared at her hands for a long moment. "I have
a lot to do, too. Don't I?"

"Yes, you do. You have a grave responsibility as well.
Your work could provide food for those hundreds of mil-

lions of starving people in the northern hemisphere. You cannot, must not, put off your research."

"Very well, then. I'll need a couple of weeks of solitude here to work out the basic theory. Then I'm going back out into the world."

"What about Ben?"

Marjorie smiled. "Yes, Mother. I'm going back to him, too."

ICE BASE ALPHA
•••••••••••••••••

11:15 a.m.–May 7th

BEN MEADE STOOD WITH his hands on his hips, his mind a thousand miles north in the Arctic as he stared at the satellite infrared image of the Gulf Stream on the video wall before him.

Flowing north toward the polar ice cap, the immense river in the sea cut across the screens in a spectrum of red-hued shades ranging from pink at the cooler outer edges of the current to deep purple in the center.

The iceberg dam was working exactly as his computer projections had predicted. The entire Gulf Stream was now moving northward at four miles an hour, carrying five billion cubic feet of warm water a second toward the Arctic basin.

Ben estimated that the head of the immense current would reach the polar ice fields two thousand miles to the north in three weeks. Almost immediately, the warm water would begin melting the leading edge of the floes. In the weeks and months that followed, the sea ice would gradually retreat, and the winds blowing south across Canada and the U.S. would begin to warm.

"Meade, you up there?" Ben heard the gruff voice of

Chief Bos'n Mate Ignatius Kowslowski bellow from the floor of the Operations Center ten feet below.

Ben crossed the command hub to the stairs leading down to the Center. Chief Kowslowski stared back at him from behind the wheel of an electric cart.

"How are you doing, Chief?"

"I got a hangover, that's how I'm doin'."

"Not surprising, considering that you drank something like a case of beer all by yourself last night."

"Hey, I hadn't had a beer in six weeks. I was like a camel soaking up water after bein' out in the desert."

The night before, Ben had thrown a party to celebrate the completion of the dam. He'd had several hundred pounds of steaks and lobsters flown out from Newfoundland, along with champagne, liquor and a hundred cases of beer. The party had gone on for half the night, with Chief Kowslowski, a can of beer in each hand, leading the celebration.

"The last time I saw you, Chief, you were doing the hula on a tabletop, wearing nothing but a ratty-looking grass skirt."

Kowslowski shook his head sheepishly. "Don't remind me. I woke up this morning with patches of that straw stuff the liquor bottles come packed in stuck all over my ass."

"You were the life of the party, Chief," Ben said, descending the stairs.

Kowslowski shook his head remorsefully. "It's going to take me years to live this one down. Years."

"You do remember promising me a tour of the base this morning?"

"That's why I'm here, Meade. Where do you want to start?"

"I'd like to inspect one of the engine rooms. I haven't had a chance to look over the Spreckles engines yet."

"Climb in and I'll take you down."

Ben got in the passenger side and the chief started the cart across the cavernous Operations Center toward one of the tunnels pocking the far wall.

"I thought you used the Spreckles engines down in Antarctica last year," Kowslowski said. "Leastwise that's what your ship's captain, Sanderson, told me."

"We did, but they were first-generation. I understand the newer engines have twice the horsepower."

"They'd have to be powerful to keep a hundred-and-fifty-mile line of bergs stationary in the Gulf Stream."

The cart entered the tunnel and began to snake down a ten-foot-wide curving passageway that reminded Ben of an exit ramp in a parking garage. "Your Seabees did a hell of job cutting out this tunnel," Ben said, appraising the glistening walls. "It looks like a perfect spiral."

"It is. My boys are tops when it comes to tunneling. Truth is, though, those laser computer programs you sent out made our work pretty easy. Basically, all we had to do was mount the laser on a robot cart, enter the distance from the Operations Center down to sea level, and the software program took over and guided the lasers down through the ice."

"C'mon, Chief, I know damn well it wasn't that easy. You still had to feed power lines in here as the lasers descended. And pump the meltwater out. That must have been a bitch. I know it was in Antarctica."

"Yeah, that was a little hairy. A couple of times the water got too deep in the tunnel and shorted the cart. Still, it wasn't as bad as when we started cutting out the Operations Center. We had up to five lasers burning away the ice at once. I had to requisition pumps from half the ships in the fleet to carry off the meltwater."

"How did the lasers work at a distance, when you were sizing bergs to fit them into place in the dam?"

"Fantastic! We were splitting bergs with those lasers from a distance of four or five miles."

"The research staff developed that long-range laser capability only last year," Ben said. "Before that, you had to be pretty close to whatever you were cutting."

"Reminds me of that 'Star Wars' program President Reagan was threatening the Soviets with back in the mideighties," Kowslowski said.

"Actually, the basic research on long-range lasers was started then," Ben said. "Most of the work was done at the Lawrence Livermore Laboratory in California."

Kowslowski guided the cart to one side as an electric

personnel carrier hummed up the ramp from the engine room.

"Hi ya, honey," one of the men aboard yelled out as they passed. "You gonna be dancing at the luau tonight?"

"Fuck you!" the chief snorted, bringing a peal of laughter from the carrier.

"Who are those guys?" Ben asked.

"Engine-room crew." Kowslowski glanced at his watch. "They just got relieved."

Ben turned in his seat. "Three men to a shift?"

"Yeah. They really need only one guy to watch pressure gauges and the like. But you know the Navy; the regs say there's got to be an engineering officer and two oilers on duty at all times."

A couple of minutes later, the spiraling ramp fed out into the engine room and both men squinted in the sudden glare of the halogen lights overhead. The chief guided the cart across the forty-foot space and stopped next to a young lieutenant junior grade who was jotting down figures from a bank of gauges.

"Well, well, if it isn't the lovely and talented Chief Kowslowski," the lieutenant grinned. "Did you bring Bob Hope with you?"

The chief turned to Ben and groaned. "I told you, didn't I? I'll never live last night down."

"It's the high price of stardom," Ben chuckled.

The young officer stuck out his hand as Ben climbed out of the cart. "Lieutenant j.g. James Kucera, Doctor Meade. I've seen you around, but I haven't had a chance to introduce myself."

"Nice to meet you, Lieutenant. How's it going down here?"

"Piece of cake. These Spreckles engines practically run themselves."

"You're being too modest, Lieutenant. The engines are efficient, all right, but things occasionally still go wrong. They can overheat, or a piece of submerged drift ice can damage a propeller. Every piece of machinery ever built still needs human supervision."

"True enough. Although these babies need less watching than most motors."

Chief Kowslowski climbed out of the cart and stood appraising the large motor set against the seaward wall of the ice chamber. "I haven't been down here since we carved out the space," he said. "How does that damn thing work?"

"It's a chemical-mechanical motor powered by an exchange of heat," Ben said.

The chief walked down to the side of the bus-sized motor and stared at the drive shaft spinning at four thousand revolutions a minute. "Look at that damn shaft. Christ, it's as big as a telephone pole."

"Got to be," the lieutenant said. "The propeller's seventy-five feet across."

Kowslowski whistled through his teeth and grinned at Ben. "An entire base carved out of an iceberg, futuristic engines large as locomotives. You ever do anything small, Meade?"

Ben laughed. "I deal with the most powerful forces in nature, Chief. Everything from volcanoes to ocean currents. I learned a long time ago that when you're trying to tap into the power of the earth, you either think big or you get into another line of work."

He looked past the chief toward the wall of ice where the drive shaft passed through to the propellers spinning in the sea water outside. "You getting any melting from the friction, Lieutenant?"

"Very little, sir. That plastic compound the chief and his Seabees injected into the berg below the waterline seems to be doing the job. At least in here. I don't know if we're getting any melting on the sea side of the wall."

"I doubt it," Ben said. "We used the same CH-Fifteen plastic on the iceberg base we built in Antarctica last year, and we had less than an inch of melting a month."

He turned to Kowslowski. "Has the Navy started injecting plastic into the Gulf Stream side of the dam yet? That tropical water will eat away the bergs if the ice below the waterline isn't treated as soon as possible."

"We've been at it for about a week now," Kowslowski told him. "Five submersibles shooting plastic in around the clock."

"How long do you think it will take to do the entire hundred-and-fifty-mile stretch?"

The chief thought for a moment. "Last I heard, each sub has been injecting about three miles of cliff face a day. Together, the five subs have probably coated about a hundred miles of bergs so far. You can probably figure another three or four days to finish the job."

"How do those little submersibles hold enough liquid plastic to coat three miles of bergs a day?" the lieutenant asked.

"They don't," Ben said. "Each sub has a tanker escort above, filled with plastic. The tankers follow along on the surface with a hose feeding down to the injection heads on the subs. We developed the system in Antarctica."

"Well, whatta ya say, Meade? You ready to see the rest of the base?" Kowslowski asked.

Ben nodded. "Yes, let's go." He turned to Kucera. "Thanks for your hospitality, Lieutenant."

"Anytime, Doctor Meade," the young officer smiled.

Ben climbed into the electric cart, and Koslowski started the vehicle back up the passageway. When they reached the Operations Center, the chief turned to the right and guided the cart across the cavernous space toward a tunnel lined with thick electrical conduits and cables.

"Where are we headed?" Ben asked.

"I thought I'd show you the power plant," Kowslowski said. "We've got the biggest generators in the U.S. Navy in there. Enough power to heat and light a city of ten thousand.

"After that, I plan to take you through the supply depot and the motor pool."

Ben looked surprised. "Motor pool? You've got a motor pool out here on the ice?"

"Hell, yeah. There are over sixty vehicles on Alpha; Sno-Cats, plows, Jeeps, trucks, electric carts. The motor pool's one of the busiest places on the base. There's the power-plant tunnel up ahead."

For the next two hours, Kowslowski guided Ben through all the behind-the-scenes work areas that kept Alpha running. Ben was impressed by the efficiency and high morale of the Navy crews that had been so suddenly transferred from their relatively comfortable base at Norfolk to an iceberg dam in the middle of the frigid North Atlantic.

The bright-eyed young enlisted men and officers were uniformly cheerful and proud of their jobs. Most were also only too ready to roast Kowslowski about his hula dance the night before.

The two had just finished a tour of the motor pool when the cellular phone on the dash of the cart buzzed insistently.

"Chief Kowslowski," the burly bos'n mate answered. He listened for a moment, then nodded. "Yeah, he's right here."

Kowslowski handed the phone to Ben. "For you. It's the captain of your research ship."

Ben took the phone from the chief. "Hi, Mel."

"I'm holding a videophone call from Marjorie, Ben," Sanderson said. "You want me to patch her through?"

"Marjorie! Hell, yes. But give me a few minutes to get back to communications."

"All right. I'll put her through in ten minutes."

"Drive me back to the command hub, will you, Chief?"

Kowslowski glanced over at the suddenly beaming Ben. "From the look on your face, this Marjorie must be someone special."

"She is, Chief. Real special."

Ten minutes later, Ben sat alone in the command hub, his fingers impatiently drumming the plastic lip of the communications console. Finally, the videophone rang and he flipped the set on.

"Hello, Ben," Marjorie said. "How are you?"

"I'm good, Marjorie." he smiled toward the lens beside the screen. "How about you?"

"Better than I've been in a long time."

"I can see that," he said, meaning it. The digitized picture showed Marjorie sitting in the library at Glennheather, rows of books behind her. A dog's head suddenly popped into the picture and Marjorie laughed.

"Freddy wants to say hello. He hasn't left my side since I got home, you know."

"Hello, Freddy, you lucky dog," Ben grinned.

"I suppose you're wondering why I called."

"It doesn't matter, so long as you did."

"I need to talk to you, Ben. I think I've come up with a way to synthesize food plants that will thrive even in the far northern latitudes."

For the next twenty minutes, Ben looked and listened, thrilled to see the animation in Marjorie's face and the fire in her eyes as she described her plans to combine chemosynthetic with photosynthetic genes. She was her old self again!

When she finished, Ben sat back and shook his head at the tiny videophone camera. "Marjorie, I think your theory's brilliant. But then, you're the smartest woman I've ever known."

"Thank you, but if I'm so bloody smart, why didn't I come up with the concept a long time ago?"

"I think maybe you were focused so intently on the genetics of photosynthetic plants that your mind was closed to other alternatives. Sometimes you just have to get away, open your mind up like a window and let the fresh ideas blow in."

"You're right of course. I've been able to think more clearly here, away from work and pressure. Perhaps some good will come of it after all."

"Tell me what I can do to help, Marjorie. Just name it."

"I'll need the *Abyss* to take me out to one of the seafloor hot-springs sites. And the *Yellowstone*, of course, to go down and collect specimens from one of the vent colonies."

"They're both at your disposal. Any time, any place, for as long as you need them."

"Where are the most promising vent sites?"

"There are several hot springs on the floor of the Pacific off western Mexico," Ben said. "And at least half a dozen sites off the coast of South America."

"Which area would you recommend?"

"South America. It would be easier to work below the equator, away from the volcanic gas clouds. It's a hell of a lot warmer down there, too."

"Thank you, Ben."

"My pleasure. Anything else you need?"

Marjorie hesitated. "Yes. I need some time with you."

"You mean that?"

"Yes, I do. I've been focused on the problems between us instead of on how to solve them. If I must lose you, I don't want it to be because I wasn't willing to try to work things out."

Ben lowered his head, his left hand kneading the furrows in his forehead.

Marjorie squinted at the screen in Scotland. "I've said something wrong, haven't I? I've just assumed that you wanted to work things out, too."

Ben looked up at the camera, his eyes brimming with tears. "There's nothing I want more in this world, Marjorie. Nothing."

"Oh, Ben. I've never seen you cry before. And now, the first time you do, you're three thousand miles away in the middle of the bloody ocean and I can't put my arms around you."

"Can I ask you something?"

"Anything."

"Why the sudden change of heart, not that I question it. I'd just like to know why."

Marjorie smiled. "I suppose part of it is the optimism that flooded over me when I realized it might be possible to develop chemosynthetic plants. Suddenly everything seemed possible. Not just new food crops and all they would mean to the planet. Everything. Even us. Does that make any sense?"

"Sure it does. One minute everything's black; nothing's working, nothing makes sense. Then, bingo, you get a break and everything else begins falling into place. I figure it's biorhythms."

"Whatever it is, I want to see you. I have about ten days of research to do here, then I'll be free to fly over."

"I'll have a Navy jet at Dundee Airport at nine A.M. ten days from today. The pilot can refuel in Iceland and land you on the task-force carrier out here before dinner."

"Are you sure you can get me on a Navy plane? I'm a civilian, after all, and a British citizen to boot."

"You're also the head scientist building Biosphere

America, not to mention the creator of new crop strains that will feed millions of people, including Americans. The plane will be there if I have to call the President personally."

"Oh, Ben, I'm excited and happy and scared all at once. We won't fight, will we? Promise me we won't."

"I promise you. I'll cut my tongue out first."

She laughed. "Don't you dare. I have better uses for that tongue of yours."

Ben laughed. "My tongue, and the entire rest of me, is yours for the asking."

"I love you, Ben. I didn't know if I could say that, but the way I feel, I can't not say it."

"Jesus, Marjorie, I can't believe all this. Half an hour ago . . . oh, hell, it doesn't matter. All that matters is that I love you, too. More at this moment than ever before."

Marjorie blew a kiss toward the camera. "I'll see you in ten days."

He brought his fingertips to his mouth and pressed a kiss against the videocamera lens. "It's going to be the longest ten days of my life."

"Of our life, Ben. From now on, it's going to be our life again."

ENSENADA NAVAL
BASE, ARGENTINA
••••••••••••••••••

2:40 p.m.–May 13th

"Is your crew ready, Captain Lobov?" Colonel General Ramon Saavedra de Urquiza asked, fixing the Ukrainian with a hard stare as they sat in the cramped wardroom of the submarine *Bukharin*.

Standing uncomfortably in the doorway, translator Julio Pena repeated the question in Ukrainian.

"No, they are not ready," Lobov said, blowing a column of cigarette smoke toward the ceiling. "As we agreed, I will have to finish their training at sea."

Pena translated, dark sweat rings spreading from his armpits. Every time he had to climb down the ladder into the submarine, his claustrophobia grew worse.

"I wish to go on the record as opposing this voyage," Admiral Juan Bautista Secchi said, a hand fanning the cigarette smoke away from his face. "We can't send an Argentine warship to sea with a half-trained crew."

When Pena finished his translation, Lobov threw the Argentine admiral a disdainful look. "You forget that I sailed the *Bukharin* to Argentina with a handful of Ukrainian officers and men. It will be far easier to operate the vessel with a full crew, even if most of them are only half-trained."

Secchi frowned as Pena translated. "I've talked to several of your officers, you know," he told Lobov. "They're nervous, afraid the crew will screw up out there at sea. What will you do, Captain, if some green sailor turns the wrong valve and the *Bukharin* starts flooding?"

Lobov toyed with his cigarette. "I'll close the valve, pump out the compartment, and arrest the stupid asshole on the spot, Admiral."

"I suppose you'll want the poor bastard shot when you get back," Secchi scowled. "Like your executive officer whom you keep insisting we execute. I don't even know why we're still holding him in the Navy brig."

"He's a fucking mutineer," Lobov said, his eyes dangerous now. "He should have been shot the day we reached Buenos Aires."

"Enough," General de Urquiza thundered. "You two remind me of an old couple squabbling over a crust of bread. We have decisions to make." He glanced at his huge gold Rolex. "We have thirty minutes until the tide turns and the *Bukharin* leaves port. Captain Lobov, have you plotted your course north to the iceberg dam?"

"I'm going south first," the Ukrainian said.

Looks of shocked disbelief crossed the faces of the junta members as Pena repeated the captain's words.

"What the hell are you talking about, you're going south?" Admiral Secchi demanded.

"Only a fool like you, Admiral Secchi, would take the *Bukharin* north through the Atlantic," Lobov said calmly, pulling a chart out of the cabinet next to the table.

Pena winced at Lobov's insulting words, a reaction Secchi caught. "What did he say? Goddammit, Pena, don't lie to me."

Pena cringed and translated verbatim.

"How dare you call me a fool!" the admiral exploded, coming half out of his seat. "You watch your goddamn tongue, Captain. You haven't sailed yet. It's not too late to relieve you of command."

"Shut up and listen to him," de Urquiza said. He didn't like Lobov any more than Secchi did. The difference was that he recognized the cunning of the Ukrainian. It was a character trait they shared.

"There are SOSUS listening posts throughout both the North and South Atlantic," Lobov said, spreading the chart out on the table. "Not to mention regular patrols by both American warships and ASW subs operating out of bases along the Atlantic coast."

He waited for the translation, then jabbed a finger at the tip of South America on the chart. "I intend to take the *Bukharin* around the tip of South America and on into the South Pacific. The Pacific is vast, and I know from many voyages in Soviet subs that there are wide areas of sea where there are no SOSUS ears and only occasional American submarine patrols."

As soon as Pena finished the translation, Lobov went on. "When we reach the northern Pacific, I shall take the *Bukharin* through the Bering Strait and on into the Arctic Ocean."

Secchi listened to Pena, then shook his head. "The Arctic Ocean? I don't understand."

"The admiral doesn't understand," the perspiring Pena told Lobov.

"It's really quite simple, Admiral. I'm going to dive the *Bukharin* beneath the polar ice pack and navigate east across the top of the world. We will emerge from under the floes in Baffin Bay, then sail south to the Labrador Sea. From there, I will stage my final run to the dam."

Pena translated.

"Why do you choose that course?" General de Urquiza asked.

"Because the ice will provide cover from U.S. reconnaissance satellites, and because the complex marine acoustics in the far northern seas will make sonar tracking by American ASW subs all but impossible. I should be able to get within a couple hundred miles of the dam without any risk of detection."

De Urquiza arched his eyebrows at Secchi. "Will this work?"

Despite his dislike of the Ukrainian officer, Secchi could not help but admire the man's plan. "I think the idea of attacking from the Arctic is ingenious. As the captain says, the *Bukharin* will have both ice and acoustic cover most of the way to the target."

"So, the course north to the American installation— word is that they're calling it Ice Station Alpha—is settled?" de Urquiza asked.

"There is one final matter to be addressed," Secchi said. "Under no circumstances is Captain Lobov to use his nuclear missiles. The installation is to be destroyed with torpedoes, fired at close range to avoid detection by any American ASW subs or aircraft in the area."

"Why are you so insistent on a torpedo attack, Secchi?" de Urquiza asked.

"Because a nuclear-missile attack would leave the sea and ice bathed in radioactivity. It would be obvious that the dam had been deliberately destroyed by a nuclear missile. The Americans would not rest until they discovered who had attacked their installation. And I promise you, General de Urquiza, that eventually their C.I.A. would find out it was us. That would undoubtedly lead to a U.S. declaration of war on Argentina."

As Pena translated, Lobov nodded in agreement. "Admiral Secchi is right. If I destroy the dam with the SS-N-Twenties, not only will the Americans have radioactive evidence of a deliberate attack, but their satellites will pick up the missiles in flight."

A cunning look came into Lobov's eyes. "On the other hand, icebergs are constantly breaking apart, splitting into sections. If I can get in close enough to avoid American sonar detection of my torpedo runs, there will be no way the U.S. can prove the dam didn't just split apart under the stress of the severe sea conditions in those waters. Torpedoes leave no trail, no evidence."

De Urquiza studied the Ukrainian as Pena translated. "You will have to get in close, Captain Lobov, very close. Can you do it?"

"I know my boat, I know the waters, and I know my adversary. Yes, I can do it."

"When?" de Urquiza asked after Pena translated. "When will the attack take place?"

"Your shipyard engineers have just finished installing the latest generation of steam turbines in the *Bukharin*.

They deliver twice the power of the older units. The *Bukharin* can now steam submerged at well over forty knots."

A glow came into Lobov's strange, flat eyes. "Steaming at full speed, the *Bukharin* will reach the target in approximately thirty days. A month from now, the American iceberg dam will cease to exist."

ICE BASE ALPHA
• • • • • • • • • • • • • • •

3:55 p.m.–May 17th

BEN MEADE STOOD AT the edge of the snow-covered helipad on Ice Base Alpha watching the Navy Sea Stallion helicopter with Marjorie Glynn aboard approach from over the towering white cliffs several hundred yards away.

She had landed on the aircraft carrier *Abraham Lincoln* an hour and a half before, and her voice was still breathless with excitement when she called him. Flying faster than the speed of sound, the Navy jet had whisked her from Scotland to a refueling stop in Iceland, then west across the Atlantic to the deck of the carrier.

A cloud of powdered snow billowed up as the chopper set down, its rotor blades continuing to whirl as the door popped open and a crewman jumped out. He extended a hand to Marjorie and she leaped down, her face hidden within the hood of a fur-lined Arctic parka that was at least two sizes too big.

Ben ran across the helipad and threw his arms around her. "Are you in there?" he laughed, pushing back the hood.

"What?" Marjorie shouted against the *whop-whop-whop* of the chopper blades.

Ben grabbed her hand. "C'mon. Let's get out of the way and let these guys take off."

"What?"

Ben laughed again and led her across to the Sno-Cat, followed by the crewman with her bag.

"Just throw it in the back," Ben told the young enlisted man.

"Yes, sir."

"Thanks," Marjorie smiled.

"Any time, Doctor Glynn," the crewman grinned, then trotted back to the helicopter. A moment later, the craft lifted off and circled out over the sea cliffs toward the carrier.

"Marjorie, I'd like you to meet Chief Bos'n Mate Ignatius Kowslowski," Ben said as the noise of the chopper died away. "There are high-ranking officers all over the place out here, but it's the chief who really runs Alpha."

Marjorie extended her hand. "Nice to meet you, Chief Kowslowski."

"Nice to meet you, Ma'am." Kowslowski glanced at Ben. "Now I know why you've been walking around with that goddamn grin on your face for the past two weeks. You sure know how to pick 'em, Meade."

Ben laughed. "In case you hadn't noticed, the chief is a blunt-spoken man."

"Like you," Marjorie said.

Ben looked into her face, searching for the sarcastic smirk that would have accompanied the remark in past months. What he found instead were smiling eyes and those teasing dimples of hers.

"Yeah," he grinned, kissing her nose. "Like me."

For a moment, the two stood close together, their gloved hands locked and the steam of their warm breath bathing each other's face.

"When you two get finished cooing at each other, whatta ya say we get back to the Operations Center?" Kowslowski said good-naturedly. "It'll be dark in an hour, and the road up there's hairy enough in daylight."

"Climb in," Ben said to Marjorie. "And for God's sake,

hold on. The chief drives like a maniac."

"That's because I am a maniac. Every one of my ex-wives told me that."

"Every one? How many wives have you had, Chief?" Marjorie asked, settling into the seat between the two men.

"Three, if I count Agnes only once. She and I got divorced, then remarried a couple of years later. Five years after that, we got divorced again. If I had all the dough I've paid lawyers, I could have retired from the Navy years ago."

"Sounds like you've had rather bad luck with women," Marjorie said, suddenly slammed backward against the seat as Kowslowski gunned the Sno-Cat forward.

"Luck's got nothing to do with it," Kowslowski said. "I just don't understand women. I mean, I can't figure how you females think. You know what I mean?"

Marjorie winked at Ben. "No, Chief, I don't know what you mean."

"The problem is, women don't think logical. That's the main thing. Not even close. I look at a situation, I see black and white. Agnes and my other wives, they saw pink and blue and aquamarine. Rainbow thinking, I used to call it."

Ben cringed inside, waiting for the feminist side of Marjorie to explode. Instead, she laughed and thumped Kowslowski playfully on the arm. "The differences between men and women are what make the world go around. You're looking at relationships ass-backward."

Kowslowski used his tongue to switch his perpetually unlit cigar from one side of his mouth to the other. "You could be right. I doubt it, but you could be."

Ben smiled to himself and settled back in the seat. It was as if Marjorie had been pricked with a pin and all the pressurized rage and resentment had left her in a rush, dissipating into thin air. Whatever had come over her standing at that stove in her parents' kitchen, it was the best thing that had happened to her in a long time. And to him.

Marjorie and the chief kept up a friendly banter as the Sno-Cat climbed the icy slope. Ben was content to hold her gloved hand in his, injecting only an occasional comment. It made him happy just to hear the lightness and laughter in her voice as she sparred with the grizzled Kowslowski.

Twenty minutes later, they reached the tunnel mouth, and Marjorie's eyes widened. "I've never been inside an iceberg before."

"Nothin' to worry about," Kowslowski said. "Hell, it's safer than a house."

They got out of the Sno-Cat and climbed into the electric cart Ben and the chief had left idling in front of the motor pool hut an hour before.

"How much ice is over our heads?" Marjorie asked as they started through the tunnel.

" 'Bout a hundred thousand tons," Kowslowski said.

Marjorie shivered. "What's holding it up?"

Ben squeezed her hand. "This berg was once part of a land glacier that formed ten or twenty thousand years ago. If the ice could hold together that long, I don't think there's any danger it'll collapse on us now."

"Famous last words." Marjorie rolled her eyes, but Ben felt the tension ease in her hand.

"There's the Operations Center up ahead," Kowslowski said, gesturing down the tunnel with his cigar. "You won't feel near as claustrophobic in there."

A moment later, they emerged into the cavernous heart of the berg and Marjorie gaped in astonishment. "Good Lord, it's as big as Westminster Abbey."

"Told ya," Kowslowski said. "Where do you want me to drop you two?"

Ben looked at Marjorie. "You've had a long trip. I imagine you could use a cup of tea and a shower."

"God, yes. In that order."

"Are Doctor Glynn's quarters ready, Chief?"

"All set. We gave her the room next to yours over in officers' country." He grinned at Marjorie. " 'Course, the rooms out here aren't really rooms; they're chambers carved out of the ice. Cold, but cozy."

"I'll tell you what, Chief," Ben said. "Drop us off at Marjorie's quarters, then send over a cart for us to use. I'll take her over to the women's shower after we've had some hot tea."

"How many women are serving here?" Marjorie asked.

"Thirty-two at last count," Kowslowski said. "Nurses, communications specialists, admin officers, you name it. Women fill just about any job in the Navy now, you know. Hell, we even got females serving on warships."

Ben pointed out the command hub as the chief guided the cart across the Operations Center. "That's where I do most of my work," he said.

"What's that over there?" Marjorie asked as they passed a thirty-foot-high electronic map of the North Atlantic, pulsing with different-colored lights. A half-dozen men and two women in light-blue work uniforms sat at a long, curving console facing the map.

"It's our meteorological station," Ben said. "That line of amber lights off the coast of Newfoundland is a weather front moving in. The numbers in white represent air temperatures; the blue numbers are sea temperatures."

Marjorie pointed toward the left of the glowing map. "What are those bands of red and green running up the left side?"

"That's the Gulf Stream coming up from the south in red, and the Labrador Current flowing down from the north in green," Ben said. "Off Newfoundland, the two currents run side by side. Notice the difference in the temperature of the seawater from one current to the other."

Marjorie studied the illuminated numbers. "Eighteen degrees! That can't be correct."

"It's accurate, all right. That will give you an idea of the incredible amount of heat the Gulf Stream is now moving north toward the Arctic."

"Good Lord, the polar floes will melt like ice cubes in a cup of warm tea."

"The base post office and bank are over there." Kowslowski pointed to two counters standing side by side against the curving wall.

Marjorie's eyebrows arched. "You've got a bank out here on the ice? What on earth for?"

"Whatta ya mean 'what for'?" Kowslowski asked. "We

may be stationed on an iceberg in the middle of the ocean, but we get paid like everyone else. We got to have a place to cash checks, send money home, buy bonds, all that stuff."

"There's the PX up ahead," Ben said. "You need anything, Marjorie?"

She gave him a blank stare. "What's a PX?"

Kowslowski's mouth fell open in disbelief. "You're foolin' me! You never heard of a PX?"

Marjorie's chin went up defensively. "No, should I have? What is it, some sort of club?"

"It's more like a general store," Ben said kindly.

Marjorie brightened. "Oh, like Harrods, you mean."

Ben laughed. "Not quite, but you've got the idea."

"The tunnel to the officers' quarters is coming up on the right," Kowslowski said. "You two will soon be home-sweet-home."

Several minutes later, the chief stopped the cart in front of a steel-shuttered door, one of a row of doors set into each wall of the tunnel at fifteen-foot intervals. The line of doors reminded Marjorie of a hotel corridor.

"Thanks for picking me up, Chief Kowslowski," she said as she and Ben climbed out.

"No thanks necessary," Kowslowski said, reaching into the back of the cart and handing Marjorie's bag to Ben. "All part of my job."

"Don't forget to send over a cart, Chief," Ben said.

"You got it, Meade. See ya later."

As Kowslowski drove off, Ben slid open the door to Marjorie's quarters. "I'll turn the heater on," he said.

"That won't be necessary," Marjorie said. "I'm staying with you."

"You're what?"

"I'm staying with you. I didn't fly across the Atlantic, make a heart-stopping landing on an aircraft carrier and then allow myself to be driven into the middle of a bloody iceberg just to sleep alone, you know. Where's your room?"

For a moment, Ben was speechless, and at the same time joyous at the thought of making love to Marjorie after so many weeks apart. He had thought there would be a period of adjustment, at least a few days of coming to know each other again. Obviously, she had already made up her mind about how she felt and what she wanted.

He jerked a thumb over his shoulder at the next door down. "Right there."

"Come along, then," she said, heading for his room. Ben slid the door to Marjorie's quarters shut and followed her down the corridor.

He put down her bag, opened the door and flicked on the light. Then he bent and picked her up. "Welcome home," he said, carrying her across the threshold.

Inside, he slid the door shut with his foot, then brought his lips down to hers for a kiss that was long and deep.

"Oh, Ben, I love you, you know," Marjorie said when their lips finally parted.

"And I love you. I'll always love you."

"I'm so sorry about all that's happened," she said as he put her down. "About the way I was."

"No, no, the way *we* were," he smiled. "We let our work drive us apart. That will never happen again."

"Promise?"

"Promise."

She kissed his cheek, then shivered suddenly. "Lord, it *is* a bit cold in here."

"I'll turn the heater on." Ben crossed the room to a control panel fed by a thick electric cable. Outlet wires ran from the panel to a large electric heater and a hot plate sitting on a small navy-style card table set against the far wall.

"It'll be as warm as toast in here in a couple of minutes," he said.

"Won't the heat melt the ice?"

"No. The walls are coated with CH-Fifteen plastic. Oh, we get a little melting, but not much." He reached for a kettle next to the hot plate and filled it with water from a large thermos jug. "You ready for that tea I promised you?"

"More than ready, darling."

Ben looked up from the kettle. " 'Darling'! That's the first time you've called me that in six months."

She crossed the room and threw her arms around him.

"I've wanted to, Ben. You'll never know how much I've wanted to."

"Probably as much as I've wanted to hear it, and to call you 'Baby' again."

Marjorie smiled. "You know, before I met you, the feminist in me would cringe when I'd hear other men call their wives or girlfriends 'Baby.' I thought it was a demeaning term, an implication that the woman was somehow inferior."

She stood on tiptoe and kissed his cheek. "But the first time you called me that, there was such love and tenderness in your voice, I realized that coming from you, 'Baby' was a term of endearment, the same thing as my calling you 'Darling.' Now I love it when you call me 'Baby.' "

"I love you, Baby," Ben whispered against her ear. They held each other for a long time, until the whistle of the kettle sounded behind them.

The ice chamber was warm now, and they took off their parkas and sat on the edge of Ben's bed, sipping tea. When they'd finished, Ben rose and put the cups on a tray for the steward to collect, then came back and sat down again next to Marjorie.

They kissed again, then her fingers went to his chest and she began unbuttoning his shirt.

"Are you doing what I think you're doing?" he grinned.

"We can hardly make love with our clothes on, can we?" she smiled back.

"What about your shower?"

She brought his head down to her lips and explored his ear with her tongue. "I can wait for my shower . . . but I can't wait for you."

BUENOS AIRES, ARGENTINA
•••••••••••••••••••••••••••

1:10 p.m.–May 18th

OLIVER FLEMING HAD BEEN in a cold sweat ever since he'd given the note to the concierge in Maria Echeverria's apartment building early that morning, asking Maria to call him on a matter of great urgency.

He could have called her, of course. The Agency had provided him with her phone number even before he'd contrived to meet her. But the number was unlisted, and she would have questioned how he got it.

When she called later that morning, he told her that it would be better if they discussed the matter in person. Could she come over as soon as possible? Maria sounded mystified, but she promised to be at his penthouse early that afternoon.

Almost two weeks earlier, the C.I.A. had informed their station chief in Buenos Aires that there was now irrefutable evidence that Argentina had purchased a nuclear-missile submarine from Ukraine.

For the past thirteen days, American ASW subs and planes had been scouring the South Atlantic looking for the *Bukharin*. Simultaneously, agents from both the C.I.A. and the Office of Naval Intelligence had been attempting

to penetrate the numerous Argentine naval installations
in their search for the sub, so far with no success.

U.S. agents had been able to get past the security measures on a half-dozen bases, but had found no sign of the
Bukharin. The largest Argentine naval installation, the
General San Martin Navy Base, was so heavily guarded—
ringed with three barbed-wire fences and choked with security checkpoints—that not a single agent had been able
to get onto the base.

The C.I.A. suspected that if the *Bukharin* were indeed in
an Argentine naval port, she was in some secret sub pen
at Ensenada. Still, there was not yet a shred of physical
evidence.

The inability of either the U.S. Navy or the intelligence
services to find the submarine had created mounting concern in Washington, and Oliver was feeling the heat. He
was under continuous pressure to find out if Maria
Echeverria knew anything about the *Bukharin.*

For two weeks, he had gently probed her, careful not to
push too hard lest she become suspicious. Yet somehow
he had always managed to bring the subject around to
submarines.

The tactic had failed several times, with Maria looking
at him blankly whenever he mentioned the subject. Then,
yesterday, when he once again steered the talk to submarines, Maria had suddenly turned pale and quickly
changed the subject.

The incident had given Oliver a hunch that she knew
something, that sometime in the past week, de Urquiza
might have told her about the *Bukharin.* He'd forwarded
his suspicions in a coded cable to C.I.A. headquarters in
Langley and received orders back within an hour to pursue the lead immediately. At all costs.

He had only one option now. He would have to lay it
all out on the table, tell her he was an American intelligence agent and that he knew she was the mistress of
General de Urquiza.

Oliver flinched at the sound of the doorbell. What
would Maria's reaction be when she learned the truth
about him? Would she hate him and stalk out? He
couldn't let her do that, not without first learning what

she knew about the *Bukharin*, not without letting her know that despite the manner in which they had met, he had fallen in love with her.

He sighed and crossed to the door. "Maria, thank you for coming," he said, drawing her to him. They embraced and kissed, as was their wont ever since that magic night when they'd first made love.

"You said it was important, Oliver. Is something the matter? You didn't sound yourself on the phone."

"Please, come and sit down. There is something we must discuss."

He led her across to the couch and forced a smile. "Would you like a glass of wine?"

"No, thank you. Oliver, please tell me what's wrong. I can see in your face that something terrible has happened."

He sat down beside her. "Maria, you're not going to like what I must tell you. None of this will be pleasant. But please hear me out. I'm hoping that you'll understand—" he looked away "—and forgive me."

"Forgive you? For what? Oliver, you're scaring me."

"I know that you don't live with your father, Maria. You live with General Ramon Saavedra de Urquiza. You are his mistress."

Maria's face fell. "So that's it. I suppose I've known all along that you'd find out eventually."

"I've known since before we met. As a matter of fact, the general is the reason we met."

She looked at him in confusion. "I don't understand."

"My first name is Oliver, but my last name is not Alberdi. It's Fleming. I'm an intelligence officer with the American Central Intelligence Agency. The purse-snatching in the market was a setup, a way for me to meet you."

Maria's face twisted in shock as the implications of the words sank in. "Then it's all been a lie? Everything? They sent you to seduce me, to use me to spy on the general!" She grabbed her purse and leaped to her feet. "You bastard! You told me you loved me. And all the while, you only wanted information on the general."

Oliver came to his feet, his hands gripping her arms. "Maria, please. You've got to listen to me."

"Listen to you! Listen to more of your lies? Do you know what you've made me feel like?"

"Maria, please."

Tears flooded her eyes. "Like a whore, Oliver. A whore to two men. At least Ramon was honest with me. He never pretended he wanted anything but my body. But you! You told me you admired my art. You told me you respected my mind. You told me you loved me."

"I do love you."

"You despicable pig! You don't know what love is."

"All I ask is that you listen to me for five minutes."

"Take your filthy hands off me. I never want to see you again!"

"Maria, you can't leave, not like this."

She jerked her arms out of his grasp. "I hope they catch you. I hope they put you in prison!" She turned and half-ran toward the door.

"Maria, if you go out that door, the C.I.A. will reveal our relationship to General de Urquiza."

She stopped and whirled around, her face a mask of fury. "Go ahead and tell Ramon. What does it matter? I haven't revealed a single thing about him."

"He won't know that. All he'll know is that his mistress has been sleeping with a C.I.A. agent. What do you think his reaction will be?"

The young woman turned pale. "I'll tell him first. I'll tell him you trapped me. I'll tell him that I never talked about him or the junta. Not once. It's the truth. He'll believe me."

Oliver took a step toward her. "No, Maria, he won't believe you. He'll have you interrogated. In Salado Prison. You're a young girl. A beautiful girl. You know what they'll do to you in there."

Maria shuddered. She had heard the stories of what happened to women in Salado: the gang rapes, the water hoses forced up their rectums, the sadistic guards who took pleasure in beating naked women.

Oliver took another step toward her, willing her not to reach for the door handle. "They'll break you, Maria. You'll tell them anything they want to hear. And when you've confessed, confessed to something you never did, they'll shoot you."

He was right, Maria knew. The room began to spin. "Oh, God, what will I do?" she sobbed, slumping to the floor in despair.

Oliver looked down at her, hating himself for having to put her through such anguish. "There's a way out, Maria," he said, crossing the room. He picked her up and carried her to the couch. "If you're brave enough to tell me the truth."

"I don't know the truth anymore," she whimpered as he lay her down on the cushion.

He knelt beside her, his hand stroking her forehead as tears streamed down her face. "Listen to me. I'm going to take you away with me, Maria. I've planned it for a long time now."

She opened her eyes. "You're lying again! I know you are."

"No, I'm not lying. And I wasn't lying when I told you I love you. I won't pretend it's what I intended. In the beginning, I was only going to use you to get to de Urquiza."

He bent and softly kissed her. "But somewhere along the line, maybe from the beginning, I began to fall in love with you. Then, the first time we made love, I knew I could never leave you."

She looked into his eyes, grasping at the hope his words offered, but still afraid, still leery.

"I wish I could believe you."

"You must believe me, for both of us. I hated having to put you through this ordeal, but I had no choice. You have information my government needs. The lives of countless innocent people may depend on what you can tell me."

Maria let out a long sigh and sat up. "Do you have a tissue?" she asked, wiping the back of her hand across her tear-streaked cheek.

"Of course," he said, taking a handkerchief from his pocket.

"Thank you." She dabbed at her eyes. "What is it you want to know, Oliver?"

"My government has uncovered evidence that the junta recently purchased a submarine armed with nuclear warheads from Ukraine. We must know where that submarine is."

"The *Bukharin*," she said.

"Then the general *has* told you about the sub!"

"Not directly. But he talks in his sleep, babbling away between snores. One night about a week ago, he went on and on about the *Bukharin*. About how the submarine was sailing north to destroy the American iceberg dam. All that talk about attacking with torpedoes. It scared me. I couldn't sleep all night."

"Jesus Christ!" Oliver breathed, his heart beating wildly. This was a nightmare beyond belief. The climate, the very fate of millions of people, depended on the success of the Arctic Alteration.

He rose and paced the room. "All right, now listen to me. I must do two things immediately. I have to cable this information to C.I.A. headquarters, and I have to get you the hell out of Buenos Aires."

Maria leaped to her feet and clasped Oliver in a desperate embrace. "Then you meant it. You'll really take me with you?"

"Everything I've told you today is the truth—the ugly part about using you, and the beautiful part about loving you." He bent and kissed her. "We'll talk, Maria. Later. Right now I have to make a call."

Oliver crossed to the phone and punched a few numbers. "Sarmiento residence," a voice answered.

"This is Oliver. I need a ride to the country store," he said. "Right away. Can you pick us up?"

"Us?"

"My friend is coming with me."

"I'll be there in ten minutes," the voice replied.

"We'll be waiting in front of the café two blocks west down the street."

"Fine. I know where it is."

Oliver hung up, hurried into the bedroom for his briefcase and wallet, then rejoined Maria in the living room. "C'mon," he said, guiding her toward the door. "We've got to hurry."

"You said on the phone that we need a ride to the 'country store,'" Maria said. "What store did you mean?"

"'Country store' is the code word for the Agency safe house near Rosario," Oliver told her as he opened the door.

"Rosario! That's almost two hundred miles from here."

"The farther from Buenos Aires I can get you, the better," Oliver said, stabbing at the elevator button. "When de Urquiza finds out that the *Bukharin*'s mission has leaked—and you turn up missing at the same time—he'll put two and two together and tear this city apart searching for you. Later, we'll find a way to get you out of Argentina."

"What about my clothes? My artwork?"

The elevator door slid open. Oliver jammed his foot against one side to keep it from closing, then reached out and took hold of Maria's arms with white-knuckled hands.

"You'd be crazy to go back to your apartment. Suppose the general's there and you can't get out again before he finds out we know about the *Bukharin*? Do you want to take that chance?"

Maria shivered. "No."

"Get in the elevator."

"Where will we go, Oliver—" she asked as the car descended "—when we leave Argentina?"

Oliver drew her close. "Home, Maria. I'm going to take you home with me."

THE BERING STRAIT
• • • • • • • • • • • • • • • • • • •

6:20 p.m.–May 28th

CAPTAIN VIKTOR LOBOV FINISHED his daily inspection of
the *Bukharin*'s reactor compartment and headed back
through the passageway toward the control room.

All was going well. The sub's two pressurized-water
reactors with new state-of-the-art steam turbines were
putting out 180,000 shaft horsepower, driving two
shrouded seven-bladed screws that were propelling the
Bukharin north through the depths at a steady thirty-five
knots.

The last stop on Lobov's inspection tour was the sonar
room, containing all the equipment and monitors for the
sub's two sonar systems.

The active sonar array was located in the bow, from
which it sent a powerful sixty-thousand-watt sound wave
radiating out into the sea in search for both submerged
and surface craft. If the sound waves encountered a solid
object in the area, the returning echo would be picked up
by the *Bukharin*'s hydrophones, allowing the sub's sonar
operator to determine the object's size, distance and direction of travel.

The *Bukharin* also streamed a large towed-array sonar

that played out from a tube in the port horizontal stabilizer. The towed array was a passive system, designed to listen for both broadband and narrowband sonar signals directed at the submarine.

"Any activity?" Lobov asked sonar operator Evgeny Vaslyshn.

Vaslyshn shook his head. "Quiet as a morgue, Captain. About an hour ago, a large freighter crossed the stern twelve miles to the south, but that's the only traffic all morning."

Lobov nodded. He had plotted a course that avoided the normal shipping lanes and the areas where his old Soviet charts listed known or suspected SOSUS sonar arrays on the ocean floor.

"Let me know at once if you get a contact," he said and left for his last stop, the torpedo room.

Many of the Ukrainian crew of the *Bukharin* had avoided the torpedo room since the two Mark C wire-guided torpedoes had hissed down the tubes and delivered death to twenty innocent Greek sailors two months before. To them, the torpedo room was like a morgue, a place associated with death. Captain Lobov had no such compunction; he drew power from his mastery of the sub's torpedoes. Along with the vertical missile-launch systems, the torpedo room justified the *Bukharin*'s very existence.

At the far end of the space, a Ukrainian noncom was showing an Argentine seaman how to polish one of the six stainless-steel torpedo tubes. The two snapped to attention and threw Lobov a salute.

"Continue what you were doing," Lobov said, touching his fingers to the tip of his cap.

"Aye aye, sir," the noncom said and went on with his instruction.

Lobov crossed to one of the double racks holding the twenty-two remaining torpedoes on board and ran his hand along one of the deadly Mark C's. The uninitiated thought of torpedoes as mere tubes with an explosive charge at the front and a propeller in the rear. Lobov knew better.

At the tip of the Mark C was a sonar seeker that used

sound waves to guide the weapon to its target. In back of the sonar was the guidance-control system, and behind that, the warhead containing over five hundred pounds of explosive. Farther back were the engine guidance computer, the fuel and, at the rear, the pump jet that propelled the torpedo through the water. In truth, modern torpedoes were among the most sophisticated of weapons.

On the way back to the control room, Lobov recognized the smell of refried beans and tostadas cooking in the tiny galley and on impulse, he climbed the access ladder and poked his head into the enlisted men's mess area.

Here the crew of the *Bukharin* had their meals, watched movies, played cards and board games and attended classes on the myriad operating systems aboard the sub. The two dozen off-duty sailors sitting at the compartment's six tables stopped whatever they were doing as the captain came in.

Lobov spotted one of the two naval interpreters whom Admiral Secchi had furnished and motioned the man over. "Ask them how the food is," the captain said.

The translator repeated Lobov's question in Spanish, bringing a round of approving nods from the crew. "Ask if there is anything they need," Lobov ordered.

"Vino," a torpedoman said when the translator finished. "Señoritas" another joked, provoking a burst of laughter from the others.

Lobov flashed a rare half-smile. "Tell them that when the mission is over, I will throw a party on shore. Wine, women and song. On me."

A cheer went up when the men heard the translation, and Lobov waved and left for the control room. The morale of the crew was important on any ship, but on a submarine, it was absolutely vital. The confined space, the endless days submerged and the monotonous routine could stoke the embers of discontent into a raging hostility toward the officers, and especially toward the captain. And a hostile crew would perform poorly in a critical situation.

Soon the real tension would begin. Tomorrow morning, the *Bukharin* would reach the frozen Beaufort Sea and turn east beneath the ice floes at the top of the world. After having traversed the length of the vast Pacific, she would hone in on her prey, now less than forty-eight hundred miles away.

THE WHITE HOUSE,
WASHINGTON, D.C.
• • • • • • • • • • • • • • • • • • • •

10:00 a.m.–May 31st

PRESIDENT KATHLEEN PIZIALI FINISHED reading the intelligence report just handed her by National Security Adviser Rob Bonham and looked across at the three Arctic Alteration advisers seated before her Oval Office desk.

"Jesus, Rob," she said, focusing on Bonham, "are these numbers right? Has your staff confirmed this stuff?"

Bonham crossed his long legs and grinned. "The figures I handed you are from our Mainland Chinese sources, of course. But we're getting the same estimates from foreign businessmen in the area. Japanese mostly."

The President turned toward Admiral Mike Mathisen, sitting beside Bonham. "What's the SEASAT surveillance showing, Mike?"

"Three weeks ago, Madam President, our reconnaissance satellites over the Pacific were picking up an average of thirty known or suspected smuggling vessels leaving ports along the South China coast virtually every day. Yesterday there were only twelve."

The President sat back in her chair and shook her head in wonder. "It's unbelievable that there could be such a drastic reduction in the number of immigrants fleeing China in so short a time."

"If you'll pardon me, Madam President," Admiral Mathisen said, "it's not really unbelievable at all. The Arctic Alteration has given the people of China renewed hope. And that hope will allow most of the Chinese to endure until the climate warms and the new food crops are harvested."

The third man sitting before the President, National Science Adviser Tom Howard, came forward eagerly in his chair. "Speaking of new food crops, Madam President, I received an extraordinary phone call from Doctor Glynn this morning."

The President's face took on a sympathetic look. "How is she? Still recuperating in Scotland?"

"No, Madam President. She's flown across and joined Ben Meade on Ice Station Alpha. Best of all, that brilliant mind of hers is back at work and she's come up with an incredible concept for bioengineering crops that can grow with little or no sunlight."

Admiral Mathisen asked, "Is this some kind of variation on those new grains we're growing in Florida?"

Howard shook his head. "Totally different concept, Mike. The plants we're testing in Florida can grow under weak sunlight conditions, but they still depend on photosynthesis. Doctor Glynn's new thesis suggests that we may be able to develop crops based on chemosynthesis."

Rob Bonham furrowed his brow. "What the hell is 'chemosynthesis'?"

"Basically, it's a system in which submarine plants and animals derive their life support from chemicals rather than sunlight. Primarily, from sulfur compounds seeping up through thermal vents in the deep ocean floor. Really, the process is far simpler than photosynthesis."

The President looked thoughtfully at Howard. "Suppose Doctor Glynn's concept proves viable, Tom. What would it mean in terms of food production in the northern hemisphere?"

Howard made a sweeping gesture. "It would be a quantum leap forward, Madam President. We could grow crops even in the far northern latitudes. Beyond that, we'd have accelerated-growth cycles because plants would continue growing even at night. Hell, we could raise corn in caves!"

Admiral Mathisen shuffled the papers before him. "What are the chances that Doctor Glynn will succeed in developing these new hybrids?"

"As you know, she's the world's foremost molecular biologist, with one hell of a track record, Mike," Howard said. "I sure as hell wouldn't bet against her."

The intercom buzzed on the President's desk and she jabbed at the On button. "Yes?"

"Director Jeung is here, Madam President," Megan Humpal said. "He insists he must see you immediately."

"Very well, send him in."

A moment later, the Oval Office door opened and C.I.A. Director Dan Jeung hurried across the room, his face pale and his eyes bulging behind his owl glasses.

"I don't think Dan's got good news," the insouciant Bonham deadpanned.

"Just once, Rob, just once, could you shut your fucking wise-ass mouth?" Jeung spit out, his hands quivering as he snapped open his briefcase.

The others looked at the director in shock. He never used language like that, certainly never in front of the President.

"Take it easy, Dan," President Piziali said. "Now what's happened?"

"A half hour ago we received a coded cable from the station chief in Buenos Aires, Madam President. It concerns the *Bukharin*."

"Your people finally find out where the junta's got her stashed away?" Admiral Mathisen asked.

"We know where she was: at the General San Martin Naval Base on the Rio de la Plata south of Buenos Aires."

"Was?" Mathisen said.

"She's gone to sea. According to our contact with de Urquiza's mistress, the *Bukharin* is headed full steam for the North Atlantic."

"Why the hell would they send a nuclear submarine to the North Atlantic?" the President asked.

Jeung took a deep breath. "The *Bukharin* has orders to

destroy Ice Station Alpha, Madam President. For obvious reasons. If the Arctic Alteration succeeds, the northern hemisphere will once again be the breadbasket of the world. The junta has invested billions in developing new agricultural lands, beef herds, roads, ships, rail lines, you name it. If Argentina loses its position as the principal supplier of food to the world, their economy will collapse within months."

"And the junta will be history," Bonham said.

The president shook her head in wonder. "De Urquiza must be stark raving mad. Just plain crazy. What would make him think he could get away with an attack on an American installation?"

Admiral Mathisen frowned. "Look at it from de Urquiza's point of view, Madam President. He's not attacking with conventional forces. He's sending out a submarine the world thinks went down ten years ago. It's untraceable. We don't have photographs. We removed her acoustic signature from our computer system years ago when she was reported sunk. She's a goddamn ghost. How the hell do we accuse a ghost of attacking Ice Station Alpha?"

The eyes of C.I.A. Director Jeung lit like supernovas. "Jesus Christ, Mike, if the *Bukharin* sends a volley of torpedoes into the Gulf Stream dam, we're going to have sonar recordings of the torpedo runs. We'll have satellite photographs of the ice exploding. Not to mention a couple of hundred dead American bodies feeding the halibut."

Mathisen shook his head. "You don't understand the sea conditions up there, Dan. Now suppose the *Bukharin* does put five or six torpedoes into the dam. The problem is with the marine acoustics in the area. The ice floes are continuously breaking apart, cracking, bergs turning upside down. It would be all but impossible to tell the difference between a hundred-thousand-ton iceberg shattering under normal sea conditions and that same berg being split apart by torpedoes."

The President turned to Bonham. "Get the secretary of state on the phone. I want him to cable our ambassador in Argentina and have him inform the junta that unless the

Bukharin is recalled immediately, the United States will take immediate action against Argentina."

"Are you suggesting war, Madam President?" Mathisen asked.

"I don't know if I would go that far, but certainly we would have to take some retaliatory action. Perhaps shell their naval installations and bomb their military airfields."

Mathisen shook his head. "In order to attack Argentina's military targets, we would have to have proof that the *Bukharin* torpedoed Ice Station Alpha. The only way we could do that would be to force the sub to the surface and capture her, or send her to the bottom and then salvage the wreck. There's no guarantee we could do either."

"Then we threaten to blockade the major Argentine ports," Rob Bonham suggested. "Bottle up their freighters and grain carriers. Without those dollars they earn from food exports, the bastards will go bankrupt in six months."

"And in those six months, one third of the northern hemisphere will starve to death," Mathisen said. "Neither the U.N. nor the European nations would support a blockade of Argentina. Hell, I doubt that even Congress would authorize it. Certainly not if based on the flimsy evidence we have so far that the junta even plans a submarine attack on Ice Station Alpha."

Director Jeung thumped the intelligence report in his hands. "We have irrefutable proof right here."

"I'll tell you what you've got there, Dan," Mathisen thundered. "You've got an unsubstantiated report from a junior intelligence officer who's been screwing de Urquiza's mistress. You really think Congress would authorize military action against Argentina, or even a blockade, on the basis of one piece of intelligence from some whoremaster in your Buenos Aires station? No way!"

"How dare you say such a thing? Oliver Fleming is the best intelligence officer we've got in South America."

The President waved an impatient hand. "Mike's right. Given the normal breakup of bergs, there's no way we could prove that the *Bukharin* attacked Ice Station Alpha

unless we capture or sink her. And it sounds to me like
the odds against either are pretty steep. Damn it, we don't
even have evidence the submarine exists."

The President turned to Admiral Mathisen. "Assuming
that de Urquiza refuses to recall the *Bukharin*, and we
can't expect Congressional or international support for
military or economic action against Argentina, what are
the practical chances our Navy can intercept that submarine before it reaches Ice Station Alpha?"

Mathisen shrugged. "We must anticipate tremendous
problems in locating the *Bukharin* in the sea off Newfoundland, Madam President."

"You're talking about the marine acoustics again?"

"Exactly. We track enemy subs through sound waves,
sonar. And there are several thermal layers off Ice Station
Alpha that totally screw up passive sonar. On top of that,
you've got the Labrador Current running in one direction
and the Gulf Stream in the other, and that creates flow
noise that totally negates sonar. Add the sounds of ice
grinding and breaking apart and what you have is an area
of sea in which even our most advanced sonar systems
are all but useless."

"Are you telling me that even though we know the
Bukharin intends to attack Ice Station Alpha, we can't do a
goddamn thing about it?"

Mathisen didn't hesitate. "I see only one solution. We
send our entire Atlantic Fleet north and surround Ice Station Alpha with warships and ASW subs."

"ASW?" the President said.

"Anti-Submarine Warfare vessels, Madam President."

Piziali stared at the chairman of the Joint Chiefs of Staff.
"Mike, I want a straight answer. If that nut de Urquiza
refuses to recall the *Bukharin*, what are our chances of
stopping her?"

Mathisen shrugged. "We must assume that the captain
of the *Bukharin* is a former Soviet submarine officer,
which means that he's familiar with the Arctic. The bastards have been operating boomer bastions up there for
years."

The President's brow furrowed. " 'Boomer bastions'?"

"Basically, they're lairs under the ice where Soviet ballistic-missile submarines hid out, undetectable by aircraft or satellites, and usually surrounded by a belt of ASW mines. If her captain has been stationed in one of those bastions, he knows the marine acoustics I mentioned—the ice grinding together, the thermal layers and all the rest. If he's smart, he'll come in at under five knots, which will make the *Bukharin* all but undetectable given the noise in the sea. We can use a technique called 'bottom bounce,' which employs active sonar to bounce sonar waves off the bottom to locate an enemy submarine. Still, I'd put our chances at finding the *Bukharin* at about fifty-fifty."

Jeung turned to the President. "Those aren't real great odds, Madam President. It might be wise to evacuate civilians from the station until this thing is resolved one way or the other."

"Agreed," the President said. "Mike, start pulling the scientists and civilian technicians out of there immediately."

Mathisen nodded. "I'll issue the necessary orders within the hour, Madam President. However, keep in mind that this is a civilian project. Technically, I can't force Ben Meade to leave. And frankly, given how vital the dam is to warming the climate—and all the work Ben's invested in it—I rather doubt he'd be willing to pull out."

The President sighed. "You're probably right." She leaned forward, her eyes taking in all three of her advisers in turn. "My decision is this: we give the junta forty-eight hours to recall the *Bukharin*. We pressure them however we can—threaten to drive down the value of the peso, cut off vital supplies like super-computers and machine parts. Whatever would hurt the bastards most. If de Urquiza refuses to comply, we send the Atlantic Fleet north and search out and sink the *Bukharin*."

Mathisen looked into the President's eyes. "You do not sink a submarine, Madam President, you kill her."

The President stared at the chairman of the Joint Chiefs. "What do you mean, 'kill her'?"

"If a surface vessel is bombed or torpedoed, there's still a chance that a good part of the crew can take to the lifeboats. Get into the water, away from the explosions and fires. But in a sub, when that torpedo or mine or depth charge comes through the hull, your world explodes and there is nothing but the rush of pressurized water, splitting plates, and the certainty of dying way down there deep in the sea. Every man dies. You don't sink a submarine, Madam President. You kill her."

The President looked at Admiral Mathisen for a long moment. "Then kill the *Bukharin*, Mike. I don't care if it takes every ship in the Atlantic Fleet. Kill her!"

BAFFIN BAY, 200 MILES
WEST OF GREENLAND
• •

1:35 p.m.–May 31st

As THE NAVY RECONNAISSANCE prop plane broke through
the cloud cover over Baffin Bay, Ben Meade turned to
Marjorie Glynn in the seat beside him and pointed down
at the ever-widening stretch of open sea.

"Just look at that," he said, elation in his voice. "The
Gulf Stream is melting the sea ice even faster than we calculated."

Marjorie squeezed his hand. "It could mean that the climate will warm months—maybe even a year—earlier
than you expected."

Ben leaned forward in the small cabin and tapped the
pilot on the shoulder. "Bring us down and do a slow circle, will you, Lieutenant? I want a closer look."

"Yes, sir," the pilot nodded, dipping the left wing toward the freezing bay below.

As the plane descended and skimmed over the ice, the
effect of the Gulf Stream waters on the floes became more
apparent. The broad, deep current was cutting an ever-
wider path through the sea ice. Miles inward from the
open water, great cracks had opened in the ice sheet, and
huge slabs of ice were breaking away and drifting south

toward the warmer, open ocean below Greenland.

Ben stared thoughtfully at the crevices in the floes. "You know, Marjorie, if we began laser runs over the ice fields at a low enough altitude, we could burn fissures in the ice and break up the floes a lot faster."

Marjorie's face lit up. "Ben, I think that's a great idea." She leaned across and kissed his cheek. "You know what I love best about all this?"

"What?"

"That we're thinking alike again. The chasm between us has closed. We've found what we lost."

He gave her a big bear hug. "I love you, Marjorie."

"And I love you, Ben. God, these days together on Ice Station Alpha have been the best of my life. The very best."

The radio buzzed in the cockpit, and the pilot leaned forward and flipped on the receiver. He listened for a moment, then turned to Ben. "It's for you, Doctor Meade. Admiral Mathisen."

"Put it on the speakerphone," Ben said.

The pilot turned on the cabin speaker system.

"Hello, Mike," Ben said. "How are you?"

"Rather troubled at the moment, Ben. I'm ordering the immediate evacuation of all civilians from Ice Station Alpha."

Ben looked at Marjorie in astonishment. "What the hell are you talking about, Mike? Jesus, we're flying over Baffin Bay now and everything's working exactly as planned. Better. The Gulf Stream's melting the sea ice at an even faster rate than I calculated."

"Ben, the Argentine junta has sent a nuclear submarine—the *Bukharin*—north with orders to destroy the dam. We're going to surround the site with warships and ASW subs, but there's no guarantee that we can stop that sub. If she gets through, she can put enough torpedoes into the bergs to blow Ice Station Alpha apart."

"Why the hell would they want to destroy the dam?" Ben asked.

"Because if we warm the climate and our new food crops flourish, Argentina loses her position as the bread-basket of the world," Mathisen said. "This is economic life or death to Argentina. The junta will risk anything."

Ben pounded the arm of his seat. "Goddammit, Mike, there must be something we can do. Threaten to launch an air strike on Buenos Aires, sink every ship in their fucking navy. Something."

"The problem is that we can't prove the *Bukharin* even exists, Ben, much less that she's been sent to destroy Ice Station Alpha."

Ben stared down at the huge crevices in the floes below. "And the way ice is constantly breaking up, we wouldn't have any evidence she torpedoed the dam anyway."

"Exactly. An attack on Argentina would be considered an unprovoked act of war. And with Buenos Aires supplying most of the northern hemisphere with food, we'd be isolated internationally. We could lose what little trade we have left, along with millions of sorely needed American jobs."

Ben threw back his head and sighed. "There must be *some* way to stop the *Bukharin* before she can reach us."

"You know the marine acoustics up there, Ben. Sonar's useless with all that water turbulence. It would be like listening for a single low voice in a room crowded with people talking loudly. No, I'm sorry, but there's too great a risk that the *Bukharin* will be able to slip past our defensive line and get in close enough to fire her torpedoes. I want you and Marjorie to evacuate Ice Station Alpha immediately."

"I'm a civilian, Mike. You can't order me off the ice and you know it."

"Dammit, I told the president you'd give us trouble on this."

"I'm not leaving, Mike. Good-bye."

Ben shut off the speakerphone and leaned forward, his head in his hands. "I don't give a shit what Mathisen says. I'm not going to let some Argentine dictator take away the only chance for survival for millions of people. I'm not leaving Ice Station Alpha."

Marjorie bent forward and put her arms around his shoulders. "Then I'm staying, too."

"Marjorie—"

"No, Ben. I left you once. I'll never leave you again."

BUENOS AIRES, ARGENTINA
• •

11:45 a.m.–June 1st

ARGENTINE GENERAL RAMON SAAVEDRA de Urquiza stared fiercely across his desk at the guarded face of Colonel Manuel Cortez, head of Argentina's Secret Police.

"Well, have you found her yet?"

"No, my General. Although we've developed several leads."

"I assume that you've questioned the sergeant I assigned to guard her. What's his name?"

"Martinez. Julio Martinez. And we questioned him forcefully. Most forcefully."

De Urquiza knew Cortez meant that the sergeant had been tortured. "And?"

"He swears he drove Miss Echeverria to her art class at the university as he always does on Wednesdays. It's customary for him to wait for her outside in the car until she returns. Only this time, of course, she never came back out."

"You said you'd developed several leads. What are they?"

Colonel Cortez averted his eyes. "Señorita Echeverria's

art professor told my investigators that she hadn't attended class for several weeks."

De Urquiza reddened. "She's been sneaking away, to see some lover, no doubt."

"There could be some other reason. You know women. They like to get together and gossip. Or she might have wanted to go shopping without her guard along. There could be a dozen other explanations."

"That's bullshit, and you know it! She's been screwing some bastard. And now she's run off with him."

De Urquiza rose and paced. "What else have you learned?"

"We questioned all the students we could find who'd been at the university that day. We finally found one art major who said he was looking out the window of his class and he saw a young woman who fits Señorita Echeverria's description get into a red-and-white taxi. That would make it one of the Urbana fleet. We went through their trip records and discovered that one of their cars had picked up a fare at the university at the same time Señorita Echeverria was seen leaving."

"Where did the taxi take her?"

"To an expensive apartment building in the Recoleta section."

"Do you know which apartment she went to?"

"Yes. When we showed the doorman her picture, he remembered her very well. She went up to the penthouse of an architect who recently moved into the building. He said she'd been there before. He wasn't sure how many times. They left together shortly after Maria arrived."

"What's this architect's name?"

"Oliver Alberdi. At least that's the name on his lease. When we checked with the Architects' Association, they'd never heard of him. As a matter of fact, there's no record of an Oliver Alberdi anywhere in Argentina. No birth certificate, no driver's license, no national identity card. Nothing."

"Have you questioned this man?"

"No, sir. He hasn't returned to his penthouse since he was seen leaving that day with Maria."

De Urquiza returned to his desk and sank slowly into

his chair, the implications of Cortez's revelation sending the blood pounding through his brain.

"If this man is not an architect, is not even an Argentine citizen, then who is he?" he asked, fearing the answer as if a knife were against his throat.

Cortez took a deep breath. "He paid his lease with checks from an account at the Bank of Argentina. All deposits to that account were made by the United States Embassy. We believe that Alberdi, or whatever his name is, is an American intelligence agent."

"Are you telling me that Maria has been seeing an American spy?"

"I'm afraid that is how it now appears."

De Urquiza pounded his desk. "The bitch! I'll kill her for this. I'll kill both of them! Both of them!"

Cortez had no doubt that De Urquiza meant exactly what he said.

"I want an immediate search of the city. Use intelligence agents, police, army units. I want them found! Do you understand? I want them found!"

"Yes, my General," Cortez said, then saluted and turned for the door.

As the Secret Police chief left, the intercom buzzed on de Urquiza's desk. "What is it?" he yelled into the phone.

"The American ambassador is here, General de Urquiza," the disconcerted secretary said.

De Urquiza glanced at his appointment calendar. "I don't have a meeting scheduled with the ambassador."

"I know that, sir. But he insists that the matter is of the highest urgency."

De Urquiza sighed. What now? "Very well. Send him in."

Ambassador Terence O'Malley looked every inch the diplomat. Tall, with a salt-and-pepper beard, he was impeccably dressed in a pin-striped suit and carried himself with an air of dignity and authority.

"Please sit down," de Urquiza said as the ambassador approached his desk. "What may I do for you today, Mister Ambassador?"

"I am here on a most unpleasant matter, General de Urquiza. I have been directed by my government to deliver this communication to you." He snapped open his brief-case and handed the junta leader a two-page letter on embassy stationery.

De Urquiza put on his glasses and began to read, the veins in his temples bulging as he grasped the missive's meaning. When he finished reading, he threw his glasses on his desk and glared at the American ambassador.

"This is preposterous," he said. "Argentina does not possess a nuclear submarine."

O'Malley stared back with open disbelief. "On the contrary, General de Urquiza, we have evidence that you purchased the nuclear submarine *Bukharin* from Ukraine, and further, that that vessel is now on its way to destroy Ice Station Alpha. If that attack occurs, the United States will take each of the retaliatory steps stated in the communication before you."

"Are you threatening me, Ambassador O'Malley?"

"Let's call it a warning, General de Urquiza. Make no mistake, my government will act, and act swiftly. The United States will drive down the value of your currency until you won't be able to buy a loaf of bread with a suitcase of pesos. We will also immediately cut off all supplies of computers, communications equipment, machine parts, and all industrial equipment you now obtain from the United States. I believe we both know that without resupplies of American material, your manufacturing base will collapse within a matter of months."

"I'll hear no more of this, Ambassador O'Malley. Leave my office at once."

O'Malley rose. "As the letter states, you have forty-eight hours in which to recall the *Bukharin*, General. My advice is that you do so."

As the ambassador left, de Urquiza snatched the phone off the hook. "Get Admiral Secchi and General Moreno over here," he ordered his secretary. "Immediately."

Forty-five minutes later, the two other members of the junta arrived at de Urquiza's office, both obviously nervous and apprehensive at the sudden summons.

"Read this!" de Urquiza ordered without greeting them, handing the American letter to Admiral Secchi. The Admiral paled as he read the ultimatum.

"How . . . how did they find out?" he asked, passing the letter to General Moreno.

"That is not a matter that concerns you. Either of you," de Urquiza said as Moreno finished reading the letter. "I called you here to consult with you on what our response should be. Do we recall the *Bukharin* or continue the operation?"

General Moreno replied first. "If they carry out their threat—and we must assume they will—it will devastate our Air Force. As you know, three-quarters of our fighters and bombers are American-made. Without spare parts from the U.S., half our planes will be unable to fly within six months. In a year, we wouldn't have an Air Force."

"The Navy would be in the same dire straits," Admiral Secchi said. "Our warships were built primarily in America."

"What is to prevent us from buying new planes and ships from other countries?" de Urquiza countered. "There are at least a dozen European nations that would gladly sell us all the war materials we ask for. The same thing applies to computers, industrial supplies and the rest. Goddammit, with the financial collapse in the northern hemisphere, they'd sell their mothers for export income."

"Which brings up the matter of the American threat to drive down the value of the peso," Secchi pointed out.

"I've already considered that," de Urquiza said. "They may be able to effect some devaluation, but if we demand payment for our food exports in dollars, what can they really do? It's an idle threat on their part, a mark of American desperation."

"There is another matter to consider," Admiral Secchi said. "Now that the Americans know the *Bukharin* has been sent to attack their installation, they will have every ASW sub, every warship in their Atlantic Fleet, searching for her."

"What are their chances of finding and sinking the *Bukharin* before she can destroy the dam?" de Urquiza asked.

"The new American ASW submarines have the most advanced sonar equipment of any submarine force in the world," Secchi said. "As well as the best-trained captains and crews. On the other hand, as Captain Lobov said, the dam is located in an extremely complex acoustical environment: ice floes breaking apart, thermal layers, an abundance of large marine mammals. The *Bukharin* may yet get through, but only if Captain Lobov is both skillful and lucky."

"If the *Bukharin* were to be tracked down and torpedoed, what are her odds of surviving?" the junta leader asked.

Secchi threw back his head and considered the question for a moment. "The *Bukharin* is a Typhoon-class submarine, General de Urquiza. It is massively constructed, with both inner and outer hulls. Even two ADCAP hits would probably not sink her."

"ADCAP?"

"Advanced-Capability torpedoes, General. The newest the Americans possess."

"Could she still complete her mission?"

"Possibly, although it is more likely that she would be forced to surface. In which case, she would, of course, be captured."

General Moreno's eyes looked frightened. "Do you realize, General de Urquiza, that if the Americans capture the *Bukharin* with an Argentine crew aboard, or sink her and then have their salvage crew discover the bodies of our sailors, they'd have a legitimate excuse to declare war on Argentina? Do you know what their Air Force and Navy could do to us? Bomb and shell us back to the Stone Age. Not to mention a military invasion. We must recall the *Bukharin*. Immediately. The risk is simply too great."

De Urquiza rubbed his eyes and sank back in his chair, weighing the terrible decision before him. On the one hand, the destruction of the American dam would guarantee continued Argentine food exports—and economic supremacy—for decades to come. Yet if the *Bukharin* were captured or sunk and salvaged, the U.S. would have every justification for declaring war, and the defeat of Argentina was a foregone conclusion. Moreno was right; the risk was simply too great.

De Urquiza sighed and looked at Admiral Secchi. "Recall the *Bukharin* immediately. I will inform the American embassy that the operation has been canceled."

Both Secchi and Moreno looked relieved.

"Admiral Secchi, you are to call me as soon as you have contacted Captain Lobov and he has turned the *Bukharin* back for Buenos Aires."

"Yes, General de Urquiza."

"That is all, gentlemen. We will meet later to discuss how to proceed, given these developments."

Secchi and Moreno rose, saluted and left the junta leader's office.

As their footsteps receded, de Urquiza rose and in one furious gesture swept all the papers off his desk onto the floor. His glorious plans for the future of Argentina—destroyed by the treachery of one woman. The woman who had shared his bed and his deepest secrets. The woman he had trusted.

When the Secret Police caught Maria Echeverria, she would die slowly . . . very slowly.

VISCOUNT MELVILLE SOUND, 1100 MILES SOUTH OF THE NORTH POLE

• •

6:00 p.m.–June 2nd

CAPTAIN VIKTOR LOBOV WAS sitting in his tiny cabin doing what he loved best in the world: planning an attack. Before, it had always been war games. Just pretend. But this time, it was for real.

Men would go to their battle stations. The torpedoes would be fired. He felt the warmth stir in his groin as he thought of listening to the sonarman read out the nearing approach of the torpedoes to their target, then the thunderous explosions as the weapons struck Ice Station Alpha.

This would be the crowning moment of his life, the event that would give meaning to his naval training, his dozens of submarine patrols, and, yes, even to his years alone at the bottom of the Black Sea.

He would, of course, use the complex acoustics of the Arctic to stalk Ice Station Alpha, cutting the speed of the *Bukharin* and letting her move soundlessly south in the middle of the noisy Labrador Current. The American Fleet was busy helping build the dam. The sounds of their propellers and noises from the machinery aboard the ships would further mask any listening U.S. sonar.

As Lobov smugly contemplated the coming attack, there was a sudden knock on his door. "Enter," he said.

"Message from the radio room, Captain," the young seaman at the door said.

Lobov took the folded sheet of paper. "Wait outside for my reply," he said, then shut the door and sat down to read. The farther he read, the more his face hardened. By the time he finished the message, he looked as if he'd been carved from stone. Even his flat eyes resembled the motionless marble orbs of a Greek statue.

The junta had ordered him to call off the attack! For a moment, he was too stunned to think. His mind reeled, alternating between a compulsion to scream and an insane desire to laugh.

It was unthinkable! They wanted to take away the greatest achievement he would ever know in his life. And what of the *Bukharin?* What was the purpose of her existence but to go to war? To attack the enemy. Instead, the junta wanted him to return the *Bukharin* to Buenos Aires. There, she would undoubtedly become part of the Argentine Fleet, endlessly patrolling the coast, playing war games, never again knowing the thrill of the attack. It would be like turning a wild tiger into a house cat.

Slowly, Lobov shook his head. No! He would not allow the junta to do this to him. He would not allow them to do this to the *Bukharin*.

He turned to his desk and wrote out a response to the radioman. First, there would be no reply to the message. He also ordered that there be no radio traffic sent from the *Bukharin* until further notice. Messages from Buenos Aires were not to be acknowledged. He ended by ordering the radioman to keep the contents of the message from the junta strictly to himself under penalty of being chained in the brig. He was to tell no one.

Lobov folded the paper and opened the door. He gave his reply to the young seaman. "Did you read the message that was just brought to me?" he asked.

"No, sir," the seaman said, obviously offended. "It is strictly against regulations to read messages to the captain."

"See that you don't read my response, either. And tell

the radioman to put my message through the shredder. Understand?"

"Yes, sir," the seaman said, then saluted and hurried down the corridor toward the radio room.

Lobov shut the door and picked up the message from the junta. Then he lit a cigarette lighter and set the paper on fire, holding it until it was almost burning his fingers. He put the remnants in an ashtray and watched them flicker out in ashes.

The junta could send a hundred identical orders a day and it would do them no good. The *Bukharin* was unreachable, unstoppable, as free to pursue her destiny as were the pirate ships of two centuries past.

And the destiny of the *Bukharin* was the destruction of Ice Station Alpha. Of course, now that the Americans knew the *Bukharin* was coming, the attack would be far more difficult. He would have to change his plans.

Yet, given the marine acoustics in the area and the fact that the south-flowing currents would carry the *Bukharin* silently most of the way to the target, Lobov believed the odds continued in his favor.

Even more, the game had now become more exciting, an intoxicating test of the powers of the *Bukharin* and his skills as a captain. What were the wants of three stupid old men in Buenos Aires when measured against a moment of history, an attack so audacious, so stupendous in its consequences, that the world would never forget it?

The attack would go on as planned.

THE WHITE HOUSE,
WASHINGTON, D.C.
●●●●●●●●●●●●●●●●●●●●

7:15 p.m.–June 2nd

PRESIDENT KATHLEEN PIZIALI SAT back and raised the glass of champagne in her hand to Mike Mathisen, Tom Howard, and Rob Bonham, sitting in deep, wingback chairs across from her in the oval sitting room of the White House family quarters.

"Gentlemen, may I propose a toast?" she smiled. "To Ice Station Alpha, and to the warmth and life it will bring to millions of people throughout the northern hemisphere."

The genesis of the celebration was the arrival an hour before of a cable from the American Embassy in Buenos Aires. The message brought the joyous news that the junta had capitulated and agreed to recall the *Bukharin* immediately. The attack on Ice Station Alpha had been canceled.

"I wasn't at all sure that de Urquiza would give in," the President said. "I've read his C.I.A. psychological profile. The guy's unhinged, a megalomanic of the first order."

"It's no wonder, Madam President," Rob Bonham said. "In Argentina, he's the king. Matter of fact, with all the food he supplies the northern hemisphere, the guy's practically an international saint. Oh, governments and people grumble about the ever-increasing cost of Argentine food. But de Urquiza himself is a Teflon leader, like Reagan was back in the eighties. When people think of him, they think of the huge improvement he's made in Argentine agriculture. An agriculture, must I remind you, that's feeding half the world."

Tom Howard nodded in agreement. "The bastard's also smart enough to play the PR card and give away free food to some of the more destitute Balkan countries. Not much, but enough to buy him a good-guy image in Europe and Asia. Millions of people think of him as the man who provides the food that feeds their families. I swear, I think that if there were such a thing as president of the goddamn world, he'd be elected."

"All of which is why he's recalled the *Bukharin*," Bonham said. "Given the risks involved now that we know he planned an attack, he had too much to lose—his throne in Argentina, his international image, the very power he thrives on."

President Piziali looked appraisingly across the rim of her glass at Admiral Mathisen. "Mike, you seem strangely subdued, given the moment. What's on your mind?"

"The message from the embassy read only that de Urquiza had recalled the *Bukharin,* not that she had actually started back. I don't trust the sons of bitches. I want to know exactly where that submarine is right now, and her daily position until she reaches Argentine waters."

The President put down her glass. "You think this is some kind of ploy, that de Urquiza still means to attack Ice Station Alpha?"

Mathisen shook his head. "No, I think Rob and Tom are right. He's got too much to lose now that we're aware that the *Bukharin* is sailing north to attack the dam. I think he's probably sent the order. The problem is, the *Bukharin* may be under the ice where she can't receive radio transmissions. Worse, the captain of the *Bukharin* is a fanatic. A lover of stealth and attack. And a man with no conscience. What other sort of human being would order the sinking of that unarmed tanker off Gibraltar and the murder of those innocent sailors aboard?"

"He doesn't sound like a fanatic, Mike. He sounds like a goddamn nut," Howard said.

"He may well be unbalanced," Mathisen nodded in agreement. "What's more, he's a Ukrainian, with little or no loyalty to the Argentine junta. At this moment, we have no guarantee that this fanatic, madman—whatever the hell he is—will call off his attack on Ice Station Alpha."

Mathisen sat back and tented his fingers beneath his chin. "Madam President, there is something about the probable psychology of this captain that must be understood. The man is a loose cannon, a rogue of the sea in command of one of the most powerful weapons of war on the planet."

President's Piziali's face clouded over. "Are you telling me that this Ukrainian captain might continue the attack on his own initiative?"

"Look at it from his point of view, Madam President. Were he to cancel the attack and return to Argentina, he would undoubtedly be replaced in a short time by an Argentine captain and sent back to the Ukraine, a nation that possesses no submarines since they sold the *Bukharin*. He would have no purpose to his life, and the rest of his days would be spent reliving empty memories."

Mathisen leaned forward. "On the other hand, a successful attack would make him a maritime legend. And if I judge this fanatic right, he'd be willing to risk his life, his crew and his boat for that."

"What do you suggest we do, Mike?" the President asked, all gaiety now gone from her face.

"I want to continue to surround the dam with our Atlantic Fleet—especially with the ASW subs—until we have visual and electronic tracking verification that the *Bukharin* has returned to Argentina. After that, our intelligence people will be watching her like a hawk."

Rob Bonham said, "I'd also like our embassy to obtain a copy of the *Bukharin*'s reply to the junta's recall order. I believe we should review that captain's response the moment we can get our hands on it."

"I think those are both wise ideas. Move on them," President Piziali said.

"Madam President, tomorrow morning I'm flying up to Ice Station Alpha," Mike Mathisen said. "Until we have positive proof that the *Bukharin* has turned south and I can put a couple of ASW tracking subs on her, I intend to take personal charge of the defense of Ice Station Alpha."

"Let's hope there'll be no need to defend Alpha, Mike, and that the *Bukharin* has canceled the attack and turned back for Argentina."

"Begging the President's pardon, but hope didn't help us at Pearl Harbor. The enemy took us by surprise and kicked the guts out of us. That will never happen to the American Navy again."

"Keep your eyes open up there, Mike."

"It won't be our eyes but our ears that we'll need sharp, Madam President. If the *Bukharin* does attempt an attack, only sonar might find her. That and a hell of a lot of luck."

ICE STATION ALPHA
●●●●●●●●●●●●●●●●●●●

9:30 p.m.–June 2nd

BEN AND MARJORIE LAY naked in Ben's bed, snuggled beneath a warm goose-down quilt that Marjorie's mother had sent over, their hands entwined as they talked of past mistakes and future dreams.

A lull came in their quiet conversation, and Marjorie suddenly grinned mischievously and propped herself up on one elbow, facing Ben. "Tell me about your first sexual experience. Do you remember?"

Ben smiled widely. "God, yes. Doesn't everyone?"

"Women always do, but I never knew about men."

"I can't speak for other men, but I'll never forget my first lover. Her name was Dee. I met her on Watermill Beach in the Hamptons, out on the ritzy end of Long Island."

"Long Island? That's off New York, isn't it?"

"Yes. I was visiting an aunt who owned a summer home out there."

"How old were you?"

"Fourteen."

"Well, what happened?"

"You don't really want to hear this, do you?"

"I asked, didn't I?"

Ben squirmed uncomfortably, much to Marjorie's delight. "God, I've never told anyone about it before. I haven't even thought about it in years."

"C'mon, c'mon, out with it."

Ben let out a reluctant sigh. "Like I said, we met on the beach. She was wearing a little red-and-white-checked bikini. And she was beautiful—light brown hair falling over her shoulders, melon breasts, long legs, and the cutest little buns I'd ever seen."

"You like buns, don't you? Your hands are always all over my bottom."

"I'm a bun freak, I admit it."

Marjorie giggled. "Don't stop there. What happened?"

"We went out that night, and a couple more times in the next few days. Up to then, it was just making out, kissing and hugging, and a lot of heavy breathing. Then, about a week after we met, we went to a beach party."

Marjorie sighed wistfully. "I always wanted to go to a beach party when I was a teenager. Unfortunately, the North Sea off Dundee was so cold, and the beach so rocky, that no one ever dreamed of having a party there. Anyway, I didn't mean to interrupt."

"You didn't interrupt much. Honestly, Marjorie, it was just one of those teenage-romance phases. The whole thing will probably bore you to death."

"Nothing about you bores me. Now go on and tell me the rest. I want to hear every little detail."

Ben took a big breath. "We got to the party about an hour before the sun set, and for a while, we lay on the warm sand just kind of kissing and holding hands. At dusk, we decided to go for a swim and when we stood up, Dee stretched out the waistband of her bikini bottom, you know, to get the sand out."

Ben suddenly stopped and reddened. "Jesus, I can't tell you this stuff."

"We promised each other we'd share every little secret. Remember?"

"God! All right, all right. Anyway, I was standing about two feet away, and when she stretched her waistband, I could see her pubic hair. It was only a half-second shot, something like that, but it was the first time I'd ever seen a girl's public hair."

Marjorie reached over and stroked his nipples. "Did it excite you?"

"Excite me? Jesus, I got an instant erection. I had to run into the ocean. Even in that cold water, it took about ten minutes for the damn thing to go down so I could come out again."

"Lord, you *were* bloody horny."

"Hell, I was fourteen. Raging hormones. I used to cop old copies of *Playboy* from the barbershop and hide them under my mattress."

"What happened when you came out of the ocean?"

"By that time, there was a big fire going, and everywhere you looked, there were couples making out in the shadows. Dee and I lay in the sand beside the fire for a while, making out and listening to the waves breaking in the dark beyond the flames. After a while, we started, well, humping each other."

"What's 'humping'?"

"You're kidding."

"No, honestly, I never heard that word before."

"It's the same motion as intercourse, moving against each other, except that you've both got your clothes on and there's no penetration. But I knew that was coming. I just knew, 'Tonight's the night.' "

"Was it 'the night'?"

Ben was silent for a moment, remembering, his mind back on the beach where he'd first made love twenty years ago.

"Yeah, it was," he said softly. "After a while, God, we were both so hot, and nothing on but our bathing suits. We dragged our beach blanket up to a little hollow on top of the dunes, beyond the firelight."

Ben laughed. "I couldn't figure out how to unsnap her top. Dee finally reached back and undid it herself. I'd never touched a girl's breasts before. I was in heaven. Heaven! It didn't take long before I had the bottom of her suit off. Then I yanked down my trunks."

Marjorie's voice was becoming husky. "Was it awkward? That first time?"

"No, that's the funny part. The rest just sort of came natural. Instinct maybe, I don't know. I'm sure I came too fast, before she could climax. God, I popped about ten seconds after I was in her."

"Did you make love to her after that night?"

"All the rest of the summer. Every night we went out. I learned to slow down. I learned a lot during those warm days and nights."

"Did you see her again after that summer?"

"No. I went back to Wyoming and Dee went back to boarding school in Connecticut. We wrote for a while, but after a few months, her letters started dropping off. Finally, just before Christmas, she sent me a 'Dear John' letter. She'd met some preppy from one of those blue-blood New England private schools. They were pinned. She was real sorry, what we'd had was special, blah, blah, blah."

"Were you hurt?"

"Damn right! I was crushed. She was the first girl I ever loved. Truth is, before you, she was the only girl I ever loved."

"But you were married once. Didn't you love your wife?"

"No. I told you about that when we first met. The marriage just sort of happened. Elizabeth started out as one of my research assistants. It was a long drive from the ranch to the town where she lived, and after a few months, she asked if she could rent a cabin I had on the place. I said, 'Sure, move in any time. No charge.' "

"And before long, she found her way to your bed," Marjorie said.

"You got it. A few months after we began sleeping together, she started bringing up the subject of marriage. At first, I backed away. I mean, I didn't love her. But there were other parts to the equation."

"Such as?"

"I'd been living alone, eating those frozen dinners and canned ravioli, that sort of junk. Half the time I'd be working in the lab until midnight or later and forget about eating altogether. Then all of a sudden, here's Elizabeth making me breakfast every morning and cooking great dinners every night. She kept the house spic and span, did the laundry, started paying the household accounts. After a while, I figured what the hell, she's doing all this wife stuff, why not get married? Looking back, I guess I thought I owed it to her."

"And she paid you back by sleeping with your brother."

"Look, Marjorie, I don't want to go into that again. I almost killed them both when I caught them screwing. Then I almost killed myself drinking to forget. It was a bad time. A real bad time."

Marjorie put her head on his shoulder. "I'm sorry you had to go through that."

"It's long over." Ben turned her face up to his and grinned wickedly. "Besides, now it's your turn. Tell me about the first time you made love."

"You beat me by a year. I was fifteen."

"Some neighborhood kid?"

"No. Actually, my first experience was with the stable boy at Glennheather. We did it in the hayloft."

Ben laughed. "Lord Glynn's daughter made love to a stable boy!"

"He was quite handsome, you know. Dark, wavy hair, flashing brown eyes and a lean, hard body. He did so much physical work that his muscles fairly bulged out of his shirt. And he could ride a horse like a Mongol. I was terribly smitten."

"I've always wondered what it was like for a woman the first time. I've heard all these stories about how it hurts, about how the girl always feels guilt and shame. I dated one woman who told me she could never climax with a man because her first time was so bad."

"It wasn't at all like that for me," Marjorie said. "First of all, I'd long since broken my hymen riding horses. And Ambrose, that was his name, Ambrose and I made out for about an hour before we actually did it. By then, I was so wet and aroused, he slipped in quite easily."

Ben felt an erection rising as he listened to her. "Did you climax?" he asked.

"Yes. Twice. And I can tell you there was no guilt involved. Quite the opposite. I loved it. After that, Ambrose and I would go out riding together. Quite often, actually. We'd find some little glade in the woods and spread out a saddle blanket and just go at it."

"How long did you and Ambrose last?"

"About a year, I think. Then I went off to the university. After that, it was the old story. I met this chap in my botany class and we started dating, then sleeping together."

"Bye-bye, Ambrose."

"Right. Poor Ambrose was uneducated, of course. It wasn't his fault. He'd never had a chance to go beyond the primary grades. At Glennheather, it hadn't mattered to me. But the boy at the university had a mind, a very sharp mind, and I found I liked that in a man. I discovered that a man's mind was far more important to me than his body."

"How did you give Ambrose the news that it was over?"

"I was a really thoughtless bitch about that. When I came home on my first vacation, I avoided him as much as possible. When we did run into each other, I'd give him one of those polite but distant smiles."

"You must have hurt him a great deal."

"I continue to hurt him to this day, I'm afraid."

"What do you mean?"

"He still works at Glennheather. Often, when I'm down at the stable, I'll turn around and find Ambrose staring at me, a look of longing and lost love on his face. I always feel like giving myself a boot in the behind for being so callous with his feelings."

"Obviously," Ben said, "Ambrose has never gotten over you. And I can't say I blame him. You're beautiful, intelligent, fun to be with, and the daughter of the Lord of the Manor to boot. To him, you must seem like a goddess."

Marjorie smiled wryly. "If that's true, I wish he'd get over his infatuation. He deserves a wife and a life of his own."

"I can't believe we're being this open," Ben said, stroking her hair. "Day by day, all our guarded secrets are flooding out."

"Do you know what I love best about our relationship now?"

"What?"

"The fact that despite how busy we are—you with your endless work in the command hub, and me with my botany research over Internet—still, we save time for each other at the end of the day. We never did that before."

"You want to know my favorite thing?"

Marjorie kissed his nose. "Yes."

"The way our lovemaking has changed. It's not the rush to climax that it was in the months before we broke up. Like tonight. An hour, two hours, of talking and touching. We've rediscovered foreplay."

Marjorie laughed and buried her face against his shoulder. "I love it when you ask me what I want—like what position, or where to touch me. You never used to ask me."

"God, Marjorie, all this talk about first lovers has gotten me—"

Marjorie brought her lips up to his. "It's excited me, too," she whispered.

They were both ready now, aching for each other. Then, like being startled out of a beautiful dream, the phone on the nightstand suddenly rang.

Ben groaned. "I'm not going to answer it."

"Good."

But the phone kept ringing. Ten times, fifteen times.

"Goddammit," Ben swore. "I told the switchboard not to call my room after ten unless it was top priority."

"Well, then it must be an important call. I think you'd better answer it," Marjorie said.

He reached across to the metal nightstand and snatched the receiver off the hook. "Ben Meade."

"Mike Mathisen, Ben."

Ben cupped his hand over the mouthpiece. "It's Admiral Mathisen."

"No wonder they put it through."

"Good evening, Admiral. I hope you're not calling again to try to convince me to evacuate Ice Station Alpha. As I told you during our last conversation, I'm staying at the base."

"Actually, I'm calling with what I hope is good news, Ben. The junta has called off the attack. They've ordered the *Bukharin* to return to Argentina—"

"That's fantastic!" Ben said. "I can't wait to tell Marjorie."

"I think it would be premature to believe the attack won't come. Even though we believe that the junta has actually sent the order recalling the *Bukharin*, we can't be sure yet that the sub has received the transmission. If she's running deep, below four hundred feet, or if she's under the ice, her communications gear can only pick up ELF, extremely low frequency, signals. And I know for a fact that the Argentine Navy doesn't have the capability to send ELF messages."

"Surely the junta must have arranged certain radio-contact times with the sub," Ben said. "Hell, at fifty feet below the surface, the *Bukharin* could receive very low frequency without exposing her radio mast. The Argentines have at least a dozen non-nuclear subs. They must have VLF transmitters."

"That's probably true, but we've got a second problem here. We believe that the captain of the *Bukharin* may well be insane. Remember, this is the man who sank an unarmed tanker. He lives for the attack. There's a strong possibility that he may ignore the junta's order and send his torpedoes into Ice Station Alpha for what he sees as his own personal glory."

"When will you know whether he'll turn back or keep coming?" Ben asked.

"It could be hours, or it could be days," Mathisen said. "We've demanded that the junta turn over a copy of the captain's reply to their order, as well as give us the *Bukharin*'s exact location. Until we're sure that the sub has called off the attack, I intend to take personal command of the defense of the dam. I'll be leaving for the ice tomorrow morning."

"I'll be glad to have you here, Mike . . ." Ben said, ". . . as long as there's no more talk of my leaving Ice Station Alpha."

Mathisen laughed gruffly. "Wouldn't do any good anyway, would it? As I've said before, technically, it's a civilian project and under your command. The Navy is playing a support role, and I don't really have the authority to order you to do anything."

"Sounds like we can work together on this."

"That's all I'm asking. See you sometime tomorrow afternoon."

"Great, Mike."

Ben put down the phone and told Marjorie what Mathisen had said. Marjorie hugged him. "Things are looking up, aren't they? If that captain obeys the junta's orders, we can get on with our work without having to worry. Right?"

Ben sighed. "Yeah, but that's a big 'if.' Mike thinks the guy may be nuts and decide to continue the attack."

"I'm nuts, too," Marjorie grinned. "Nuts about you. Let's not worry about it anymore. What will happen will happen. Let's just think about the two of us now."

"That's the best idea I've heard all day. Let's see. Where were we . . ."

BUENOS AIRES
●●●●●●●●●●●●●●

4:45 p.m.–June 4th

WHEN ADMIRAL JUAN BAUTISTA Secchi walked into the huge office of the junta leader, his face was ashen and his briefcase shook in his trembling hands.

General de Urquiza sat behind his ornate desk in a barely controlled fury, his eyes hard and unblinking and the muscles bunched along his massive jaw.

"Well?" de Urquiza demanded, not bothering to invite the admiral to sit down.

"Lobov missed his scheduled radio-contact time again this morning," Secchi said. "He has not responded to a single one of the repeated messages we've been sending out for over two days now."

"Have you heard from the *Bukharin* at all?" de Urquiza asked. "A coded position transmission? Anything?"

"Nothing, my General."

"Is it possible he's under the ice and can't send or receive?"

"There are always open leads in the ice. Or places where the floes are thin enough for a submarine the size of the *Bukharin* to break through and send and receive radio transmissions. Certainly that is what I would expect him to do, if only at the scheduled contact times."

"Are you sure that Captain Lobov received our first transmission ordering the *Bukharin* to return to Argentina?"

"Yes, positive, General de Urquiza. The radio operator aboard the vessel acknowledged receipt of our transmission. Standard procedure. He radioed that he would send Captain Lobov's reply as soon as he received it. Of course the reply never came."

General de Urquiza sat back in his chair, his hands clasped tightly before his chest. "You realize that the Americans are apoplectic. They have demanded a copy of Captain Lobov's reply to our order. They also want to know the exact position of the *Bukharin*. Ambassador O'Malley calls here every goddamn hour asking why they have not received this information. What do you suggest I tell him?"

Secchi braced himself. "As I have been telling you for some time, General de Urquiza, I believe Captain Lobov to be insane. You will recall that I strongly advised against this mission."

De Urquiza shot forward in his chair and slammed a fist on his desktop. "What is done is done. I asked you what the hell we should tell the Americans."

"I believe that Captain Lobov intends to ignore our orders and continue the attack on Ice Station Alpha. I suggest we tell the Americans the truth, that we have a rogue submarine on our hands and there is nothing we can do to stop the assault."

"You realize the position this puts us in with Washington?" de Urquiza asked. "We're trapped. We've already admitted that we sent the *Bukharin* north to destroy the dam. If Lobov succeeds and torpedoes Ice Station Alpha, the Americans will have a legitimate excuse to attack our military installations."

"There is one thing we can do, General."

"What is that?"

"Help the Americans find and sink the *Bukharin* before she can get to her destination. We will still be condemned by the Americans for having planned the attack, but at least we may escape retaliatory action."

"How the hell do we help the Americans find the *Bukharin* when we don't know where she is ourselves?"

"We can reveal that the *Bukharin* is presently somewhere under the Arctic ice. That Captain Lobov plans his approach down through Baffin Bay and the Labrador Sea. That will allow the Americans to concentrate their naval forces north of the dam. If the Americans know the direction the attack is coming from, it will give them a far better chance of finding and sinking the *Bukharin*."

De Urquiza blanched at the thought of losing his prized nuclear submarine. "You don't believe there is some technical or other reason that Captain Lobov has not responded to our command?"

"The *Bukharin* has a backup radio, General. If the primary radio failed, they could always use the spare set. And if they had a reactor or other mechanical problem, they would, or should have, notified us. No, Captain Lobov has ignored our transmissions because he plans to carry out the attack."

De Urquiza thought for a moment, then sighed and sagged in his chair. "I think you're right, Secchi. Lobov is undoubtedly mad, and we have far more to lose than a submarine if he succeeds in his attack. I want you to go personally to the American Embassy and tell Ambassador O'Malley exactly what you have told me—that the *Bukharin* is now a rogue submarine under the command of a captain we believe to have gone insane. Also give them Lobov's approach course from the north."

The admiral was visibly relieved. "I will go to the embassy at once, General," he said, then saluted and left the junta leader's office.

For a long moment, de Urquiza sat motionless, weighing the possible consequences of the coming naval action in the far north. If Captain Lobov succeeded in his attack, the junta leader could expect immediate retaliatory action from the U.S.

And even if the American Navy found and sank the sub, de Urquiza would be condemned by every nation on the planet for having planned the attack. It was probable that even the Argentine press and people would be so appalled that he would be driven out of office.

Whatever happened, Ramon Saavedra de Urquiza knew that he was doomed.

ICE STATION ALPHA
●●●●●●●●●●●●●●●●●●●●●

7:30 p.m.–June 4th

"OUR MAJOR PROBLEM IS that we simply don't know yet whether the *Bukharin* will continue the attack," Admiral Mike Mathisen said to Ben and Marjorie as the three dined in the officers' mess on Ice Station Alpha.

"We don't even have a clue as to where the goddamn sub is. And we won't have answers to either question until we receive a reply to our ultimatum to the Argentine junta."

"Let's take the worst-case scenario," Ben said, "and assume that the captain is mad enough to attack on his own initiative. Which direction will he come in from?"

Mathisen finished chewing a bite of steak. "I'd give all four of my stars if I knew the answer to that. The shortest course from Buenos Aires to the dam is up through the Atlantic, of course."

"So you think he'll pass north somewhere off the U.S. eastern seaboard?" Marjorie asked.

"No," Mathisen replied. "I believe he went the other way, around the tip of South America and then north through the Pacific and the Bering Strait. Unless I miss my guess, at this moment he's somewhere under the Arctic ice. He may even have reached Baffin Bay or the Labrador Sea by now. It all depends on when he left Buenos Aires and how fast he's traveling."

"What makes you think he's coming that way?" Ben asked.

"Because this man is not just crazy, he's canny as well. If he came up through the Atlantic and attacked from the south, he'd risk detection by one of our ASW subs on routine patrol. As a former Soviet submarine officer, he'd also be aware that we have numerous SOSUS listening posts off the East Coast."

"Couldn't he swing far enough east to avoid our ASW subs and SOSUS posts?" Marjorie asked.

"He could, but he'd still have to turn west toward Newfoundland at some point, and he undoubtedly knows that the Canadians have their own ASW patrols and SOSUS stations. But there's a second reason I believe he'll come at us through Baffin Bay and the Labrador Sea."

"Marine acoustics," Ben said.

"Exactly. If he brings the *Bukharin* down through those waters, he's got flow noise from both the Labrador Current and the Gulf Stream covering the sound of his propellers."

"Not to mention the tremendous noise of the ice floes breaking up," Ben added.

Mathisen nodded. "You've got it."

Ben thought for a moment. "Mike, if you're so convinced he's coming in from the north, why not send your ASW subs and warships up there and blockade Davis Strait at the southern tip of Baffin Bay? You'd have the *Bukharin* bottled up."

The admiral shook his head negatively. "I thought of that, but it's too risky. The *Bukharin* might pass through Davis Strait and be somewhere in the Labrador Sea before we can set up a blockade. If that sub gets south of our fleet, Ice Station Alpha would be left defenseless."

A messenger crossed the room and approached their table. "Excuse me, Admiral Mathisen," the young seaman said, "but the President will be calling on the videophone in the command hub in ten minutes. She wishes to speak to you, and to Doctor Meade and Doctor Glynn."

"Very well," Mathisen said. He turned to Ben and Marjorie. "I assume that the President's heard back from the junta. Let's hope she has good news."

The three rose and followed the messenger out of the mess. As they climbed into the electric cart, Marjorie said, "I can see why the President would want to talk to you two, but I wonder why she would want to speak to me."

Admiral Mathisen grinned. "Are you kidding, Marjorie? When the President learned of your breakthrough concept for crop chemosynthesis, she grasped its enormous significance immediately. I'll give you ten to one she wants to congratulate you."

Marjorie looked worried. "So far, it's only a theory, Mike. Congratulations may be premature."

Ben put his arm around her shoulders and hugged her. "You've shown me all your research, and the positive assessments coming in over Internet from botanists around the world. Your concept is brilliant, and it's going to work."

"I hope so, Ben, but remember that it has never been attempted before. I could screw up."

"Nonsense," Mathisen said good-naturedly. "You're going to succeed, and the new grains and vegetables you create will feed half the world."

The electric cart crossed the vast Operations Center and stopped beside the stairs leading up to the command hub. The three got out and climbed the steps, crossing to the communications console.

The Navy communications specialist on duty rose and saluted Admiral Mathisen. "The channel to the White House is on standby, Admiral," the young woman said. "The President should be calling any moment now."

"Thank you, sailor," the admiral said. "Why don't you go over to the snack bar and get yourself a Coke? I'll let you know when we're finished here."

"Yes, sir," she said, then saluted again and descended the stairs.

The three made small talk for the next couple of minutes, until the videophone screen flickered and the face of the White House operator came on the screen. "Good evening, Doctor Glynn, gentlemen. The President is waiting to speak to you. I'll switch you over now."

The screen went blank for a moment. Then a live picture of the President sitting at her Oval Office desk came on.

"Good evening, Mike. Good evening, Marjorie, Ben."

"Good evening, Madam President," the three replied in unison.

The President looked tired, and obviously troubled. "I've just gotten off the phone with Ambassador O'Malley in Buenos Aires," she said. "I'm afraid we've got problems. One of the junta members, Admiral Secchi, arrived at the embassy there an hour ago. He told Ambassador O'Malley that they haven't received a reply from the *Bukharin* since ordering her to return to Argentina."

"Nothing at all, Madam President?" Mathisen asked.

"Not a word, Mike. Equally ominous, the *Bukharin* has missed all of her scheduled contacts with Argentine Navy headquarters in Buenos Aires. Secchi thinks the captain has deliberately severed all communication with the junta."

"Did Secchi give O'Malley a reason why the captain would shut down his radio?" Ben asked.

President Piziali nodded glumly. "Secchi confirmed the suspicions Mike voiced at our last meeting. Like you, he believes that the captain, a Ukrainian named Lobov, has gone mad. They think he intends to continue the attack on Ice Station Alpha."

Marjorie's hand went to her face. "Dear God!"

"Did Secchi give our ambassador the position of the *Bukharin*?" Mathisen asked.

"When Argentine Navy headquarters received their last communication from the sub, she was under the Arctic ice. The battle plan is for the *Bukharin* to come at you from the north, down through Baffin Bay and the Labrador Sea."

"Jesus, Mike, you were right," Ben said. "He's going to use the marine acoustics up here to mask his approach."

"It wasn't hard to make that assumption," Mathisen said. "I used to command an ASW sub, and that Ukrainian captain is planning his attack exactly the way I would."

"At least now we know his course," Marjorie said.

Mathisen shrugged. "That's true, but it still leaves a lot of sea to search. And with only half the Atlantic Fleet on station and our sonar all but useless up here, the *Bukharin* retains the edge."

He turned back toward the small videophone camera. "Madam President, did Admiral Secchi reveal when the *Bukharin* left Buenos Aires?"

"Yes. The sub slipped down the Rio de la Plata into the South Atlantic twenty-two days ago."

Mathisen made a quick calculation. "Depending on the *Bukharin*'s speed, she could well have reached the Labrador Sea by now."

"I've called both the president of Russia and the Canadian prime minister," President Piziali said. "Each has promised naval support."

"That will help, Madam President," Mathisen said. "But we're up against an insane sub captain in command of one of the most powerful weapons of war on the planet. Because of her double hulls and massive bulk, it will be all but impossible to sink the *Bukharin* with a single torpedo hit."

"So even if our forces find her and put a torpedo into her, the sub could continue the attack?" the President asked.

"Yes, Madam President. And from what we now know of Captain Lobov, that's exactly what he'll do. He'll sacrifice his boat, his crew and himself to destroy Ice Station Alpha."

"Those Typhoon-class subs also carry nuclear missiles, don't they?" Ben asked.

Mathisen nodded. "Each boat is armed with twenty submarine-launched ballistic missiles. But I don't believe that Lobov will use them."

"Why do you say that?" the President asked.

"Because everything I know about this man tells me he thinks of himself as a warrior, a soldier of the sea who likes to stalk and kill his enemy close in. If he launched his missiles from several hundred miles out, it would make

him a button-pusher instead of a fighting man taking on
the enemy in personal combat. It would deprive him of
the excitement of the attack, the thrill of hearing his sonar
pick up the sound of his fish striking the dam and the ice
exploding into hailstones."

"I wish I could do something more to help you, Mike,"
Piziali said.

"You've done all you can, Madam President. Now it's
up to us to find the *Bukharin* in time to put more than one
fish into her."

The President looked grave. "Keep me advised, Mike. I
want reports morning, noon and night until this thing is
over. Whatever happens."

"I'll keep in constant contact, Madam President."

"There's one thing I especially wish to say to you, Marjorie," President Piziali said. "First, I want to congratulate
you on your latest breakthrough in plant genetics. Your
concept of grafting photosynthetic and chemosynthetic
plant life is brilliant."

Admiral Mathisen gave Marjorie an "I told you so"
wink.

"Thank you, Madam President," Marjorie said.

"The second thing I want to tell you is that I intend to
hold a televised news conference tonight to announce
your achievement. I intend to use the new food plants
you're going to develop as an insurance policy."

A perplexed look came over Marjorie's face. "An insurance policy? I'm afraid I don't understand, Madam President."

"If the *Bukharin* gets through and succeeds in destroying Ice Station Alpha, it will be a terrible blow to the people of the northern hemisphere. I'm not talking about just
the loss of a warmer climate that the Arctic Alteration
promises to bring about. Perhaps even more disastrous
would be the damage to the morale of millions of freezing, starving people from China to Europe."

"We'd probably see a resumption of massive immigration," Ben said.

"That's precisely what I'm talking about. And that
would mean turning the country into Fortress America.
The only way we could prevent millions of aliens from

flooding across our coasts would be by armed force. And that could well result in the death of countless innocent immigrants."

The President smiled. "Perhaps you understand now, Marjorie, why I referred to your work as our insurance policy. It's something—call it hope, call it a new chance at survival—that we can still give the people of the northern hemisphere even if we suffer the loss of the iceberg dam."

"I'll do everything in my power to prevent that loss," Admiral Mathisen promised.

"I know you will, Mike. Good-bye, and may God watch over all of you."

As the video screen went blank, Ben smiled wryly at Marjorie and the admiral. "An insurance policy! You've got to hand it to the President, she covers all the bases."

"That she does," Mathisen said. "Now I have to try to do the same thing. The only trouble is that with only half the Atlantic Fleet on station so far, it's like trying to win a game with no one to cover second and third."

"How long before the rest of the Fleet arrives?" Marjorie asked.

"I've recalled ASW subs and warships from as far away as the Eastern Mediterranean and the Persian Gulf," Mathisen said. "They're all headed for Ice Station Alpha at flank speed. Still, I won't have the majority of the Fleet on-station for at least another seventy-two hours."

"Seventy-two hours!" Marjorie exclaimed. "God, it's going to seem like an eternity."

"If the *Bukharin* gets here first, it could quite literally mean eternity," Mathisen said. "For every man and woman on Ice Station Alpha."

THE LABRADOR SEA, 950 MILES
NORTH OF ICE STATION ALPHA
••••••••••••••••••••••••••••

8:20 a.m.–June 11th

CAPTAIN VIKTOR LOBOV ENTERED the control room of the
Bukharin with a heady confidence bordering on euphoria.
For the past several days, he had worked on his plan for
the coming attack on Ice Station Alpha, refining details
until he was satisfied that the scheme was foolproof.

He crossed to where Sonarman Evgeny Vaslyshn was
sitting at his station listening through earphones for the
sound of any nearby enemy subs or surface ships. Vaslyshn saw the captain's reflection in the scope glass before
him and took off his earphones as Lobov approached.

"No contacts, Captain," he said, assuming that was
what the captain would want to know.

"I didn't think there would be," Lobov said. "We're far
north of the shipping lanes, and any Allied warships will
be well to the south. My question concerns icebergs."

"Icebergs, Captain?"

"Yes. Are there any icebergs in the sea above us?"

Vaslyshn shrugged. "The sea is littered with them, sir.
There must be a dozen within ten miles of our position."

"Excellent. I want you to find the largest one in the area
and give its position to the helmsman."

"Very well, sir," the sonarman said, although he had no idea why the captain would issue such an order.

Lobov turned and recrossed the room to where the helmsman stood at his post, his hands on the brass navigation wheel. Junior Officer Ivan Zhulinsky had the watch, and he stood beside the helmsman, continuously checking the course and the depth settings.

"In a few minutes, Vaslyshn is going to give you the location of an iceberg in the area," Lobov said to the helmsman. "I want you to set a course for the berg."

"Aye aye, sir."

The captain turned to his junior officer. "When we reach the berg, bring us up to radio antenna depth, as close to the ice as you can get us."

Zhulinsky blanched. Everyone knew that icebergs were not smooth-sided and that ledges and lateral tongues of ice often jutted out from them. Nevertheless, he was not about to argue with the captain. No one on the boat was stupid enough to cross swords with a man they were all now convinced was utterly mad.

"I'll have to coordinate the maneuver closely with the sonarman, sir. You're familiar with the configuration of bergs. It may take some time to locate a suitable place to bring the sub up."

"You're to carry out the order as quickly as possible. You'd do well to keep in mind that we are on an attack mission and time is vital. I will be in my cabin. Let me know when we've reached antenna depth beside the ice."

"Aye aye, sir," Zhulinsky said.

Lobov returned to his cabin and went over his attack plan yet again. By bringing the *Bukharin* up near the surface close beside a berg, he all but eliminated the risk of detection. Of course it was possible for an orbiting infrared satellite to pick up the heat emanating through the hull, but that was a chance he'd have to take.

It was vital to reach antenna depth not to send a radio message, as the control-room crew undoubtedly assumed, but to listen in on Allied radio transmissions. He needed to know the location of the ships towing icebergs south toward Ice Station Alpha. It was fortunate that Chief Engineer Mykola Onopenko spoke English. When

they reached antenna depth, Lobov would have Onopenko eavesdrop on the messages that were undoubtedly
being sent between the ships of the task force building the
dam.

Lobov was certain that the Americans had somehow
discovered that the *Bukharin* was headed north to destroy
Ice Station Alpha, and that they'd pressured de Urquiza
into canceling the attack. What other reason could there
be for the junta to recall the *Bukharin?* Especially since the
very future of the Argentine economy depended on a successful mission.

No, there was no question but that the Americans knew
of the *Bukharin's* planned attack. And it was almost certain they knew that the sub was somewhere in Arctic waters, and their Fleet would be maintaining radio silence as
they searched for her.

The seagoing tugboats and civilian vessels towing the
icebergs to the dam site were another matter. There
would be no reason for them to cease communication, for
the Americans would be aware that they were not the
Bukharin's target. And it was for one of these ships that
Lobov was searching.

Half an hour later, he heard the main ballast tanks vent
and felt the *Bukharin* begin to rise. He left his worktable
and headed back for the control room.

When he arrived, he found Zhulinsky tight-lipped and
pale. Obviously, the junior officer was nearly scared out
of his wits by the responsibility of surfacing the *Bukharin*
so close to a berg.

"We will reach antenna depth in about three minutes,
Captain," Zhulinsky said, his voice cracking.

"How near are we to the ice?" Lobov asked.

"We will come up within approximately fifty feet, Captain."

"Not good enough. Bring her in closer, no more than
twenty feet from the berg. Any farther out and a satellite
or an ASW could distinguish her shape."

Zhulinsky's Adam's apple bobbed. "Captain, as you
know, the currents are extremely strong in these seas. We
could be driven into the ice."

"Twenty feet. That's an order."

For a fleeting second, the junior officer was on the verge of objecting. Then he remembered the arrest and detainment of Oleg Pynzenyk when he had balked at obeying the captain's order to fire on the supertanker at Gibraltar. When they'd left port, Pynsenyk had remained in an Argentine Navy brig.

"Very well, Captain. Twenty feet." He turned to the helmsman. "Rudder five degrees left."

"Rudder five degrees left," the helmsman repeated, his brow covered with sweat despite the sixty-five-degree temperature in the control room.

Lobov turned to his chief engineer. "Onopenko, get to the radio room and as soon as we reach antenna depth, start listening for transmissions from the ships towing bergs south. I am specifically searching for a vessel nearing the dam site, a ship navigating south within the Labrador Current."

"Yes, sir," the chief engineer said and turned for the radio room aft.

"Antenna depth," the radioman's voice came over the control-room speaker three minutes later.

"Level off. Maintain depth and position," Zhulinsky ordered, his heart beating wildly. He could almost feel the submerged wall of ice now only twenty feet from the outer hull of the *Bukharin*. One mistake on his part and the sub could strike the berg, split her steel skin and share the grave of the *Titanic* on the floor of the icy sea.

For the next ten minutes, there was silence from the men in the control room as they waited for the chief engineer to report from the radio room.

Finally, the voice of Onopenko came over the speaker. "I've picked up three ships so far, Captain. Two tugs and a larger freighter. They're all towing bergs south."

"Are any of them within the Labrador Current?"

"Yes, sir. One of the seagoing tugs. She's Russian."

"How far is she from Ice Station Alpha?"

"Their radioman just reported to their Operations Center that she was approximately three hundred and forty nautical miles north of the dam, coming in at six knots."

Lobov ran the numbers through his head. If the *Bukharin* continued south at thirty knots, her speed would produce more noise than he was comfortable with. Still, the sub was in the Labrador Current where flow sounds, coupled with the creaking and splitting of the bergs moving south, should cover the noise of the propellers.

The captain rubbed his hands. By maintaining their speed of thirty knots, he could catch up with the towed berg approximately a hundred and seventy miles north of Ice Station Alpha.

He would then slow to six knots to match the speed of the tug, and bring the *Bukharin* up as close under the berg as possible. The sounds of the ice, along with the tremendous noise of the tug's diesel engine, would completely cover the *Bukharin*'s propeller and hull noises, totally negating any chance the Americans might have at acoustic detection and tracking.

The second advantage to his plan was that by approaching Ice Station Alpha hidden beneath the towed berg, it would be impossible for American satellites or ASW aircraft to spot her. The *Bukharin* would be invisible to the eyes and inaudible to the ears of the Americans. She would remain the ghost she had been for the past ten years.

"Get a position and course-fix on that Russian tug," Lobov ordered the radioman.

He turned to Ivan Zhulinsky. "As soon as we have a fix, take her down and steer for that tug's position. Full speed."

"Aye aye, Captain," the junior officer said, deeply relieved that they would be getting away from the danger posed by the icy sub-killer twenty feet off their starboard side.

Euphoric, Lobov turned for his cabin. There was now nothing the Americans could do to stop him. In fifty-six hours, his ghost sub would fire a volley of torpedoes into Ice Station Alpha, and he and his beloved *Bukharin* would know the greatest moments of their existence.

ICE STATION ALPHA
• •

8:00 a.m.–June 14th

A CLOYING SENSE OF doom hung over Ice Station Alpha, turning the spirits of everyone present as gray as the ash-laden sky and slate-hued sea around them.

It had been twelve days since the *Bukharin* was last heard from, more than enough time for the rogue submarine to emerge from the cover of the polar-sea ice and travel south beneath the berg-strewn surface of the Labrador Sea.

No one on Alpha doubted that the huge Typhoon-class sub was somewhere near, using the complex marine acoustics in the North Atlantic off Newfoundland to mask her approach. When the *Bukharin* struck, she would come in like a stalking shark, using stealth and cunning to hide her movements until the final furious moment of the attack.

"This waiting is driving me bloody mad," Marjorie Glynn said as she and Ben were getting dressed for the day in Ben's quarters. "I can't concentrate on my work."

"I know what you mean," Ben said, pulling on a pair of fleece-lined jeans. "I'm having a hell of time keeping my mind focused, too. Yesterday, when I made that helicopter inspection of the dam, I kept worrying that the *Bukharin* would attack while I was airborne. I had this horrible mental image of torpedoes blowing Alpha and you to pieces while I flew safely overhead."

"So that's why you were back here so early. I wondered."

Ben threw his arms around her. "I couldn't live without you. If the *Bukharin* gets through and the end comes, we'll go out together."

Marjorie pulled away. "Stop it, Ben. You're being maudlin. Good God, I'm scared enough without you dwelling on our death. There's still hope that the Navy will intercept the sub before she reaches Alpha."

"We have to face reality, Marjorie. That Ukrainian captain may be mad, but he's an experienced submarine officer. And from what Mike tells me, he undoubtedly served in the Soviet submarine fleet and knows these waters, including the acoustics, like the back of his hand. The odds are stacked against us."

Marjorie shivered. "Why talk about it, Ben? I mean, we really don't have a choice, do we? Our work is too important for us to abandon Alpha."

"It's not just our work. Think of what it would do to the collective psyche of the people of the northern hemisphere if we pulled out of here. Can't you just see the headlines: 'Scientists Abandon Arctic Alteration.' "

"I don't want to hear any more of this. Now finish getting dressed. We're supposed to meet Mike for breakfast in fifteen minutes."

"You're right. Sorry I went off the deep end there." Ben gave her an admiring grin. "You keep cool at crunch time, Marjorie. You've got more courage than me."

"No, Ben. If anything, perhaps I have a bit more faith that there's a god and He or She won't allow that madman to destroy the future of millions of people. It may be my Church of England upbringing. Or maybe I'm just being naive, I don't pretend to know. All I'm certain of is that we have to go on, no matter how bleak things look at the moment. Now, come on, get dressed. I could do with some tea."

Fifteen minutes later, Ben and Marjorie joined Admiral

Mathisen at his table in the mess hall. After they were seated, Ben asked, "Any word on the *Bukharin?*"

Mathisen shook his head. "Nothing. No sonar contacts, no radio transmissions, no infrared satellite sightings. Nothing."

"Any chance she might have experienced mechanical problems and stopped?" Ben asked. "Or maybe struck submerged ice and been too damaged to continue?"

Mathisen threw back his head and stared silently at the arching ice ceiling. "I've spent the past few days mulling over those very possibilities, Ben," he said finally. "And, yes, there's a chance that one of those scenarios occurred."

Marjorie studied the admiral's face. "But you don't think so, do you, Mike?"

"No, I don't, Marjorie. If the *Bukharin* experienced a mechanical problem too serious to repair at sea, Lobov would have been forced to radio Buenos Aires for an ice-breaker to tow him back to Argentina. And I doubt the *Bukharin* struck ice, not with an officer as experienced with the Arctic as Lobov is."

"So you think she's still coming at us," Ben said.

"Yes, I do. And given the time that's passed, I think she's close. How close, I don't know."

A white-jacketed steward approached their table. "Good morning, Admiral Mathisen, Doctor Glynn, Doctor Meade. May I take your breakfast orders?"

"Just toast and tea for me," Marjorie said.

"Make mine bacon, scrambled eggs and hashbrowns," Ben said. "And coffee with cream."

"Sausages, a poached egg and black coffee," Admiral Mathisen said.

As the waiter turned for the galley, Marjorie leaned her elbows on the table. "I've done about all the research I can do over Internet," she said. "The next step is for me to become familiar with the retrieval systems aboard the *Yellowstone*. I can't dive on those seafloor thermal vents without knowing how to bring plant specimens up."

She looked at Ben. "Is the submersible ready to dive?"

Ben shrugged. "It would take a couple of hours to charge up the batteries and top off the oxygen tanks.

Other than that, yeah, she can go down any time."

"I'd like to dive today," Marjorie said. "Is it okay if I call Mel and tell him I want to go down as soon as the batteries and oxygen tanks are ready?"

A look of alarm spread over Ben's face. "You'll dive the *Yellowstone* today over my dead body. The *Bukharin* is out there somewhere. I can't let you take a submersible down with a goddamn killer sub prowling the depths out there."

"Don't be silly, Ben. Captain Lobov's target is Ice Station Alpha. He's not going to bother with a small, unarmed submersible. Mel and I will be perfectly safe."

"No way!"

Admiral Mathisen polished a water-spotted knife with his napkin and glanced sideways at Ben. "If you don't mind my butting in, I think you're overreacting. Marjorie's right. Lobov's after Alpha. If he fired on the *Yellowstone*, he'd reveal his position and our ASW forces would pounce on him within minutes. He knows that."

"Suppose he mistakes the *Yellowstone* for one of our subs," Ben countered.

Mathisen shook his head. "That's highly unlikely. Your submersible's what, a tenth the size of an ASW sub? If the *Bukharin*'s out there and their sonar picks up the *Yellowstone*, Lobov will recognize her as a small research craft. He's not about to risk detection just to torpedo an insignificant target like the *Yellowstone*."

"I still think it's risky," Ben said dubiously.

"Ben, you promised to let me dive in the *Yellowstone*," Marjorie said. "Your exact words were 'any time, any place.' Do you recall promising me that?"

"That's not fair. When I made that promise, I didn't think you'd want to dive in a goddamn war zone."

"Are you going to keep your promise or not?"

Ben turned to Mathisen for support. Mathisen raised his palms. "Don't look at me. I told you what I thought. This is between you two now."

Ben turned back to Marjorie. "You're determined to do this?"

"Yes."

He sighed. "All right, all right, if you're dead set on

risking your ass down there playing hide-and-seek with a killer sub, who am I to stop you? You're going to do what you want to anyway."

Marjorie smiled brightly. "Thank you, Ben. I'll call Mel and tell him to get the *Yellowstone* ready."

"Here comes our breakfast," Mathisen said as the steward approached with a brimming tray. "What do you say we move on to another subject? I want to discuss Alpha's defenses."

While they ate, Mathisen outlined the antisubmarine measures he'd mapped out. "I've set up a defense ring of ASW surface ships, subs and patrol aircraft fifty miles to the north and south of the Operations Center," he said. "The crews have been at their battle stations for the past week."

"The waiting and the constant strain must be taking their toll on your people, Mike," Ben said.

"I'm sure they're all tired and tense," Mathisen acknowledged. "But every man and woman out there was trained for a mission like this. I've talked to several of my captains, and the morale of the crews remains high, despite some frazzled nerves."

"If we only knew where the *Bukharin* is," Ben said. "That's the worst part. Not knowing where the attack will come from. Or when."

Captain Viktor Lobov felt the adrenaline coursing through his veins as he entered the hushed control room of the *Bukharin*. The immense submarine was now only twenty-nine kilometers west of Ice Station Alpha's Operations Center.

Twenty-five hours before, the *Bukharin* had slipped beneath the berg being towed south by the Russian tug, the sounds of her approach masked by the flow noise of the Labrador Current and the loud diesel engines aboard the civilian vessel.

As the *Bukharin* neared the ice, the sonar officer had reported that the berg had not one keel but two, with a long, deep trench between them. Hidden up between the keels, the Typhoon-class sub would be virtually undetectable by American sonar.

It was an extraordinary piece of luck, a stroke of fortune that confirmed to Lobov his belief that the *Bukharin* was predestined for this mission. Five hours before, Lobov's attack plan had faced its first test as the boat approached the American defense ring eighty kilometers out from the Operations Center.

Although the sea around them had pulsed with the pings of searching American sonar beams, nothing had penetrated the *Bukharin*'s frozen lair, and the Typhoon had passed through the defense ring undetected. If before, Lobov had felt a heady confidence, now he experienced an intoxicating sense of invulnerability.

"Is that Russian tug still on course?" he asked the Argentine officer on duty.

One of the three interpreters assigned to the control room around the clock translated the question into Spanish.

"Aye, sir," Lieutenant Commander Domingo Calvo said. "There has been no change during my watch."

The interpreter repeated the answer in Ukrainian.

"Time to target?" Lobov asked, then waited impatiently for the translation.

"Three hours, five minutes, sir."

"Assuming the tug maintains her heading, how far off the ice dam will we pass?"

"Approximately fifty-five hundred meters, Captain."

Lobov rubbed his hands together. "Excellent," he said. Fired from the close range of fifty-five hundred meters, the *Bukharin*'s wire-guided Mark-C torpedoes would score direct hits on the American Operations Center. It would be like shooting a rifle at an elephant ten feet away.

"Tell Commander Calvo that I'll be in my cabin for the next hour plotting our escape course," Lobov ordered the interpreter. "Also, Junior Officer Zhulinsky is to take the conn. We're closing for the attack, and I don't want to take any chances that you'll translate an order incorrectly."

The interpreter stiffened, obviously offended. "Beg-

ging the captain's pardon, but I happen to speak fluent
Ukrainian. Have I even once made a mistake?"

"No, your Ukrainian is fine. But during the heat of the
attack, emotions rise. Thought processes often suffer.
Suppose you get a mental block at the moment I order a
sudden turn to evade an incoming torpedo or a dive to
escape a depth charge. One wrongly translated word
could mean our lives."

"I assure you, Captain Lobov, that I have never lost
control of my mental state."

"Have you ever been in a submarine attempting to
evade an incoming torpedo?"

"No, sir."

"Have you ever been through a depth-charge barrage?"

"No, sir."

"Then you have no right to assure me of anything.
We're about to attack an installation guarded by the most
formidable navy on earth. The moment we fire our first
torpedo, the Americans will counterattack with every
weapon in their arsenal. No man knows how he will react
in combat until he's been through a battle. Can you understand that?"

The young Argentine interpreter studied his shoes in
defeat. "Yes, sir."

"Good. Now get Zhulinsky up here. Tell him I'll relieve
him in an hour or so."

"Aye aye, Captain."

The eyes of the control-room crew followed Lobov as
he left for his cabin. Unlike the exhilaration the captain
felt as the moment of attack drew near, both the Argentine and Ukrainian members of the crew suffered a uni-
versal sense of apprehension and building fear.

But for the communication necessary to run the sub,
there had been little conversation among the men for
hours past. Instead, each man had withdrawn into himself, each aching with thoughts of families and homelands they would likely never see again.

For now, the iceberg being towed east above them continued to provide them with cover from detection. Yet, as
Captain Lobov had warned the interpreter, once the *Buk-*

harin fired her first torpedo at Ice Station Alpha, they would instantly become a target themselves, vulnerable to American depth charges and torpedoes.

Their most formidable opponent would be the Los Angeles-class ASW subs armed with wire-guided MK48 Advanced Capability (ADCAP) torpedoes. The ADCAPs had a range of fifty thousand yards, and an advanced combination seeker head/computer that used electronically steered sonar beams to guide the torpedo to its target.

The head allowed the torpedo to "see" across a hundred-and-eighty-degree arc ahead of the weapon, and the computer made the MK48 the world's most accurate and deadly torpedo.

If an ADCAP locked onto the *Bukharin*, they were certain to take a crippling hit. After that, the crew's only hope for survival would be if Captain Lobov ordered an emergency blow that would pop the sub to the surface, where they could raise a white flag of surrender.

No one believed that their mad captain would issue such an order. Even with a massive wound in the side of the sub and freezing seawater flooding compartments, Lobov would never give up his beloved *Bukharin*. Instead, he would undoubtedly continue the attack, using his undamaged torpedo tubes to fire on the Operations Center berg.

There could be little question that Captain Lobov would succeed in destroying Ice Station Alpha, but the price would be their own lives. What had started out for the crew as a great adventure had turned into a suicide mission.

And every man aboard the *Bukharin* knew it.

Marjorie Glynn jumped down from the helicopter that had flown her out to the *Abyss*, waved her thanks to the chopper crew, then ran across the fantail helipad in a half crouch.

As soon as she was clear, the Sea Stallion lifted off and banked back toward Ice Station Alpha, three miles away across the choppy gray sea.

As the chopper grew small in the distance, Captain Mel Sanderson rounded a corner of the deck, a wide grin on his beefy face. "Hi ya, Marjorie. Welcome aboard," he said, giving her a bear hug.

"Hi, Mel," Marjorie smiled, hugging him back. "Is the *Yellowstone* ready to go?"

"Rich Kaneko's still charging the batteries. Be another couple of minutes."

"Give it to me straight, Mel," Marjorie said, studying the old sea dog's face. "Do you have any problem with going down today? I mean, with the *Bukharin* out there somewhere in the depths."

"I have to admit that when you first called, it gave me pause for thought." Sanderson shrugged. "But when you told me about the conversation you and Ben and the admiral had at breakfast, I could see the logic in Mathisen's view. Hell, the *Bukharin*'s not going to come after us."

"Ben still thinks we'll be taking a chance."

"You know Ben. He's just worried about you."

Marjorie smiled. "It's that old male double standard, isn't it? It's all right for him to go poking around erupting volcanoes and boiling geysers, but let me suggest a dive in the *Yellowstone* and he's wringing his hands."

Sanderson grinned. "That's Ben all right. He likes to take all the risks himself." He looked at his watch. "Rich ought to have the batteries charged by now. You ready to go down?"

"I'd like to use the ladies' room first. When Ben and I dove to the floor of the Irish Sea last year, he never bothered to tell me there wasn't a W.C. aboard. If we'd been down another ten minutes, I swear I would have wet my pants."

Sanderson laughed. "There's a head down the first passageway on the starboard side. The *Yellowstone*'s amidships, near the crane. I'll meet you there."

Five minutes later, Marjorie found Captain Sanderson standing beside the orange-painted submersible talking to a short, bullnecked machinist's mate.

"Marjorie, this is Rich Kaneko. He'll get us launched with the crane, then stand by the radio."

"Good morning, Doctor Glynn." Kaneko touched the tip of his cap.

"Nice to meet you, Rich," Marjorie smiled. "Well, are we all ready?"

"Let's do it," Sanderson said. "Up you go."

Marjorie climbed the U-shaped rungs attached to the side of the submersible, then swung her legs through the open hatch and descended a removable aluminum ladder leading down into the cabin.

Sanderson followed, then handed the ladder back up to Kaneko. The mate closed the small hatch, and Sanderson swung the wheel attached to the underside, securing the airtight seal.

Then he worked his way forward to where Marjorie had already strapped herself into the copilot's seat. Sanderson plopped himself down in the pilot's chair, facing the floor-to-ceiling plastic bubble that formed the front of the cylindrical sub.

He grunted as he worked his buttocks into the small seat and strapped the harness over his bulky frame. "These goddamn submersibles aren't built for a tub of lard like me," he complained. "I feel like a salmon in a sardine can."

Marjorie grinned and looked around the submersible's cramped interior. Both the pilot and copilot had butterfly-shaped control wheels with which to steer the craft. Between the wheels and the bubble bow there were two small, illuminated panels crammed with gauges, systems monitors and electronic terminals.

Behind the pilots' seats, the *Yellowstone*'s curved walls were lined with instrumentation that gave the cabin the look of a cockpit aboard a supersonic aircraft.

"Launch chief to *Yellowstone*," Rich Kaneko's voice came over the cabin speaker. "You two ready to go play with the whales?"

Sanderson turned on the oxygen system and the submersible's electric motor, then put on a radio headset and handed an identical pair of earphones and throat mike to Marjorie.

"Ready, Rich. Put us in the water."

"You got it, Captain. Good luck down there."

A moment later, Marjorie and Mel felt the *Yellowstone* lift off her wooden chocks. They watched through the plastic bubble before them as the crane hoisted the submersible above the deck, then swung the tiny craft out over the choppy gray sea.

For a long moment, the *Yellowstone* hovered over the waves, twisting in a slow half-circle. Then the submersible started down as the crane let out line. There was a sudden bump, after which the craft began to roll from side to side as four-foot waves washed against her hull.

"I'm casting off the line, Rich," Mel said into his throat mike, reaching up to hit the cable disconnect switch.

"Cable free," Kaneko replied.

Mel turned on the submersible's lights, then flicked several switches on the control panel to his left. Marjorie started as a loud hissing sound filled the tiny sub, then relaxed as she realized it was only the ballast tanks flooding.

Slowly, the *Yellowstone* began to descend into the icy depths of the North Atlantic, her powerful searchlights illuminating a cloud of bubbles as air from the ballast tanks rose toward the surface.

"Ben asked me to take a look at the submerged section of the Operations Center berg during the dive," Mel said. "He wants to be sure that the CH-Fifteen plastic is preventing any melting below the waterline."

"Just as long as it leaves time for me to practice with the manipulator arms," Marjorie said. "I have to be sure I know what I'm doing before we dive on one of those seafloor thermal vents."

Sanderson nodded. "No problem. We'll have a look around Alpha, then head for the bottom."

"How long will the dive take, Mel?"

"I figure about two and a half hours."

As the *Yellowstone* descended into the inky depths, Marjorie began to feel the same soothing serenity she'd experienced the year before when she'd gone down into the womb of the Irish Sea with Ben.

"It's so peaceful down here, Mel," she smiled. "As if we're floating in a vacuum, with all our cares and woes left behind on the surface."

"I know what you mean," Mel said. "Funny. There's nothing between us and a cold, quick death but three-quarter-inch walls of plastic and steel. Still, I've always felt safe in the *Yellowstone*."

Marjorie stared through the plastic bubble three feet in front of her. They were passing through a thick soup of plankton, and the *Yellowstone*'s searchlights illuminated millions of minute animal and plant life drifting slowly with the current.

A school of codfish swam into the light, then suddenly turned as one and darted off into the inky blackness. A half second later, a great white shark flashed through the light, close on the trail of the cod.

Marjorie sat back and breathed a sigh of resignation. Even down here, the eternal struggle between hunter and hunted went on. Suddenly the sense of peace left her. Suddenly she wondered where the *Bukharin* was.

Ben Meade stood beside Mike Mathisen in the command hub, staring up at the video-wall display of the ASW defense ring the admiral had set up fifty miles from the Operations Center.

"That satellite feed is as clear as a bell, Mike."

Mathisen nodded. "It's computer-enhanced, of course. Still, it's hard to believe we could get definition like that from an infrared radar scan. When I started my navy career thirty-five years ago, technology like that wasn't even on the horizon."

"One more time, Mike. The blue blips are our ASW subs. Right?"

"Right. Ten Los Angeles-class boats, and a half dozen Ohio-class subs."

"And the red?"

"Surface warships. We've got thirty-two destroyers, cruisers and frigates out there."

"What are those white lines looping back and forth across the perimeter?"

"Those are the search patterns of patrolling ASW aircraft, primarily Harriers, Vikings and sub-hunting helicopters."

"I don't care how good that Captain Lobov is," Ben said, impressed by the formidable array of warships and aircraft. "I don't see how a walrus could slip through your defense ring, much less a huge Typhoon-class sub like the *Bukharin*."

"You're forgetting the cardinal rule of warfare, Ben."

"Which is?"

"Never underestimate your enemy. Lobov's like a fox being pursued by hounds on his home turf. The bastard knows these seas. He knows how to use the acoustics, the thermoclimes, the currents and the ice to mask his movements. All I've done is put up a fence. And as any farmer will tell you, fences don't always stop foxes."

Ben turned back to the video wall. "What's that surface vessel coming in from the west? Looks like she's not far off Alpha."

"That's the *Murmansk*, a Russian tug assigned to iceberg-towing duty. You can see the radar image of the berg about a mile behind the tug."

The admiral looked at Ben. "I've been meaning to ask you why you're still having bergs towed in. I thought the dam was complete."

"It is," Ben said, "but there are three or four places to the east where the ice doesn't have the breadth I'd like. If we get a bad gale, I want to be sure the dam won't breach in the heavy seas."

Ben studied the radar image. "Funny. That berg has almost the same configuration as the ice we're on. Notice how it's plateau-shaped on one side, then rises to an ice mount on the other."

Mathisen looked pensive. "Didn't you ask Captain Sanderson to inspect the ice below Alpha while he and Marjorie are down in the *Yellowstone*?"

"Yeah. I want to know if that CH-Fifteen plastic is working. If the Gulf Stream is melting the ice below the waterline, we'll have to recoat the cliffs."

Mathisen pointed at the video wall. "That Russian tug is on a course that will take her between the *Abyss* and Alpha in a couple of hours. Isn't that about the same time the *Yellowstone* will be on her way back up from the bottom?"

"Jesus, I never thought of that."

"I suggest you radio Marjorie and Mel and warn them they're going to pass under ice on the way back. Quite a few of those Arctic bergs have narrow ice keels extending down below the main body of ice."

"Mel will have the *Yellowstone*'s sonar on, Mike. If there's a keel under that berg, he'll see it on the screen."

Mathisen shook his head. "Not necessarily, Ben. Remember, that berg's being towed through the sea at six knots. At that speed, the turbulence beneath the ice would distort sound waves. If there's a keel below, the *Yellowstone*'s sonar may not even pick it up."

"You're right, Mike," Ben said. "I'll call the *Abyss* and get a patch through to the *Yellowstone*."

Ten kilometers to the west, Captain Viktor Lobov entered the control room of his ghost-quiet submarine. The attack on Ice Station Alpha was now only ninety minutes away. It was time to address the crew.

He crossed to the commander's large leather chair and for a long moment sat with his eyes closed, rehearsing what he would say to his men. He knew that they feared him, and because of that fear, they would obey his every order.

It was not enough. He wanted to inspire his men as a great conductor inspires an orchestra, to wield not a club but a baton, a wand of words that would instill in the crew of the *Bukharin* the same fervor that burned in him. To Lobov, the coming attack was not a brutal act of war, but a magnificent moment in history, a crossing of the Rubicon that would mark the inevitable decline and fall of the superpowers of the northern hemisphere.

Finally, he cleared his throat, made raw after years of chain-smoking harsh Russian cigarettes, and put on his intercom headset.

"Attention, men of the *Bukharin*," he said. "Our destiny is at hand. Ice Station Alpha is now but fifteen kilometers to the east."

The control-room crew watched Lobov in total silence, their faces and necks glistening with nervous sweat. In every compartment of the mammoth submarine, Ukrainian sailors huddled around intercom speakers while their Argentine shipmates strained to hear the translation from their interpreters.

"We are only a hundred and fifty men. Yet we possess a power that no military force on earth has ever known. When our torpedoes have destroyed the great ice dam, the Gulf Stream will once again flow southeast away from the Arctic. The Earth Winter will go on. For decades to come."

Down the length of the mammoth submarine, crewmen stared at the loudspeakers in rapt silence as the passion mounted in Lobov's voice.

"Without the promise of the Arctic Alteration, the corrupt cultures of the northern hemisphere will collapse. Millions will flee their freezing homelands. Great cities will be abandoned. Crop fields will lie fallow beneath the snowdrifts. And the United States, the colossus of the north, will drown in blood as her armies are forced to slaughter the legions of refugees seeking haven in Biosphere America."

Junior Officer Zhulinsky shuddered violently. For the first time, he realized that Lobov was not only insane, but a nihilist who denied any moral truths, a terrorist who believed that destruction was desirable for its own sake.

"For centuries to come, the world will marvel over our audacity, our cunning, our bravery," Lobov said, his voice rising to a fevered pitch the crew had never heard before. "Cast away your fears. Embrace the challenge of the combat to come. Ahead lies glory. Ahead lies an immortality other men may only dream of."

Lobov's strange, flat eyes glowed like the luminous fish that inhabited the deep, dark depths. "We attack in ninety minutes."

Marjorie Glynn grinned as she surveyed the collection of mollusks in the retrieval tray jutting out from below the plastic nose of the *Yellowstone*.

"Not bad for the first try, huh, Mel?" she asked.

"You did a great job with the manipulator arms,"

Sanderson said. "A couple more practice dives and you'll
be using those robotic hands like a pro."

The radio suddenly chimed, signaling an incoming call.
Sanderson leaned toward his console and flicked the
radio switch on. *"Yellowstone."*

"Mel, Ben. How's it going down there?"

"Hi, Ben. It's going great."

At the sound of Ben's name, Marjorie broke into a wide
smile and turned her headset on. "Oh, Ben, I wish you
could have been with us. All the retrieval systems worked
just perfectly. We have a whole basketful of specimens."

"You're going to be proud of Marjorie," Mel said. "By
the time we were through, she was picking mollusks off
the bottom like gumdrops off a table."

"I'm already proud of her, Mel."

"I really don't deserve any credit," Marjorie said. "Mel
maneuvered the *Yellowstone* in so close that a child could
have plucked those shellfish off the bottom."

"I know how difficult it is to manipulate the arms accu-
rately," Ben said. "Depth perception's the hardest part.
Anyway, that's not what I'm calling about. There's a berg
being towed directly across your course back to the *Abyss.*
Mike and I are concerned that there might be an ice keel
extending down to your depth."

"I've got the sonar on short range," Mel said. "Let me
switch over to a long search pattern."

Sanderson keyed a command into the sonar computer,
then studied the screen for a moment. "I see her, Ben. Big
berg. And you're right. There is an ice keel." He squinted
harder at the screen. "Well I'll be damned. From the sonar
reading I'm getting, she's got a double keel."

"That's not unusual with Arctic bergs, Mel," Ben said.
"Still, you two might find it interesting. Why don't you
aim your searchlights up as you pass under the ice?"

"I'd like to take some pictures," Marjorie said. "Is there
a camera on board?"

"My old Nikon's in the top storage compartment back
near the hatch," Ben said. "There should be eight or ten
shots left on the roll."

"Hang on," Marjorie said. "Let me check."

She unbuckled herself, went back to the storage area

and opened the top compartment. Sure enough, Ben's camera sat on one side, flanked by electronic testing equipment and spare parts.

Marjorie made her way back to her seat and put on her headset. "I've got it, Ben. Thanks."

"My pleasure. Look, Marjorie, I need to get out of here for an hour or two. I want to feel the wind on my face and smell the salt air off the sea. I'm going to fly out on the chopper that's scheduled to pick you up."

"I think that's a wonderful idea, Ben. You've been cooped up in that command hub far too long. Besides, it will give us that much more time together."

"Just what I was thinking. Mel, when do you figure you'll have the *Yellowstone* back aboard the *Abyss*?"

"In about an hour and twenty minutes."

"Okay, I'll start for the helipad in ten minutes. I'll see you two on the ship."

Mel switched off the radio and looked down at the sonar screen again. "We'll be passing pretty close below that berg, Marjorie. You should get some good shots."

Marjorie nodded absently, absorbed with Ben's Nikon. "Good Lord, this thing has a manual focus and range setting. I didn't think they made anything but auto-focus cameras anymore."

"They don't. Ben's had that thing since he was a kid."

Marjorie laughed. "I love that man. He spends ten million dollars building the world's most advanced submersible, then equips it with an antique camera."

Sanderson shrugged. "It's a damn good camera, if you know how to use it. Problem is, Ben's the only one I know who can get the settings right."

Marjorie studied the camera intently. "Well, I have news for Doctor Meade. His exclusive camera club of one is about to get a new member. If Ben can take pictures with this relic, so can I. I'm going to get some close-ups of those ice keels if it kills me."

It was Vladimir Razin's forty-third birthday, and the radio operator aboard the *Murmansk* was getting gloriously drunk with his best friend, cook Nicholas Stolypin.

If the *Murmansk* had been on a routine tow job in the crowded Baltic shipping lanes, Razin would have waited until the boat reached port before he began celebrating. But for the past two boring weeks, the tug had been far to sea, towing an iceberg south from Baffin Bay.

Except for routine check-in calls and an occasional personal message for one of the crew, the radio had remained silent for most of the voyage. The next check-in wasn't until six in the morning, and, Razin told himself, by then, he'd be sober again.

"Forty-three!" Razin said to Stolypin as he threw back his fourth glass of vodka. "Do you realize that in seven years, seven short years, I'll be fifty? An old man."

"Drink, Vladimir," the cook laughed. "Drink and forget that life is passing you by."

Razin held out his glass and Stolypin filled it to the brim.

"All my life I have had bad luck, did you know that, Nicholas? I have never had a good-paying job, never met the right woman. And now I'm getting old. I think it is my fate to die poor and alone."

"Fuck fate." The cook clinked glasses.

"You're right, Nicholas, fuck fate," Razin slurred, and poured the glass of vodka down his throat.

Ben Meade could smell the sea air as the electric cart neared the exit to the Operations Center. He turned in his seat and grinned at Chief Bos'n Mate Ignatius Kowslowski behind the wheel.

"It's going to feel good to be outside again. As big as the Center is, the walls start to close in on you after a while."

"I know what you mean, Meade. I get out at least once a day and just sit in the cart and stare at the ocean for an hour or so. Reminds me I'm a sailor, not some igloo-bound Eskimo."

Ash-muted daylight washed the tunnel walls and floor ahead, and a moment later, the cart emerged from the ice. Kowskowski swung the wheel toward a small, level area where three Sno-Cats were parked, their motors idling to keep the engine blocks from freezing and cracking in the below-zero air.

A young seaman came out of the motor pool hut near the Sno-Cats. "Morning, Chief. You headed down to the helipad?"

"Yeah. These puppies all fueled up?"

"I top them off every hour. Take your pick."

"Is One-thirty-five up here?"

"Last one on the right. Why do you always want One-thirty-five? They're all the same."

"In a pig's ass," Kowslowski scowled. "One-thirty-five's got beefed-up shocks."

The seaman's eyebrows arched. "Beefed-up shocks? Who installed those?"

Kowskowski moved his unlit cigar around with his tongue. "Me. I made 'em in the machine shop."

"What the hell did you do that for?"

" 'Cause I got hemorrhoids, Sonny. Not that it's any of your fuckin' business."

Ben and the seaman burst out laughing, sending Kowslowski stalking off toward the Sno-Cat. "You comin', Meade?" he yelled over his shoulder.

"Delicate subject, hemorrhoids," Ben said to the seaman, then followed Kowslowski over to One-thirty-five.

Kowslowski glared as Ben strapped himself into his seat. "I'll have you know that hemorrhoids are a serious medical condition, Meade."

"Oh, I know, Chief. Hemorrhoids are no laughing matter."

"Then why are you grinning?"

"I'm guess I'm just naturally lighthearted."

Kowslowski yanked the cigar out of his mouth and spat tobacco juice over the snow. "Shit!" he swore, then jammed his foot down on the accelerator and spun the Sno-Cat down the icy track toward the helipad on the plateau below.

Sonar Officer Evgeny Vaslyshn started suddenly and pressed his headset against his ears. He listened intently for a moment, then rang the control room.

"Sonar to command. The passive array is showing a small submersible approaching our position from the north."

In the control room, Lobov's eyes shot to the sonar screen before him. "I see the image. Are you certain she's a submersible and not a Long Angeles-class sub? The thermoclimes up here can distort images."

"She can't be a Los Angeles, sir. The acoustic signature is all wrong. The computer I.D. says she's some sort of civilian craft."

Lobov chewed his lower lip in indecision. If he ordered the stranger pinged with active sonar, he'd have a clear picture of what was coming at him. But he would also be taking a chance that an American ASW sub would pick up the pings and plot his position.

He'd have to trust that the computer was right, that the intruder was a small, unarmed submersible. "Command to sonar. Plot her course. If she keeps coming at us, I want to know."

"That double-keeled berg's dead ahead at the twelve-o'clock position," Mel Sanderson said, pointing at a shadowy gray mass just visible in the glare of the *Yellowstone's* powerful searchlights.

Marjorie squinted at the bottom of the ice, now only a hundred yards ahead. "I see only one keel."

"That's because we're coming at the berg broadside. We'll pass under the keel to the north first. There'll be a trench between them, then we'll see the southern keel."

Marjorie brought the Nikon up to her eye and practiced focusing. "Bring us up a hundred feet or so, Mel. I want to get some close-ups."

"All right, but no nearer than that. There's a lot of turbulence down here. I don't want to take a chance that we'll get slammed into one of those keels."

"Sonar to captain. That submersible's headed directly for us."

Viktor Lubov's face betrayed no emotion. "Range?"

"Eighty meters, sir, and closing."

"Continue to track." Lubov hit the button for the radio room. "Command to radio."

"Radio here, sir."

"Put your ears on down there. If that submersible transmits a radio message, I want to know immediately."

"Aye aye, sir."

Lubov hit the disconnect button and sank back in the commander's chair. To the control-room crew, he appeared calm and composed. But inside, his adrenaline-fueled blood pumped madly through his heart like gasoline through a race-car carburetor.

The Americans would never send out an unarmed research craft to search for the *Bukharin,* not with a dozen or so Los Angeles-class ASW subs at hand. No, the sudden appearance of the submersible was a fluke, a stroke of bad luck.

Still, the Typhoon might yet escape detection. The sonar aboard a tiny submersible wouldn't be nearly as sophisticated as the arrays aboard a nuclear submarine. Even if the research craft were pinging the bottom of the berg, the *Bukharin* might simply appear on their screen as part of the ice.

Then suddenly, like a nightmare piercing the cocoon of a peaceful sleep, it struck him that a research submersible would have view ports. Some submersibles even had plastic bubble bows that gave the pilot a three-hundred-and-sixty-degree view of the sea ahead.

Lubov knew that if the submersible had her searchlights on, the *Bukharin* would cease to be a ghost in the dark sea.

"We're passing under the first keel now," Mel Sanderson said, leveling off the *Yellowstone* thirty feet beneath the knife-shaped ice above.

"Lord, it's beautiful," Marjorie breathed, her eye glued to the Nikon viewfinder as she snapped away. "Isn't it amazing, the things that nature can—"

She stopped in midsentence and yanked the camera away from her eye. The *Yellowstone*'s searchlights were

playing across a huge black shape hidden deep between
the ice keels.

She rubbed her eyes and looked again, then sucked in a
sharp breath. It was a submarine. A submarine with
Cyrillic lettering near the bow! Only the Russians still
used the Cyrillic alphabet.

"Oh God, oh God, oh God!"

Sanderson snapped his head up from the inertial navigation screen he'd been studying. "What the hell's the
matter?"

Marjorie pointed toward the top of the plastic bubble,
her hand trembling violently. "Look, Mel! Between the
keels. It's the *Bukharin!*"

Sanderson squinted upward toward the ice. After looking at the bright screen, it took a second for his eyes to
adjust to the water-blurred searchlights. Suddenly he saw
the huge Typhoon, and the blood rushed from his face.

"Holy shit, I don't believe it! I just don't believe it. No
wonder the Navy couldn't find her. The *Bukharin's* snuck
right up to our goddamned front door hidden under that
berg."

Sanderson spun the wheel and threw the control switch
to full speed ahead. The submersible heeled hard aport
and sped east, away from the ice.

"Get on that radio, Marjorie. Call the *Abyss* and have
Rich patch us through to the command hub. Fast!"

The Ukrainian radio officer aboard the *Bukharin* suddenly
stiffened and pressed his headset against his ears. The
submersible was sending a radio message. He cursed
himself for never learning English, then hit the intercom
button for the control room.

"Control, radio room. That submersible is transmitting
a message to her mother ship."

"Radio, command," Lubov answered. "Are you certain
the transmission is coming from the submersible?"

"No question, Captain."

"Keep listening. I want to know immediately if there is
any return transmission."

"Aye aye, Captain."

As soon as Lobov disconnected, the intercom buzzed again.

"Command, sonar. The intruder's made an abrupt turn to port and picked up speed, Captain. She's running east by southeast at full speed."

"Maintain tracking, sonar," Lubov ordered.

"Aye aye, Captain."

Lobov sat back, deep in thought. The sudden radio transmission and the flight away from the berg could mean only one thing: the submersible had spotted the *Bukharin*.

Within minutes, the entire American ASW defense force would know his position. He realized that he could no longer afford the luxury of firing from six thousand meters out. He would have to launch his torpedoes the moment the *Bukharin* was within the ten-thousand-meter range of her Mark C torpedoes.

"Engineering, control. Flood forward and aft ballast tanks. Bring us down twenty meters below the ice keels."

"Aye aye, Captain. Flooding forward and aft ballast tanks."

The sound of pressurized water forcing air from the tanks reverberated through the huge sub, and the *Bukharin* began to descend slowly from her lair between the keels.

Admiral Mike Mathisen was working off stress in the Ice Station Alpha gym when he suddenly heard his name blare from a large intercom speaker in a corner of the room.

"Admiral Mathisen, please phone the command hub immediately. You have a top-priority call. Repeat, top-priority call for Admiral Mathisen."

The gray-haired flag officer grabbed a towel and wiped the sweat off his face and neck as he crossed the gym floor and pushed through a set of double doors to the corridor outside.

He tossed the towel on the seat of the electric cart and yanked the cellular-phone receiver off the small dash.

"Alpha operator."

"This is Admiral Mathisen. Put me through to the command hub."

"Aye aye, sir."

"Command hub, Specialist Forest," a female voice answered.

"This is Admiral Mathisen. You holding a call for me?"

"Yes, sir. It's from Doctor Glynn aboard the *Yellowstone*. She and Captain Sanderson have spotted the *Bukharin*."

"Jesus Christ! Patch me through immediately."

"I can't, Admiral. The transmission's too weak. I've got our receiver cranked all the way up and I can barely hear her."

"What the hell's the problem?"

"The *Yellowstone*'s apparently several hundred feet down, sir, and running at full speed."

"Is Doctor Meade in the hub?

"No, sir. He and Chief Kowslowski are in a Sno-Cat on the way down to the helipad. I believe Doctor Meade plans to fly out to the *Abyss*."

"Balls!"

"I beg your pardon, sir?"

"Nothing. I'll be there in three or four minutes."

"I'll keep the line open, Admiral."

Mathisen vaulted into the cart and sped down the tunnel toward the command hub.

"Search northeast on all active sonar," Captain Lobov ordered. "I want the exact range to their Operations Center."

The sonar officer pushed the button. "Searching forward with active bow array, Captain."

Lobov lowered his head and pressed his fingertips to his throbbing temples. How long would it be before the American ASW force reacted? If the sonar computer was right and the submersible was a civilian research craft, she would have had to radio her mother ship first.

From there, the *Bukharin*'s position would be transmitted to Ice Station Alpha's Operations Center, and only then sent on to the carriers, surface ships, and subs manning the perimeter ring.

It would take five, perhaps as long as ten, minutes for word of the *Bukharin*'s position to reach the American Fleet. It would buy him a little time, and time was now what he needed most.

"Sonar to command. Range seventeen point five kilometers, Captain."

Lobov sat back in the commander's chair and set the timer on his watch. In forty-five minutes, they would be in range of the Operations Center.

Admiral Mike Mathisen sped his electric cart across the Operations Center and screeched to a halt beside the command hub. In a moment, he was up the steps and standing beside the communications console.

"You still have radio contact with Doctor Glynn?"

"Just barely, Admiral. The *Yellowstone*'s passing through several thermoclimes. The transmission keeps fading in and out."

"Which line is she on?"

"Number two, Admiral."

Mathisen snatched the radiophone receiver off its cradle and pressed the button for line two.

"Marjorie, this is Mike Mathisen."

"Hello, Ad . . ."

"Marjorie, I can hardly hear you. Can you speak louder?"

"I'm yelling my bloody . . . out, Mike."

"All right, we'll make this short. Are you sure, absolutely certain, that you saw the *Bukharin*?"

"No question, Mi . . . There was Cyrillic lettering on . . . and Mel spotted double bronze props . . . a Typhoon."

"Where, Marjorie? Where is she!"

"Hidden . . . the keels of that berg . . . Russian tug is . . ."

"That's all I need to know. Your transmission's breaking up bad. Call me when you get back aboard the *Abyss*."

"All . . . Mike."

Mathisen lowered the receiver and turned to Specialist Forest.

"Where's that Russian interpreter assigned to the command hub?"

"I'm right here, Admiral."

Mathisen turned to find a thin, sallow-faced Russian Navy lieutenant regarding him with a quizzical half-smile.

"I want you to call the captain of the *Murmansk* and tell him to cut all lines to that berg he's towing. Tell him that's a direct order from Admiral Mathisen."

The Russian lieutenant snapped to attention. "I'll put through the call at once, sir." He saluted, then turned for a radiophone on the communications console.

"Specialist Forest, get me Captain Travers aboard the *Abraham Lincoln*."

"Aye aye, sir."

Mathisen stared up at the ship-deployment display on the video wall. If the *Murmansk* continued on her present course, she'd tow that double-keeled berg right past the Operations Center. And Lobov would be able to fire his torpedoes at Alpha without exposing the *Bukharin* to attack from the air.

"I have Captain Travers, Admiral."

Mathisen snatched the receiver out of her hand. "Jerry, this is Mike Mathisen. We've found the *Bukharin*."

"Jesus Christ. Where?"

"She's approximately ten miles east southwest of the Operations Center."

"That's impossible, Admiral. There's no way a Typhoon-class sub could have gotten through our defense perimeter."

"We have visual confirmation, Jerry. She came through hidden between the double keels of that berg the *Murmansk* has in tow. I've got our Russian interpreter calling the tug captain now. I've ordered him to sever the tow lines."

Travers let off a string of profanities, then abruptly quieted, his pride and professionalism deeply wounded. "I guess I blew it, Mike. If you want to relieve me, I'll understand."

"I'm in command of the defense of Ice Station Alpha, Jerry. If anyone's at fault, it's me. And when this is over, I'll take the fall. Right now, all I'm concerned with is killing the *Bukharin*. I want every ASW fixed-wing aircraft and helicopter you've got in the air in five minutes."

"If the *Bukharin*'s still under that berg, we don't have a prayer of killing her with depth charges, Mike. And I don't think we'll have much luck with torpedoes, either, not if that bastard Lobov's got decoys aboard."

"I know the odds, Jerry. But we've got to try. Get those aircraft up."

"Aye aye, Admiral."

Mathisen hung up and looked at the Russian interpreter. The young lieutenant was rubbing his forehead in obvious agitation.

"You get through all right?" Mathisen asked.

"We have a problem, Admiral," the interpreter said, avoiding the American's eyes.

"What is it?"

"The radio operator aboard the *Murmansk* is drunk, sir. I've asked to speak to the captain three times, and each time he's slurred something incomprehensible, then hung up on me."

"Jesus Christ!"

"On behalf of my countrymen, I offer my deepest apologies, Admiral. I assure you that the man will be arrested and disciplined severely for this."

"That doesn't do us any good right now, does it?"

"No, sir, it doesn't."

"All right, all right. I want you to call the captain of that Russian carrier that joined the fleet last week. Tell him to fly someone with a bullhorn out to that tug immediately. The *Murmansk* has got to sever those tow lines."

"Yes, sir."

Mathisen whirled toward Specialist Forest. "Get Ben Meade on the phone."

The Sno-Cat was descending the snaking track leading down to the base helipad when the cellular phone on the dash buzzed insistently.

"Do you mind answering that, Meade?" Chief Bos'n Mate Kowslowski asked. "There's a hairpin turn up ahead; I'll need both hands."

"Sure," Ben said, reaching for the receiver. "Sno-Cat."

"Doctor Meade, Please."

"Speaking."

"Doctor, this is Communications Specialist Forest calling from the command hub. Admiral Mathisen is waiting to talk to you."

"Put him through."

"Ben, we've found the *Bukharin*. Marjorie and Mel spotted her hidden under that double-keeled berg being towed in from the west."

Ben's fingers tightened around the receiver. "Are Marjorie and Mel all right? The *Bukharin* didn't fire on them, did she?"

"No, no, they're both fine, Ben. They should be back aboard the *Abyss* in a half hour or so."

Ben let out a relieved breath. "Has that Russian tug severed the tow line?"

"No. I haven't been able to contact it yet."

"What the hell's the problem?"

Mathisen sighed wearily. "Their radio operator is drunk. I've ordered a Russian chopper to fly out there with a bullhorn."

"Jesus Christ, Mike, what the hell do we do now? The last time I checked the video wall, that berg was just west of the Operations Center."

"I've called in an air strike, Ben. Our aircraft should start dropping depth charges and torpedoes in ten minutes or so. I don't expect the depth charges to do much more than temporarily deafen the *Bukharin*'s sonar and hydrophones. But we may get lucky with one of the torpedoes."

"Suppose Lobov fires his own fish before our aircraft can get there?"

"He's too far out, Ben. The *Bukharin* carries Mark C wire-guided torpedoes. Theoretically, he can fire from twenty or even thirty thousand meters away. But he's only got ten thousand meters of wire."

"You've lost me, Mike."

"The older Soviet Mark Cs have notoriously unreliable on-board homing computers. Left to run on their own, three out of five times they'll miss their target. So the only way Lobov can be sure his torpedoes will run true is to guide them in from the *Bukharin*. He's got to get within ten thousand meters of the Operations Center."

"What about our ASW subs, Mike, those Los Angeles-class boats you've got patrolling the defense ring? Can't they flush the *Bukharin* out from under that berg?"

"Under normal conditions, our Los Angeles-class boats could fire their ADCAPs from fifty thousand yards and be fairly confident of a kill. But a long-range shot like that's impossible with the goddamn marine acoustics up here. It will take our subs at least an hour to get close enough for a sure kill."

"How long before the *Bukharin*'s in range?"

"I just ran all the data through the mainframe—the *Bukharin*'s present position, the tow speed of that berg, winds, currents. The computer says Lobov will fire his torpedoes in exactly thirty-five minutes, twenty seconds."

"Jesus, Mike, you'd better get your people the hell off Alpha," Ben said, setting his watch.

"I'm afraid it's too late to evacuate," Mathisen said, his voice somber. "The only way off the ice is by air, and we have neither the Sno-Cats nor the time to get to the helipad."

Ben's heart felt like a lead window weight in his chest. "Alpha's my creation, Mike. You and your people are out here on the ice because of me. I'm coming back. We'll face those torpedoes together."

"No, Ben, you can't do that. If the *Bukharin* succeeds in destroying Ice Station Alpha, you're the only one who can rebuild, the only one who can put it all back together."

"I'm not sure that's possible, Mike. There's no way I could even begin until the iceberg season next spring. And by then, there'd be fleets of smuggling ships landing hordes of refugees along our shores. The Navy would need every ship afloat just to guard our coasts."

"Sacrificing yourself isn't going to save my people, Ben. You've still got time to make the helipad. Fly out to

the *Abyss*. Take Marjorie back to the States and build as
many mini-Earths as you can. Lobov may destroy the
Arctic Alteration, but Biosphere America will live on.
Hope will survive among the people of the northern hemisphere."

"Mike—"

"Good-bye, Ben. And may God keep you."

"God keep you, Mike," Ben whispered as the disconnected phone buzzed in his ear.

His mind numb, Ben hung the receiver back on its
mount and for a long moment stared out over the gray
sea below them.

Chief Kowslowski drove on down the track in silence,
Ben's terrible pain hanging next to him like a shroud.

"You heard," Ben said finally.

"Yeah, I heard."

"You've got a lot of friends on Alpha, don't you,
Chief?"

"Yeah, Meade," Kowslowski said, maneuvering the
Sno-Cat from side to side as they started down a steep in-
cline. "A lot of friends."

The sudden sound of supersonic aircraft approaching
reverberated off the frozen slope around them, and the
men looked up as a flight of Harrier jets swooped in low
over the sea.

A moment later, they could hear muted explosions as
the navy ASW planes dropped their depth charges
around the double-keeled iceberg.

"Are there any binoculars in here?" Ben asked.

"Yeah, in that small storage compartment under the
dash."

Ben found the glasses and swept the sea to the west.
For a moment, he could see only slate-gray waves topped
with plumes of wind-whipped foam. Then he caught a
white blur on the horizon and adjusted the focus.

The double-keeled berg looked bigger than it had appeared on the video wall. It was at least two and a half
miles long and three-quarters of a mile wide.

As Ben watched, a flight of ASW helicopters came in
from the west and began dropping a second barrage of
depth charges along the perimeter of the ice. The sur-

rounding sea erupted with dozens of watery volcanoes as the explosive charges detonated beneath the waves.

"Mind if I have a look?" Kowslowski asked.

Ben handed him the binoculars and the chief brought the glasses up to his eyes. "You know, the configuration of that berg looks a lot like the ice the Operations Center is on. A plateau on one side and an ice mount on the other."

"I said the same thing to Admiral Mathisen."

"Goddammit, Meade, if that sucker were an ice floe instead of a berg, we could cut it apart with our laser-equipped Sea Stallion. That laser's been working like a charm in Baffin Bay, slicing up two hundred square miles of floes a day."

Ben had forgotten about the helicopter-borne laser that had been cutting apart the Baffin Bay ice for the past two weeks. Carried south by the Labrador Current, the segmented ice began to melt when it reached the warmer waters of the North Atlantic.

"No way, Chief," Ben said gloomily. "The ice floes are only ten to twenty feet thick. That berg probably extends down eighteen hundred feet below the sea. In the time we have left, the most we could do is maybe cut it in half with the las—"

Ben suddenly shot bolt upright in his seat and grabbed the binoculars back from a startled Kowslowski.

"That's it!" Ben said, studying the berg through the glasses. "Jesus Christ, Chief, that's it!"

"What's it? What the hell are you talking about?"

"Later, Chief. Is that laser-equipped chopper down at the helipad?"

Kowslowski looked at his watch. "She was scheduled to make a run over the ice fields in Baffin Bay this morning, but she should be back by now."

"How long will it take us to get to the helipad?"

Kowslowski surveyed the corkscrew track leading down to the plateau. "I don't know, forty-five, fifty minutes."

"Too long. We need to cut that in half."

"The only way to do that is to go straight down the slope."

"Do it!"

"That's a thirty-five-degree angle, Meade. There's a fuckin' good chance the Sno-Cat will turn over on top of us."

"Get out, then. I'll take it down the slope myself."

Kowslowski chewed belligerently on the stub of his cigar. "Like hell you will. If you've got the balls to do this, so do I."

The chief yanked the wheel to the right and gunned the tracked vehicle over the lip of the track. Ben grabbed the dashboard before him and hung on, the freezing wind stinging his face as the Sno-Cat gathered speed down the steep slope.

The gut-churning sound of depth charges exploding in the surrounding sea reverberated through the two-hundred-and-eighty-foot *Bukharin*. In every compartment, men turned terror-stricken eyes upward, as if they could see through the steel plates and, seeing, somehow escape their fate.

In the control room, a young Argentine apprentice seaman vomited in fear, drawing a disgusted look from Captain Lobov. The depth-charge attack didn't worry him. Sheltered under the berg, he was confident that the double-hulled Typhoon could survive the bombardment.

A moment later, his cool confidence was tested by the voice of the sonar officer. "Control, sonar. High-speed screws in the water."

Lobov's hand shot to his intercom mike. "Sonar, control. What's the bearing?"

"Ten degrees off our starboard bow, Captain. Closing fast."

"Keep tracking," Lobov ordered, then hit the button for the bow torpedo room.

"Torpedo room, control. Enemy fish coming in. Ten degrees to starboard. Launch a decoy."

"Control, torpedo room. Aye aye, Captain."

A red light blinked on a monitor to Lobov's right as a blast of compressed air sent the decoy out into the sea. The projectile's electric motor came quietly to life, and thirty seconds later, the decoy began sending out sound waves that imitated the machinery noises aboard the *Bukharin*.

The control room was thick with a silent dread as the seconds ticked by. Finally, the voice of the sonar officer crackled over the intercom speaker.

"Control, sonar. The fish is homing in on the decoy. Distance three hundred meters."

Lobov tensed. Waiting. Waiting. Then he heard it. Every man in the control room heard it. A muffled explosion from the direction of the bow, followed instantly by the excited voice of the sonar officer.

"Control, sonar. Torpedo neutralized, Captain. She went for the decoy."

A spontaneous cheer went up from the control-room crew. Lobov allowed himself a small smile of satisfaction. The attacking ASW planes obviously did not carry the advanced ADCAPs. The dozen decoys in the *Bukharin*'s torpedo room should be more than sufficient to protect the Typhoon from any further torpedo attacks from the air.

Lobov's earphones crackled. "Control, navigation. Five kilometers to firing position."

Lobov glanced around the control room, wondering if his hybrid crew of grizzled Ukrainian submarine veterans and raw Argentine recruits would be able to function as a team during the attack.

His answer would come in exactly thirty minutes, sixteen seconds.

His eyes ice-caked slits against the freezing headwind, Chief Ignatius Kowslowski struggled for control as the Sno-Cat careened down the thirty-five-degree slope toward the plateau below.

They had plowed through several deep drifts on the way down, and both he and Ben were covered with a thick layer of powdered snow. Kowslowski's teeth snapped his cigar in half as the Sno-Cat barely cleared an unexpected crevasse, then gathered speed down the final stretch of slope.

Finally, they were down, the ice level beneath them, and the chief jammed the accelerator to the floor. As they

sped across the ice plateau, Ben pushed back the cuff of
his coat and looked at his watch. In twenty-four minutes,
the *Bukharin* would reach torpedo range. He brought the
binoculars to his eyes and studied the double-keeled
berg. The ice mount towered at least three hundred feet
above the plateau, its sharp peak like a dagger poised to
strike.

He caught a blurred movement in the sky to the west of
the berg and focused the glasses into the distance. It was a
lone helicopter with the flag of the Russian Republic em-
blazoned on the fuselage. As he watched, the chopper
flew past the ice, then banked sharply and hovered over
the Russian tug towing the berg.

A moment later, the helicopter door slid back and
someone leaned partly out of the aircraft. Ben zeroed in
on the figure. It was a woman in a Russian Navy uniform,
a bullhorn at her mouth.

He brought the glasses to bear on the tug below. Several seamen were gaping up at the chopper. A moment
later, they turned and stared at the berg. There was an excited exchange. Then four of the men ran toward the stern
with axes and began severing the three tow lines attached
to the berg.

"Looks like the *Murmansk* is finally turning that berg
loose," Ben said.

Kowskowski scowled. "It won't make a fuckin' bit of
difference now, Meade. The ice is so close, it'll drift into
torpedo range on its forward momentum."

Ben nodded glumly. "What's the number for the communications shack at the helipad?"

"One-five-oh," Kowslowski said.

Ben punched the buttons.

"Alpha helipad. Lieutenant Rawlings."

"Lieutenant, this is Ben Meade. Chief Kowslowski and
I are in a Sno-Cat about fifteen minutes from the pad. I
want that laser-equipped Sea Stallion warmed up and
ready to fly the moment we get there."

"I'll have to file a flight plan, Doctor Meade. Can you
tell me what your mission is?"

"We're going out to kill the *Bukharin*, Lieutenant," Ben
said. "We've got to kill her before she kills us."

* * *

Seawater poured off the sides of the *Yellowstone* in sheets as the crane aboard the *Abyss* lifted the submersible out of the freezing North Atlantic and swung the craft over the deck.

Machinist's Mate Rich Kaneko pushed a lever forward, carefully lowering the *Yellowstone* down on her chocks. The submersible was still rocking when the hatch popped open and Mel Sanderson boosted Marjorie Glynn out onto the hull. She reached back in to give Mel a hand up, then scrambled down the rungs on the side and tore across the deck toward the radio room while Mel headed for the bridge.

Marjorie snatched the ship-to-shore phone off its cradle and punched in the number for the command hub.

"Alpha Communications," Specialist Forest answered.

"This is Marjorie Glynn. Do you know where Doctor Meade is?"

"I believe he's in a Sno-Cat on the way to the helipad, Ma'am."

"Can you patch me through?"

"Right away, Doctor Glynn."

For several moments, static filled the line; then she heard his voice above the sound of the Sno-Cat engine.

"Ben Meade."

"Ben, it's Marjorie. We're back aboard the *Abyss*."

"Thank God," Ben breathed. "When Mike told me you'd spotted the *Bukharin*, my heart stopped. You must have been awful damn close to catch that sub in your lights."

"We came in about fifty feet below her keel. Good God, Ben, she's immense. Like some huge black sea monster lurking beneath that berg."

"The *Bukharin*'s the last of the old Soviet Typhoon-class, Marjorie. She's the biggest goddamn submarine in the world."

"I talked to Admiral Mathisen on the way up. He told me there's no way to stop the *Bukharin* now." Her voice cracked. "He said Ice Station Alpha was expecting to come under torpedo attack within minutes. Oh, God, Ben,

Mike doesn't think anyone on Alpha will survive."

"Listen to me, Marjorie. There's still hope. I think I have a way to kill the *Bukharin*."

"What? How?"

"The chief and I are almost to the helipad. I don't have time to explain. I want you to tell Mel to close all the hatches and watertight doors, and turn the bow of the *Abyss* toward the berg. In about twelve minutes, there'll be thirty- or forty-foot waves radiating out from the ice. If those waves catch the *Abyss* broadside, they could send you to the bottom."

"Ben, whatever you're planning to do, please be careful. Promise me you'll be careful."

"I promise."

"I love you, darling."

"I love you too, baby. Good-bye."

"Good-bye, Ben."

For a long moment, Marjorie held the disconnected phone tightly against her chest, not wanting to let go of the link to Ben. Then slowly she lowered the receiver to its cradle, wiped the tears from her eyes and left to find Mel.

Captain Viktor Lobov pressed the intercom button for the engine room. "Engine room, control. Bring the reactor up to full power; I want steam in ten minutes."

"Control, navigation. Aye aye, sir."

Lobov turned off the headset and glanced at his watch, then swiveled his chair toward Chief Engineer Onopenko. "Fourteen minutes, Mykola."

The fire-control officer stared back at Lobov with infinitely sad and fatalistic eyes. This madman before him had already forced him to murder twenty innocent Greek sailors.

And now, within minutes, he must kill again. Kill because he hadn't the courage to die himself. Yet Mykola Onopenko knew that he was already dead. The moral man who had sailed from Sevastopol, the human being who had never harmed a soul in his life, had drowned in a sea of fire and blood at the gates of Gibraltar.

* * *

With a blown head gasket pouring acrid smoke, the ice-encrusted Sno-Cat skidded to a stop beside the Sea Stallion helicopter. Ben Meade and Chief Kowslowski leaped out and dashed for the open door of the chopper. A crewman reached down to give them a hand up, then slammed the cargo door closed behind them.

"Take her up," Ben yelled at the lieutenant j.g. at the controls.

"Sir, you'd better strap—"

"Now, Goddammit!"

The pilot whirled around and pressed the stick forward. The huge helicopter lifted off in a cacophony of whirling blades and straining engine, throwing Ben and the chief against their seats.

The crewman held onto the door handle with a vicelike grip as the Sea Stallion rose to three hundred feet and leveled off.

The pilot looked back over his shoulder. "Where to, sir?"

"Head for that berg three miles to the southwest," Ben shouted above the *whop-whop-whop* of the props above. "And then get Admiral Mathisen on the radio."

"Aye aye, sir." The pilot banked the chopper toward the sea, then put in a call to the command hub.

Ben turned to Kowslowski. "Get that laser warmed up, Chief."

"You mind telling me what we're goin' to do, Meade?"

"You'll know soon enough."

"I have Admiral Mathisen on the line," the pilot said, handing Ben a headset.

Ben put on the earphones and throat mike. "Admiral, it's Ben. We're going out after the *Bukharin*."

Mathisen could hear the staccato sound of the helicopter blades through the open line. "I take it you're in a chopper?"

"Yeah. The chief and I just lifted off from the helipad."

"Forget it, Ben. We've already tried helicopter assaults. Our birds have dropped bombs, depth charges, torpedoes. We've thrown everything we had at the *Bukharin*."

"Not everything, Mike."

"What's left?"

"Ice, Mike. I'm going to kill the *Bukharin* with a mountain of ice."

"What the hell are you talking about?"

"Just bring that berg up on the video wall, Mike, then sit back and watch the show."

"Goddammit, Ben, you listen to—"

"So long, Mike."

Ben pulled the headset off and looked at Kowslowski, adjusting dials on the laser. "You have full power yet, Chief?"

"Be two or three minutes."

Ben had developed the long-range laser at his research lab in Wyoming. Designed to slice bergs apart, the laser had originally used power from a conventional electric generator.

Then, in May 2000, a team of Hungarian nuclear physicists perfected the world's first cold-fusion reactor and Ben had immediately grasped its potential as a source of almost limitless power for his new laser.

Unlike a conventional nuclear-fission reactor, with its uranium rods, heavy water, coolants and control rods, the Hungarian fusion reactor had relatively few parts, consisting primarily of a plasma fuel contained in a compact "magnetic bottle."

The simplicity of the fusion process allowed the physicist to design compact models the size of a home refrigerator. Ben had purchased two fusion reactors eight months before, and one of these was now secured to the belly of the Sea Stallion.

Ben looked at his watch. They had seven minutes left.

"Laser's ready," Kowslowski said.

"Full power?"

"I got her maxed out, Meade."

"Sonar to command. Six minutes to firing range, Captain."

"Sonar, command," Viktor Lobov said. "Send target information to the fire-control computer."

"Aye aye, sir."

Lobov half-turned toward Fire-control Officer Onopenko, but said nothing. He didn't have to. Onopenko hovered over his computer console, his nerve ends raw as he awaited the feed from sonar. Finally, the screen began to blink with numbers and letters, and he quickly went to work on his firing solution.

Lobov hit a second intercom button. "Command to torpedo room. Load bow tubes one through six."

The torpedo officer typed a command into the torpedo-room computer, and hydraulic levers automatically took over, moving the deadly Mark Cs from their racks into the torpedo tubes and then sealing the doors.

"Command, torpedo room. All six bow tubes loaded, Captain."

Ben Meade lowered the binoculars and looked at his watch. They had less than five minutes before the *Bukharin* fired her torpedoes at Alpha.

He switched on the intercom. "What's our distance from the berg, Lieutenant?"

"A mile and a quarter, sir."

"I want to fire the laser from one mile out. When we're in range, descend to a hundred feet and keep the chopper as steady as you can. You got that?"

"Affirmative, sir."

Ben turned back to the window and swept the glasses across the huge mass of ice sheltering the *Bukharin*. He estimated that the frozen white cliffs rose two hundred feet from the sea, with the ice mount on the western side soaring another six hundred feet above the plateau.

The laser was most effective from the distance of a mile, and an altitude of a hundred feet would allow him to work the burning beam up and down the cliff in equidistant pulses.

He turned to Kowslowski. "Time to go to work, Chief. We're going to cut that berg in half."

"What? What the hell for?"

"It's a simple matter of physics. The ice mount makes the western half of the berg top-heavy. The only thing keeping it from rolling over is the counterbalance of the plateau to the east."

"Yeah, I understand that part, Meade. But I still don't . . . Holy Shit!"

Kowslowski's face suddenly lit with cognition. "When you slice away the plateau, the ice mount will turn turtle!"

"You got it."

"Right on top of that fucking Typhoon."

"That's the theory, Chief. Let's see if it works."

The voice of the pilot crackled through Ben's earphones. "We're in position, Doctor Meade."

"Hold her steady, Lieutenant."

"Aye aye, sir."

"I want you to time my laser runs, Chief."

"You got it, Meade."

"Okay, open that goddamn door."

Kowslowski grabbed the handle and shoved the door open. A freezing wind whistled into the cabin, bringing with it the smell of salt air and ancient ice.

Ben yanked his parka hood over his head and sighted on the ice cliff dead ahead. Then he took a deep breath and stabbed at the power button.

Instantly, a beam of intense light—hotter than the surface of the sun—shot across the sea, burning a yawning crater three hundred feet deep in the face of the ice cliff just below its summit. A Niagara of boiling meltwater and steaming blocks of ice cascaded into the sea as Ben worked the burning beam down the frozen white wall.

When the laser neared the waves below, Ben returned it to the top of the plateau. "How long did the run take?"

Kowslowski looked at his watch. "Thirty seconds. Jesus, you're never going to be able to burn all the way through before the *Bukharin* launches her torpedoes."

Ben started the laser down again, deepening the crevasse another three hundred feet. "I don't have to cut all the way through, Chief. That ice mount's so heavy that the berg should crack apart of its own weight once that crevasse reaches the halfway mark."

"How wide is the berg?" Kowslowski asked.

"About three-quarters of a mile. I figure I need six more passes."

"I hope it's six, Meade. We've only got a little over three minutes left."

"Command, sonar. Range ten thousand, three hundred and thirty meters. Estimated time to target, two minutes."

"Sonar, command," Lobov replied. "Sing out at one minute."

"Aye aye, Captain."

"Navigation, report."

"Escape course plotted, Captain."

Lobov leaned back in his commander's chair. Nothing could go wrong now. Nothing.

Admiral Mike Mathisen stared at the video wall in astonishment. The satellite infrared display was showing the Sea Stallion firing a laser at the berg sheltering the *Bukharin*. What in the name of God was Ben Meade up to?

Mathisen punched in a command for a close-up shot. A moment later, the ice filled the wall of screens, and now he could see the deepening crevasse the laser was cutting into the berg. It looked like Ben was trying to cut the ice in half. But why? Then the admiral's eyes went to the frozen peak towering above the stern of the berg, and suddenly he knew exactly what Ben was doing.

Communications Specialist Forest came half out of her chair at the sound of the admiral's raucous war whoop reverberating off the video wall behind her.

"Is there something the matter, Admiral?"

"Just the opposite, Specialist. Get on the public address system. I want every sailor on Ice Station Alpha gathered around the command hub in two minutes."

"How we doing, Chief?" Ben asked, finishing his fourth pass down the steaming face of the berg.

"We've got a minute 'n forty-two seconds left, Meade,"

Kowslowski said, chewing hard on his cigar butt.

Ben started the laser back up the cliff. "Three more runs and we'll pass the halfway mark."

"That's all we've got time for, Meade. Three more runs."

"Control, navigator. Sixty seconds to firing range."

"Navigator, control. Begin countdown at ten seconds."

"Aye aye, Captain."

Lobov spun his chair toward his fire-control officer. "Recheck firing solution."

"Rechecking firing solution," Onopenko said.

"Torpedo room, control. Flood torpedo tubes."

"Control, torpedo room. Flooding tubes, Captain."

"Time?" Ben yelled out as he started the laser on its seventh run up the face of the ice cliff.

"Forty seconds, Meade. This is the final pass."

His blood pounding in his ears, Ben fought to keep the burning ray in the middle of the now eighteen-hundred-foot-deep crevasse. If the berg hadn't split apart by the time he reached the top, Ice Station Alpha was doomed.

"Control, sonar. Twenty seconds to firing position."

"Firing solution confirmed, sir," Onopenko said without being asked.

"Prepare to fire torpedoes," Lobov ordered.

The laser beam was nearing the top of the ice cliff when Chief Kowslowski suddenly yelled from the door. "Ben, Jesus Christ, I think she moved!"

"What moved?"

"The ice mount. The peak's beginning to tilt away from the plateau. Look! Look!"

Ben leaped for the door.

* * *

Mykola Onopenko heard it first. An ominous sound like brittle thunder coming through the control room's hydrophone speaker. The hair rose on the back of his neck.

"Captain," Onopenko said. "Did you hear that?"

Lobov looked at Onopenko. "Hear what?"

"Control, sonar. Nine seconds to firing position."

The sound came again, louder now, echoing eerily through the hushed control room. The eyes of the terrified crew shot toward the steel-plated double hull above them.

"Nine seconds."

Lobov rose slowly from the commander's chair. He had spent most of his submarine career in the Arctic. He recognized the sound of shattering ice.

"Eight seconds."

"The berg," he whispered, so low that only Onopenko heard him. "The berg is breaking apart."

Ben and the chief watched wordlessly as the two-and-a-half-mile-long berg began splitting in two. The crack had already severed the surface of the plateau, while unseen beneath the waves, the ever-widening fracture raced downward toward the bottom of the ice.

Seawater was sucked into the yawning chasm, creating a vacuum that became an instant whirlpool as the surrounding water rushed in to fill the void. The already rocking ice peak tilted crazily toward the sea as the turbulence built below.

"Four seconds," the sonar officer reported an instant before the Typhoon suddenly lurched upward, sucked toward the fractured berg by the immense whirlpool above.

Men and equipment slammed into the deck plates, then slid toward the stern as the Bukharin's bow jerked up at a thirty-degree angle, making the forward torpedoes totally useless.

"Abort torpedoes," Lobov screamed at Onopenko.

The fire-control officer scrambled to his feet and slammed a hand down on the torpedo-abort button.

"There she goes!" Kowslowski yelled as the ice mount dipped its peak into the waves and rolled over into the churning sea. "You did it, Meade. Jesus H. Christ, you did it!"

"But was I in time, Chief?" Ben asked, searching the sea toward Alpha for torpedo wakes. "Was I in time?"

The huge Typhoon was rolling madly when the terrible noise suddenly changed. Now it was the sound of tons of water rushing past the hull, sweeping the huge submarine sideways.

Something in the sea was moving the water. Something big. Something very close.

An instant later, the ice peak swung into the *Bukharin* from the starboard side, slicing open the sub's twin hulls just forward of the sail. The Typhoon was pushed far over on her port side by the force of the impact, sending the crewmen in the control room smashing headlong into the equipment-lined wall.

Men screamed in agony as arms and legs snapped like matchsticks. Mykola Onopenko found himself sprawled across the inertial navigation monitor. There was an unbearable pain radiating up from the base of his smashed spine, and he had lost the feeling in his legs.

Onopenko knew he was going to die, and suddenly he wasn't afraid anymore. For the first time since he'd boarded the *Bukharin*, he was free of the satanic grip of Viktor Lobov.

"Flood starboard ballast tanks," the mad captain screamed from four feet away. "We've got to right her!"

Onopenko clenched his teeth against the agony radiating from his spine, and clawed his way across the debris between himself and the captain, who lay prone amidst the wreckage, a bloody gash across his forehead.

Lobov looked up, new hope in his eyes at the sight of

his loyal lieutenant. "Mykola, we've got to flood the starboard tanks. We've got to right her."

"No," Onopenko spat, his right hand yanking the pistol from Lobov's holster."

"What are you doing, Mykola?"

"It's over, you crazy fucking bastard. The *Bukharin* is about to die. She's going to the bottom. And you're going to hell!"

Onopenko jammed the barrel against the captain's head and pulled the trigger. Blood oozing from his shattered brain, Viktor Lobov stared upward in death, up toward the surface of the freezing sea he had sought to rule.

For a hushed moment after Lobov died, the *Bukharin* lay helpless on her side, the sea pouring in through a sixty-foot gash in her hull. As the compartments filled, the screams of the doomed crewmen were drowned one by one beneath the freezing water.

Then the huge Typhoon turned upside down and sank slowly toward the bottom of the North Atlantic, a grizzly flotsam of dead men and shattered debris trailing upward above her.

"Debris at two o'clock," the pilot of the Sea Stallion shouted from the cockpit.

"Take us down," Ben said.

"Aye aye, sir."

"Jesus, there are bodies in the water," Kowslowski said as the helicopter swooped low over the carpet of carnage sucked from the bowels of the shattered *Bukharin*.

"I wish there'd been another way," Ben said softly.

The chief turned from the window. "But there wasn't, Meade. You didn't kill those men. Lobov did. Their blood is on his hands, not yours."

Ben nodded. "Thanks, Chief. But it's going to take me a while to accept that."

He turned toward the pilot. "Do you think you can land this thing on the *Abyss*, Lieutenant? The waves are still high down there. She'll be rolling all over the sea."

The pilot looked back at Ben, "If you can kill a Typhoon

with an iceberg, Doctor Meade, I can sure as hell land on a rolling ship. Buckle yourselves in."

"Put me through to Doctor Glynn on the way, will you?"

"Aye aye, sir."

As the Sea Stallion banked, Ben put on his headset. A moment later, Marjorie came on the line. "*Abyss*, Marjorie Glynn speaking."

"Marjorie, it's Ben."

"Ben, I've been waiting here by the radio for your call. Mike Mathisen just phoned. He told us that SEASAT satellite was picking up debris from the *Bukharin*. I'm so proud of you. So very proud."

"I had to kill a lot of men today, Marjorie."

"That billions of others might live, Ben. Can't you see that?"

"I'm trying to."

"I'll help you, Ben, when we get home."

"Home's a long way away, baby."

"No it isn't, Ben. Home's a chamber carved out of ice, or a lonely geothermal rig in the middle of nowhere. Home is anywhere we're together."

EPILOGUE
● ● ● ● ● ● ● ● ● ●

A TUMULTUOUS CHEER WENT up from the sailors based on Ice Station Alpha as the cart carrying Ben Meade and Marjorie Glynn entered the Operations Center.

"Did you know about this, Chief?" Ben asked as Kowslowski eased the cart slowly through the throng surrounding the command hub.

"Sure did."

"Thanks for the warning."

"You two better get used to the limelight. Scuttlebutt is that every nation in the northern hemisphere wants to shower you with honors."

"Shower Ben, you mean," Marjorie said. "He's the hero around here."

Ben put his arm around her. "Like hell. If you hadn't discovered the *Bukharin* under that berg, none of us would be here."

"I figure you're both heroes," Kowslowski said.

Admiral Mathisen was waiting at the top of the stairs as the cart finally reached the command hub.

"It's about time you two got here." Mathisen grinned down from the top of the stairs. "C'mon up. My people

have been standing around for a couple of hours waiting
to welcome you back."

Ben and Marjorie mounted the steps and followed Mathisen to a railing overlooking the Operations Center. As
soon as they appeared, the cheering started again, rising
to a crescendo of whistles and clapping.

"This really isn't necessary, Mike," Ben protested.

"Not necessary? Let me tell you something, Ben. Those
men and women aren't down there cheering because I ordered them to. They're here because they want to be, because you two have given them back their future."

"We were only doing our jobs, Mike," Marjorie said,
her voice barely audible above the continuous cheering
from below.

"Speech, speech," someone in the crowd yelled, and
the call echoed from a dozen other throats.

"Looks like you're on," Mathisen grinned at Ben.

"Mike, I'm no good at speeches. You talk to them."

"And get pelted with eggs? No way. It's you they want
to hear, Ben. You and Marjorie."

Marjorie threw up her hands. "Oh, no, not me. Ben can
speak for both of us.

"Thanks a lot."

"I'll be right here giving you moral support."

"I'd prefer vocal support."

"Go on, go on. They're waiting for you."

Ben sighed and stepped up to the microphone. The
cheering rose again, and he raised his arms to quiet the
crowd.

"I want to thank you . . ." he began, then waited for the
last of the applause to die down. "On behalf of Doctor
Glynn and myself, I'd like to thank all of you for turning
out. We're honored that you've come, just as we've been
honored to have worked with you these past weeks."

Ben paused for a moment and glanced somberly at Admiral Mathisen, then turned back to the crowd and went
on.

"We killed a submarine today," he said. "The *Bukharin*
now lies broken and lifeless in the depths of the sea. It's a
fitting grave, for the *Bukharin* wasn't just a submarine.
She was the incarnation of the dark side of mankind, the

embodiment of an avarice and thirst for power that knew no limits. The suffering and starvation of millions of innocent people mattered nothing to the junta that sent the *Bukharin* north, and even less to the madman at her helm."

The crowd was quiet now, faces somber and intent.

"Because of your work here on Ice Station Alpha, the Gulf Stream will continue to melt the Arctic Sea ice, and the northern hemisphere will warm. The Earth Winter will turn into spring. And as Doctor Glynn's new crop strains ripen in the fields, the starving people of the northern hemisphere will harvest not just food, but hope."

Ben reached back for Marjorie's hand and held it aloft in his as the crowd below broke into the loudest cheers of all.

Finally, the tumult died down and Admiral Mathisen stepped up to the microphone. "As of this moment, you're all on twenty-four-hour shore leave. You'll find all the food you can eat and all the beer you can drink in the mess hall. Well done, men and women of Alpha, well done."

"See you later, Mike," Ben said as he and Marjorie started across the command hub.

"Hold on, you two. You can't just take off. There are messages pouring in from every nation north of the equator. And the President's waiting to talk to you."

"Bye, Mike," Ben grinned as they descended the stairs and climbed into their electric cart.

Admiral Mathisen looked at them from the top of the steps. "What the hell am I supposed to tell the President?"

Ben turned on the motor. "Tell her we went home, Mike," he said as Marjorie's hand crept into his. "Just tell her we went home."